CHRISTM...
DR DE...

BY
SUE MacKay

ONE NIGHT
THAT CHANGED
EVERYTHING

BY
TINA BECKETT

MILLS
BOON

With a background of working in medical laboratories and a love of the romance genre, it is no surprise that **Sue MacKay** writes Mills & Boon® Medical Romance™ stories. An avid reader all her life, she wrote her first story at age eight—about a prince, of course. She lives with her own hero in the beautiful Marlborough Sounds, at the top of New Zealand's South Island, where she indulges her passions for the outdoors, the sea and cycling.

Born to a family that was always on the move, **Tina Beckett** learned to pack a suitcase almost before she knew how to tie her shoes. Fortunately she met a man who also loved to travel, and she snapped him right up. Married for over twenty years, Tina has three wonderful children and has lived in gorgeous places such as Portugal and Brazil.

Living where English reading material is difficult to find has its drawbacks, however. Tina had to come up with creative ways to satisfy her love for romance novels, so she picked up her pen and tried writing one. After her tenth book she realised she was hooked. She was officially a writer.

A three-times Golden Heart finalist, and fluent in Portuguese, Tina now divides her time between the United States and Brazil. She loves to use exotic locales as the backdrop for many of her stories. When she's not writing, you can find her either on horseback or soldering stained-glass panels for her home.

Tina loves to hear from readers. You can contact her through her website or 'friend' her on Facebook.

CHRISTMAS WITH DR DELICIOUS

BY
SUE MacKAY

MILLS & BOON

This book is dedicated to all my extended family. You've always been there for me through all those blips life tosses up. Love you all. And to the Cancer Society of New Zealand, especially the Blenheim and Christchurch branches. You are awesome. Thank you so much for your care and concern.

First published in Great Britain 2012
by Mills & Boon, an imprint of Harlequin (UK) Limited.
Harlequin (UK) Limited, Eton House, 18-24 Paradise Road,
Richmond, Surrey TW9 1SR

© Sue MacKay 2012

ISBN: 978 0 263 89213 0

Harlequin (UK) policy is to use papers that are natural, renewable and recyclable products and made from wood grown in sustainable forests. The logging and manufacturing process conform to the legal environmental regulations of the country of origin.

Printed and bound in Spain
by Blackprint CPI, Barcelona

Dear Reader

Welcome to Nikki and Fraser's story. These two have their share of issues to resolve, stemming from those uncertain teenage years when they, like the rest of us, were finding out about themselves and putting their toes in the dating waters.

I've set this story around the ambulance service as I have a lot of admiration for the people who regularly face situations that would have most of us hiding under a blanket. The exacting standards of care and service are a credit to each and every member of the New Zealand St John Ambulance Service.

I personally spent time working with the crews at Blenheim Station, but for the purposes of this book have used fictitious characters and events.

But in the end this story is about Nikki and Fraser finding their way back to each other. I hope you enjoy it.

Until next time…

Cheers!

Sue

PS I'd love to hear from you, so drop me a line on sue.mackay56@yahoo.com or visit my website at www.suemackay.co.nz

**These books are also available in eBook format
from www.millsandboon.co.uk**

CHAPTER ONE

'OKAY, everyone, listen up.' Mike, the Blenheim Ambulance Base manager, strode purposefully into the staffroom and straddled a chair. 'I've just been talking to the boffins in Nelson.'

Nikki lifted her head from her laptop where she had been engrossed in her studies. Any conversation between Nelson, where their overall boss worked from, and Blenheim stations usually had a direct effect on everyone. 'What now?' she asked with a grin. 'Got to cut back on our coffee intake?'

Mike grinned back as he shook his head. 'Nothing so drastic. We've employed a paramedic, starting in eight days' time.'

Good news for once. 'That's going to lighten the workload for some of us.' They had plenty of volunteers working as ambulance officers but few full-time paramedics and advanced paramedics, which meant she was always being called in to work extra shifts. Not that she minded most of the time. More shifts meant more pay to spend at the fashion shops.

Mike hadn't finished. 'Gavin, I intend putting the two of you together so you can mentor him as he trains for his Advanced Paramedic qualification. I think you'll get on well with him. He comes across as confident and competent, as well as likeable.'

Gavin's face turned thoughtful. 'Why not Nikki? She's just as capable as me.'

Unused to Gavin questioning anything, Mike looked taken aback. 'She is, but at the moment this is how I want it to run. Okay?'

'Sure.' But Gavin looked worried.

To give him a break Nikki asked, 'So who is this person? Anyone we know?'

'I doubt it. He's been in Dunedin for years, but has decided to move back home. His credentials were too good not to take him on immediately. He could get a job anywhere in New Zealand if he wanted.'

Nikki shivered. A guy returning home from Dunedin after years away. Why should that raise her antenna so quickly? Quite a few people from here had gone to university in Dunedin and not come back. She glanced up at Mike but saw nothing more than enthusiasm for his new staff member. Another shiver tripped through her. 'Do we get a name for this guy?'

Mike's gaze remained fixed on her. 'Fraser McCall.'

The air left her lungs in a whoosh. The warning shaking her body had been right. 'That doesn't make sense. Are you talking about Fraser Ian McCall? Twenty-seven years old?'

'The same man.' Mike frowned. 'Problem?'

Yes. A big one. Panic squeezed her, turned her skin icy. Fraser could not work here, in this station, with her. He could not. It was too small. They'd always be running into each other, even if they were on opposing shifts. Did he know she worked here? If he did then it was unfair of him to even contemplate joining up. Why had he? 'He's a doctor, not a paramedic.'

Mike stood up. 'Wrong. McCall's been working on the ambulances for three years.'

Really? Why? Five years ago Fraser had just finished his fourth year at med school so that left two years between then and now unaccounted for. Of course, she hadn't heard anything about him since she'd returned home from Dunedin but he must've finished his studies at university in that time. Swallowing hard to push away the sudden blockage in her throat, she croaked, 'What was he doing before he joined the ambulance service?'

'You know I can't give out confidential information about any of the staff, including you, Nikki.' There was a warning, a message, in Mike's eyes just for her.

Hadn't Fraser mentioned to Mike he knew her? That they had history not easily dismissed? Hell, that they couldn't possibly work together? For five long years Fraser had shown he didn't give a damn about what had become of her. Why would he start now?

'Does he know I work here?'

'Yes. He seemed surprised. Said he knew you when you were a chef, and that you hadn't had a medical thought in your head.'

She dipped her head in acknowledgement. 'True.' Unexpected pain lashed at her. Was that all he admitted to remembering about her? What about the part where he had been her fiancé? Or that they'd lived together for three years? Been high-school sweethearts?

Her brain ran into overdrive, trying to assimilate the one piece of news she'd never, ever expected to be told. Or wanted to hear. Her hands clenched in her trouser pockets. How could she work with the man who'd once sworn he loved her so much he'd broken his own vow and proposed before he'd finished his training?

The man who had not shown up for their wedding, leaving her looking a complete fool, shaking in her high heels and beautiful silk gown, clinging to her father's arm as they'd stood on the top step ready to walk the aisle. To her love, her bright and exciting future.

They'd waited, and waited, she and her dad. Slowly her mother had joined them, then her four brothers had surrounded them, protecting her from the buzz of questions rising from the guests also waiting.

At the time she'd been frantic, thinking the worst, imagining him in a hospital bed after an accident, but he hadn't been there. Or anywhere she'd called. It had been as though he'd vanished into thin air. Then late that night he'd called her from who knew where. It had been the call she'd have given anything not to receive.

'Nik, I'm so sorry. About today, about everything. I won't be marrying you. Not ever. I'm sorry.' Fraser had choked and then the line had gone dead. As far as she knew, he hadn't been seen in Blenheim since.

The pen in Nikki's fingers shook, creating wonky lines as she filled in the weekly checklist for Blenheim One ambulance. Her teeth pressed into her top lip, inflicting a sharp pain. 'What's wrong with me this morning?' She couldn't blame the icy chill from the late winter frost blanketing Blenheim.

Fraser McCall. That's what's wrong.

'I know.' Her teeth dug harder.

So what are you going to say to him first? Hi, and welcome. Or, where've you been hiding for the past five years since you ran out on me?

'Definitely not that. That'd be telling him how much I still care and that's a non-starter.'

Since hearing from Mike that her worst nightmare was coming true she'd lived in dread of this day. Her stomach had been rioting continuously, barely tolerating even the tastiest food. The belt on her trousers was a notch tighter. Her mind had refused to shut down at night, giving a constant recital of all the reasons why she did not want to work with Fraser.

There'd been little sleep, causing her head to ache continuously. The headache pills she'd swallowed an hour ago hadn't worked, as they hadn't for the past eight days. And now her hands had started this crazy shaking that made her writing look like a two-year-old's.

How challenging could working with Fraser be? How difficult was it to run a marathon over mountains with no preparation? Her hands shook harder. Mike had put them on the same four-day roster, and no amount of pleading had changed that. She'd even baked Mike's favourite coffee and walnut cake, but had got zip, *nada*, nothing. At least she'd be working days while Fraser did the nights, and vice versa. Hopefully they'd only see each other at shift changeover. Still, far too often.

Toughen up. Use the opportunity to finally ask him why he left. Why he couldn't face marrying you. Why he didn't have the gumption to face up to you that day and tell you straight. Then you can tell him exactly how much you hurt at the time and that you're now totally over him.

'I am?' Of course she was. 'I'm older and wiser. I've learned not to trust as easily—which has to be a good thing, right?' Whatever. But she did have her future all mapped out, which went to show how far she'd moved on from Fraser.

A lonely future without a husband or children of your own.

'There's a wee niece or nephew due in six months' time. How cool's that?'

Not the same as your own. True. One day she'd love to

have a baby, to feel it grow inside her, to push it out into the world and then smother it in love.

'Talking to yourself again?' Mike asked from the internal garage door.

'Only way to get a sensible answer,' she quipped automatically, while bending down to check the tread on the rear tyres. She didn't want Mike to see the pain and worry that must surely be swimming in her eyes.

'You're early. There's fifteen minutes until you clock on at seven.'

'I was up and ready so decided I might as well come in.' She'd figured it would be better to already be working when Fraser arrived. That way she could acknowledge his presence and then immediately carry on with the job. She straightened up slowly, made a show of ticking another box.

'Like you do that often.' When she glanced across the garage, Mike's calm, knowing smile beamed at her. 'Our newest crew member's also early.'

'What?' Fraser was here already? Shouldn't she have sensed his presence? Breathe in deeply, breathe out. In, out. It was too soon to front up to him. She wasn't ready. She'd never be ready. The next tick on the checklist skewed sideways. 'Dang.' She could do without this ridiculous thumping in her chest and the sudden lump blocking her throat. What did she say to him? It wasn't as though they could ever become friends again. Could they? No, too much pain sat between them.

'Nikki, you'll be fine. Whatever your problem is with Fraser, you're a very professional AP and I know you won't let anything come between you and your job.' Mike's words soothed her a little. If he believed she could manage then she'd do her best to live up to his expectations.

'I wish I was as confident as you.' She'd even mentioned

resigning to Mike a couple of days ago but he'd known it for the halfhearted gesture it had been. She loved working as an AP and this was the only full-time ambulance station within a hundred kilometres. Her plans for owning a catering business were for the future, not now when she could help so many people when they were ill or distressed.

Mike stepped closer, the concern in his eyes worrying. 'Fraser's in the tearoom. Come and have a coffee, break the ice while everyone's around. You have to get past this moment, whatever's causing it.'

Gulp. There was another option. She could run away. *So you're a coward now? Face it, Fraser can't hurt you any more. That's done and dusted. And he was the one who did the running away, remember?* Pushing her shoulders back, sucking in another deep breath, she plonked the checklist down on the front seat of the ambulance and squeaked, 'You're right.' She owed this man who'd given her a break and taken her on at a time when he'd had many applicants, some far more qualified than her. Tapping his shoulder, she gave a weak smile. 'Thanks.'

At the tearoom door her shaky resolution backed off. Standing with his back to her, talking to Chloe and Ryan, who were about to take over on Blenheim Two for the day shift, was Fraser. Her first glimpse of him since she'd come home from Dunedin to get ready for their wedding, fully expecting him to follow her three weeks later.

Her heart bumped hard against her ribs as she drank in the sight of him. Fraser's tall, lean body had morphed into a broader, more muscular version of the body she'd known intimately. On Fraser the very ordinary uniform looked like something out of a style magazine. The black pants hugged his mouth-watering butt in a way that made her fingers itch.

What had seemed difficult had just become darned near

impossible. Right now her heart was squeezing tight with raw longing, and her eyes were filling as an alien tenderness overtook her. Transfixed, she drank in the sight of this man who'd dominated her thoughts one way or another for all her adult life.

She swallowed, hard. 'Hello, Fraser.'

He turned slowly. Nervous? Unwilling to face her? It had never occurred to her over the past few days that he might find this situation as difficult as she was. But maybe he did. After all, he still owed her an explanation, not to mention an apology.

'Nikki.' He gulped. 'You're looking good.' His rich, golden-honey voice washed over her, bringing with it a storm of sweet memories.

Memories that until this moment she'd believed she'd deleted from her mind. Fraser murmuring to her as they'd lain tangled in the sheets of their small double bed in the cosy flat they'd shared with two other med students in Dunedin. Fraser egging her on to beat him at strip poker then laughing like crazy when she'd lost.

Stop it. Focus. Concentrate. Remember everything else. The burning humiliation, the pain in her heart so big she thought she'd die.

Nikki stared at him, speech impossible. He looked… different. That full, generous mouth, strong jaw line, the autumn-brown eyes all were tight with wariness instead of the constant laughter she remembered. But that was the least of the changes. His face had deep lines running either side of his mouth. A jolt of shock ripped through her as she looked further. His once straight, thick, chocolate-brown hair was streaked with grey, and curls spun over the tops of his ears, coiled at the edge of his collar.

What had happened? Was that why he'd done a runner? No. She refused to accept that as an excuse for his actions.

If anything had gone wrong he'd have told her, and they'd have sorted it—together.

From somewhere a long way away Mike said, 'Let's have coffee while it's quiet. Fraser, you'll be pleased to know Nikki puts her cooking skills to great use and keeps us supplied with yummy treats.'

Nikki jumped. For a brief moment she'd forgotten where she was. A quick look around the staffroom showed Gavin and Amber watching this meeting with interest, as were the other day crew, who'd just arrived. Amber, her friend and flatmate, should've clocked off by now, but had probably hung around to meet the new guy. Questions blazed from her eyes, warning Nikki there'd be an interrogation later.

Fraser spoke into the silence. 'My stomach's doing flips already.'

Nikki looked into his eyes, really looked, and locked gazes with him. She saw pain and resignation, determination and wariness, all tumbled together. None of the extreme confidence she'd known before. Again, shock tilted her sideways.

'So, how are you?' he asked softly.

Her chin pushed forward. 'Fine, good, busy.' *Dumbstruck, clueless about how to deal with you.*

'It is really good to see you. You look different somehow.' Fraser's tone sounded genuine, as his eyes appraised her slowly.

Too darned slowly. Making her skin heat. Drying her mouth. Huh? What was going on here? Had to be the sleepless nights catching up with her. Why else would she be feeling these odd sensations for a man she no longer trusted enough to make her a coffee?

Fraser moved forward, his arms lifting in her direction. To hug her?

Yikes. No way. Not now, not here. Not ever. Quickly

shoving her right hand out, she gripped his, shook it perfunctorily and let go. But not before something she hadn't felt for five years zinged up her arm. Desire.

Fraser heard Nikki mutter, 'Dang.' She spun away, her thick dark blonde plait swinging across her back as she added, 'I need coffee.'

Fraser grimaced. He could relate to that. Strong, black coffee might just fix what ailed him. Temporarily.

As if the mess he'd created way back when he'd learned he wasn't invulnerable could ever be fixed. Even with the best reasons in the world there was no denying he'd mucked up big time. Especially with this woman standing within reaching distance and looking as remote as the top of the Himalayas.

He couldn't prevent himself watching every movement Nikki made as she crossed to the whiteboard where case studies were written up for everyone to read and learn from. Despite the bulky green jacket she wore she seemed leaner than he remembered. Her steps were more deliberate, as though she'd lost the constant spring in her walk. Nikki Page. The girl he'd cherished at school. The woman he'd desperately wanted to marry. The lady he'd walked away from. Walked? Sped from, more like. He'd broken her heart. He'd also broken his own. Completely.

But he'd eventually got over her. Or so he'd thought. He'd truly believed that or he'd never have come to work here, despite how much he needed to become an AP for his father's sake.

'How do you take your coffee, Fraser?' Mike waved a mug at him, thankfully shifting his focus for a second.

'Black, thanks.' His gaze instantly returned to Nikki. Hell, a few moments ago he'd nearly hugged her. Why? Trying to prove that seeing her again was easy, that he had no hang-ups from the past? Proving it to Nikki? Or himself? Suddenly he felt unsure of everything—his plans to remain in Blenheim and settle down, his yearning to claw back the friendships he'd known before he'd messed up.

'I've got some cereal here for our breakfast,' the girl introduced to him as Amber told Nikki. Then waved the box at him. 'Fraser?'

Nikki's shoulders rolled. 'Not hungry at the moment.'

'Me neither.' He'd forced some toast down before leaving home twenty minutes ago, nearly gagging as it had stuck in his throat. Tiredness dragged at his body after he'd spent half the night pacing the house, keeping away from his parents' room in case he woke his light-sleeping mother. He'd asked himself repeatedly if coming to work here was the right thing to do, and had repeatedly come up with the same answer. It wasn't, and yet it was if he was getting on with his new life.

Amber shook the cereal box. 'You've got to have some food, Nikki. You've hardly eaten anything for days now.'

Nikki winced. 'Okay, just a little to appease you, bossy.'

So Nikki's appetite had disappeared lately. Since she'd heard he was coming to work at the same station? Strange, but he couldn't possibly affect her any more, could he? Not after the damage he'd done before. The way he'd treated her had been truly bad, despite his justifiable reasons.

'I'm bossy?' Amber chuckled. 'That's rich.'

'That's what friends are for. Keeping you in line.' Nikki shrugged eloquently and rubbed out a word on the board, rewrote it spelled correctly. 'Gavin, your spelling is atrocious. And don't go blaming your Welsh background. We might speak funny in New Zealand but the words are the same.'

Gavin looked up from the paper and spoke in what sounded like a put-on broad Welsh accent. 'You're right,

Amber. She's nothing if not officious.' His wink showed how unfazed he was by Nikki's comments. 'So, Fraser, what brings you back to Blenheim? If you don't mind me asking, that is?'

'Family.' And getting on with the life he'd believed for so long he'd never get the chance to live. A second chance. 'My dad's not well so I want to be around to help out with things like keeping the house and section in order, making sure my mother's coping okay.'

Nikki's hand stilled on the board. Listening carefully? She asked without turning around, 'What's wrong with Ken?'

'He's got dementia.'

Nikki gasped, turned to look at him, sympathy in those wide azure eyes. 'That's terrible. Hard for your mum too, I imagine. I'm sorry, I didn't know.'

None of Nikki's family had had anything to do with his parents since that dreadful day when he'd hurt not just Nikki but two families who'd cared about him. He'd lost a lot of people who'd been important to him that day, but he only had himself to blame.

'Mum's managing but I think she's reaching her limits now that Dad's getting very argumentative and wanders a bit. That's why I've decided to live at home and not get my own place yet.'

Nikki nodded. 'I can hear your mum now, checking what time you get home at night, making sure you put your washing out. She'll be enjoying having you to watch over.'

There was a lot Nikki didn't know but she'd got that spot on. His mum had been devastated that he hadn't come home when he'd been diagnosed, but she certainly seemed intent on making up for that now.

Gavin leaned back in his chair. 'You can't beat having your family around. They take precedence over everything else.'

There's no wedding ring on Nikki's finger. The thought blazed through him. *She's still single.* Hang on. No ring meant nothing. She could be in a relationship. Why not? A stunning-looking woman whom everyone adored would attract any red-blooded male. He should feel happy for her, not empty and sad. And maybe a tiny bit hopeful.

'Are your parents still living in Redwood Street?' Nikki stared at him. 'Fraser?'

He shook away those bewildering thoughts. 'Same old house that I grew up in. It's looking a bit tired now.' His mum was struggling with the maintenance. He should've come home sooner but no one had told him he was needed. Not until the night last month when he'd phoned his parents to give them the good news that his five-year tests had shown no sign of the cancer returning. The specialist had virtually given him an all-clear and a new lease on life.

His good news had been tempered with the information that his father had dementia and had had it for two years. It hurt that his mother had decided not to mention it while the cancer cloud had hung over him. Another black mark against him.

There'd been no time yesterday to track Nikki down and make contact prior to starting here. Neither had he found out anything about her, so he asked now, 'Are you living on the farm? Or in town somewhere?'

'Amber and I share a poky flat not far from here.'

No address, then. But what had he expected? An invitation to dinner? 'Most of town isn't far from here.'

Mike coughed. 'Can I see you two in my office? Now?'

Nikki's azure eyes blinked. 'Shouldn't Gavin be joining you? He's the one going to work with Fraser.'

Mike answered brusquely, 'No. Bring your coffee with you.'

At the table Gavin appeared totally absorbed in the newspaper.

What was up? Suddenly Fraser sensed he was about to learn something he definitely would not like. He knew that feeling. It started deep in his belly and writhed outwards, upwards, cold and insidious, taking over his body and then his mind. He'd known it once before and that time the news had been grim. He wanted to call out to Mike, to stop him before any words were uttered, but Mike had disappeared into his office.

At the door Nikki turned back to him, a huge question in her eyes. So she was worried too. He wished he had it in his power to take away that dread blinking back at him. Hell, she was still gut-wrenchingly beautiful. His heart slowed, his throat filled as he headed in the direction of the office they'd been summoned to. She still turned his head, still made him want to hold her and run his hands over her satin skin. Talk about bad timing for remembering those particular sensations. Nikki Page was a no-go zone.

Closing the office door was a mistake. He'd shut the three of them into the small space and there was no getting away from Nikki. He drew a deep, steadying breath. And inhaled her scent. The one that had always reminded him of summer gardens; of roses and freesias and peonies. For a brief moment his head spun, almost taking his feet out from under him. Placing a hand on top of the filing cabinet, he waited for his heart rate to slow to normal. And tried to concentrate on the dull, grey carpet under his black workboots.

Then Mike began to speak and he forgot everything as the dread he'd felt minutes ago became reality.

'Gavin handed me his notice last night. Patricia has been homesick for a while now so they're heading back to Wales next month.' Mike sat on the edge of his desk, his feet stretched between them. 'Nikki, you're taking his place as Fraser's mentor.'

'C-can't Gavin do it until he leaves? A month's a long time.' Her bottom teeth bit into her top lip and her wide eyes gleamed desperately at her boss. 'I can take over in September.'

'No, Fraser deserves continuity while he's training.' Mike hesitated, looked from Nikki to him and back to Nikki. 'Look, you two have obviously got history but if you're working here then you leave it at the door. Our patients deserve one hundred per cent concentration from all of us, all the time. I can't have you warring on the job.'

'That won't happen,' Fraser rushed to assure him.

Nikki's head snapped up and the glare that pierced him told him he shouldn't be so sure of that. But she did say, 'As long as we keep everything on a professional basis, it should work.' A breath escaped between her lips. 'I guess,' she added softly, the glare softening as worry and uncertainty took over.

Mike continued to outline what was expected of them both, then handed Fraser a folder, a key and a pager. 'Your rosters, course notes and timetable, and access codes.' He then shoved out his hand and clasped Fraser's. 'Again, welcome aboard. It's great to have someone experienced joining us. Isn't it, Nikki?'

Shaking Mike's hand, Fraser watched Nikki as she hauled herself off the chair. 'Yes, a change from training someone right from scratch.' Her voice was a monotone, as though she'd put a tight rein on herself. Was she barely keeping from yelling at him to go away, get lost?

Ah, Nik, if only you knew how much I regret having done that to you once already. On everyone's belts pagers beeped simultaneously. Relief poured across Nikki's face as she snatched at hers. 'Priority one. We're on, Fraser.' And she was gone, charging out the door and into the garage before he'd taken a step.

He followed quickly, equally glad of the interruption while they both assimilated the new situation. But, damn, working in the same truck with Nikki would make everything a hundred times more difficult. They weren't being given any time to get used to being around one another. No time at all. Straight into the fire. Might be the best way.

CHAPTER TWO

NIKKI raced for the ambulance, leaving Fraser to follow. He might be used to a different station but the drill would be the same. Snapping her seat belt in place, she turned the ignition key as he slid into the passenger seat. 'Did you unplug the truck?' she asked, without looking at him.

'Yes. Having you drive off with the power supply still attached wouldn't be a good look on my first day.'

'It's been done before.' Mainly by new recruits eager to leap aboard, on their way to a call, and completely forgetting about all the truck's many batteries being kept topped up while on standby. With so much equipment on board that needed power, the batteries drained very quickly.

Fraser tapped the computer screen, bringing up the details of the callout. 'Ashleigh Rest Home. Eighty-seven-year-old woman found lying on bedroom floor. Conscious but groggy.'

'And probably very cold because of this morning's frost.' Putting on the lights and siren, she eased the ambulance out of the garage, nodding thanks to the car drivers giving way to them. If she concentrated on the details of the job and the traffic she was weaving the heavy vehicle through she might be able to pretend that wasn't Fraser sitting on the other side of the truck.

Who was she kidding? It was Fraser. No getting away

from that. His size dominated the cab. The tantalising citrus smell of his aftershave teased her senses. He hadn't used aftershave before, not that she could remember, and she remembered most things about him. He liked scrambled eggs soft and made with cream, his toast underdone, his steak rare, and would refuse point blank to eat lumpy mashed potatoes.

Fraser fumbled around behind her seat. 'Where's the PRF kept?'

'Under your seat.'

He found the patient report form and copied in details from the screen, appearing totally impervious to the situation.

Why couldn't she act as though he was any other crew member she had to mentor? She tried. 'Patient's name?'

'Mavis Everest.'

'Don't know her.' In a town the size of Blenheim she often attended people she knew, which added a personal, and not always welcome, factor to the situation. 'Is Mavis in a unit or the hospital wing?'

'A detached unit, number three. She must be capable of looking out for herself, then. Not bad at that age.'

'Probably has a caregiver.' Nikki hated the idea of anyone she loved ending up in a retirement village. A lot of people liked the security and companionship but she couldn't see her parents there after spending their lives on the farm. Not that they were even close to having to think about that but, still, she already knew she'd look after them if the need arose.

'Is this a good rest home?' Fraser asked, peering through the windscreen as the entrance came into view.

'I've never heard any complaints or noticed anything untoward. Why? Looking for somewhere to live?' Dang, why crack a joke? She was supposed to be keeping aloof and discussing work only.

Fraser's smile flicked on and off so fast she nearly missed it. 'No, thinking about my dad.'

'He's too young for this place.' She recalled Ken McCall as being years younger than her father. 'But I guess dementia doesn't take note of age.'

'Isn't that a fact? He's decades too young. But soon Mum has to face reality and put him into care. He's already a handful for her.' A haunting sadness filtered through Fraser's voice and into the cab between them.

'But she loves him. It can't be easy, making that decision.'

'No, it can't,' he snapped.

Whoa, what had she said wrong?

Then he said in a milder tone, 'Sorry. I'm still trying to get my head around it all.'

Nikki negotiated the narrow entranceway, her mind focused almost entirely on Fraser. His sadness made her want to do the strangest of things. Made her yearn to put her arms around him and hug him tight; made her wish his worries away.

Stop it. Let Fraser in at all and you're back where he left off with you. It was a long enough haul getting over him the first time. Just remember the black hole of depression you fell into and that'll keep you well away from him.

With a hitch in her throat she drove into the parking area. How could she even be contemplating touching him or wanting to help him? That's what partners, husbands and wives, lovers did. Not estranged couples.

Finding unit three, Nikki prepared to back up to the tiny pathway leading to Mavis Everest's front door, checking as she went how low a nearby tree hung. Wiping off the emergency lights with a branch never went down well back at the station. A car was parked close to where she wanted to put the truck. She sighed. 'Why couldn't the staff have asked the car owner to shift?'

'Want me to direct you?' Fraser's hand was on the door-handle.

'I've got it.' She backed up neatly and stopped. Jumping down, she headed for the back of the truck and pulled the doors open, tugged out the stretcher in readiness for their patient.

When Fraser picked up the defibrillator and the pack containing their equipment, she nodded silently. He knew what he was doing.

A tall, gaunt woman in her late fifties opened the front door. 'Judy Mathers.' She sighed exasperatedly. 'I came around when Mum didn't answer her phone. We talk every morning at seven while I'm getting ready for work. I found her on the floor and I can't lift her back into bed.'

They squeezed into the stifling, tiny bedroom full of large furniture. At least their patient hadn't got hypothermic but how she'd found a space to fall was beyond Nikki. 'Mrs Everest, I'm Nikki and this is Fraser. How long have you been lying down there?'

'Been here all night.' Mavis Everest's voice was weak but there was a twinkle of mischief in her faded eyes. 'Long time since I spent the night on the floor alone.'

Unzipping her jacket, Nikki squeezed down beside the prostrate woman and smiled as she reached for Mavis's wrist. She hated seeing elderly people in this sort of predicament. It seemed so undignified and lonely somehow. 'Can you remember what happened?'

'Got up to go to the bathroom and felt a bit dizzy. Must have blacked out because that's all I remember. Woke up some time about two.' When Nikki raised an eyebrow, Mavis added, 'The radio was on. The talkback show and some silly man complaining about his ingrown toenails and how the doctor wouldn't fix them.'

Mavis was alert and her speech coherent. All good indicators. Amazing, considering how long she'd been lying there. Nikki counted the steady beats under her fingertip as her watch ticked over a minute. Sixty-three. 'Normal,' she assured Mavis.

Fraser took Mavis's other hand. 'I'm going to check your blood-sugar level so just a wee prick in your finger, Mrs Everest.'

'Ooh, dear, don't go to any fuss. Just help me back into bed and I'll be good as gold.'

From the doorway Judy said in her exasperated tone, 'Do what they say, Mum, for goodness' sake. They know best. The sooner they've done with you, the sooner I can get off to work.'

Blimey, show some concern for your mother, why don't you? Nikki kept her face straight with difficulty.

Fraser deftly took a small sample of blood from the elderly woman's thumb, speaking softly as he did so. 'We need to find out why you were dizzy, Mavis. Nikki's checking all your bones in case you did some damage when you fell.'

Nikki ran her hands over their patient's head, down her neck, feeling for contusions or abnormalities. Down Mavis's arms, torso and on down her legs. 'Looking good.'

'For an old duck,' Mavis quipped.

'You're only as old as you feel.' Fraser shoved the glucometer back in its bag. 'Glucose is four point six. No problems on that front.'

But a few minutes later he told Nikki, 'Blood pressure's low.'

Nikki nodded. 'That could explain how she ended up

on the floor.' Looking up at Judy, she asked, 'Has Mrs Everest got a history of low blood pressure?'

'Doesn't look like it.' The woman held four pill bottles in her hand. 'Only arthritis drugs here.'

She doesn't know? 'Can you pop them in a bag for us? And some overnight clothes.' Nikki turned back to Mrs Everest. 'Mavis, have you ever had any problems with your blood pressure before?'

'Not that I'm aware of.'

'Okay. The doctor will do some more tests. We're going to take you to hospital now.'

'No, love, I don't want any fuss. My GP can visit when she's got time later today.'

'For pity's sake, Mum, just do as they tell you. If you weren't so stubborn about going into the partial-care wing of this place, we wouldn't be here now.'

Nikki felt her blood beginning to simmer but bit down on the retort itching to escape. This had absolutely nothing to do with her. 'Your GP would probably send you to hospital anyway, Mavis.'

'My daughter will be happy with that. Save her having to check up on me.' The yearning in the old lady's voice saddened Nikki.

'I'm sure she'll find time to visit you.' Or was that unrealistic? Nikki mightn't know anything about Judy or her own family commitments but she couldn't understand people who neglected their parents. Look at Fraser. His parents' woes had brought him home when nothing else had.

Fraser straightened up. 'I'll bring the stretcher inside. Mavis, you're going for the trip of your lifetime. First-class bed in the ambulance.' He winked down at the little lady in her winceyette nightgown.

'Do you serve meals as well?' Mavis rallied, a tired smile lifting her mouth.

'This is the drinks run. Saline via drip.'

Nikki gave Fraser a reluctant smile. This was the man she used to know. The man who'd always made people laugh with his light-hearted banter. 'Keep it up. You're making her feel better. I'll get the stretcher.' Laughter was definitely the best medicine. 'We need to get Mavis into her dressing gown to keep her warm outside. I'll also brush her hair to spruce her up a bit.' Warmth and dignity would be equally important to the elderly lady.

'Thanks, love. Can't go out looking like something the cat dragged in.'

Fraser picked up the thick robe and began to gently slip a sleeve up Mavis's arm. 'You're going to wow those doctors in ED by the time I've finished with you.'

Nikki strode outside for the stretcher and gasped. She'd been smiling. At Fraser, and how he handled Mavis so well. For a very brief moment she'd forgotten the past. Dang.

Thirty minutes later their patient had been delivered into the kind care of the ED nurses and Nikki pulled away from Wairau Hospital's ambulance bay. 'You were good with Mavis.'

Fraser picked up the handset. 'Why do you sound surprised?'

Gulp. Yeah, why did she? 'I'm not, really. You were always brilliant with patients.' She'd observed it first hand when he'd been training and she'd dropped by the hospital to see him. Changing the subject away from anything close and personal, she said quickly, 'Some old folk are so lonely. I wonder how they get that way. Mavis's daughter doesn't exactly seem overly caring and loving.'

'Maybe they've had a bust-up in the past. Life doesn't always pan out how you expect it to.' Fraser pressed the button and spoke to the call centre in Christchurch where all 111 calls in the South Island were dealt with.

Was she talking about his father? Or their relationship? Her life had certainly gone off course because of Fraser. But his voice had been harsh with knowledge, with deep understanding of things going wrong. Had he faced something terrible since before he'd left her? Or had it been the prospect of getting married that had distressed him so much? Not for the first time she wondered if he'd got cold feet at the thought of being tied to her for ever. Or had he thought her unattractive? Overweight? Not good in bed? Found another woman? All the insecurities she'd learned to deal with now flashed up in her head, but she quickly shoved them away. She was at work, not the place to be thinking about the past.

'Blenheim One departing Wairau ED, en route to Base.' His tone was measured, professional as he relayed details to Coms. It was the voice he used to calm distraught patients before he started gently teasing them and making them smile. The times she'd seen him on the wards he'd been completely at ease with patients and their families, making them feel they'd had his undivided attention for as long as they'd needed it.

'Did you finish your medical degree?' The words were out before she could stop them.

'No.' His fingers whitened as they pushed the handset back onto its hook.

'Why not? All you ever wanted to be was a doctor. Even when we were kids you'd tell everyone that's what you were going to be when you grew up.'

'I changed my mind.'

Stunned, she again spoke without thinking, 'You changed your mind after four years of study? Why?'

'I wasn't ready.'

'Not ready? For what? You loved medicine. I remember all those endless nights you put in studying and not begrudging a single second. You couldn't wait to get to university or the hospital every morning to learn more. You loved it all. There was the day you came home shouting with excitement, saying you wanted to be a surgeon, that surgery was amazing. Then months later you decided paediatrics was the greatest, all those little kids needing your care. Then—'

'Drop it,' Fraser snapped at her. 'Just leave it, will you?' The eyes he turned to her glittered angrily. His fists pounded his thighs. 'I had a change of heart, Nik. That's all.'

Perversely *her* heart swelled. He'd called her Nik, his pet name for her. No one else dared call her Nik. Until Fraser she'd hated it. Had he used it to drive his point home? Or because he still cared a little about her?

Idiot. Even if he does, it means nothing. You're not interested in getting back with him, only in finding out why he took off in such a flaming hurry without a word of explanation.

Nothing had changed in that respect. He'd made it very clear he had no intention of telling her anything about what he'd been up to in the intervening years. She needed to mind her own business, even with Fraser. But she'd like some closure, even after all this time.

The radio squawked to life. 'Blenheim One, stand by.'

Snatching up the handset, Fraser acknowledged, 'Roger, Blenheim One standing by.' His relief at the diversion throbbed between them.

Nikki pulled the ambulance over to the side of the road to wait until they found out where they were needed next. Her fingers drummed on the steering-wheel as she waited for the details. Her stomach cramped as it squeezed around yet more disappointment about Fraser. The silence between them was heavy with all the things they'd left unsaid. Had he ever really loved her? Had he got caught up in the excitement of their relationship and popped the question without thinking the ramifications through? Unlike her. She'd always loved Fraser, had always wanted to marry him and have his babies. She shot a quick glance in his direction, saw his face in profile as he glared outside, his chin pushed forward, the corner of his mouth white with tension.

'Blenheim One, male, nineteen years old, severe abdo pain,' the dispatcher intoned over the radio, her voice sharp in the frosty air of the cab.

Thank goodness. With a patient to deal with they could forget everything else for a while. Forget? Or postpone?

'Roger, Coms.' Fraser tapped the screen to bring up the patient details.

Nikki noted the address and made a U-turn, making a mental list of the obs she'd do for a patient with abdominal pain.

Fraser appeared fascinated with the passing houses. Then he surprised her further. 'I'm not the only one to change careers. You always talked of being a chef, and had a goal to work in a top-class restaurant. What happened to that, Nikki?'

He'd turned the tables on her. She turned them back. 'I never went back to Dunedin after you dumped me. I quit my job and stayed at home on the farm.' She'd never have survived returning to the city where they'd lived. 'You must've noticed that much.'

His mouth tightened. Regretting asking about her past now? 'Who do you think packed up all your gear from our flat and sent it up to your parents' farm?'

She deflated like a balloon suddenly let go. 'I never knew it was you. I just thought it would've been one of our friends.' So it had been Fraser who'd put into one of the boxes her favourite photo of them together at St Kilda beach. It now lay at the back of the wardrobe in her old room at the farm. 'Did you leave university then? Or later?'

He ducked that one. 'What made you choose the ambulance service?'

She sighed. 'Dad had an accident, rolled the tractor at the back of the farm. Luckily he was thrown clear but still copped a broken femur and a punctured lung.' Nikki paused, reliving the scene she'd come across when her dad hadn't come in for lunch on time. 'At first I thought he was dying, he looked so still and pale. I freaked.' She'd wished Fraser had been there because he'd have known what to do.

Fraser had turned to look at her. 'A frightening situation.'

'Terrifying. The ambulance crew were fantastic and I began to see something else I might consider doing for a job. I volunteered the next week and gave them every hour I had free.' It had also made her feel closer to him—for a while.

'But you always hated the sight of blood.' Fraser shook his head.

'I got over that really fast.'

'But you gave up your passion. I remember those fantastic meals you created. There was never a time when there wasn't something tasty in our fridge. Our friends used to draw straws to see who came to dinner in our cramped flat because you loved giving them gastronomically divine treats…' His voice trailed off. 'Oh.'

'Exactly.' There hadn't been a lot of fun in cooking after they'd broken up. Cooking was her way of expressing love and friendship, and for a long while she had struggled with the whole concept. She'd got a job as junior chef at one of Blenheim's vineyard restaurants but it had been a drag, a way of earning an income, not a lot of fun. Because her passion for food had disappeared.

Moments later Fraser said, 'Here's our stop. That narrow driveway by the hedge. You'll have to park on the roadside.' He stood and pushed through to the back, no doubt to get the pack. His hip brushed her shoulder lightly.

She braked sharply. Sucked air through her teeth. It was only a hip. An unintentional touch.

'Hey,' Fraser called out.

'Sorry,' she muttered, and eased the heavy vehicle alongside the pavement. She was toast if she went hyper every time Fraser inadvertently bumped against her, because it was going to happen often working together with a patient in the crowded confines of the ambulance. She shoved her door wide, dropped to the ground with a thud, jarring her teeth. Not even halfway through day one of his training and she was going stark raving bonkers with emotions all over the place.

A girl aged in her late teens let them into the untidy house. 'Col's in a lot of pain. He can't move at all.'

Nikki followed her through to the lounge, trying not to breathe deeply as the rancid stench of body odour swamped her nostrils. Looking for a clean spot to put down the pack, she asked the young man sprawled across the couch, 'Col Hargreaves? I'm Nikki. I hear you've got a pain in your stomach.' She had to shout over the din from the enormous television.

'It's agony,' the man groaned.

'Can you show me exactly where it's hurting?' Nikki crouched down beside the couch and, picking up the remote, lowered the noise level.

Tugging his sweatshirt up, Col stabbed the right side of his belly with his forefinger. 'Here.' Another poke on the left side. 'And here.'

'How long has this been going on?'

'Since last night.' Col moved sideways and foul language followed.

Wrapping the pressure cuff around his upper arm, Nikki kept up the questions, trying to ignore everything else. 'Have you had something like this before?'

'Yeah, last week. Your lot took me to hospital but the doctor couldn't find what was wrong. Are you going to take me there again?'

'Yes, after we've taken some readings.' She wrote the normal blood pressure results on her glove. 'What were you doing when the pain started?' She could hear Fraser pushing the stretcher through the door behind her.

'Watching TV.' Her patient gave a loud and drawn-out groan. 'I get giddy too. Ahh,' he squealed.

'Take it easy. On a scale of one to ten how strong is the pain?'

'Ten.'

Then he should be writhing in agony. 'Is it hurting anywhere else?'

'Nah, only in my gut.'

'Okay, Col. We need to get you up onto the stretcher. Reckon you can do that by yourself?'

'Lady, I'm in pain here.'

Fraser stepped around the stretcher. 'Right, bud, we'll take an arm each to help you up. On the count of three, ready?' When Col grunted, Fraser continued, 'One, two three.' And he hauled the guy upright.

Nikki helped get Col onto the stretcher and covered him with a blanket. She had a shrewd suspicion Col was more than able to walk out to the ambulance if he had a mind to. His symptoms were hard to pin down and he'd groaned before she'd touched his stomach, making her suspicious about what he was up to. But she could be very wrong. They'd make Col's shift to their vehicle as comfortable as possible.

Fraser pressed the stretcher's brake off and pushed the stretcher out to the ambulance. 'We'll soon have you in ED and the doctors can check you over.'

'What about my girlfriend? She's got to come.'

Col's belligerence was beginning to annoy Nikki but she offered a lift to the girl and indicated the front seat. The trip to the hospital was punctuated with loud groans and intermittent swearing.

After handing Col over to the ED staff, Fraser commented dryly, 'That guy bounced across from the stretcher to the hospital bed. What happened to the level-ten pain? He's having everyone on.'

'Not our problem any more. But maybe he needs someone to take notice of him, for whatever reason.' She stepped into the back of the ambulance. 'You drive. I'm going to wipe down the stretcher with antiseptic and see if I can't get rid of that overpowering stink of sweat.' It had taken over their vehicle.

What she wouldn't give for a shower and a clean uniform. She began scrubbing every surface she could. Funny how that particular odour hung around long after the cause had gone.

Nikki's cellphone rang as Fraser backed into the garage bay back at Base. Flipping it open, she smiled. It was Jay, her big, bad brother, who'd recently joined a rural vet practice close to the farm they'd grown up on. Nearly two years older than her, he was the youngest of her four brothers. He'd also been Fraser's best friend at one time. Jay had taken it almost as hard as she had when Fraser had gone away. 'Morning—'

'Did I just see McCall in the ambulance with you?' Jay's deep voice rumbled in her ear.

It had taken all of two hours for the news to get out, quite slow for Blenheim. 'Yes, the one and only.'

'What's he doing here? When did he return?'

The ambulance stopped and Nikki quickly slipped away to head outside the garage. This was one conversation she didn't want Fraser overhearing. 'I only found out last week when Mike told us he'd got a job here.'

'He's not working as your partner, is he?'

'Yeah, Jay, he is. It's not like I had a choice. Believe me, I tried to get out of it but Mike insisted we work together.'

'Work together? What's this about? Why would a doctor want to work on the ambulances?'

'Thanks, Jay. Our job isn't for the brain dead.'

'I know that.' Jay paused then went on, 'So what's going on? Is McCall here for a week? Or for ever?'

'I'm not sure. Definitely more than a week.' She quickly filled Jay in about Fraser's father, before telling him, 'Fraser didn't finish med school.'

'No way! He was destined for a great career. No, sis, you've got it wrong.'

'He told me himself.'

'Did he say why?'

'You think he would?'

'I think he should,' Jay growled. 'So he's still hiding things from you. Wait till I see him. It's time he knew exactly how we all feel about him.'

She surprised herself by saying, 'Jay, leave him alone for now. Give him a chance. Who knows? He might turn up at the farm one day with a six pack of lager under his arm and apologise to us all for the trouble he caused.'

'Sis, if you believe that, then you believe in the tooth fairy.'

Fraser plugged the electricity source into the ambulance, wincing as Nikki's words reached him. He was going to have to move a lot faster than he'd intended. Apologising to the Page family was on his latest to-do list. Only he'd figured it wise to first let them get used to the fact he was back.

But if Jay was on the case he'd be breaking down his mum and dad's front door by sundown tonight. The Page men were known to be very protective of their sister. Especially Jay, who carried his own demons about the sister who'd drowned years ago.

Fraser drew a deep breath. Gawd, he'd missed Jay. They'd done a lot together—getting into trouble as teens, surviving their first hangovers, learning to drive, racing motorbikes on the Page farm, playing in the school first fifteen and the cricket team. So much of his wonderful life and friendships back then had been tied up with Nikki's family. All had gone down the gurgler because he hadn't known how to handle the terrifying situation he'd suddenly found himself thrown into five years ago.

When the garage door rattled downwards Fraser realised Nikki had finished her phone call and was standing beside him. 'Are you happy with the way those callouts went?' she asked, one hand on her hip.

'Absolutely. So far everything works the same way it does in Dunedin.'

'Good. Do you know when you'll be starting your courses?'

'Online workshops start in a couple of weeks and my first week away in Christchurch is next month.'

Nikki was deliberately showing him that their relationship was strictly professional. He'd have gone along with that if she hadn't discussed him with Jay.

Tonight. Tonight he'd visit Nikki and lay the past to rest. A cold sweat broke out on his brow. All those years and he still wasn't prepared for her reaction to what he had to tell her. He did not want to see pity in her eyes. He did not want sympathy. He just wanted a clear conscience.

Tonight. After they knocked off for the day. He'd get her address and pay her a visit.

CHAPTER THREE

'Why are we doing a Life Flight pick-up?' Fraser negotiated the ambulance through the lunchtime traffic the next day. 'Surely two paramedics for this job is overkill?'

'Blenheim Two's already out on a job so there's no one else.' Nikki didn't look up from her paperwork. 'But if there's a priority one call we'll ditch the pick-up.'

Fraser rubbed his aching head. Another sleepless night tossing and turning after his plan to see Nikki had gone awry. He'd wheeled Nikki's address out of Amber when she'd come on for the night shift and had headed straight around there, only to find the place in darkness. He'd returned after dinner with his parents but Nikki still hadn't come home so he'd had no choice but to forget about talking to her last night. But he would try again tonight, and every night until she was at home and ready to listen to him.

As he drove down Middle Renwick Road towards the airport, they passed row after row after row of grapevines, some still being pruned. 'The vines always look naked at this time of year. I'd forgotten how I always knew the season by the vines and the activities in the vineyards.' A pang of homesickness struck Fraser, despite being back here. This was one of the things he'd come back to Blenheim for, he suddenly realised. A sigh trickled past his lips. He was home physically, but in any other respect he had a long way to go.

'Remember when it used to be cherry and apricot orchards, and paddocks filled with carrots and peas that you drove past.' Nikki glanced out at the passing scenery.

'Not many of those left now. I heard that the council rates have been driven up with all the vineyards creating high prices for the land.'

'Yep, and that's a sore point with some of the older farmers.' Nikki touched the icons on the screen in front of her. 'Our patient's been having chemo and radiation in Wellington. Bowel cancer.'

'Ouch.' An old, familiar tug of horror and fear grabbed at Fraser. The fear that had receded over the years since his treatment still managed to raise its ugly head at times to twist his gut. Like a warning not to get too complacent as it could come back. But, no, it would not. Must not.

Nikki continued reading aloud. 'Glen Wright. Twenty years old. Hell, that's terrible. He's so young. How does someone deal with that? He's got his whole life ahead of him.'

You have no idea. Fraser pressed his mouth tight, kept the words in. Now was definitely not the moment to be revealing his secret. Gawd, if Nik had been at home last night she'd know the answers to her questions.

She hadn't finished. 'I hope he's got a good prognosis. At twenty he'll have hardly done a thing with his life.'

Nope, he won't have. But he sure as hell will hurry on with it the moment he's fit enough. 'It must've been dreadful for him to learn he had cancer.'

It would've blown the guy's mind wide apart with fear and disbelief and shock. It would've stopped him eating and sleeping for days. He'd have looked out at the world with a deep longing for all that he could be deprived of.

He'd wonder what he'd done so wrong to be thrown into this situation.

'You planning on snapping that steering-wheel?' Nikki's eyebrows rose cutely.

'Not today.' He tried to relax his fingers and his brain. A return mental trip to those bleak days would achieve absolutely nothing but darkness. And the darkness was over. With the all-clear, he'd been given a fresh start on life, which he mustn't waste.

Stopping at the security gate leading onto the tarmac, he punched in the access code Nikki reeled off and watched the gate slowly pull back. 'I called round to see you last night.'

Nikki jerked around in her seat, her beautiful azure eyes darkening with worry, panic even. 'Why? I thought we agreed to keep everything on a professional level.'

Why had he opened his goddamned mouth? Now he'd have to give her some reason or she'd niggle away at him all day to find out what he'd wanted to see her about. The truth but nowhere near the whole truth? 'Thought we might discuss how we're going to make this crewing together work without too much aggro.'

'We can do that on the job.' She wasn't giving him any leeway. 'Move, or the gate will close on us again.'

Fraser blinked. When had the gate opened fully?

Pointing to the left, Nikki told him, 'Keep your speed at ten k's an hour and park between that hangar and the painted circle on the tarmac.'

Easing the ambulance onto the edge of the tarmac, he watched the plane rolling along the taxiway, the wintery sun highlighting its bright red paintwork. Beyond the flat ground of the airport the rolling curves and sharp edges of the Wither Hills wore their winter green.

Fraser dropped down onto the tarmac, asked over his shoulder, 'What's our role here?'

'We help transfer the patient and drive him to hospital. He's accompanied by two nurses, who take care of him. They'll return to their plane by taxi once they've handed over to the ward staff.'

'That's it?'

Nik came around the front of the truck and looked up at him. 'Guess you never had to do this in Dunedin where there's a big hospital with all the bells and whistles. Unfortunately there are many instances when local patients are sent away for major surgery or treatment. These flights save them an awful lot of discomfort getting home.'

The sound of the engines of the advancing plane drowned out anything else she might have said. As soon as the props stopped spinning a side door popped open and an elevator with a platform attached began sliding out.

Nikki told him, 'You can move the truck closer now. Come from the back. The pilot gets antsy if he thinks his wingtip is in jeopardy.'

Yes, boss. Keep it professional. Absolutely. Fraser felt a wry smile tugging his lips. 'On my way.'

He'd barely braked to a halt when Nikki had the back doors open and the stretcher out. A chill wind edged under the collar of his thick uniform jacket, making him shiver. 'The sooner Glen's inside the ambulance the better.' The guy's resistance to the cold would be low if he'd just finished a round of chemo. Fraser shivered, this time not from the cold but from the melancholy memories of his own chemical-ravaged body in the days after treatment.

On the platform at the plane's side was a stretcher with Glen strapped on. He was looking around with dull, tired eyes, barely acknowledging what was going on.

'Hey, Glen, you're nearly home,' one of the nurses dressed in blue overalls commented.

'Sure,' the guy muttered.

'Hospital ain't home, is it?' Fraser gave Glen a knowing smile.

Glen's eyelids lifted. 'You're damned right, mate.'

'Let's get you out of the wind.' Fraser snapped buckles together to keep their patient from moving. With Glen quickly installed inside the vehicle, Fraser slid behind the steering-wheel and eased the vehicle forward, vowing to make the trip as smooth and bump-free as possible. *As you do every trip.*

Yeah, but this one's special.

Nikki had just added the mussels to her paella when the door chime rang. She dropped the wooden spoon and rice splattered over the stovetop. 'Dang. Who's calling at dinnertime?'

Her heart stuttered. Not Fraser, surely? He'd been around last night when she'd been out at the movies. Unfortunately Amber, sensing something going on between Fraser and her, had been quick to give him their address.

Another ring from the door. 'All right, hold on.' She swung the front door wide. And leaned against the doorjamb as casually as tight nerves and shaking hands allowed. 'Fraser. I thought we'd agreed to keep work at work.' Talking was difficult with a mouth as dry as dust.

'A six pack of lager, I think you said.' Fraser held the pack out.

'You overheard me talking to Jay yesterday.' And she'd have to find a tooth to put under her pillow for the fairy.

'But if you're not into lager then I've got this.' In his other hand was a bottle of very good Chardonnay. 'Not knowing what you drink these days, I'm covering my options.'

'You need me on side that much? Is this where you tell me why you didn't turn up for our wedding?' Gripping the edge of the door, she held herself upright through sheer determination. She'd wanted to know this for ever and yet now she shook with nerves. She could learn bad stuff that would shatter her carefully restored confidence.

'Nik, let me in.' His tone was gentle. 'Please.'

Every time he called her Nik she softened towards him. Did he know that? Was that why he used her pet name? Sucking in her stomach and straightening her back, she waved him inside and shut the door. Shut Fraser inside with her. Too late to say no now. She breathed in the tang of lime aftershave and regretted her capitulation. Anything to do with Fraser always became too hard too quickly. So much for remaining calm, aloof, non-involved. It wasn't possible whenever he came near.

So she would hear him out and move on. Then maybe she'd even manage to be happy working with him. As she pushed past him in the narrow hall, her arm slid over his, but she clamped down on the instant surge of longing that contact brought.

A strong burning smell. 'The risotto,' she screeched, and raced into the kitchen to snatch the deep pan off the gas ring. 'Great, there goes my dinner.'

Fraser peered around her at the risotto. 'Can't you lift off the top layer carefully? It'll only be burned on the bottom.' His tongue did a lap of his lips. 'It looks damned good from here.'

She raised her gaze to glare at him. 'Help yourself.'

A wee smile lurked at the corners of his mouth. 'You're not afraid I'll tell everyone you served me burned food? That could ruin your reputation as a great cook.'

'If you're talking about the gang at work they'll ignore you for fear they won't get their weekly quota of home-made cakes and biscuits.'

'True. The way to anyone's heart is through their stom-ach.' Fraser put down the wine and beer and scooped up a mouthful of risotto with the wooden spoon.

She watched as the spoon slipped into his mouth, saw his tongue clear the rice off the wooden surface. She leant against the bench for support. For the second time in two days desire spread through her like wildfire, heating her in long-chilled places, suffocating her in need. Heaven help her, it was only paella, and yet the guy made it the sexiest food out.

'Divine. A little smoky but absolutely delicious.' He took another spoonful, his eyes rolling and that tentative smile growing.

Resignedly, Nikki found a plate and a fork, handed them to him. 'Help yourself.' Tugging a bottle from the six pack, she twisted the cap off and took a long, cold drink. It cooled her throat, but nothing else. Why had she opened her front door so wide and invited Fraser in? This had not been what she'd expected, this deep need clawing its way down her body, teasing her, taunting her.

Bang. The bottom of the bottle cracked on the bench as she put it down. 'Come on, let's get this over with.' Her voice came out light and squeaky. Clearing her throat, she tried again. 'Why are you here, Fraser?'

The fork that had been about to slide into his mouth stopped, held still as Fraser studied her frankly, closely, for a long time. Like he was looking for something.

'What?' Goose-bumps lifted on her skin in forebod-ing as she saw the sorrow and trepidation begin filtering into his eyes.

Finally, Fraser dropped the fork back onto the plate

and pushed it all aside. He turned away, stared around the kitchen/dinning room, turned back to her. His chest lifted as he drew a breath.

Nikki began to shake. This was nothing like the breezy 'I'm sorry' she'd expected. This was serious. 'You're frightening me.'

'I had cancer.'

She gasped. Her Fraser had cancer. Fear bounded through her, turned her legs to jelly, made her head swirl, her hands open and close, open and close. Reaching for the closest chair, she hauled it near, dropped down onto it.

'Are...?' She swallowed, tried again. 'Are you all right?' Dumb, dumb question. As if. He's got cancer, idiot. Of course he's not all right. He could be dying. Never in a million years had she imagined anything so dreadful, so terrifying. Deep shudders racked her. Nausea rose, soured her mouth. Fraser? Cancer? Oh, no. It couldn't be true. It mustn't be.

'I'm fine now.'

'What?' She blinked at him. How could he sound so calm? Didn't he understand how serious cancer was?

She told herself to get a grip. If anyone in this room knew the answer to that it was Fraser. He'd been there.

He straddled the chair opposite, propping his hands on its back. 'I *had* cancer. It's gone. The all-clear came through last month.'

Relief poured through her. She slumped farther down her chair. Fraser was fine. Not sick, not dying. He was as healthy as he looked. Phew. Her shaky hand brushed over her banging heart. It was all right. Fraser was going to make it. She lifted her gaze to his face. Saw again the new lines around his mouth, the seriousness in his eyes. Now she understood the change in his hair. 'You had chemo.'

When hair grew back after that treatment it could be a different colour and sometimes it turned curly.

'And radiation,' he told her.

Hang on. 'It takes five years for an all-clear.' She couldn't focus on one thing at a time as she struggled to take it all in.

Sadness filled his eyes, turned his mouth down. 'Yes, it does.'

'So, around our wedding date?'

He understood her question. 'Three weeks before.'

'Three weeks?' The air hissed out of her lungs. The old, familiar pain of humiliation slammed into her. How could he not have wanted her there with him? Not wanted to share his pain with her? 'Why didn't you tell me?' she whispered.

'I mucked up. Big time. But you have to believe me when I say I thought I was doing the right thing. For you. For us.' Fraser shoved off the chair, strode to the window to stare out into the night. 'It was incredibly difficult. I had testicular cancer. I struggled to deal with it myself, let alone tell anyone else. Especially you.'

Her eyes squeezed shut. A new pain clutched at her. Pain for Fraser. Any cancer was bad, but for some reason this seemed worse. She couldn't explain it but knew it was all tied up with his virility, his very essence. He'd been a sexual man, enjoyed making love. What man didn't? But this had happened to Fraser, her Fraser.

'Why especially me?'

He reached for the wine bottle. 'Got a glass?'

She found two, put them on the table and returned to her seat, still trying to get her head around this nightmare.

Fraser filled both glasses, pushed one towards her. 'I was afraid that you'd leave me, that you'd find excuses because I was no longer the man you'd loved. Often I tried to ring you but every time I picked up the phone and dialled I'd hear you in my mind telling me you wanted no part of it so I'd hang up before you answered.'

The wine was cool and beautiful on her tongue. Swallowing, she pushed the glass aside. It was out of place at the moment. 'So you got in first and left me.' She squeezed her eyes tight. He hadn't had a lot of trust in her love, then.

'Nikki,' he called softly. 'It wasn't like that. Believe me.'

Slowly, she opened her eyes and looked at him. Really looked, looking for the man he'd become, not the man she'd thought she still knew. And her heart broke again. For them both. So much had happened, things they should've shared and hadn't. Of course her depression didn't compare to his, and it probably wouldn't have happened if she'd known the truth behind him leaving her. Fraser should have told her, no matter how hard it would have been.

'You went away without a word. That short phone call was hardly an explanation.'

She'd still had to face people, return their gifts, pack up her wedding gown, eat the food already prepared and paid for and delivered to her parents' home. And the whole time the tears had kept sliding down her face, soaking into her clothes, exhausting her.

He came back to the chair, sat opposite her and reached for her hands. 'I am so sorry for how I treated you, for what I did.' His fingers were trembling as they squeezed her hands. 'When I heard about the cancer I was terrified. I thought I'd been given a sentence. There was so much to think about and my mind was such a mess I was completely unable to make the right decisions. And I didn't want your pity.'

'As if.' Another thought hit her. 'Was I in Dunedin when you found out?'

He shook his head. 'I found out three days after you left to come up here to sort out all the last-minute things for the wedding. I'd been tired and irritable but put it down to all the study and exams, and our upcoming wedding. But after falling asleep on duty one night I decided to see a doctor to get a prescription for something to give me some energy. I got more than I'd bargained for.'

She pulled a face at the thought. Her skin felt clammy. Her stomach quaked at the fear for him. 'Finding out must've been horrible.' On his own. 'I could've been with you.'

'I didn't even know the doctor had asked for a PSA test. He'd only ticked the boxes for anaemia on the blood test request form. Apparently, he rang the lab and added the prostate test as an afterthought. Damn him.'

When Nikki raised her eyebrows, he added, 'It's kind of like the ostrich syndrome. If the doc hadn't asked for the test I'd never have known I had cancer and therefore it wouldn't have existed.'

'Yeah, sure.'

'Very scientific, I know.' Fraser squeezed her hands and put them back in her lap. 'It's a big ask but I hope one day you can forgive me.' The glass he lifted to his lips was unsteady. One mouthful and half the wine had gone. 'The oncologist told me I had to have surgery urgently, followed by chemo and radiation. He also mentioned that I'd be sterile after that treatment.'

'Oh, Fraser. I'd have coped with that. It was you I wanted, loved, not any future children.'

'Nikki, Nikki.' He shook his head again. 'You loved kids, always made jokes about having a dozen. Your own cricket team with a reserve, you used to quip. How could I take that away from you?'

'How about letting me make up my own mind about

it? Huh? Ever think of that? I'm not denying it would've been disappointing but nothing in comparison to what losing you was like. I wasn't marrying you to have children. I wanted to spend my life with you because I loved you.'

'I did have my sperm frozen for later, but it felt all wrong to be asking you to deal with that at the time.'

'Easier to leave me on the day of my wedding?' The bitterness was unexpected and wrong. Fraser had been through hell and it didn't matter how badly he'd treated her. He deserved better. Who knew how they'd have dealt with his situation unless they'd faced it?

Ashamed, she glanced across. 'Sorry, that was uncalled for. You must've been going through hell. I only wish I'd known. That's what relationships are about—sharing the good and the bad. I'd have been with you the whole way through, fighting for you when you didn't have the strength, boosting your morale when you didn't think you'd make it. That's what my love for you meant.' Tears streamed down her cheeks, but she ignored them. 'I'd have done anything for you back then.'

He stood up, ran a hand over her head, down her cheek, cupped her chin. His eyes were deep, anguished pools, not brown, not black, a nothing dark shade of despair. 'Exactly. I couldn't handle that.'

Then he was gone, closing the front door quietly behind him. Leaving her shocked and shivering. With questions crashing around her skull. Sadness mixed with anger. Self-righteousness laced with despair. And seeping through it all a dawning understanding of the man she'd once loved more than life itself.

Fraser walked along the edge of the Taylor River where it meandered through town. His hands were shoved into the pockets of his trousers, his chin almost touching his chest. His mind held an image of Nikki opening the door, dressed in designer, hip-hugging jeans and a fluffy blue sweater the colour of her eyes. Stunned at how gorgeous she'd looked, he'd struggled not to haul her into his arms and kiss her. Temptation in clothes.

Then the other images overtook him. The images he'd expected right from the beginning. Her shock at his revelation. The sadness, the fear. Her anger at him for not sharing the news with her back at the beginning.

Nikki owned his heart. She always had. At some time between being a kid and turning into a teenager he'd fallen in love with his best friend's sister. She'd stolen his breath away with her easy smile and twinkling eyes, her cute nose and smattering of freckles. Only as he'd grown up had he learned that those feelings swamping him were all to do with love.

She'd hated those freckles and covered them with a hefty layer of make-up whenever she could. And nowadays the smile and twinkle had gone. Because of him?

He'd effectively killed her love. But he'd saved her a load of anguish. While he regretted how he'd broken off with her, he couldn't regret doing it. For her sake. He'd loved her too much to ever ask her to give up her dreams for him. And now? When he was home, ready to pick up his life?

Now was too late. For him and Nik. She'd moved on, made a life that would never include him. She'd become totally self-sufficient, self-reliant. She didn't need him. He didn't need her. Right? Right.

Loud laughter had him snapping his head up, gazing at the restaurant that stood at the top of the bank overlooking the river. People sat around tables, enjoying themselves, each other, sharing meals and wine. Surprised at the longing gripping him, he hesitated. He'd missed that kind of intimacy ever since he'd left Nikki. Not even his close friends had filled the gap made by her absence. Neither had the parade of forgettable women he'd been with to test himself, to assess the true level of his loss, to try to blank out his past.

If this was his new life then he was damned if he'd stand on the outside looking in and feeling sorry for himself. Striding up the steps, he entered the restaurant and took a seat at the bar, ordering a glass of cabernet merlot and a rare steak from a passing waitress.

'Hey, Fraser McCall, is that you?' The barman placed the wine in front of him.

Fraser studied the man on the other side of the counter before shoving his hand out. 'Mark Stevens, how the hell are you, man?'

'Heard you were back in town. On the ambulances, aren't you? With Nikki. You two got together again? That's great news.'

Ouch. The reality of small towns, home, was that everyone thought they knew your business. 'No, we're only working together.'

'Aw, shucks, man. I couldn't believe it when I heard you'd split. Everyone knew you were made for each other.'

Fraser swirled the wine in the glass, tasted it, nodding his approval for the wine, not for the way the conversation had gone. Maybe he should've kept walking. Walking away from life? 'So, Mark, what about you? I see you're wearing a wedding ring. Who's the lucky woman?'

He was home, with all that entailed. Tonight he'd apologised to Nikki. Two steps forward. And Mark had underscored what his own heart knew but had recovered from—Nik and he had belonged together. One step back.

CHAPTER FOUR

'THIS one's yours,' Nikki told Fraser as they responded to a priority call. Being a mentor had its benefits. By putting Fraser in charge of the job she could observe his techniques. And keep him busy so he wouldn't have time to talk about anything other than work.

'Sure thing.' Fraser looked up from the PRF he held, as though waiting for her to say more. When she didn't, he began filling in details on the page.

Dang, she was tired. If she'd got five minutes' sleep last night, she'd have been lucky. Fraser's words, all of them, had gone round and round and round in her mind until finally just before 4:00 a.m. she'd got up and made a hot chocolate and watched mindless TV, crying for Fraser and what he must've been through, until Amber had come in a little after six.

It was shift changeover day, which meant Nikki and Fraser had had the day off in preparation for working the next two nights. Nikki had skulked around the flat most of the day, venturing out for her run late in the morning. Her head had ached so much her skull had felt as though it would split in half and she'd returned home after only twenty minutes, deciding ibuprofen and a hot shower were more likely to set her up for work than running for an hour. Tomorrow, she'd make up for the lost kilometres.

A car pulled out from the kerb directly in front of the ambulance, forcing her to brake hard. Her hand slammed the auxiliary horn. 'Moron. Can't you hear the siren? We're right behind you.'

'Their stereo's probably heaving.' Fraser read aloud, '"John Gemmell, male, twenty-nine, fell out of a tree."'

'What was he doing up a tree in the dark?' she snapped. 'It's after seven o'clock. Got to be nuts.'

Fraser outlined his approach to the call they were attending. 'I'm thinking there could be spinal and or head injuries, fractured limbs. Depending on whether the guy landed on flat ground or obstacles lying around he could also have internal injuries.'

'Yes.' He knew all that, so why run it by her? Making conversation? As she sped down Renwick Road she tried not to think any more about his revelations from the previous evening. There was nothing to be gained by it, but it was very hard to stop considering all the ramifications.

'Two hundred metres to Jackson's Road,' Fraser intoned.

That golden voice reminded her of things she didn't want to remember. Whispers of sweet nothings that had led to kisses to die for. Kisses that had led to exquisite lovemaking. Her hands tightened on the steering-wheel while her tongue slid across her lips. Disturbing when she was actually angry at him.

Fraser peered through the gloom. 'Looks like that's the place. Plenty of lights on. According to Coms there's a small track we're to follow next door to the winery entrance.'

'Right.' Nikki focused entirely on navigating the wide vehicle down the narrow, rutted driveway, finally reaching a ramshackle cottage where lights blazed through the dark. After lots of negotiating backwards and forwards in the small area, with a woman who'd been waiting for them on the porch directing her, she got the truck backed around and ready for an easy departure.

Hopping out, she snapped on gloves and asked, 'Where's Mr Gemmell?'

'Around the other side of the house,' the woman told her. 'He's bad, not moving and groaning all the time.'

'We'll check him over before taking him into hospital,' Nikki said.

'My sister, John's wife, is with him. You might need to give her something to calm down as well.'

'Hopefully she'll feel better when we've got John in the ambulance,' Nikki said quietly as she reached for the stretcher at the same time as Fraser. Her hand snagged on his. Snatching her hand away, she kept her face blank, hoping the flare of heat cooking her brain wasn't warming her cheeks.

'Want to show me the way?' Fraser asked the woman, and headed around the side of the house without a backward glance.

'He wasn't affected at all. Which means he doesn't have any residual feelings for you.' Nikki muttered to herself as she pulled the stretcher free, letting its wheels fall to the ground so she could lock them in place. 'Not that you want to go down the Fraser track again either.' He might've had a very plausible explanation for his desertion but she'd never completely trust him again. No way. And without trust she had nothing.

Placing the backboard and a collar on the stretcher, she headed in the direction Fraser had gone, looking for hazards on her way. At least headlights from a parked car lit up the area, making it easier to see.

Fraser was asking, 'Is John conscious?'

'Yes, has been all the time.'

'How long ago did he fall?' Fraser unzipped his bag.

'It must be nearly an hour. He went outside to feed the dogs and when he didn't come back after a few minutes I went looking for him,' the woman who'd met them replied.

'Are the dogs tied up?' he asked, glancing around.

'Yes.'

'Why did he climb the tree?' Nikki pushed the stretcher to the side, out of the way until they were ready to shift John.

'It wasn't a tree. He came off the roof and crashed through the fence,' the woman explained.

'Sorry, we've been given the wrong details.'

'He'd been muttering about tomorrow's predicted frost freezing the pipes. The lagging came off in the wind yesterday so he climbed up to tie it back.'

Glancing upwards, Nikki could see the corrugated iron gleaming with moisture. The sky was clear, the stars twinkling through the freezing air. It wouldn't be long before ice began forming.

Fraser introduced himself to the man sprawled on his back on a muddy patch of long grass and covered in blankets. Beside him knelt a thin young woman, gripping his hand so hard his bones were in danger of more trauma.

'He's real bad,' she gasped.

'John, are you in any pain?' Fraser asked.

'My head hurts, and my leg and back.' John's voice was very soft and Fraser had to lean close to hear him.

'On a scale of one to ten, ten being the worst, how bad is the pain in your head?'

John murmured, 'Bad. Eight.'

'And your leg and back?' Fraser continued his visual appraisal of John.

'Leg ten,' John gasped as he inadvertently tried to shift his legs. 'Back five.'

'Okay, John, I'll give you something for the pain in a moment. I just need to run my hands over your body, checking everywhere for injuries you might not be aware of,' Fraser continued. 'Try not to move your head. We'll put a collar on shortly as a safety measure.' Beginning at the head, Fraser began examining John thoroughly.

Nikki eased close beside the woman on the opposite side. 'I'm Nikki. Are you John's wife?'

'Yes. My name's Alison.'

'Okay, Alison, can I get you to move a bit so I can reach John? There are some tests I have to do.' She noted the smell of alcohol on John's breath as she pushed up his jersey and undid his shirt. How could anyone even think about clambering onto a slippery roof after having had alcohol? But all she said was, 'John, I'm going to take your pulse and heart rate.'

'Pulse is weak, Glasgow coma scale is ten,' Nikki soon told Fraser, meaning that John was responding moderately well to their questions with speech and eye contact, and was reacting to pain by withdrawing from any stimuli. 'Mild hypothermia, too.'

'Not surprising. It's freezing out here,' Fraser acknowledged. 'Fractured lower leg. Possibly tib and fib.'

As Fraser gently worked his hands down John's left leg his patient cried out and then swore. 'Sorry,' John muttered a minute later. 'I didn't mean to curse you. It's just that it's bloody painful.'

Nikki unzipped her drugs bag. 'Let's give you some morphine for starters. That'll help ease the pain.' The defibrillator printed out some figures. 'Blood pressure mildly elevated. Oxygen saturation still at eighty-five per cent.'

When they'd got the plastic collar around John's neck Fraser hunkered down where he could be seen by John without him having to move at all. 'We're going splint your lower leg to prevent movement when we slide you onto a board. Even with the morphine it's going to hurt a bit, I'm afraid. If the pain's too bad tell us and we'll give you a suck on the Entonox.'

'What's Entonox?' Mary asked.

'Laughing gas.' Fraser was handling the situation perfectly.

Nikki's mouth dried. He was so good at anything he set his mind to. Even at shutting her out. That hurt. A lot. Now that she'd got past the shock of him having cancer, other emotions were taking over.

Disbelief that she hadn't sensed something was so wrong, hadn't noticed he hadn't been well. Could all the excitement and preparations of the wedding have dominated her mind so much she hadn't been taking any notice of the man she was supposed to marry?

Resentment and anger at not being trusted with Fraser's own fear, at not being allowed to support him or make decisions with him about their future.

'On the count of three.' Fraser nudged her attention back to their patient.

With John sucking gas, they carefully rolled him onto his right side and slid the board as far under him as possible, then rolled him onto his back and gently but firmly tugged him into the centre.

Fraser placed everyone at a corner of the board. 'On the count of three we'll lift and move John to the stretcher. One, two, three.'

Alison stumbled as she took the weight of her corner. John squealed with agony, and his wife looked ready to cry. 'Oh, John, I'm so sorry. This is awful. I can't do it.'

'You're doing fine,' Fraser placated her. 'Keep coming this way, small, steady steps. That's it. Okay, everyone, put the board on the stretcher.'

Quickly, Nikki attached the straps to keep John stable while Fraser placed the defibrillator at the end of the stretcher. When he began wheeling the stretcher towards the back of the ambulance, Nikki collected up the pack and drugs bag.

'Can I go with John in the ambulance?' Alison asked hesitantly. 'I don't want him to be on his own.'

'Of course you can.' Nikki touched the worried woman lightly on her shoulder. 'You'll have to sit up the front with me so Fraser's got room to move as he keeps monitoring John on the way.'

'Think I'd prefer that. Seeing those machines and cords and things makes me queasy.' Alison climbed aboard and snapped her seat belt in place.

Nikki shut the back doors and squeezed through the middle, pushing past Fraser as she headed for the front. Through gritted teeth she asked, 'Are you ready to go?'

'As John's not critical I'll do another set of obs first.' Fraser glanced at her, a query in his eyes.

'Easier while we're stationary,' Nikki agreed. 'I'll call ED to let them know our ETA and what we've got.'

Waiting for ED to come back to her, she again contemplated Fraser as he worked hard to keep his patient comfortable and his condition from deteriorating. He knew his stuff. He'd have been a brilliant doctor. It came through in everything he did with their patients. He had an almost instinctive feel for their needs, emotionally and physically. He should never have quit his training.

It was blindingly obvious now why he had. Because of the cancer. But why hadn't he returned to university after his treatment? They'd have given him leave for that, even for a whole year, if he'd wanted it. More questions. Would she ever have all the answers?

* * *

Fraser filled the kettle. 'Want a coffee, Nikki?'

No reply.

He glanced around the staffroom and sighed. Not here. Again. Nikki would be upstairs in one of the bedrooms allocated for night crews. Giving him the cold shoulder.

Yep, that's exactly what she was doing, had been doing since he'd been round to her flat to explain and apologise two days ago. Last night and so far tonight all she'd talked to him about had been work and then only when he'd asked her something.

Had he expected anything else? He'd hurt her so much, why should she roll over the moment he explained his actions? She believed he should've told her everything five years ago. He still hadn't told her everything. Hell. He'd been protecting her from having to make impossible decisions. He'd been looking out for himself as well, not wanting her to stay with him out of pity. Not when he'd loved her so much. He'd done a brilliant job of turning her against him, and there was no way of undoing the damage.

What if he told her the rest? Would she go easy on him then?

The kettle clicked off, the small sound loud in the empty room. Reaching for a mug, he shovelled in coffee granules and two spoonfuls of sugar. His sweet tooth had got sweeter over the years.

'Hey, Fraser, make a couple more of those while you're at it, will you?' Chloe bounced into the room, bringing with her a blast of cold outside air. 'It's freezing out there. There'll be ice on the bridges tonight.'

'We've already picked up a woman who skidded near the river.'

Chloe grinned. 'At least our call was an inside job, a wee kiddie having an asthma attack.'

Chloe's crew partner, Ryan, strolled in, rubbing his

hands. 'Good, I can smell coffee.' He glanced around. 'Where's Nikki?'

'Upstairs, I guess.' Fraser stirred the drinks ferociously. Last night whenever they hadn't been out in the ambulance Nikki had been holed up in a bedroom, the door firmly shut.

'Again?' Ryan frowned. 'Is she working on her university papers?'

How would he know? 'I didn't know she was studying anything.' Fraser handed around the drinks. He didn't know much at all about Nikki these days. And whose fault was that?

'She's doing a commerce degree.' Ryan flicked the TV on. 'Seems a waste to me when she can make food like this.' He held up a piece of lemon coconut slice he'd taken from a cake tin on the table. Damn it. Fraser punched the switch on the kettle and grabbed another mug. He couldn't stand this silence from her. They owed each other more than that.

Nikki clicked on her email folder. Hopefully there'd be something from her tutor at the extramural university regarding her last submission.

Knock, knock. 'Nikki, I've got you a coffee.'

Fraser. Didn't he get it? She didn't want to talk to him. 'Nikki, can I come in?'

No. Go away. Leave me to digest my emotions without taking them out on you. But he wouldn't. He could be the most stubborn person when he wanted something. Best get it over with. Pushing off the bed, she opened the door wide enough to take the mug Fraser held out to her. 'Thanks.'

He put his foot in the opening. 'Nik, talk to me. Please.'

'Talk to you?' She stared at him. The anger she'd been trying to suppress welled up, making her voice rise, her hand shake so that coffee spilled over her fingers. 'Talk to you. That's rich.'

Fraser stepped forward, effectively forcing her back into the room. As she sat down on the only chair available he closed the door and leaned back against it. 'You're right. I've got a hell of a nerve asking you to share your feelings with me. But we have to get on. It's a bizarre twist of fate that we're both here working side by side, but I'm not leaving. This is what I do, just like you.'

Not what she'd expected. But her anger didn't lessen. 'I'm trying to get my head around it all.'

'I can understand that. It took me weeks.'

'I'm not talking about the cancer, though…' She paused, calmed down a notch, put her mug on the floor. 'That's bad enough. No, what really gets me is that you didn't tell me a thing. Not even when you phoned and told me to call off the wedding. You gave no reason why you didn't want me any more.'

'I always wanted you, Nik.'

'How was I to know that? I'm not psychic.' The words gathered, spewed out. Selfish words coloured with the hurt, bewilderment and humiliation she'd carried for a long time after he'd gone. And she'd thought she'd got past most of this. Who had she been fooling?

'Did it ever occur to you that by telling me about the cancer you'd have saved me years of grief, of wondering if you'd found someone else better-looking, or more exciting in the sack or on your level of intelligence? Did you even have the tiniest clue how I might cope with your shock withdrawal from what I believed to be a mutual relationship?'

Fraser reached for her hand.

She swatted him away, picked up the mug again to wrap her shaking hands around it. Tears streamed down her face.

'The truth would've hurt but at least I'd have known. You made decisions for both of us, and that's the hardest part to understand. Why couldn't you tell me something so important? Not even the possibility of never having children excuses that.'

Fraser crossed to the bed, sat down. Placed a box of tissues beside her. Picked at the cuff of his jersey. Opened his mouth, closed it again.

She watched him closely, trying to read on his face, in his eyes what he obviously couldn't say to her. Then told him, 'I don't know that I'll ever again trust anyone not to do that to me.'

Fraser again reached for her hands, and this time she didn't pull away, hoping the contact would help him tell her what was on his mind.

But he moved his head from side to side. 'I'm just so damned sorry I hurt you. I really am.' He tugged free and stood up. 'I'd better let you get back to whatever you were doing when I barged in.'

Nikki stared at him, disappointment squeezing her. 'You're still doing it. Keeping things from me.' Suddenly she wanted him to know a little more about what she'd been doing in the years they'd been apart. It might help bring them back on an even keel so that at least they could work together smoothly. It might eventually help Fraser talk to her.

'I'm doing a commerce degree. I've got this idea of having my own baking business some time so thought I might as well be prepared for that eventuality.' She gave him a small smile. 'Actually, it's kind of fun, studying. And keeps me off the streets and out of the shops, where I tend to spend too much.'

'I don't remember you being keen on shopping.' He stood near the door, looking genuinely puzzled.

For the first time since he'd arrived back in her life Nikki laughed. 'Oh, boy. You have no idea. Ever since I lost weight I've discovered clothes. And shoes.'

'Guess we didn't have a lot of spare cash when we were living together.'

No, she'd been the breadwinner once she'd completed her chef course. And bread had been about it some days, her wages having been minimal. At least now, since her inheritance from her grandmother, she had more than enough money to indulge her passions. Passions. Cooking still ranked number one, and there was money set aside for the shop she dreamed about.

'So you do want to go back to being a chef one day?'

'When scraping people off roads or picking them up from floors gets too much for me I'll think about it. Some nights after particularly ghastly jobs I want out, but I usually manage to work through that. One day, though, I'll know it's time to move on.' Hesitating, she nibbled her top lip, then dived in. 'Was your decision to quit medicine tied up with having cancer?'

Surprisingly the tension in his shoulders disappeared and he answered easily. 'Yes. Suddenly faced with the knowledge I mightn't live for ever, I couldn't see the point in spending the next years tied down studying.'

She lifted her eyebrows in acknowledgment. 'That's understandable. But going into the ambulance service instead must've been difficult after giving up your ambition. You must think you could do so much more as a doctor.'

'Sometimes.' He looked wistful.

'Did you join immediately after your treatment?'

'No. I went travelling with a couple of mates. Do you remember Kevin and Nigel? They always dropped in as you were making dinner.' When she nodded, he continued, 'The three of us went to Europe, Asia, South America. Had a blast for nearly two years. Worked when the cash ran out, then carried on travelling. I joined the service when I got back to Dunedin. Having done four years' medical study I was fast-tracked through the system and given a permanent job straight away.'

His face was animated, the stress lines ironed out for a few moments. His usually tight mouth lifted in a smile. Those missing years obviously held some great memories for him as well as the bad ones.

'You don't ever think about going back and completing your degree?'

Snap. The smile was gone, the lines were back. 'No.'

Nikki watched Fraser turn and leave the room, his shoulders taut again, his tread heavy on the stairs. Why did she get the impression he was being untruthful?

CHAPTER FIVE

'AHH,' sixty-five-year-old Jeremy Day moaned, kicking out at the bottom of the bed. His elbow connected with Nikki's arm just as she was about to stab his thumb with a sharp.

Ouch. 'Mr Day, please lie still so I can get a drop of blood.' She held back her exasperation, knowing that the man probably couldn't help his attitude right now. A known diabetic, his behaviour suggested his glucose level would be very low, which could be confirmed if they could get a blood sample to test it.

'Hey, Jeremy.' Fraser put a restraining hand on the man's shoulder. 'Take it easy, mate. We're trying to help you.'

The woman in the doorway cried, 'Jeremy, do what they say.'

Nikki asked her, 'How long's your husband been like this?'

'I don't know. He was asleep when I left to do the shopping at nine this morning. When I got home half an hour ago I found him acting funny.'

A three-hour gap. 'Do you know if he had any breakfast? Or lunch?'

'I left food on the bench but he hasn't touched it.' Mrs Day stared at her husband, despair and love all mixed up on her expression. 'He's so stubborn at times.'

Snap. The sharp pressed into the ball of Jeremy's thumb

and a drop of blood oozed out. Nikki quickly used the filter paper to suck up the sample and sighed with relief as she waited for the glucometer to read the blood-sugar level. 'Has this happened before?' she asked Mrs Day.

'Three times. He's not very good about taking his readings. Says if he feels all right then he's fine. The doctor tells him it's very serious not to do everything properly but he won't listen.' Mrs Day looked close to tears.

Beep. The meter showed a glucose reading of two point three. 'Far too low.' Nikki nodded to Fraser, who already had an oral dose of glucose ready.

'Here, Jeremy, let's get this into you then you'll soon start to feel better.' Fraser held the tiny plastic cup to their patient's lips.

Jeremy jerked his head aside, knocking the liquid down his shirtfront. 'Don't want it.' He rolled onto his side and drew his knees up to his chest.

Calmly, Fraser reached into the medical pack for a second dose. 'Yeah, you do,' he drawled, 'otherwise we take you to hospital for the doctors to sort this out.'

'No. Not going to hospital.'

Nikki sighed. 'We might have to sedate him.'

'Jeremy, here, drink this.' Fraser held the sample cup firmly this time. 'Or we'll put a needle in the back of your hand.'

Slowly, the man opened his eyes and glared at Jeremy. 'I don't want it.'

'I know, but you'll feel so much better when you do. Swallow this then your wife can get you some food.' Fraser pressed the cup gently against Jeremy's lips. 'Please.'

The room was quiet for a moment then Mr Day opened his mouth and Fraser quickly tipped the liquid in.

The tension in Nikki's shoulders relaxed. Very soon

Jeremy would start behaving rationally and they'd be able to discuss what to do next.

'Let's see how you cope walking to the kitchen,' Fraser told the man once he was sitting up and looking more alert.

'I'll be right as rain, you watch.' Jeremy's legs wobbled as he pushed up off the bed but became stronger as he shuffled out of the room.

'Never have figured out that saying,' Fraser muttered he followed their patient, suddenly grabbing the man by his arm. 'Whoops, steady on. You're not in a race, Jeremy.'

'Young man, are you challenging me?' Jeremy looked ten years younger when he smiled.

Nikki grinned. She hadn't found a patient yet that didn't adore Fraser. They were eating out of his hand most of the time, especially once the medication or painkillers started doing their job. He had a way that everyone related to. Even her. No matter how hard she tried to keep him at a distance, he was slowly getting under her skin.

As they drove away Fraser ran his knuckles down his cheek. 'I felt like a bully back there, trying to get Jeremy to take his meds.'

'You? A bully?' Nikki rolled her eyes. 'As if.'

'I was pushing him to do something he didn't want to do.'

'You were saving his life. You were being firm but caring.' He was nothing like his father.

Fraser stopped rubbing his cheek, relaxed back into his seat. 'Thanks for that.'

They made it back to Base and had time to top up glucometer sharps, defib pads and gloves from the store, but not enough to get lunch, before the next call had them scrambling.

'I didn't get to check out that shortbread you brought in,' Fraser groaned.

'Get over it.' She grinned unsympathetically. But when she saw the details of their next call her grin faded. 'Six-year-old girl, unconscious after hitting head on jungle gym at Fairhall School. Charlotte Stevens.' Nikki's stomach plummeted. 'Ella and Mark's little girl. Do you remember them? Ella Wood.'

'I was talking to Mark the other night. Hard to shut him up. Heard everything about Ella and the two kids. Gawd, he's going to be tipped sideways when he hears about this.' Fraser sped through the traffic, the siren blaring. 'Considerate drivers get out of the way,' he roared as he swung wide to avoid a car that had stopped in the middle of the road. 'Ever heard of pulling over?' he yelled.

Thankfully they had a straight run once they left the outskirts of town. As they raced past the vineyards, Nikki filled in a PRF for the child. 'Charlotte Stevens.' Her heart was in her throat. 'I hate going to kids. And this is worse because I know her. She's such a cutie with a mop of curls and a button nose, always talking so fast I can't understand her.'

'Ella and Mark will be glad it's you attending as you know her so well.'

'Talk about pressure.' Nikki nibbled a rough fingernail. 'It freaks me out a bit, hoping I can help them but always wondering if my knowledge is going to be enough. They're so small and I keep thinking about their parents and what I'd say if I couldn't help their baby.'

'You'll be fine. If anyone can save a child it's you,' Fraser commented. 'Seriously, if you ever want a career change, go for emergency nursing. You'd be fantastic.'

'You're kidding? I couldn't do that. I get all hot and flustered whenever I go to serious emergencies.'

'I'm not aware of that and I work with you. You're known as Miss Cool, Calm and Awesome back at Base.'

She blinked. 'Me? Who said that? I've never heard a thing.' Cool, calm and awesome? Her chest swelled. 'I can live with that.'

Fraser rolled his eyes as he slowed for the school entrance. 'I bet you can.'

They grabbed everything they could possibly need and raced after the teacher, who'd been waiting anxiously for them.

'We haven't moved her at all,' the woman called over her shoulder. 'She fell about twenty minutes ago and still hasn't opened her eyes. Her parents are on their way.'

Nikki swallowed. This didn't sound very good. She glanced across at Fraser as they ran and caught him watching her.

'Miss Cool, Calm and Awesome,' he mouthed as they reached Charlotte.

Blood pooled on the ground beneath Charlotte's head from a large gash above her left temple. Her face appeared whiter than white. Her little body had twisted as she'd fallen and thankfully no one had tried to straighten her. Who knew what damage could've been inflicted when she hit the concrete?

Nikki looked at Fraser. 'You check her head. I'll take her pulse.' The pulse was impossible to find. Nikki's heart sank as she kept trying to feel the tiniest beat under her fingers. Refusing to give up hope, she was about to ask Fraser if he could try to find it when she felt a ridiculously light movement under her fingertip on the carotid artery. 'Yes,' she muttered, and studied her watch as she began counting. 'Dangerously low,' she muttered a minute later. The blood-pressure reading gave her no more hope.

'Deep compression at the back.' Fraser spoke quietly and with no sense of urgency in his voice, yet she knew he'd be frantic to save this girl.

'We'll load and go. Charlotte needs urgent, expert care. We can't afford to waste time checking her vitals out here.' Basically they'd do all they could to keep her alive while getting her to expert care—fast.

'Definitely. Intubate, collar, transfer to stretcher, and we're gone.'

'If only it was that easy.' Nikki carefully slid the airway tube between Charlotte's teeth and tried to slip it down her throat. Felt relief when the tube finally went into place on the third attempt. Fraser had the oxygen ready. Between them they quickly secured the collar in place. And then Charlotte was carefully shifted onto the stretcher, with as little movement as possible before being transferred to the ambulance.

'Phone her parents, tell them to go to ED immediately,' Nikki told the teacher as she closed the doors. Charlotte would most likely be flown to Wellington for specialist care and Ella and Mark would want to go with her.

'Ready for me to start driving?' asked Fraser.

'Go.' And don't spare the engine, she thought, her heart thumping in trepidation for their tiny patient. The trip took for ever and yet it flew past at a breakneck rate. Seeing the doctors and nurses waiting at the ambulance bay doors was the most welcome sight of her career. Charlotte stood a much better chance now.

After handing over, she turned to Fraser and walked into his arms, laid her cheek against his chest. 'That was scary.'

'But we made a difference. Now it's up to those guys.' His hand stroked her back gently. 'Come on. Let's hope we get back to Base without any further calls. I don't know about you but I could do with a very strong coffee.'

She remained a few more moments in Fraser's arms, trying and failing to wipe out the image of Charlotte's immobile face. She could still feel on her fingertip the child's light pulse. And her heart held anguish for a young girl she adored. Finally, she drew back. 'Very, very strong coffee it is.'

'How do parents cope with something like this?' Fraser said as they drove away. 'When I see accidents like that one I think I'm glad I haven't got kids. I'd be locking them up all the time.'

'To think I wanted to have twelve. I'd have turned grey in no time at all.' Nikki sighed. 'Actually, I only wanted two, a boy and a girl. Funny how things turned out.'

'Nik, you're talking as though it's too late for you to become a mother.'

'It is.' *Because I can't have them with you. We're not getting together again. And there isn't anyone else I'd like for the father of my kids.*

Pushing into her seat, she stared out the window, not really seeing anything. She'd let her guard down with Fraser for a moment, and look where it had got her. Thinking of unattainable things. Like babies and Fraser all in the same sentence.

At the end of their shift Nikki stretched her back, rolled her shoulders. 'Yee-haa, a day off tomorrow.' Then two nights on. The time was flying past. It was hard to believe Fraser had been here ten days now.

Amber strolled through to the staff lounge, coffee in one hand, a sandwich in the other. 'Are you going shopping tomorrow?'

'As in groceries?' It had been Amber's turn to get those in.

'Done. But there's a sale on at your favourite shoe shop.'

'You're kidding!' Excitement sizzled along Nikki's veins. 'How did I miss that?'

'I'm asking myself the same thing.' Amber grinned. 'They've got the most amazing boots that you're going to want. Black, extra-long to above the knee, with the cutest slender and very high heels.'

'Nikki, you're dribbling,' Fraser called from the doorway. His eyes looked slightly misty. Did boots turn him on? So what if they did?

Nikki grinned despite her tummy suddenly tightening. 'What would a guy know about these things?'

But as Fraser's eyes turned a roasted-coffee-bean colour she decided this guy knew quite a lot, even if only how boots looked on tall, slim women. Her bubble burst. She was of average height and definitely not slim so his fantasy, if that's what it was, wasn't about her.

'Guess you'll be up early to fit your run in before the shoe shop opens.' Amber bumped the table with her hip, splashed coffee over her forest-green uniform jersey. 'Great.' As she wiped at the spill she asked, 'Did you two have a quiet day?'

Nikki shook her head. 'Nope. We hardly stopped.' After Charlotte they'd been up the Awatere Valley for a broken femur and torn artery, followed by a car versus tree that had involved a family of four and required two ambulances. 'Any news on Charlotte?' she asked the room in general.

Gavin looked up from the newspaper. 'The little girl flown to Wellington? Not a word so far.'

Fraser still waited at the door, his day pack slung over his shoulder, his gaze on her. 'Can we phone anyone?'

'I don't want to bother Mark and Ella's families. I'll check with ED later to see if they've heard anything.'

'Come on, let's get out of here. We're already an hour past sign-off time.' Fraser jerked a thumb over his shoulder. 'We could join Mike and the others for a beer at the pub. Wind down a bit before going home.' His voice was soft, quiet, as though afraid of frightening her off the idea.

'Sounds like a plan.' Shrugging into her jacket, she saw Amber watching her with a knowing smirk on her face. 'What?'

'Nothing.' Her friend grinned.

'Good.' Checking Fraser wasn't within hearing, she added, 'Drop it, Amber. We barely speak in the truck, so we're not going to have a rave at the pub.'

'Where's your SUV?' Fraser asked as he closed the outside door behind them.

'Along Scott Street a bit, under that old oak.'

'I'll walk with you. Mine's a bit farther on.' Then he asked, 'Why an SUV? Why not a zippy little car?'

'My brothers.'

'Pardon?'

'All part of the making sure Nikki is safe programme.' Which was all well and good at times. 'But I didn't argue too much as I do like my vehicle. It's cool.' Hurrying along the footpath, Nikki tugged the zip of her jacket higher. 'Dang, but it's cold out here.'

'You've got a flat.' Fraser stepped off the pavement and bent down on the far side of her four-wheel-drive vehicle. 'I'll change it for you.'

'No need. I can manage.' Not that it would be fun in the dark and the light drizzle that had just begun.

'Nikki, I'm not walking away and leaving you to change a tyre. Got a torch?'

'Yep.' Waving her electronic key, she popped the locks, found the torch and opened the back door to retrieve the wheel brace and jack. 'You're not taking the slightest bit of notice of me, just like my brothers.' Fraser being the forceful, caring male wasn't the Fraser she wanted to remember. Too close to home.

He brushed past her. 'I'll get the spare wheel out.' His shoulder sliding against hers should've been innocuous. It wasn't. She felt as though she'd been zapped with a high-voltage electric shock.

Leaping back, she dropped the brace. As she bent to pick it up her head bumped Fraser's thigh. Talk about turning everything into a circus. 'Sorry,' she muttered.

Fraser's hand gripped her shoulder, tugged her close. In the gloom he peered into her face. 'Hey, Nik, take it easy. We're changing a tyre here, nothing more exciting than that.'

That was the problem. She didn't want anything more exciting either, but after days spent driving around Blenheim with him beside her, or sitting in the common room at the station talking cases, her hormones seemed to have a different opinion from the sane side of her brain. Shocked, she stood staring at the back of his head as he wrestled with undoing the wheel nuts, willing the goose-bumps lifting her skin to lie down.

'Hold the torch so I can see.' Fraser handed her the nuts and hunkered down again, his big hands making easy work of removing the offending tyre.

Her tongue cleaved to the roof of her suddenly dry mouth as a vivid memory came to mind of those hands, those fingers making easy work of bringing her alive as she and Fraser had rolled around their bed in the flat. Why now, after an awful day, did she have to recall that particular picture?

Slumping against the side of the vehicle, she struggled to keep the torch pointed exactly where Fraser wanted it. The beam shook. Her head buzzed and her tummy tightened with unbelievable longing.

'Now for that beer.' Fraser clipped the old tyre into place in the back of Nikki's vehicle and slammed the door shut.

He turned and bumped up against Nik. Why hadn't that peony scent warned him how close she was?

He had to touch her, hold her. Like he had earlier outside the ED. Nothing like that. That had been platonic, or as near platonic he was capable of being with Nikki. Which was diddly squat. But right now he wanted—no, needed—to wrap his arms around her and hold her tight, feel her chest rising and falling, her hands on his back, her fingers pressing firmly. He ached with the need. She stood so close he could feel her sharp, quick breaths on his chin.

An urge to kiss her gripped him, too strong to be denied. Placing his arms around her waist, he gently drew her nearer, afraid that at any moment she'd slap him away. At last his lips covered her sweet mouth. His tongue slid slowly inside, tasting her, stirring up so many wonderful, warm feelings and memories from the past.

Nikki didn't pull away. Instead, she leaned into him, a soft groan slipping over her bottom lip. One hand clasped the back of his neck. To prevent him getting away? She needn't worry. He wasn't going anywhere. His legs didn't have the strength required to walk.

He deepened his kiss, sliding his tongue farther into that warm mouth, exploring her sweetness, her heat. Sending his hormones into overdrive. When his arms tightened further Nikki's breasts pressed hard against his chest. Even through the thick layers of uniform they both wore he was aware of her shape, her heat, her body.

'I want you.'

Fraser blinked. Had he just said that? Then why wasn't Nikki leaping out of his arms and locking herself inside the SUV?

'No,' Nikki growled against his mouth. But didn't pull away.

Nikki had heard him. The words had been real, hadn't

been in his head. He wanted, needed her. But this was Nikki, the woman who'd been avoiding him for days other than to discuss emergency procedures. She was kissing him back. The woman he should be staying well clear of— for her sake. He knew he had to step away from her. But she tasted so good, how could he let go of her? Twisting his head for better access to her mouth, his hands on her chin, thumbs rubbing lightly, the world shrank to this spot. No one, nothing else mattered.

The drizzle turned into a downpour.

They sprang apart. Nikki leapt for her SUV.

'See you at the pub,' Fraser yelled as he slammed her door shut and raced for his vehicle ten metres farther down the road.

Inside his home-built truck he slumped over the steering-wheel, banging his head with his fist. What an idiot he was. Nikki wouldn't be at the pub when he got there. Not after he'd lost his cool and kissed her. She might've been kissing him back but he'd bet his best cricket bat she was already regretting it. She'd be berating herself for giving in so easily when she'd spent every day they'd worked together making absolutely sure that he understood there was nothing between them any more.

Reaching for the ignition, he sighed. Might as well have a beer anyway. He needed it now, even if Nikki didn't.

'Wakey-wakey, sleepyhead.' Amy's voice crawled into Nikki's head, dragging her into the morning.

Rolling onto her back, Nikki groaned as pain slammed into her eyeballs and threatened to blow the top off her head. 'Ahh, what happened?' She squeezed her eyes tight.

Amber tugged the curtains wide open. 'I'd say you drank too much at the pub last night.'

That could explain the bongo drums in her head. That

probably had as much to do with her state as the three vodkas. Nothing to do with the fact she'd lain awake for hours dissecting that bone-crunching, mind-shattering kiss after all. 'I didn't eat much yesterday because we were so busy.' Nikki partially opened one eye. 'Shut those curtains, will you? The light's hurting me.'

Amber sounded disgustingly cheerful. 'So nothing to do with kissing Fraser?'

'How do you know that?' The drums picked up their pace. So it hadn't been a bad dream. It had been real. And it hadn't been bad either.

Amber plonked down on the end of the bed, tucking one foot under her bottom. 'Gavin and I drove past on our way to a call.'

Nikki swallowed hard. 'Do me a favour and keep that to yourself. It won't be happening again.' What had she done? Kissing Fraser was worse than running stark naked down Market Street on a busy Friday night.

Tugging her pillow from under her head, Nikki pulled it over her face. She couldn't bear to think about last night. Whatever had possessed her to return Fraser's kiss instead of pushing him away? It would be so humiliating when she next saw him. He'd think she was an easy touch. That she'd enjoyed kissing him and had wanted more was completely irrelevant. They weren't getting back together.

'Nikki.' Amber leaned forward to stab her shoulder with a finger. 'Come on. You've got to get up.'

'Go away,' she muttered into the pillow as tears began squeezing out her scrunched-shut eyes. 'I can't believe I did that.'

'Want a coffee?'

Nikki eased the pillow aside and glared at her friend. 'Leave me to sleep for the next ten years, will you?'

Hopefully by then Fraser would have left town again and she'd be able to step outside her front door.

'Can't do that. Your brother's coming around any minute.'

'Which one?' Her stomach rolled unpleasantly.

'Jay.'

Nikki stared at Amber, trying to see her properly through the fog in her eyes. 'There's a hint of red in your cheeks when you say Jay's name.'

'I've just had a hot shower.' Amber looked away, fiddling with the bedspread.

'You've got the hots for my brother.' Nikki's head pounded harder. She needed to warn Amber about Jay. Another time, she decided on a tender breath.

'Lover boy's here.'

'What?' Nikki's skull split wide as she screeched, 'Who do you mean?' But she knew. Fraser had turned up. Why?

'He brought your car round.' When Nikki squinted at her, Amber added, 'Apparently you were adamant you weren't driving last night.'

Nikki flipped her hand left, right. 'I'd never risk it. I've seen too many alcohol-induced road smashes.' She shut her eyes again. 'Tell him thanks and I'll see him at work.'

'No can do. He's sitting in the kitchen with take-out coffees for us all. Says he's not leaving until he's seen you.' Amber stood up, a sly smile on her face. 'I suspect he'll come in here if you don't make an appearance soon. He's that determined. You've made a hit, Nikki.'

You have no idea what I've done. None whatsoever. Another thought crashed into her skull. 'Jay's coming around.'

'So?'

'Ever seen a match thrown into a drum of petrol?' Jay was the most protective in a bevy of protective brothers.

She could almost feel sorry for Fraser, except he was big enough to fight his own battles.

Fraser paced the length of the tiny kitchen. Five steps to the wall with a shoebox-sized window that looked out onto the damp concrete square that served as the back yard. A washing line was strung from one side to the other, with underwear hanging from it. Gulp. Nikki's?

In an effort to blank that sight from his head he turned, took five steps back to the door leading into the hall. This tiny flat had surprised him. He'd expected something roomier, sunnier, like the enormous, rambling homestead Nikki had grown up in.

Reaching the door, he heard the girls murmuring in one of the rooms off the short hall. He turned back to the window. Would Nikki make an appearance? If she refused to come out of her room he'd go to see her. He had to make sure she understood last night had been a one-off. His fingertips tingled, vividly reminding him of her satin skin as he'd caressed her neck, her cheeks. Unfortunately. He stopped. Stared around. Unfortunately? Since when did he want to get back with Nik?

Only since you left her five years ago.

His head spun. Really?

The back door burst open, letting in a draught of icy air—and one of four men Fraser definitely did not want to come face to face with yet.

'McCall, what the hell are you doing in my sister's flat?'

'Waiting to see Nikki.' Fraser stood straighter, taller. At six-one he mightn't quite measure up to Jay's height but he was damned if he was going to let that bother him. He would not be intimidated by the Page brothers. He needed them back on side, like they used to be before the wedding debacle, which meant proving he was looking out for their sister and in no way upsetting her.

Which meant explaining and apologising for the past. By the angry gleam in Jay's eyes it was obvious Nikki hadn't said a word about the cancer. Which was good. It was up to him. He didn't believe for a minute that the Page family would immediately forgive him but hopefully none of them would want to beat the crap out of him either.

'She won't see you.'

He was probably right. 'You know we work together—'

'Hey, Jay.' Nikki slunk into the cramped kitchen, Amber following.

Nik looked tired and dishevelled; that gorgeous mane of dark blonde hair free of its usual constraints and falling haphazardly over her shoulders. She wound her arms around her brother and gave him a brief peck on his cheek.

If only she'd do the same to me, Fraser thought. 'Hi, Nikki,' he croaked, his tongue so thick it filled his mouth. He'd give a year's pay to run his hands through her hair, to feel its softness sliding across his skin. Her classy, satin dressing gown outlined her fabulous bottom perfectly and switched on his desire. Just like that. Bad timing. If he stood absolutely still, maybe no one would notice his re-action to the goddess standing before him.

'Fraser.' Nikki barely acknowledged him.

So he was back out in the cold. Two steps forward, three back today.

Jay kept a protective arm around her waist as he asked, 'What's McCall doing here?'

Nikki blinked, nodded perfunctorily. 'Fraser brought my vehicle home. Everyone from work went to the pub and I didn't want to drive afterwards.'

Jay grunted, relaxed a tad. 'Oh, thanks, McCall.'

'Yeah, thanks.' Nikki picked up a coffee. 'This for me?'

'Yes. It's probably gone cold by now.'

'Thanks anyway.' She sipped cautiously, before pouring the coffee down her throat. Next she opened a cupboard, removed a pan and placed it on the stove. From the fridge she removed a carton of eggs and a bottle of cream, moving carefully as though she hurt. 'Breakfast, anybody?'

'Count me in,' Amber looked at Jay, hope in her eyes. 'You staying?'

'If Nikki's cooking, I am.' Jay squashed himself down at the tiny table and folded his long legs under the chair.

Crack. Crack. Crack. Slowly the pan filled with eggs.

Amber asked Fraser, 'Do you need a ride somewhere after breakfast?'

He hadn't said he was staying. 'I'll walk home.' A five-kilometre hike would be good for what ailed him. He should have put his running gear on.

Nikki turned, fixed him with those azure eyes that had haunted his sleep last night. 'I'll drop you back.' The whisk in her hand dripped egg on the floor.

Fraser gave her a tentative smile. 'Thanks, but you're cooking breakfast. Besides, you're not dressed for going outside.' He reached around her for the dishcloth, bent down to wipe up the mess.

'You can stay for some food,' Jay drawled, his gaze crossing from his sister to Fraser and back, a distinct question in his eyes. 'Got enough eggs in that pan, Nikki?'

Why was Jay suddenly okay with him being there? Had Nikki told him about the cancer after all? Fraser hoped his old mate wasn't feeling sorry for him. That was the last thing he wanted. But he was getting an opportunity to be on speaking terms with his old friend. 'I'll stay.'

'I've got more than enough.' Nikki glanced at Jay then back to him before slowly turning back to the pan and whisking cream into the eggs. When she added chopped fresh herbs to the pan his mouth watered. He remembered this process. Nik made the most delicious scrambled eggs ever. Then he saw the whisk slow and stop as Nikki stared out the window. Seeing what? Thinking what? About them? Last night?

Behind him Jay asked, 'Are you back permanently, McCall?'

Dragging his gaze away from Nikki, he faced her brother. 'Yes.'

Jay studied him with a worrying intensity. His gaze shifted to his sister for a moment before returning to bore into Fraser. A warning?

He hurried to explain. 'Dad's got dementia and Mum needs me here. Besides, Blenheim's home and that's where I want to be these days.'

Nikki's head had lifted, tilted slightly to one side. Listening carefully.

So he added, 'I also want to qualify as an AP while Dad's capable of understanding. It's something I owe him.' It would never make up for the medical degree he'd dropped out of, but at least he'd have finished something for once in a long time.

Suddenly a similar smell to burning paella teased his nostrils. 'The eggs are burning.'

Nikki spun around and snatched up the pan. 'I never burn eggs. I'm a good cook.'

He was almost relieved. Now he could get away from the daunting questions in Jay's eyes. He'd tell Jay what had happened to him, but he intended telling all Nikki's family, just not one person at a time. 'Guess that's breakfast, then. I'll head home now.'

The pan clattered into the sink and the sound of vigorous scraping filled the room. 'I should never have started to cook this morning. Too many distractions,' Nikki muttered, loud enough for only him to hear.

Jay spoke over the noise. 'I'll give you a lift, McCall.'

Nikki paled, and the pot scrub in her hand came close to snapping. 'No, it's all right. I'll get dressed and take him.'

'Sis, I've got to go to the pharmacy and pick up some drugs I've ordered for a dog anyway. It's no problem to take Fraser with me. Right, McCall?'

What could he say? *No, I'd rather crawl all the way?* 'Thanks.' He wanted his old life back, right? And that meant playing sport with the local teams, going to the pub with old mates. He couldn't win Nikki's heart back, but if he mended some bridges with old mates, especially Jay, he could settle down here where his roots were.

CHAPTER SIX

NIKKI rushed into the farmhouse kitchen, tugging her jacket off and tossing it on a hook by the door. The scent of fresh rosemary from the roast lamb wafted tantalisingly around the kitchen. 'Sorry I'm late, Mum. Amber and I went shopping. I also got highlights put through my hair and had my nails done. Time got away from me.' Glancing down at her new ankle boots, Nikki grinned. They were so cool. 'Plus the torrential rain forced me to drive slowly.'

'Never mind, I'm just glad you made it.' Her mother, Rose, smiled as she handed Nikki a wooden spoon. 'Just in time to make the gravy.'

'No problem.'

Just then a shout of familiar laughter snatched her attention, wiped her smile away. 'Fraser?' She turned to stare into the games room off the side of the kitchen, where three of her brothers stood shoulder to shoulder at the pool table. Fraser was lining up a shot. Beau and Jay were heckling him. 'He's here? With the boys?' Her voice lifted in a shrill squeak. They seemed almost relaxed with him, not trussing him up like a chicken so they could take turns hurting him. 'But—?'

'Jay invited him to stay for dinner.' Rose stood beside her, looking in the same direction. 'It's a bit like old times.'

No. Nothing like that at all. Old times meant everyone

got on, meant she and Fraser were in love, meant they had a joint future ahead of them. She'd been so happy then. There was no going back now. Worse, her family were supposed to support her, not let Fraser back in. Despair shook her. 'Thanks a lot, everybody,' she muttered.

'Took some guts, walking in here, I'll give him that,' Nikki's dad muttered as he carved the enormous leg of lamb on the meat platter. 'He told us he'd talked to you the other night, and then he apologised for his behaviour the day of your wedding.'

Wow. Fraser really did mean to clear up everything that had gone wrong. Nikki nodded, her gaze still fixed on him. 'Did he just turn up out of the blue? Were all the boys here?'

'Yep, about an hour ago when everyone but you and Jordan had arrived. Had a couple of six packs with him. Told us about the cancer, too.' Her dad continued carving. 'He filled Jordan in on the facts when he turned up.'

Nikki shook her head slowly. 'How did the boys take Fraser's story? Is he back in favour now?' Had her brothers all accepted the situation and put the past behind them as easily as that? This was her territory. Those big men in the games room with Fraser were her over-protective siblings. Where did this leave her? Was she wrong to hold out on him?

Pulling her gaze away, she concentrated on heating the basting juices from the lamb, slowly adding seasonings until she was happy with the flavour.

Her dad watched her, love for her in his eyes. 'I know it still doesn't make it right how he treated you, but I guess we've got to cut him some slack. Fraser was a part of this family until then.'

Nikki swallowed. There had been moments over the past few days when she'd thought the same thing, but then she'd think that if he'd really and truly loved her, she'd have been the first person he'd have told. 'Yeah, well, that's why he should've felt comfortable talking to us.'

Stirring the gravy, letting it thicken slowly, she glanced over at the man who had kissed her a few days ago. A short kiss as far as kisses went, but potent. Fraser's lips on hers had reminded her of some of the good times they'd had. Memories she wasn't sure she needed now, because they gave her hope. Hope for something she wasn't anywhere near ready to think about. Or was even sure she wanted to follow up on.

Her dad tapped the carving knife on the edge of the plate. 'Fraser's got a good heart, lass. He's come home to help his mother take care of Ken. Which—' her dad carved another slice of meat '—considering how Ken used to treat Fraser, is nothing short of a miracle.'

'You mean because Ken bullied Fraser?' Fraser had told her about being taunted by his father if he ever failed a school test or didn't score enough runs in a cricket match. Not meeting his father's demanding expectations had made Fraser's childhood harsh. 'I guess that shows Fraser's good nature.' Dang.

'It does.' Her dad sighed sadly. 'I always figured your man over there left town the very day he finished school to get away from his old man. The rumours were rife when he was young. I remember finding him in the implement shed here one day, sobbing because he'd missed out on the maths prize and his father would be angry. He was seven, for pity's sake.'

'He's not my man.' Her response was automatic, but also the truth. It didn't matter why they'd broken up, but they had, and that was that. But what her dad had said was true. Fraser hadn't said much but she'd seen the hurt in his eyes whenever he'd mentioned his father.

Fraser straightened and challenged Jay with a long drink from his bottle of beer. Bloke speak. Then he glanced sideways and locked eyes with her. The air leaked from her lungs. Fraser. He'd been badly hurt, as badly as she had, if not worse, by his illness and who knew what else. Caution hovered in the back of his eyes, as if half expecting someone or something to snatch away his happiness. In the past she'd have said, 'Serves him right', but now she only wanted to hug him and take away that wariness, to assure him everything was all right. Which was strange. She wanted to hug Fraser? As in comfort him? She shook her head. Weird.

Her mother tapped her shoulder. 'Mind that gravy, love.'

Too late. 'It's split.' Heck, take her mind off the pan for one moment and look what happened. Fraser happened, that's what. Once again, she'd made a basic cooking error because he'd distracted her. At this rate she'd have to give up cooking.

'Not much you can do with that now. We'll have to go without.' Nikki's mother handed her a plate laden with roasted vegetables. 'Put that on the table, will you? And relax. Fraser's not going to hurt you tonight or any other night.'

Nikki turned back to her parents. 'You're both so sure. He's apologised and suddenly the front door's open again.' The plate was heavy and she gripped the edges.

Her mum leaned closer. 'Come on, my girl. He's faced up to a family he knows he treated badly. And he's done it with good grace, honestly and openly. Everyone's entitled to a second chance at least once in their life.'

'Hey, Nikki. Bet you weren't expecting to see me before Tuesday.' Fraser had appeared in front of her. He leaned close, asked quietly, 'Are you okay with me being here? Because I can go if you'd prefer it.'

A second chance, her mother had said. What did that mean? Give Fraser another chance with her? Or the opportunity to be a part of her family again? To play sport with Jay and his mates? To turn up to join in whatever was happening here? Like tonight?

The heavy platter tilted precariously in her hands. Reluctantly, she looked into his eyes, saw nothing but honesty. Which made it hard to tell him to go. With a hesitant smile she held the dish out. 'Put that on the table, will you?'

'I take it I'm staying.'

'You should.' Amazing, but she meant it. Must be something in the air.

Glancing in the direction of the dining room, Nikki noticed her two sisters-in-law watching them, nothing but genuine concern for her in their eyes. Or was it for Fraser? Turning back to him, she asked, 'How hard was it to walk in here after all this time?'

'A little easier than rifles at sunset would've been.' Fraser smiled that delicious smile that had always got to her, making her putty in his hands. And now made her think he did deserve a second chance. Oh, boy. As she blinked, Fraser continued, 'I'm a useless shot.'

She smiled tentatively, suddenly wanting to move forward, step over the past lying between them. 'Then I'm glad it didn't come to that.'

'Come on, you two. We're starving in here,' Beau called out.

'And that food's getting cold, Fraser.' Jordan, brother number two, added his bit. 'Talking of cold, I'll throw another chunk of wood on the fire. That rain hasn't eased off all day and the temperature's dropped further.'

'The river was higher than I've seen it in years when I came out,' Nikki said, suddenly glad to get back to talking about ordinary, everyday things. 'So much for spring pushing winter out of the way. Just hope there haven't been too many lambs born yet.'

'There've been a few out this way recently.' Jay looked around the many dishes on the table. 'Where's the gravy?'

'I wrecked it.'

Jay grinned. 'First burnt eggs last week and now ruined gravy. You need cooking lessons, sis.'

'Still giving you a hard time.' Amusement glinted at her from Fraser's eyes.

'Brothers can be such a pain at times.' Nikki grinned and relaxed completely for the first time all evening. 'But Beau's going to have to start behaving sensibly soon. He and Yvonne are pregnant.'

Fraser reached a hand out. 'Congratulations, Beau, Yvonne. That's fantastic news.'

'Auntie Nikki has already drawn up a babysitting roster so that she gets more turns than anyone else.' Yvonne grinned and gave Beau a peck on his bristly cheek. 'But she'll have to wait a few years until we're in need of a break. I can't imagine ever wanting to let someone else look after my baby.'

Rose smiled knowingly. 'You'll be glad of a night out with Beau after sleepless nights and full-on days, believe me.'

Fraser winked at Nikki. 'Auntie Nikki, eh?'

'Just wish the rest of them would get on with producing heirs for me to play with.' And fill the gap in her heart that should've been filled by her own children.

There were only two vacant seats at the table, side by side, apart from those her parents always sat in. A manipulation by her family? Or coincidence? She'd go for the latter, and try not to question what those big oafs who claimed to care so much about her were up to. Or were they silently telling her to take another look at Fraser?

That they'd vetted him and found him good enough for their sister after all? Totally confused, Nikki sat down and deliberately immersed herself in the light banter flowing around and over the table. This was how families behaved. At least, hers did, and always had.

As the meal progressed Nikki became increasingly aware of the man sitting beside her. It seemed that every time she moved she brushed against him. 'Salt, please.' And her thigh touched his as she reached to take the shaker. 'Peas, ta.' Her arm moved over Fraser's. Her elbow nudged him as she cut her meat. When she tapped her foot in exasperation, her toes tapped the top of his foot.

This was far worse than being shut in an ambulance with him all day. And that was bad enough.

'How are you finding being back in Blenheim?' her father asked Fraser when he could get a word in around his sons' banter—about halfway through dessert.

'At first everything seemed exactly the same as the day I left for university. But Blenheim has changed, Allan. More people live here, the vineyards have spread farther out from the town, and now it's the people I grew up with who are working on the land, running the businesses. I'm very glad to be back.'

Out in the hall the phone rang and Jay pushed his chair back. 'I'll get that. Might be someone remembering it's my birthday.'

'How could anyone forget when he told the whole town?' Beau grinned.

Jay was back, his face bleak. 'That was the police. The bridge is out. The river's burst its banks. Our four-wheel-drive tractor's needed up by the bend to pull a campervan out from where it crashed over the railing into the water.'

'Sounds dangerous, son.'

'It gets worse. Two people are trapped inside. Nikki,

Fraser, I took the liberty of saying you were here and the SARS co-ordinator wants you to attend. There could be injuries.'

'Not a problem. I'll change into workboots.' Nikki stood up. 'Jay's in the search-and-rescue team these days,' she informed Fraser while mentally running through what might be available in the house to take to the scene in case of injuries. 'Mum, I'll take your first-aid kit and some blankets.'

Fraser pushed his chair back. 'Has the ambulance been called?'

Jay answered over his shoulder as he headed for the back door. 'Yes, but they're going the long way. There's another breach of the river bank closer to town that's causing chaos.'

Nearly an hour would be added to the crew's trip, then. 'Guess it really is up to us.' Nikki grimaced.

Beau was already at the door. 'I'm coming, too. Might be something I can do to help.' Within moments three brothers were kitted out in wet-weather gear and stomping through the rain to one of the large four-wheel-drive vehicles parked by the shed, while Jay headed to the shed and the tractor. Allan called to Fraser, 'Keep an eye on my girl, will you? I know what she's like when she thinks someone needs her help.'

'I'll be glued to her at the hip.' Fraser took the pile of blankets Nikki's mother handed him and stuffed them into plastic bin liners for protection from the rain. He nodded at Nikki. 'We'll take your SUV. My little heap will sink in the first puddle we come to.'

'Glued to me at the hip?'

'Where you go, I go.' He grinned that wicked grin of his that turned her toes upwards, fizzed her blood.

Thank goodness it would be chilly out in the rain.

Fraser drove, following the guys down the long drive

and out onto the sodden road, surprised that Nikki had tossed him the keys. Normally she would be proving that she was as good as any of her brothers.

Slap, slap went the wipers. *Whack, whack* went his brain. He'd gone out to her family home that afternoon, not really knowing how well he'd be accepted by Nikki's family despite Jay's genuine invitation after he'd heard his story. No one had mentioned the past, which had perversely put him on edge, tightening his gut, tensing his shoulders.

They'd just waited for him to say his piece, which had been hard to do with those men all lined up, hands on hips, waiting. Everybody but everybody knew you didn't fool around with Nikki or else those brothers would be down on you like a load of hay bales. But Jay had stood beside him.

Parking on the edge of the hard by the group of people clad in waterproof gear peering over the edge into the raging waters of the usually quiet Wairau River, Fraser commented, 'Those spotlights on that farm truck give the whole place an eerie look.'

'There's the campervan.' Nikki pointed to the van bobbing precariously in the river, water lapping at the bottom of the windows. 'Those poor people must be terrified.' She jumped out of the vehicle and stomped through the puddles to join her brothers.

Fraser followed, pausing at the river's edge, the sight making him whistle through his teeth. 'Hell, those folks are lucky not to have been swept away.'

'The current could still roll the van at any moment.' Beau appeared at his elbow.

Jay joined them. 'It's going to be a job and a half getting those people out of there. I doubt I can pull the camper back onto land. It's too far over the edge and I'll be pulling against the current. A crane might do the trick tomorrow. In the meantime, I can anchor the van while the guys evacuate those people.'

Nikki stood on Jay's other side. 'If that was me stuck in there, I'd be screaming in fear.'

Fraser grimaced. If it had been Nikki in that van *he'd* be screaming with fear. And there'd be no stopping him moving mountains to get her out. 'Do we know exactly who's inside the camper?' he asked Jay.

'A woman and a teenager. They'd been parked on the river bank most of the afternoon but must've decided it was time to move away from the river. Pity they didn't make that decision hours ago.' Jay stomped off to his tractor.

Fraser turned to Nikki. 'Why don't you wait in your vehicle until we're wanted? No point in getting soaked unnecessarily.'

'Because then I wouldn't know what's going on.' She glared at him. 'As soon as Jay's secured the van I'm going to see if I can reach those people. There's a strong possibility one or both were injured when they tipped over the edge. Either of them could've slammed headfirst into the windscreen or dash.'

Fraser's blood chilled, slowed. 'You are not going anywhere near that vehicle. Or the bank.'

Beau stepped in front of her. 'No, Nikki. I don't think so. What if the bank gives out completely and the van gets washed away?'

'You could be hurt. Drowned.' Fraser added his fears.

Jay had spun around and stomped straight back to Nikki. 'Where did you get that dumb idea from, sis? You are not going near that river.' Even in the dim light his fear for his sister was easy to see. 'You think we haven't got enough to deal with without you getting into trouble? Try climbing down to the front of that van in this rain and see

what happens. You'll slip for sure. Stay with Fraser and
Beau until we can bring those people to you.'

Nikki laid a hand on Jay's arm. 'It's okay, I'll be careful.'

Jay shrugged her hand away. 'You're not going there.'

'You could tie a rope around my waist.' Defiance tightened her voice and stabbed Fraser in the gut.

'No way,' he all but shouted, and was rewarded with
rolling eyes and a tight mouth.

'You think we're not going to do everything we can to
get those two out of there?' Jay snapped. 'We've got spe-
cially trained people to do this.'

'None of your lot can do more than basic first aid. I
can.' Nikki glared at her brother. 'I understand why you're
worried but this is different. I can look after myself, Jay.
And your guys will make sure nothing happens to me.'

Jay grunted. 'You want me scared witless?'

'No, I don't.' Some eye contact went down between
Nikki and her brother before she turned her fiery glare
on Fraser. 'Our job is to help people.'

Fraser responded quickly. 'No, Nik. It's the job of the
SAR's guys to get them out of there. Then you can do your
magic medical stuff.'

Jay prodded Nikki's shoulder. 'Seriously, sis, I want you
safe on firm ground, not giving me a heart attack while
you're hanging over that wild river in a vehicle that's rely-
ing on a rope to keep it out of trouble.' He raced towards
his tractor.

Just then shouts came from below them. 'Help me.
Mum's not waking up.' The young voice from the camper's
now open skylight was filled with terror.

'That does it. I can get in through that skylight.' Nikki
charged after Jay, calling, 'Hurry up with securing that
van. I'm going in.' She approached the other men and

whatever she said quickly had them fixing her into a harness attached to a long safety rope on pulleys.

Fraser's heartbeat was all over the place. She couldn't go out there. What if she slipped? He stepped forward. 'I'll go.'

'Like you're going to fit those shoulders through that gap.' Her eyes glittered at him then suddenly softened. 'Can you get the first-aid stuff that I brought from home?'

He wanted to tie her to her SUV so she couldn't do such a damned-fool thing, not be aiding her in this crazy scheme. But she wasn't about to listen to him.

'Okay,' he acquiesced, but it should be him going. He wanted to help those people as much as she did, and at least then she'd be safe.

'Fraser,' she said softly, 'I'll be fine. These guys will make sure of that.'

And I'll be terrified every single second until you're back on firm ground. 'You're right.' He strove for a normal voice, speaking around a huge blockage in his throat. Nikki needed him focused on the job. 'I wish we had the ambulance and all its gear.'

Her hand was shaking when he handed her the bag of supplies. He changed tack. She needed support, not argument. 'You can do this, Nik. You'll be just fine.'

Please, his heart begged. *Please don't slip, fall, hurt yourself. Please put your safety first*, but he knew that was a hopeless request so he kept it to himself and stood with Beau, watching while his heart thumped continuously.

The SAR men wouldn't let Nikki go until Jay had the wire cable secured from his tractor to the camper and one of them had gone over to perch on the van's roof first. The moment they gave her the nod she was moving down the bank as fast as possible, crossing the raging water. Using the spare wheel attached to the back of the van, she began hauling herself up. She slipped, grasped the wheel and hung for a moment, her feet kicking at the water. The rope did its job, holding her safe, although at an awkward angle.

'Hell.' Fraser stood on the edge of the bank, mindless of his own safety, holding his breath. Even knowing about the safety rope, his mind tossed up pictures of Nikki being washed away, rolling and bouncing down the river. Then she began hauling herself upwards again. Slowly, one hand grip at a time. He'd give anything to swap places with her.

'Damn it, Nikki. Be careful,' Beau muttered beside him. 'Why couldn't she wait until the guys brought those people to her?'

'Because she cares too much,' Fraser admitted. 'Hell, I want to go and help them, so why wouldn't Nik?'

'You ambos are all the same, needing to make everyone better.'

'Yeah, and you're not? Coming out in these conditions to rescue these people?' Fraser nudged Beau in the arm. 'Eh, Dr Page?'

'A lot of use being a gynaecologist is,' Beau retorted before calling to Jay, 'How are your lot going to get everyone off that campervan?'

'The same way Nikki and Andy went on board. Ropes and pulleys.'

It took for ever to evacuate the boy, Bryne, who'd had his left arm strapped across his chest by Nikki. When he was on firm ground Fraser led him to the SUV and settled him on the back seat. 'Let's take a look at that arm.'

'The lady said it's broken,' Bryne told him. 'Here.' He tapped his lower arm.

Beau joined them. 'Did Nikki give you anything for the pain?'

Bryne shook his head. 'Do you think Mum's going to be all right? She's unconscious and her head's bleeding.'

'I'm sure she'll be good to go as soon as we get her to hospital. What did she bang her head on?' Fraser asked.

'I don't know. I was in the back when we went over the bank. It was scary. I thought I was going to die.'

'Hey.' Fraser lightly tapped Bryne's hand. 'You're safe now, okay? Think of the story you can tell your mates.'

Nikki poked her head in the door. 'How are you doing, Bryne? Mum's safe now. My brother, Beau, he's a doctor and he'll see to your mum.'

Fraser couldn't help himself. He reached for Nikki, ran a finger down her frozen cheek. 'Glad you're back,' he whispered.

'So am I. It was darned freaky out there.'

It had been darned freaky here, too.

Flashing lights announced the arrival of the ambulance. 'Here comes the cavalry.' It was easier to focus on that than think about the danger Nikki had put herself in. She was safe and that should be all that mattered. The fact that his heart was still knocking hard against his ribs was irrelevant. Wasn't it?

Nikki called through the rain still pouring relentlessly out of the sky, 'Hey, guys, typical. Wait till the hard work's done before turning up.'

'I think we've been to Christchurch and back, trying to find a way through,' Mike said as he and Rebecca jumped down and splashed across to them. 'What have you got for us?'

'Bryne here has a broken arm and lots of bruises. His mum needs a nice warm bed for the night in hospital.' Beau gave them a quick rundown.

Fraser led the boy around to the back of the ambulance and helped him aboard, while Rebecca and some of the SAR guys loaded Bryne's mother onto a stretcher.

Finally, Fraser held open the SUV's door. 'Come on, Nikki, let's go home and get dry.'

'Home, as in Mum and Dad's place,' she muttered. 'I don't fancy driving back to town with all that water on the roads.'

Disappointment flooded Fraser. For one crazy moment he'd forgotten they weren't a couple. They weren't even having a relationship so they didn't do things like go home together. 'I guess you're right. It's probably crazy to be on the road tonight if you don't have to be.'

'There's plenty of room for you to stay too,' Nikki murmured, staring fixedly out the windscreen. 'I'm sure Mum will be happy to put you up for the night.'

Warmth trickled through Fraser at the offhand invitation. Three steps forward, none back. Progress?

CHAPTER SEVEN

FRASER pulled into the drive of his parents' home just after six the next morning. He'd left a note on the bench back at Allan and Rose Page's house, thanking them for putting him up the previous night.

Quietly closing the truck door, he headed up the path in the dark to the front door. Hopefully his dad had had a quiet night.

His father's newly querulous voice shattered that wish. 'What do you think you're doing, skulking around here, you scoundrel?'

'Dad? What are you doing outside this early?' Fraser stared at the semi-naked man sitting on the top step. 'You need more than pyjama pants to protect yourself against the cold and damp.' At least the rain had finally stopped.

'Keeping an eye out for you, Henry Broad. You needn't think you're getting past me to Molly. She's mine now. She don't want a bar of you, so beat it.'

Shock slammed into Fraser, forcing the air out of his lungs. *Dad doesn't recognise me.* Knowing that this would happen didn't lessen the impact or the pain. *He's really lost all sense of what's real.*

'Dad, it's me, your son.' Fraser spoke evenly, quietly, pretending his heart wasn't pounding his ribs like a battering ram. He needed to make his father come back from wherever his mind had wandered. 'Dad, I'm Fraser,' he said as he slipped his jacket off and around his dad's shivering shoulders. This was the man who'd tormented and bullied him all his childhood and yet Fraser would give anything to bring back the father he was more familiar with.

'Go home, Broad.' His dad's voice dipped, wavered, as though he wasn't sure what was going on.

Fraser grimaced. *How long has Dad been out here?* His skin was icy. Hypothermic? Shivering and confusion were symptoms. But the confusion was more likely due to the dementia. 'Come on, let's get you inside and warm.'

Where was Mum? Finally getting a desperately needed full night's sleep? This would rattle her, and cause more sleepless nights as she kept one eye open to watch over the man she'd spent all her adult life with.

His dad stood up slowly. 'Don't get funny with me, Broad. I know you've been sneaking around, trying to win Molly away from me.' He swung an arm in Fraser's direction.

Carefully catching the arm, which wasn't as muscular as it used to be, Fraser tried to turn his father round and lead him inside, all the while aching for this once strong man. The man who'd been a hard father, who'd pushed him around, taunted him over any shortcomings, and yet had sat with him for every single round of chemo.

Twisting out of Fraser's hands, his dad yelled, 'Don't you touch me. Get off my property and don't come back, you hear?'

Fraser reluctantly tried another tack. 'Ken, get your butt in the house now before Molly comes looking for you. She's going to be mad as hell if she finds you out here.' It was a crappy state of affairs when a man had to speak to his father like this, but if it meant getting him inside and wrapped up in warm clothes then it would be worth it.

His father glared at him then suddenly peered sheepishly over his shoulder at the front door as though expecting Molly to appear suddenly. 'She'd give me a bollocking, wouldn't she, son?'

Son. Fraser's heart tripped. *Thank you, Dad.* But there were going to be more and more instances when he wasn't recognised by the man who'd reared him, who'd been the reason he'd left Blenheim. Who'd made him the person he was. Because of his father he'd spent years polishing his skills at beguiling people, bringing them onside so they liked him. But suddenly his eyes moistened. Families were meant to be about loving and caring, whereas he'd always believed his father was an adversary.

With his mum everything had been different, all about love and caring. His dad had bullied her as well, but she'd accepted it, whereas he'd fought back. And won his father's love along the way.

'Come on, Dad.' Taking his father's elbow, Fraser directed him inside, closing the door on the outside world. As he and his mum had done for as long as he could remember.

'Ken? Fraser? What's going on?' His mum came towards them, tying a belt around her robe, looking bewildered. 'Where have you been, Ken? I didn't notice he'd gone,' she added in an aside to Fraser.

'It's all right, Mum. I'll get him dry and dressed in something warm. Maybe you could turn on the heaters and make us all a cup of tea.'

Seeing the weariness in his mother's face made the tears prick harder at the backs of his eyelids. This disease was so unfair. Thank goodness he'd come back to Blenheim when he had. His mum couldn't have managed alone for much longer. Even with him here it wasn't easy, but he knew better than to mention rest homes and dementia units again. She'd send him packing for sure.

Not that Fraser could blame her. If he loved someone as much as his mum loved his dad, despite everything, then he'd be dead set against handing over her care to strangers. A picture of Nikki clambering up the camper van last night slipped into his head, along with the chill he'd known as he'd watched her. He'd feared for her, been terrified something dreadful would happen to her. He'd wanted to be the one on the end of the pulleys and ropes, holding her safe.

Sighing, Fraser dropped a kiss on his mum's wrinkled forehead. 'Who's this Broad character?' he whispered.

'The man your father charmed me away from.' His mum smiled softly, her eyes misty. 'Thank goodness.'

'Really?' Shock rippled through him. He'd never understood how his mum could love his dad despite the bullying and demands he'd made on her. Yet now her face shone with it. She wouldn't change a thing. He could see that in the steel at the back of her eyes, in the hand that rubbed his dad's arm.

'Absolutely.'

'Sorry.' He kissed her soft cheek, knowing she wouldn't understand he was apologising for trying to belittle that love when he'd been a teen and thought he knew everything. But setting Nikki free had been just as loving. In a back-to-front way. Must have picked up some of his mother's good characteristics.

'We all used to go to the dance hall in town and your dad was a better dancer than Henry.'

'I got that skill from him, then.' Fraser was very sorry for hurting his mum, but his parents' relationship was not one he wanted to emulate. Sometimes, in the deep of the night, he worried he'd turn out to be no better than his father. What if he had married Nikki and spent their whole life together putting her endeavours down, humiliating her? What if he'd had all those kids he yearned for and then spent for ever making them wish they'd never been born? Or did love really conquer all those fears?

'Fraser.' His mum's gentle voice cut through his questions. 'Dad needs to get warm. Now.' Her steady gaze said she did understand.

With a brief nod Fraser turned back to his father and took his arm again. 'Come on, Dad.'

To concentrate on helping his parents properly he had to ignore the bubble of anguish that had arrived in his belly when he'd seen his dad sitting outside. This disease was never going away. It was going to end in tears and it was his job to cushion the impact for his mum. All part of resuming his place in his family, in his home town.

Nikki flipped open her phone, squeezed it between her ear and shoulder, and continued loading the washing machine. 'Hello?'

'It's Fraser.' Two words. Two very tired words.

Her heart stopped. The very person she'd been thinking about. But why was he ringing her? 'What are you up to?'

'Have you been for your run yet?'

Yes, she had, hours ago. But she hesitated. Something in Fraser's tone suggested he desperately needed company. 'I was about to head out. Want to join me?' Two runs in one day would be hard on her legs but she'd manage. Maybe they'd take it easy. As if. Fraser was a regular runner, too, and she already knew how competitive he was at everything.

'I'd like that. Where shall I meet you?' he asked.

'I'll pick you up in ten, if that suits. We can head up to Wither Hills Farm Park.'

'That works perfectly. See you shortly.' Fraser hung up.

Nikki stared at her phone. Something was up, but why had he asked her to go for a run with him? It wasn't as though he told her much about himself these days. They'd managed to make working together possible by not sharing any personal information.

Ten minutes, she'd said. Minus sixty seconds already. Nikki turned the washing machine on and raced to her bedroom for a clean set of track pants and sweatshirt.

At the foot of the Wither Hills Farm Park they did warm-up stretches before running up the track that would eventually edge around the side of the hill. Nikki took the lead. 'Come on, slowcoach,' she taunted over her shoulder. So far Fraser hadn't said a word about why he'd wanted to join her and her nerves were winding tighter by the minute.

'Slowcoach, eh?' Fraser gave a tense smile that didn't reach his eyes as he lengthened his stride to pass her.

Nikki immediately upped her pace, feeling the strain in her calf muscles as she passed Fraser, only to have him tap her shoulder as he raced past her again. At the top of the hill they collapsed against the fence, gasping cold air into their lungs.

Finally, Fraser muttered, 'Next time I have a rush of blood to the head and suggest going for a run with you I'll go to the gym instead. You're very fit.'

'You're not so bad yourself.' Nikki straightened up, hands on hips as she stretched her back. The wind was chilly, rapidly cooling her down.

His gaze cruised over her, slowing at her breasts. 'When did you take up running? You never used to own a pair of sports shoes, let alone know how to use them.'

Embarrassment warmed her cold cheeks. About to avoid the question, she hesitated. One of her biggest complaints about Fraser was that he didn't tell her anything important. Hauling in a lungful of air, she told him, 'After you left me I got depressed. Like really depressed. I had to take drugs for a while.'

The eyes that Fraser turned on her were dark caramel and full of guilt and concern. 'That explains the way you walk now.'

'What?'

'You used to have a spring in your step, as though nothing could keep you down. Your love of life flowed through everything you did.' His gaze remained fixed on her. 'I took that away from you.'

Blimey. He carried so much guilt. She reached a hand out, touched his lightly. 'Don't. It's over now. You've explained and I have the answers I'd been looking for. I have to own some of what happened to me, too.' Could she have prevented the depression? Should she have knocked on Fraser's door and demanded answers, instead of hiding away feeling sorry for herself? She'd never know.

Fraser turned his hand over, laced his fingers with hers, shook his head at her. 'That's too easy.'

Probably. Striving for a lighter tone, she smiled. 'There was nothing easy about taking up running, believe me. I hated it at first, but my doctor kept insisting I not give up.' She pulled her hand free, away from the temptation to hold on tight, to try and find that connection they used to have.

'What kept you going?'

'I'd lost a lot of weight and didn't want to find it again so in the end that's why I persevered. For weeks I ached from top to toe, then one day I woke feeling great and knew I'd never give up running, or some form of exercise, again.'

'It agrees with you. You look fantastic. But you always did.'

I did? Really? She stared at Fraser, but could see nothing in his eyes that refuted his words. Wow. But it didn't matter what he'd thought, it was still too late. Rubbing her hands up and down her arms, she said, 'Let's walk a bit. It's too cold to stand still.'

Fraser nodded but remained staring out over the town for a long moment. Finally, he turned to her. 'My father's getting worse, and there's not a thing I can do about it. It's like watching a coil of wire unwinding under its own volition. I can't stop it. I can't change anything. And worst of all, it's too late to tell him the things I've wanted to tell him most of my life.'

The helplessness in his eyes caught at her, making her heart ache for him. 'What would you say to him if you could?'

She had to strain to hear his reply. 'I'd tell him I forgive him.'

'I'm sure he knows. You came home for him. That says what words don't.'

Fraser turned to face her. 'I know he loved me. He just didn't know how to show it. Until I was ill. Then he spent months with me. Still tried to tell me what to do, though.' Fraser's smile was poignant. 'Guess that'll never change.'

Nikki asked, 'So what happened today? Did your dad take a turn for the worse?'

'When I got home this morning Dad was sitting on the front porch dressed in nothing but his PJ bottoms. He didn't know me.' Fraser's Adam's apple bobbed and he ran his knuckles down his cheek. 'Called me Henry Broad. Accused me of trying to steal his wife from him. Turns out Broad's an old flame of Mum's. The whole thing would be funny if it wasn't so damned sad.'

Nikki tossed caution to the wind and stepped in front of him to wrap her arms around him. 'I can't begin to imagine how you cope. What about your mother? Is she okay?'

He stood absolutely still, hands at his sides. Waiting for

her to let go? She didn't, instead hugging tighter. This was what friends did, and she could be Fraser's friend. For now.

Finally, he relaxed into her hold, and his hands came up around her back. Against her cheek he murmured, 'Mum's good. Exhausted, but she's good.'

When they began shivering from the cold he pulled away and began jogging slowly. 'Mum's so patient with him, not to mention stubbornly determined to keep Dad at home with her.'

'How much longer can she realistically do that?' Nikki followed, feeling warm on the inside despite the chill wind making her shiver. A hug with Fraser had lifted her spirits no end.

Fraser shrugged. 'How long's a piece of string? There's no way of knowing with this disease. She swears he's been okay up till now.'

'I bet your mother's just happy you're here now.'

'I guess.' Then he tossed a challenge over his shoulder. 'Last one back to the car buys lunch.' And he was gone, racing down the track like a greyhound.

'If you think I'm buying, think again…' But as she sped down the narrow path after him she knew there was no way he'd let her beat him. It wasn't in his nature.

Fraser hurdled over the last fence and slapped his hand on the vehicle first. 'I won.'

Nikki slipped between the fence wires. 'You cheated.'

His eyes rolled skywards. 'Excuses, excuses.' He opened the car door, leaned his arms on the roof. 'Thanks for coming out with me. I needed to let off steam.'

Nikki gazed into those serious eyes and her breath hitched in her throat. He'd chosen her to spend the morning with when he'd wanted to put the pain of his father's illness out of his mind. That made her feel warm and soft inside. Special, even. Like they were getting close again.

'Nikki.' Fraser strode around the car to her. 'Nikki, I...' His hands gripped her upper arms.

'You wh-what?' There was an unfamiliar yet very familiar look in those beautiful eyes gazing at her. He wanted to kiss her, but he was wary. Heat and longing stared out at her, turned her insides soft, exploding all thought of keeping her distance. Her legs stretched, lifting her onto her toes. Her hands gripped the front of his windbreaker jacket and hauled him closer.

'Kiss me, Fraser,' she demanded, secure in the knowledge he wanted it as much as she suddenly did.

His eyes widened and he grabbed her to him. 'I've missed you,' he murmured against her mouth.

Then his lips covered hers, slick, forcing her mouth wide. His tongue pushed inside, teasing, tasting, dancing with hers. Driving her crazy with desire.

Pressing her body length against Fraser, her breasts hard against his chest, her belly against his, thigh to thigh, excitement wound tightly deep inside her womanhood. She needed to touch his skin. Her hands slipped under his shirt, fingers spreading wide on his back, his skin smooth and warm under her fingertips.

She pressed even closer and he wound his arms tighter around her. His shaft, hard, pressed against her belly. It had been so long since she'd known this need. Every muscle in her body shook as his kisses deepened, became hungrier. Shaking with need for him. She wanted him. She wanted Fraser? Yes.

No. She jerked her mouth free. No. They couldn't do this. She wasn't ready. She'd never be ready for him.

Fraser took her face in his hands. The eyes that met hers were full of concern and slowly evaporating need. 'You want to stop?'

Unable to speak, she nodded slowly. And bit back the denial threatening to break from her mouth.

He leaned in, placed the softest of soft kisses on each cheek, then her mouth. 'Okay.' And he stepped away, around the SUV to the other side, never taking his gaze off her.

She stared at him, her hands trembling. How could she have let that kiss happen?

How had she stopped it?

As Nikki pulled into the driveway of his parents' home a little later she gasped. 'That's Mum's car. What's she doing here?'

'Seeing if there's anything I can do for Molly and Ken.' Rose Page answered her daughter's question when they went inside. 'Fraser said last night he's going to Christchurch next month for training so I dropped by to see if Molly might want some company or help with the chores while he's away.'

Nikki gaped at her mother. Yesterday, her brothers seemed to have accepted Fraser back into the fold all too easily, and today her mother had turned up to see Molly McCall.

Yeah, and twenty minutes ago who had been kissing Fraser like a starved woman?

Fraser smiled. 'Thanks, Rose.' Then he turned to his mother. 'Where's Dad?'

'Right here.' Mr McCall loomed up in the doorway. 'Just been catching the midday news and weather. Last night's storm did a lot of damage all over the top half of the South Island.'

It seemed that morning's episode of forgetfulness had passed. Until next time. Pain for Fraser lanced Nikki's heart. It must be dreadful never knowing what offbeat thing his dad might do next. Right now, if she hadn't known, she'd never have guessed Mr McCall had dementia.

Did Fraser ever worry he might get dementia? One glance at him, laughing and chatting with everyone, and she'd have to say no.

'They got that campervan out of the river this morning.' Her mum's voice cut through her thoughts. 'It's a mess. All that poor woman's possessions have been under water all night.'

Molly was looking from Fraser to Nikki. She asked in such an innocent voice that had Nikki wondering if she had 'I've just been kissed by your son' written over her face. 'What are you two doing this afternoon?'

'I'm taking Nik out to lunch.'

Nikki shook her head. 'No, you're not.'

His eyes instantly filled with disappointment. 'I thought that was the deal.'

'The deal was the loser shouts lunch. I believe I came second.' A rush of pleasure warmed her as the disappointment cleared and he smiled a toe-curling smile. 'Even if you did cheat.'

'For that I'll buy the wine. Which vineyard do you recommend?'

The sun had at last cleared the sky of clouds and its warm rays made the garden at the vineyard restaurant very appealing to Nikki and Fraser. They selected a table out in the open, away from the shade of the trees.

'This is definitely something I didn't get to do very often in Dunedin.' Fraser stretched his long legs under the table. 'And definitely not at this time of the year.'

'I've never missed those freezing winters, all that snow and ice. I still remember the first year we moved down there. I thought I'd never survive the cold.' Nikki shivered exaggeratedly.

'You used to hate leaving the kitchen where you worked to come home at night.' The intensity in his eyes made her blush with memories of how they'd got warm when she had finally got back to their flat. She reached for her glass, sipped the crisp Sauvignon Blanc and nodded. 'Excellent.'

'It is.'

Finally, Fraser looked away, and she was able to draw a full breath. So many good times between them. All ruined by one thing. She shivered. Time to take a break from the past and enjoy this time with Fraser, enjoy today. Leaning back in her chair, Nikki looked around the garden.

'The daffodils are in bud. And over the fence there's green showing on the grapevines. Spring is definitely on the way.' The new growth always lifted her spirits. It was like a new beginning. Was that what was happening here with Fraser? Was that what she wanted?

I don't know. But I'm not uncomfortable with him any more.

'Can I take your orders?' A waitress hovered at her elbow and Nikki refocused, ordering the smoked salmon terrine and salad.

Fraser leaned his elbows on the table and studied her over his clasped hands. 'Don't you miss the kitchen at all?'

'I miss putting together a beautiful meal that someone's paying for and therefore expecting the best. I miss being around other foodies all the time. But the daily grind of producing the same thing over and over, of not being able to be creative?' She shook her head. 'I'd rather strap an oxygen mask on a seriously ill asthmatic patient and save their life.'

'Maybe you should've been the one going to med school. There's room for more than one doctor in your family.'

'I don't think so.' Between her fingers her glass twisted back and forth. 'Would you ever consider finishing your degree? I can't accept you won't ever become a doctor.'

'Funny thing, but since I've come home on a permanent basis I've started thinking about that and wondering if I should try and qualify. But I'm not sure I want to go into debt for it when Mum's going to be paying huge fees for Dad to go into a rest home soon.' When she opened her mouth he held his hand up. 'Nik, it's not possible. I've said I'll be around for Mum now that Dad's ill. I won't break that promise. Or any others I get to make in the future.'

'Fair enough.'

'I meant that, Nik.' He was watching her with wide eyes, as though he might miss any nuances in her expression. 'I'm done with letting down the people I care about.'

'I believe you.' *I doubt I'd trust you with my heart again, but I believe you mean what you say.* She deliberately returned to his medical career. 'So you've signed on for life at the Blenheim station, then.'

He blinked, turned that intense gaze away. 'I hadn't thought of it like that. Just as well I really enjoy being a paramedic. It's edgy, fun and helping people in stressful situations. Which reminds me, have you heard how Charlotte's getting on?'

'She's out of her coma but the doctors aren't saying yet if she'll be all right.'

'How are Mark and Ella? I can't imagine what they're going though.'

'They've moved into a motel unit next to the hospital, and George is with them now.' When Fraser's eyebrows lifted in query she added, 'George is their son. He's two years younger than Charlotte.'

'Weird how things turn out. Mark and Ella couldn't stand each other at school, yet now they're married with kids and helping each other through what has to be the worst time of their lives.'

Yes, they're sticking together, sharing the pain. 'They've grown closer and closer over the years since they married. Charlotte came along before they married, and Ella always says that was the best thing that could have happened to them. She brought them together.'

Wariness slipped into Fraser's eyes, but he didn't say anything, just let her carry on talking.

'I hope more than anything Charlotte makes it.' *I worry that there was something more I could've done to save her.*

'We did our best, Nik. You were awesome with her.'

'I'm that obvious?'

'You forget how well I used to know you.' His smile was tender, almost sad.

'No, I haven't forgotten.' It was time to return the conversation to safer ground. Sitting up straighter, she looked around. 'I wonder where our meals have got to.'

The meals were scrumptious when they arrived. 'Want a second wine?' Fraser asked as they put down their knives and forks.

'Yes, it's so lovely out here I'm not ready to leave.' And now that they'd managed to talk about everyday things for a while she'd relaxed even more with Fraser.

'Two glasses of Sauvignon Blanc for two of my favourite people.'

Fraser looked up into the face of Isabella Fowler. He leapt up and grabbed her in a hug. 'How are you?'

'I'm good.' Isabella hugged him back then moved to Nikki, hugging her extra tight. 'I hope you were going to poke your head into the kitchen before you left.' She grinned at Nikki. 'Got a spare apron if you're tired of saving people.'

Nikki laughed. 'Not yet. Anyway, there was never room for both of us in your kitchen.'

'You worked here?' Fraser stared at Nikki. 'You didn't say.'

'Why do you think I chose this restaurant?'

Isabella sat down between them. 'I heard about your dad, Fraser. I'm sorry. Is that why you're back home?'

'One of the reasons.' He quickly changed the subject, not wanting to talk about the past and knowing how Isabella wouldn't hesitate to ask awkward questions. One thing he'd learned growing up next door to her was that nothing but nothing was a secret with her. 'Are you head chef here?'

'I own the restaurant, along with my partner, André, from Paris.' Her face filled with love. 'He drove into town one day, had a meal at the bistro I worked at and the rest is history.'

'She tied André from Paris down so he couldn't leave.' Grinning, Nikki turned to Isabella. 'Or did you remove the sparkplugs from that old clanger he drove? I can't remember.'

Isabella touched her nose with a forefinger. 'I had my ways.' Then she went on, 'I'm glad to see you two out together. I never understood why you split.'

Fraser saw the instant denial in Nikki's eyes and rushed in to save her from more difficult questions Isabella was capable of tossing up. 'We're not back together, just having lunch. I work on the ambulances too.'

Thankfully, a waitress appeared. 'Isabella, you're needed in the kitchen. André's arguing about a delivery.'

She jumped up. 'I'd better sort this out. André's not known for his patience. Great to see you two. And if you can, work on getting back together. I'd love to dance at your wedding.'

The silence was deafening. Fraser stared into the depths of his glass, waiting for Nikki to explode. When she didn't he looked up slowly and was taken aback by the look of shock on her face.

'She's too much, isn't she?' he tendered.

'Yep.' Nik nodded. 'Way out there.'

So what do you think about Isabella's suggestion? Is it too awful to contemplate? He took a mouthful of his wine. 'Of course, there's a lot she doesn't know.'

Nik's mouth flattened into a line. 'Can I ask you something?'

Why did his stomach tighten? 'Sure.'

'Are you really home for good? When your dad's in care and your mum no longer needs your help, won't you want to leave again? Go back to university or Dunedin?' Her finger scratched at a knot in the wood of the tabletop.

His heart slowed, settled heavily. Nikki still didn't trust him one hundred per cent. He wouldn't have minded too much if he hadn't kissed her again and finally woken up to the fact that he loved her, had never stopped loving her. He'd done a damned fine job of hiding his feelings from himself, but they were only lurking in the dark recesses of his mind, waiting to pounce on him when he least expected it.

'I'm really home for good,' he reiterated. 'I'm no longer that teen who left Blenheim to get away from things I couldn't face. I've learned family and friends are more important than anything. And this is where they are.'

'I see.' Her tone held too much doubt for that to be true.

CHAPTER EIGHT

NIKKI stopped two metres from the door into Gavin and Patricia's leaving party, apprehension suddenly gripping her, twisting her stomach. 'Mistletoe? In September? Who's dumb idea is that?'

As if she couldn't guess. Standing directly beneath the green, plastic ornament with its tiny white berries, Fraser looked too darned smug for his own good, waiting to kiss every female going through that door. He looked too darned good for her equilibrium.

Unbelievable how much she'd missed him while he'd been in Christchurch. Work hadn't been the same without him in the truck beside her, those all-seeing brown eyes not there watching her, without his easy way of cheering up patients.

I missed Fraser. What did it mean? She couldn't quite accept his assurances that he wouldn't be leaving some time in the future and that kept a brake on her delving too deeply into what she might want with Fraser.

Beside her Amber giggled. 'It's great. Only Fraser would come up with this idea. He's also the only man on the staff worth kissing. As I'm sure you are aware.'

Very. But she couldn't begrudge him a few kisses with all the women. She had no right to exclusivity. They weren't a couple. Dang. Her mouth watered. Dressed in jeans that must've taken hours to squeeze those muscular thighs and tight butt into and a black open-necked shirt that exposed just enough chest to make her fingers itch, Fraser was the best sight she'd seen since—since she'd last seen him more than a week ago. At that moment Fraser turned round from charming the newest recruit and smiled at them. 'Hey, ladies, welcome to Christmas in spring. Slip those jackets off and come in.'

Amber nudged past her, digging an elbow into her waist. 'Come on. This is fun.'

Fraser didn't notice Amber. His eyes were appraising Nikki slowly. Too darned slowly. As if he might've missed her too. Had he? Nikki sucked her stomach in, tugged her shoulders back. And stepped forward. 'Evening, Fraser. How'd the course go?'

'Nik, we're not talking work tonight. But I'm glad you're here. I'd have had to pull down the mistletoe if you hadn't made it.' A slow-burning smile lifted his mouth, caressed and teased her.

'You don't think you've got your seasons muddled up?' Her return smile was slow and wide and caressed him back. Blimey, she couldn't believe how good it was to be with him. Ten days since she'd last worked with him and she was slobbering like a puppy.

Used to be you never wanted to see him again.

'Only way to get a kiss from you so early on in the evening.'

'You're flirting with me.' Double dang. This was over the top. Be truthful. There were too many days when she felt a strong pull towards him. The fierce physical attraction she'd felt that first day had not gone away, instead gnawing at her like a dog did at a bone. The fierce physical attraction she'd had for him since her teen years. Her brain and her body had regularly been at loggerheads over

Fraser. Even more so now, when she knew better than to give in to his look that turned her knees to something with the strength of syrup.

'If it works,' he murmured.

Amber tapped his shoulder. 'I'm waiting for my mistletoe treat.'

Fraser blinked, finally pulled those potent, earthy eyes away from Nikki. Draping an arm over Amber's shoulder, he dropped a light kiss on her cheek.

Amber chuckled loudly. 'Aw, shucks. I guess you're saving the best for Nikki.'

Nikki scowled, suddenly afraid of where her emotions were taking her. On a ride to nowhere with Fraser? She'd be safer going home and washing her already clean hair. She may have forgiven him but she was not ready for anything more than the two kisses they'd already shared.

'Nikki, come on.' Amber's voice boomed across the gap from where she was hanging up her jacket inside the room decorated with red and green baubles and streamers. 'Give Fraser a smacker of a kiss. All in the party spirit, of course.'

Shrugging out of her jacket, Nikki made to step through the doorway and was stopped slap bang in the middle by two firm hands on her shoulders. Under her top her skin tingled. Her heartbeat went into overdrive. Great. So much for regaining control over her hormones.

'Not so fast, Nikki.' His deep yet soft voice stroked her, cranked up the heat in her skin.

Her stomach twisted tighter than a knotted rope. Her teeth jarred as her mouth snapped shut. But her heart seemed to clap encouragement to her brain for the crazy ideas suddenly forming about kissing those full lips just inches away. Forget keeping her distance. She suddenly wanted to be close to Fraser. Again.

'You okay?' he asked softly, too softly. His words caressed her cheek, squeezed her stomach, sent her senses spiralling with desire.

Help. She gulped. 'Why wouldn't I be?' she asked in a strange, childlike voice, while trying to ignore that sexy light stubble accentuating his strong chin.

'How have you been?' Fraser's full mouth curved into a sweet, friendly smile. A harmless smile. Or was it beguiling? His eyes twinkled at her. 'I missed you.' He lowered his head towards hers and gently pulled her close, then those intriguing lips were caressing hers. In a tantalising, erotic way. Soft yet demanding, pliant yet strong.

Nikki couldn't have moved if someone had yelled, 'Fire!' Her senses filled with the scent of Fraser's aftershave; subtle and alluring. Her shoulders felt branded where his fingers pressed. His breathing was light and quick. Her lips felt the manliness of his lips, and her mouth opened under his.

Big mistake. Kisses weren't meant to be so diverting, so dangerous. *Pull away.* She would. In a moment. One more second of tasting this man. Of feeling his lips, his tongue. Oh, wow, nothing, no previous kisses had prepared her for the weightlessness overtaking her now. Nothing had prepared her for the sheer need crawling up through her bones, her muscles, through every cell. Fraser was back.

'Hey, you two, mind if we come in?'

Nikki leapt backwards, out of Fraser's embrace, her face turning scarlet. And stared into Mike's grinning face.

'Glad to see you've patched up your differences,' Mike added. 'Fraser, I don't think you've met my wife.'

Nikki escaped, going to sit at a table with Amber, who pushed a glass towards her. 'Vodka with a twist to cool you down after that hot smooch.'

'Danged mistletoe.' She gulped a large mouthful.

'And absolutely nothing to do with the hottest guy here, of course.' Amber grinned.

Nikki turned away as yet more heat scorched her cheeks. Her eyes found Fraser, latched onto him as he headed over to the jukebox. His strides were confident, the swing of his arms relaxed. Her tongue traced the edges of her lips, tasting him. The urge to run her fingers through his hair shining in the gleam from the rotating disco lights was sudden and fierce.

'His choice is perfect for dancing,' she muttered as music suddenly filled the hall. Her feet began tapping the rhythm as it filled her ears.

Amber grinned. 'He knows his stuff.'

Tell me about it. My blood's zinging around my body. My heart rate's so high it's dangerous. Again Nikki's tongue traced her lips. 'And doesn't he know it.'

Amber stood up. 'Let's start dancing. We'll get everyone on the floor and make this party rock.'

'Good idea.' Better than ogling Fraser. Nikki looked around and her eyes locked with Fraser's as he moved towards her.

'Want to dance?' he asked, the intensity in his gaze rocking her back on her heels. 'You used to enjoy dancing.'

The floor tilted dangerously. 'You remember.'

His hand caught her elbow for the second time tonight. Without the barrier of her thick jacket his touch scorched her, dried her mouth. 'I remember a lot of things.'

Before Nikki could ask what, she was swung around in Fraser's arms and danced across the floor. The words dried in her throat as his arms held her effortlessly and his thighs pushed against hers to direct her in their dance. She hadn't danced like this since quitting the ballroom-dancing team at the same time she'd left Dunedin. And

Fraser had been the only dancing partner who'd held her as though she might break. And the only man who'd made her want to shimmy in his arms so she could feel his hands move over her skin.

The tempo of the music changed and Nikki reluctantly slipped out of his arms. Wriggling her hips, she was totally aware of him watching her with thought-diverting intensity. Her skin melted, her mouth tasted like a desert, and deep inside a hot, raw need poured through her. Desire so intense she thought she was about to explode.

'I could do with a cold drink.' She turned, pushed through the other dancers, making her way to the table where she glugged down the rest of her vodka.

'Like another of those?' Fraser asked from beside her.

She blinked. 'I'll make it a lemonade this time.' Sinking down onto a chair, hands clasped tightly in her lap, she watched him skirting the crowd as he strode purposefully towards the temporary bar, barely stopping to talk to anyone who tried to waylay him. As if he was focused on looking out for her, and no one else mattered.

'Idiot,' Fraser muttered. 'Why the hell did I go and kiss Nikki like that? Here? Now? So much for trying to win her back by taking things slowly.'

The devil of it was once he'd started he hadn't been able to stop. Who knew what would've happened if Mike hadn't arrived at that moment? He'd been lost in her. Her scent that reminded him of summer gardens, her beautiful face and stunning figure, that mass of shining hair spilling down her back. She was something else. Roasting hot. So sexy it was a wonder every man here wasn't queuing up to dance with her. Except he'd beaten them all to her, unable to stay away.

'Something else you've got in common with Nikki—talking to yourself.' Gavin winked at him.

Fraser winced. 'Only way of getting the answers I want.' Not.

'Our Nikki stirring your blood, is she?' When Fraser gaped at him, Gavin added, 'I presume that's who you're muttering about.'

Was he that obvious? 'Need a hand here? I'm not into dancing all night.'

Gavin's eyebrows rose. 'Really? With those moves? Go away.'

'I guess that's a no, then.' Fraser picked up the drinks and headed for Nikki to hand hers over before going to socialise with someone else.

Instead, he sat down right beside her, unable to walk away. He looked up at the ceiling to see if there was a puppeteer pulling his strings. Nope. Dropping his head, his gaze clashed with Nikki's wide stare. Those azure eyes teasing, heating him, reminding him of making love to her after other dance nights. Dragging his eyes away from temptation, he noted the tension in her upright stance and her tight shoulders as she leaned back to put some distance between them. But the message in her eyes was in direct contrast to her body posture. That kiss had got to her too. Silently, he waved a mental fist in the air. Yes.

'Want to dance some more?' His feet were tapping in time to the music, his body humming with this muscle-tightening need to be holding her. To have her in his arms, to touch her, feel her sexy body moving in time to the music.

'No, thanks.' But she was already standing up, balancing easily in those knee-high black boots with heels that were taller than him. His brain short-circuited. The air got hotter when his gaze cruised up from the boots, over her thighs clad in black stockings to the edge of a very short denim skirt. Up to layers of tight-fitting tops that accentuated her stunning curves.

Nikki Page. The girl who'd haunted his sleep for years. All the times he'd cried for her, for them, when life had got too tough to handle alone. He'd never been able to let her go from his heart, from his soul.

'You happy to sit there like an old man?' Nik stood, hands on hips, smiling down at him. His breath stuck in his throat. Her skirt and boots showcased those stunning legs. A few extra kilos used to cover her hips and he wished she hadn't lost them. All that running she did had thinned her down too much. But she was still so lovely he wanted to weep.

'Or do you want to dance with someone else?'

He heard the surprising hurt in her voice, knew she still held deep concerns over her attractiveness. Because of him. He jumped up and grabbed her hand. 'Old man, eh? You're so going to regret that comment by the end of the night.'

A new tune filled the air, a much slower pace than they'd had for a while. Nikki glanced up into Fraser's eyes and stilled.

His gaze was fixed on her, so intense, so full of something she wasn't sure she should believe. Desire. For her. Slowly shaking her head from side to side, she tried to step back.

His hands were on her waist, holding her, pulling her so close she had to tip her head back to keep watching him, his gaze obliterating all thought processes. His face came slowly closer and closer until his lips brushed her forehead, down her nose and, at last, her mouth. Her lips were trembling as she pushed up on to her toes to get more of his mouth. Her hands gripped his shoulders. To hold him as near as possible. To hold her upright on suddenly lifeless legs.

Fraser's mouth stole across hers, opening on her lips. His hands slid around her back and he hauled her in against him so close she could feel all of him. His chest was rock solid under her breasts. His thighs were hard muscle against hers. His rigid reaction to her pressed firmly into her belly.

Someone bumped into them. 'Sorry, guys.' Amber laughed.

Nikki jerked back, glanced around the room. No one else seemed to be taking the slightest bit of notice of them.

'Let's go somewhere quieter,' Fraser murmured by her ear.

She nodded, her tongue suddenly glued to the roof of her mouth. She wanted more of that kiss. It would be so unfair to stop now. Her fingers laced with Fraser's as they sped to the door and out into the hall's entry area, where he stopped their hasty retreat and picked up where he'd left off kissing her.

Her mind sparked and melted. All reason disappeared in a heartbeat. Her body became liquid, moving only to keep her lips pressed to Fraser's, to keep her breasts rubbing against his chest, to hold him tight.

'Nikki,' he murmured against her mouth. 'You're driving me insane.'

Welcome to her world. Insane about described it. Wonderfully, beautifully, sexily crazy. She was in Fraser's arms and she did not want to back off. The tiniest warning sounded somewhere inside her skull, but she shoved it aside and focused entirely on kissing Fraser. Sliding her tongue across his lips, she sought his taste, his mouth. Their tongues danced around each other, teasing, promising, rediscovering.

He slipped his hands up to her face, held her closer, his eyes slumberous with yearning. For her? Suddenly he tore his mouth away and snatched her hand. 'Come on. We need privacy.'

They ducked into a tiny room off to the side and Fraser banged the door shut, sliding the lock into place. Then he leaned back against the door and lifted Nikki into his arms. Stretching up on her toes, teetering on the tips of her boots, she ran her fingertips across his mouth.

Fraser groaned as she slipped each finger over his bottom lip. He sucked them into his mouth, rolled his tongue over their pads. Needles of desire zipped through her hands, up her arms and spread out over her body, bringing every nerve ending to life, awakening her body.

He turned her round so she leaned back against his body. His hands slipped under all her tops up to her bra, pushing beneath the lacy fabric to find her nipples.

Nikki sucked a breath through her teeth at the onslaught of raw longing slamming into her, pounding her. Her nipples were exquisitely tight under the ministrations of his thumbs. Two small peaks, one massive wave of heat rolling through her. How much more of this could she take without melting into a puddle?

Frazer nibbled a line of soft, teasing bites down her neck, making her back arch and pushing her breasts further into his hands. Against her backside pressed his need for her, hard and strong, insistent.

'Fraser?' she croaked.

His mouth stilled, his body tensed. 'Yes?' he breathed against her skin.

'Don't stop.' What had she really been going to say? Her mind had gone blank, taken over by a growing sense of urgency.

His groan excited her further. 'For a moment there you

had me worried.' He spun her round, his hands sliding from her breasts to her sides to her back, then down over her buttocks, taking his time to savour every cell on the way. 'Your skin's so soft, like satin.'

Was that a good thing? Must be. His tone sounded hungry.

'And firm muscles.' Excitement ramped up in his voice. 'Very firm.' His mouth trailed a line of moist kisses down the side of her mouth to her neck to her cleavage.

Nikki straightened under his touch, tried to undo the buttons of her tops, and when they wouldn't go through the holes she gave up and tugged the offending garments over her head, dropping them at her feet.

Fraser unclipped her bra with one hand, his other busy teasing a nipple and driving her to the edge of the precipice. Her legs shook as she reached for the buckle of his belt. When his manhood sprang free she wrapped her fingers around it.

'Niiikkiii.' Her name fell slowly off his tongue as his eyes widened, his fingers trembling on her skin. There had been times when this moment had only been a fantasy in his mind, when he'd been afraid it would never happen again, especially not with Nikki. But now it was real. She was here, and in his arms. Fraser let out a sigh.

With her free hand Nikki pushed those tight jeans down enough to make it easier for her to hold all of his sex.

Fraser gasped, his body shuddering. She loved the power she had over him at this moment. And then he was picking her up, pressing her against the wall, pushing her skirt up to her waist and tugging her panties aside. His fingers slid across her moist centre, stroking her slowly, slowly. Then faster and faster until it seemed she was floating.

The tension grew inside her, tightening, twisting, filling her to the point she thought she'd explode with need. Suddenly her body rocked against his hand as she split in two.

Then Fraser entered her, hard and strong, hot and slick. And when he cried out his passion it was her name on his lips.

Stunned, Fraser let Nikki down so her boots reached the floor. Her uneven breath heated his chest. Her hands trembled on his waist.

She tipped her head back to peer up at him. 'What just happened?'

Her eyes, usually light, were darker, bigger and dazed. His heart jolted, banged his ribs. His hold tightened, brought her so near it was as though they were one. 'I don't know.' But he did know he wanted to do it again. Soon. When he got his breath back, when his body had the strength to begin all over again.

Her cheek settled on his chest. She had always done that afterwards.

He returned to running his thumb over the exposed skin on her lower back. Silky skin, warm skin. Nikki's skin.

On his waist her fingers were pressing softly, one after the other as though playing a tune on a piano. A sensual tune that had a direct line to his libido. Not possible. It was too soon. He'd hardly begun to recover. But south of his waist his body hadn't heard of restraint, didn't realise it was supposed to take a break before coming out to play again.

Under his hands Nikki's body swayed, moving softly left then right, as though to get maximum sensation from his hands. Shock delighted him. Nikki was more than ready for a repeat performance.

Lowering his head, his lips found hers, softly swollen from his kisses. As his tongue swept across them then delved inside her sweet mouth, she groaned and all but climbed into him.

He rocked as the hot sensations clawed at his gut, at his manhood. This was unbelievable, this was Nikki. This brought hope for the first time in years.

CHAPTER NINE

STANDING under the jets of hot water, rinsing the shampoo out of her hair, Nikki felt drained of energy. Her emotions had been through a blender and were now all mixed up and messy ever since the night of the party.

She'd had sex with Fraser. Twice. And loved every exquisite, nerve-tightening, sweet moment.

Which was the problem.

Because she wanted more. But…

But.

They weren't getting back together. She needed to know he'd always be open and honest in the future. Going by how she had to drag things about the past out of him still, she didn't feel confident that he'd always do that.

He'd had five years to get in touch and tell her why he had walked away. He needn't have waited for the all-clear to do that. Had it never occurred to him that she'd needed closure, had a load of self-doubt that only he could dispel by telling her the truth?

No. Obviously it hadn't.

But.

She'd missed him when he'd gone to that course in Christchurch. She'd enjoyed working alongside him since he'd returned. She even joked with him now. And since the party a fortnight ago neither of them had referred to what had happened between them. It was as though it hadn't happened. Weird. Like the tension between them since Fraser had joined the Blenheim staff had evaporated in a cloud of passion. Weird.

Yet there was still tension deep within her. How could there not be? Dang, she'd made love with him. Twice. More than enough to crank up the fires of desire smouldering inside her.

I will not be distracted. I want more than great sex. I need to know he will always be there for me. And I don't.

She suddenly shivered. The water had gone cold. How long had she been in the shower? Fraser had distracted her.

Outside the shower she sniffed. Something was burning. The brownie. Snatching her towel, she wrapped it around her as she raced for the kitchen. Her cellphone rang. The smoke alarm shrieked a warning.

'Okay, okay, I'm coming.' Tugging on an oven mitt, she quickly took the offending cake from the oven and dumped it in the sink.

Hunting in the utensil drawer for the rolling pin while answering her phone, she swore silently. Yet again she'd ruined something she was cooking because of Fraser.

'Hello?' She spoke into the phone as she jabbed the off button on the alarm.

'Hey, girlfriend, what took you so long? I haven't interrupted anything going on between you and lover boy, have I?' Amber giggled.

'How many times do I have to tell you not to call him that?' Amber didn't have a clue what had happened in that storeroom at the party. Did she?

'As many as it takes to convince me nothing's going on between you two. And considering the way Fraser's always looking at you as though you're the best thing since cellphones were invented, I'd say you haven't got a chance.'

'Thanks, *pal*. It takes two, you know.'

Amber only laughed. 'Did you know it was Mike's birthday?'

'Yes, and I've just burnt the brownie. I'll have to go shopping for more chocolate drops, cocoa and eggs.'

'How many cooking debacles is that since Fraser turned up?'

'Too many.'

Amber's tone changed. 'Nikki? You are all right, aren't you? It's just that you've been very distracted all week. I'll stop teasing you if Fraser is becoming a problem.'

The real concern in her friend's voice brought tears to her eyes. 'I'm fine. He is a problem of sorts but nothing I can't handle.' One way or another. 'After I've been shopping and made more brownies. Tell the guys I'll be in with a treat later this morning.'

Fraser clicked off the online ambulance service study site and rubbed his eyes. 'That's doing my head in.'

'How's this assignment going?' Mike asked.

'Not too bad. Doing the practical course last month certainly helped make sense of it all. Sometimes I think the trainers deliberately make the online notes hard to follow.'

'Wait until you take your practical exam. Then you'll really see how difficult they can make it.'

'I was afraid of that.' On the chair Fraser stretched his hands behind his head and touched his feet to the wall at the back of the desk.

'You'll hose in. You know your stuff, and don't get in a flap on the job. As long as you show that, you'll be an AP in no time.'

Then what? He wouldn't be working alongside Nikki. They'd each have their own crew. Although it made sense not to waste resources, the thought saddened him. Working with Nik was fun. He appreciated her knowledge and skills on the job. This wasn't about loving her. This was about having found something new that they both enjoyed doing.

'Hey, happy birthday, Mike,' the woman right now churning his brain to mush said from the doorway. 'I've brought something for your lunch.'

Watching Nik as she crossed to their boss and gave him a hug, Fraser sighed. She was downright gorgeous. And confident about her role here as an AP and in her colleagues' lives. She was more relaxed with him these days, despite their hot night in the storeroom. Would they ever get back that easy, loving relationship they'd once had? Or was he destined to watch her from the sidelines?

Mike took the proffered cake tin, tugged off the lid. 'Brownies? My favourite.'

'Any cake's your favourite.' Nikki flicked his arm before filling the kettle.

Amber asked, 'Coffee, everyone?' After a chorus of requests she lined up six mugs and spooned in coffee and sugar.

Nikki sat at the table and glanced his way. 'Did you hear Charlotte's coming back to Wairau Hospital tomorrow?'

He sat up. 'Really? That's fantastic news. Isn't it?'

'The best. She still needs a lot of care and rehabilitation but the Wellington doctors think it's best she gets that here now that she's on the mend. She'll be able to see friends and other family members. Ella and Mark are thrilled.'

'I bet they are.'

The phone rang in Mike's office. 'Don't touch that brownie till I get back.'

Then Mike charged back. 'Fraser, turn your phone on. That was the police. It's your father. He's gone missing.'

'What? Dad's missing?' Fraser's stomach churned. Tugging his phone out of his back pocket, he stabbed the keys. 'When did I turn this off?' One ring and his mum answered. 'Mum, what's happening? How long's Dad been missing? I'm on my way.' He barely gave her time to answer before snapping the phone shut, his face grim.

Nikki stood in front of him. 'I'm coming with you.'

Of course she would. 'Mum only noticed Dad wasn't there when she went to get him for breakfast. He could've been gone for hours.'

As Fraser headed out the door, Nikki grabbed his hand. 'I'll ring my mother on the way. She can sit with Molly while this is going on.'

His fingers tightened around hers as they ran to his vehicle. His heart thudded against his ribs. Where could his dad be? What had been going on in that warped mind today? 'Dad, give me a clue, will you? I need to find you. For Mum's sake. For mine.'

Nikki stayed with Fraser as he ran up the footpath at his parents' home and hauled Molly into a tight hug. Her heart broke all over again as he gently wiped the tears from his mother's face.

'I'll find him, Mum. I promise.'

Stepping forward, Nikki also hugged her. 'Mum's on her way to keep you company. And Dad's going to join the searchers.'

'Thanks, Nikki.' Molly squeezed her tight. 'Stay with Fraser, won't you?'

'Try keeping me away.' She smiled softly then turned to dash back into Fraser's truck just as he banged it into gear.

He raced down the drive, along Redwood Street, taking the first road on their left. His head flicked from side to side as he searched. His foot lifted from the accelerator as he peered down driveways then pressed down, making the little truck surge forward, only to slow again.

'Fraser, you look on the right, I'll take the left.'

'Makes sense.' The truck raced forward, stopped.

'And maybe go easy on the pedal,' she added quietly as her head jerked forward and her neck cricked, doubting he'd take any notice. She refrained from pointing out that they should stop and make a plan, approach this in small increments, not race around like headless chooks.

But Fraser would only tell her she didn't know what she was talking about. Which, in terms of the fear and worry for his dad, she didn't. But she did know her heart was hurting for him, that she wanted to make everything right for him. And there just wasn't much she could do.

Tugging her phone from her pocket, Nikki called Jay. 'We need help.'

Fraser lurched the car around a corner, the tyres squealing. 'Where the hell would he go? Damn it, now Mum has to listen to reason and put Dad into care.'

'Jay's already on his way. SAR has been notified. Blake's with Dad.'

'Right.' Fraser's head was still flipping back and forth, left and right, as he drove down the road. Not trusting her to look as carefully as he did? Fair enough. She'd probably do the same.

'Want me to drive so you can concentrate on looking out the window?' *Before we crash into something.*

'No, I'm fine.'

'Then slow down. Please.' Nikki squinted at an old man disappearing around the corner of a house. Too short to be Ken McCall. 'Fraser, think about places your dad used to go, places that were important to him. Where did he work?'

'The sawmill, which is too far away for him to have walked to, then the building centre.' Fraser did a U-turn. 'Might as well check it out. Nothing else to go on.'

'What about sport? Did he go to Lansdowne Park to

watch rugby? The racecourse? Which was his favourite pub? Did he go fishing?'

More than an hour later they'd drawn a blank at every site Fraser could think of. 'Call Jay, find out where they're searching and where we should go next.' Despair filled Fraser's voice. 'Because I'm right out of ideas.'

'We're doing a house-by-house, street-by-street search out from Ken and Molly's property,' Jay informed her. 'You two could try town, see if he's in a café or wandering around the shops. The police are combing the river banks.'

A chill lifted bumps on Nikki's arms. *Please, not the river.* 'Keep us posted.'

They drove up and down every street in the centre of town, peering at people and in shop doors. Nikki jumped out and looked into every café with the same result. Ken McCall had vanished.

Fraser pulled over, the engine idling. His fingers tapped the steering-wheel, his head tilted back against the head-rest. 'Gawd, Nik, what if I don't find him? What if—?' He choked off the next words.

'Don't even think that,' she chided gently. 'He's out there somewhere and half the town's searching for him. It's only a matter of time.' If only she believed herself. A vision of the police on the river banks flashed up in her head, and she bit down on the cry threatening to break from her throat. That wouldn't help Fraser at all.

'Let's be realistic, Nik. Anything could've happened to him.'

His sharp tone pierced her but she continued anyway. 'At least it's a warm, late-spring day, not like that time you found him on the steps in his PJs.'

'The day he mistook me for Henry Broad.'

Nikki spun around to stare at him.

Fraser's head snapped forward.

'That's it,' they cried in unison.

'It has to be, please,' Nikki whispered.

Fraser snatched his phone and punched redial. 'Mum? Where was that dance hall you used to meet Dad at?'

A week later, after they'd found his dad dressed in his suit and tie, standing on the old site where the hall used to be, Fraser backed the ambulance into the garage and turned off the engine. The door rattled down and he winced. 'That should wake Chloe and Ryan.'

'Serve them right for having a perfect shift so far. And since it's just gone four they're very unlikely to get a call now.' Nikki yawned. 'There are advantages to being on truck two during the night.'

'Feel like a hot drink? Or do you want to get some shuteye?' He could do with her company, even so early in the morning. He was unable to explain it, but ever since his dad's disappearing act he'd felt like this, wanting to spend as much time as possible with Nikki.

Nik turned those tired but beautiful eyes on him. 'Tea would be great. There might even be a slice of coffee cake in the pantry to go with it.'

'At this hour?' He jumped out and went to plug the power supply into the ambulance.

'I'll run it off before lunch.' At the supply room she tapped in the security code and opened the door. 'I'll replace the drugs and equipment if you're boiling the jug.'

Handing Nik a steaming mug ten minutes later, Fraser sank into one of the armchairs and stretched out, crossed his feet. 'What've you got planned for your days off?'

She dropped into the chair beside him. 'Not a lot. Probably go out to the farm one of the days. What about you?'

'Driving Mum and Dad to Nelson tomorrow. They're

staying at a hospital unit while Dad's assessed for placement in rest-home care.'

Nikki sighed. 'That must be really hard for you and Molly.' She sipped her tea and studied him over the rim. 'But no surprise, huh?'

'Not after the other day's event. Even Mum admits it's time, but she's not liking it one bit. I can't blame her. It will be hard, a bit like separating yet not really.'

Her brow furrowed. 'Does this mean Ken's going to be living in Nelson?'

'No way. But all the assessments are done there at the moment. Mum's found a place here for him that'll be available before Christmas.'

'Christmas. That's not too far away. Surely you can have Ken at home for that?'

'That'll be up to Mum.' Fraser swallowed some tea. 'She just wants to get this assessment out of the way before making too many plans.' It wasn't going to be easy, even though he knew this was the right thing to do for his father.

'Want me to come with you tomorrow?' Nik's soft voice covered him like a blanket, soothing out the tension in his shoulders, warming the cold place in his heart.

'I'd love you to.' It would be so much easier having someone to share the day with, to make that trip back from Nelson with. He was done with trying to do things alone. Especially if Nik was offering to be there for him. 'Thanks.'

'If I've ever earned a beer, it's this one.' Fraser groaned. 'What is it with women and shopping? There can't be an outfit left in town.'

'Get over yourself.' Nikki smiled happily.

Fraser had finally relaxed. After an hour with doctors and nursing staff they'd left his parents at the medical unit that dealt with dementia patients, his mother tearfully shooing them away. 'Go. I'll be all right. It's only for three nights. And think of the sleep I'll get with the nurses watching over your father.'

After promising Fraser a beer if she could take a peek in the shops, Nikki had dragged him around town and loaded his arms with parcels.

Finally, he'd growled, 'That's it. Time for that drink you promised. How many new clothes can you wear at one time anyway?'

She laughed. 'That's a man comment. There's no such thing as too many pairs of boots. Or too many clothes. Come on, drink time.' Despite the reason for being in Nelson she was enjoying herself. Fraser was always good company and hopefully she'd managed to cheer him up for a while.

'So there are some perks to being a pack horse.'

'A few small ones.' She tucked her hand around his elbow and stretched her stride to equal his long one.

Just like old times.

She gasped. Yes, it was, wasn't it? Being together, ribbing each other, going for a drink. She'd missed all that as much as the love-making, the planning for their future, the big issues every couple faced. It had been a long time without someone close, someone of her own. If only this day could last for ever.

Really? Really.

At the top of Trafalgar Street they turned into a pub where tourists and locals leaned against the bar or sat around tables.

'What are you having?' she asked. 'Beer? And a late lunch?'

'Yes and yes.' He chose a local beer from the list on the blackboard. Then added, 'Seafood chowder for me.'

Seated in a corner, Nikki rested her elbows on the table and her chin in her hands. 'This is the life. I feel so removed from work, it's wonderful.'

Her gaze travelled over the patrons, finally pausing on a couple in their thirties. The woman nursed a wee baby wrapped in a blue blanket and sipped an orange juice while her husband enjoyed a lager. Nikki watched with a sense of longing that had recently begun expanding within her. What would it be like to hold your own child? To be a mum?

'You've gone all dreamy.' Fraser nudged her.

Oops. She shook away those thoughts. 'People watching.'

'The couple with the baby?' His eyes narrowed.

She tried for nonchalance. 'Well, he is cute.' She sipped her beer and didn't look at Fraser. 'At home everyone's excited about Beau and Yvonne's baby, even though it's not due until Christmas.'

'I bet they are.'

'Yvonne let me touch her tummy when the baby kicked. It was amazing. Made me realise that's a real person inside there.' When Fraser's eyebrows rose she grinned. 'Yeah, I know a baby's a real person, but feeling his kicks really brought it home to me how wonderful the whole process of having a baby really is.'

Fraser's jaw had dropped. She blushed and reached for her glass, taking a mouthful of beer to stop herself from saying anything else. But she'd been ecstatic after that moment, had even started wondering if she'd ever know the joy of motherhood.

'Their lives are going to change for ever.'

'Change in a good way, surely?' She blinked. Didn't Fraser want children? He must. He'd put sperm on ice, hadn't he?

'Sorry. Did I sound glum? It's this thing with Dad. You're so right, life goes round in circles.'

Absolutely. The past couple of days had brought it home to her in a way she'd never considered before. Her parents and brothers had always been there for her, supporting her, looking out for her, as she had for them in her own way. And now there'd be a new generation in her family. 'It's exciting.' Someone for her to take care of.

She'd driven back to the flat last night thinking about her future. Until now she'd truly believed that her work could satisfy her completely and that not getting married and having babies didn't matter. She'd been playing safe. Fraser's return had started her questioning everything in her life and feeling that tiny kick against the palm of her hand made her want more. A man to love, a baby in her arms and a house she could call home. The stuff that life was really about.

'Time to hit the road.' Fraser was watching her, looking as handsome as ever, as familiar and lovable as he always had. The man of her dreams?

As long as it wasn't the impossible dream.

Fraser smiled across at Nikki as her eyelids drooped. He spoke quietly so as not to wake her. 'Hey, sleepyhead, you're supposed to be chattering to me, keeping me alert as I drive.'

'Hmm.' Jerking her head up, she stared out the wind-screen before shuffling her shoulders against the seat to get more comfortable. Her chin fell forward and her eyes closed again.

Warmth stole through him as he took quick glances at her. Nikki. Nik. She'd been there for him today. Not inter-fering or taking over with his dad, just there with a smile or a touch. As she had when his dad had gone missing last week. He liked it that she didn't made a song and dance about anything. He liked it that she felt she could stand by him. Maybe she was beginning to accept him again, to want to be with him in the rest of his life outside work.

He slowed for the first of many tight corners on the road going over the Whangamoa hills as they headed away from Nelson. And recalled the misty look in Nikki's eyes as she'd talked about Yvonne's baby. She wanted children of her own. That had been apparent as she'd kept glancing across at the tiny baby in blue. Would she be prepared to have them his way? In vitro.

He braked. 'Hell, man, look out.' The car in front weaved across the middle line, and Fraser drove even slower, keeping his distance.

Nikki stirred, lifted her head, peered around. 'What's going on?'

'The guy in front's driving very erratically. A moment ago he was half across the median.' Fraser gaped in astonishment. 'And now he's overcompensated and his wheels are in the loose gravel on the outside of the road.'

They both flinched as stones flicked back at them. Fraser held the horn down for a long moment. 'Come on, man. You shouldn't be on the road.'

'Hope he keeps to his side of the road when there's traffic coming the other way. Especially any freight trucks. That would be messy.' Nikki watched the saloon in front. 'Is he drunk?'

'Quite possibly.'

'Nothing we can do if he won't pull over,' Nik muttered. 'No cellphone coverage in these hills.'

Rounding a sharp bend, Fraser braked hard. Nikki jerked forward, gasping loudly. Ahead, the saloon scraped along the rocky bank and stopped abruptly.

'Are you all right?' Fraser asked Nikki as he flicked on the hazard lights.

'I'm fine. Got a fright, that's all.' She was already half out of the car. 'Let's check this guy out.'

When Fraser pulled the driver's door open, ready to give the man a blasting for his appalling driving, Nikki automatically bent to catch the man as he slid half out of his seat.

'Hey, careful, I've got you.' She spoke quietly, confidently.

Fraser took the man's weight and helped Nikki ease him back inside before turning the ignition off.

Then Nik opened the back door and clambered inside, squeezed between the seats to the front. 'Sir, are you all right?' Automatically, she reached for his wrist, feeling for a pulse. 'Sir, my name is Nikki and this is Fraser. We're both ambulance paramedics. Do you mind if we check you over?'

'My chest hurts.' The words were drawn out and slurred. His free hand tapped his chest in the vicinity of his heart. 'Here. And here.' His hand slid carelessly down his left arm.

His face was grey and sweaty. His pulse was too slow and he was struggling to breathe. She glanced at Fraser and shook her head. 'We need help,' she told him very quietly.

'Onto it. I'll stop the next car heading into Nelson and get them to call 111 the moment they get phone coverage.'

'There are houses at the bottom of the hill and a store another couple of kilometres along.' Then Nikki returned her attention to the man, her lips moving as she started counting his respiration rate.

Fraser turned as another car pulled up, followed by a large truck and trailer unit. 'Yes, trucks have radios.' He crossed to the truck and asked, 'Can you call the emergency services?'

'Sure can, mate. What do you need?'

'Ambulance and traffic. One patient.' Fraser gave the bare details he had. 'That car's going to need towing too.' Then he returned to Nikki, who'd need his help if the driver was really ill. From the sound of loud voices someone had started to sort out the traffic snarl already developing.

Poking his head inside the car, he told Nikki, 'A truckie's calling up on his radio so that should speed things up a bit. What have we got here?'

Nikki glanced up. 'This is Roy Constable, and he's been feeling unwell for a while.' Looking back at her patient, she added, 'Resp rate is down.'

As Fraser watched he saw Roy gasping as though he wasn't getting enough oxygen. If only they had a tank with them.

Roy spoke slowly between gasps. 'I felt crook. Before I left my daughter's in Nelson. Thought it was indigestion.'

Fraser squeezed Roy's shoulder. 'Have you ever had anything like this before?' Indigestion and heart attacks were often mixed up, the pain initially similar.

'Not really.' He winced. 'Ahh. It's getting worse.' His lips quivered as he tried to suck in a lungful of air. 'I wanted to get home.'

Silly man. Why hadn't he pulled over? He was extremely lucky not to have had an accident involving another vehicle. But it wasn't his place to point that out. 'Where's home?'

'Rai Valley.'

Great. A few houses, one café, a petrol station and a farming supplies store. No doctor. No ambulance. No help. 'Okay, Roy, I want you to stay still and try to relax. We're getting an ambulance to come out for you.' But that was going to take forty-five minutes at least, he calculated. Hopefully Roy wouldn't work it out. That would definitely increase his anxiety level. Fingers crossed, Roy didn't have a full-blown cardiac arrest before the arrival of a fully equipped truck. But if he did then he and Nikki would be able to start CPR immediately.

Nikki sat back. There was nothing for her to do but keep an eye on Roy and wait for help to arrive. 'What were the odds of us being right behind the guy when he crashed?'

Fraser grimaced. 'What were the odds he'd slide into the bank and not go over the edge on the other side?'

Roy's eyes were closed, and his respiration rate had slowed further.

A screech of tyres made Nikki jump. 'Idiot,' she muttered. 'We need a traffic cop here before we're dealing with more patients.'

Roy groaned long and loud, his hands grasping at air. Nikki took his wrist and began counting his pulse again.

At least he still had one, Fraser thought as he straightened up. 'I wonder what's in the back of his car that we could lay him on if we have to.' He reached in and popped the boot before disappearing round the back to take a look. 'Nothing.'

He returned to hunker down by the car and talked quietly as they waited for the ambulance to arrive. 'Days like these I'm glad I'm medically trained.'

The *whoo-whoo* of a siren screeched through the air. 'That was quick.' Nikki glanced along the road to the corner but Fraser saw her hope fade as the familiar white car with yellow and blue strips pulled up. 'Not the ambulance, then.'

The traffic cop who got out of the car shoved his hat on his head and strode across to them. 'The ambulance is about five minutes behind me. What happened?'

Fraser quickly filled him in on details of the accident. Within moments the cop was directing the traffic one way at a time on the narrow road.

When the ambulance pulled up Nikki made the handover while Fraser helped extricate Roy from his car onto the stretcher.

'Let's try for home again.' Fraser draped an arm over Nikki's shoulders and turned her towards their vehicle. 'Blenheim, here we come. I hope.'

Under his arm Nik twisted to look at him. 'We make a great team.' She raised one hand, high-fived him. 'We both knew what to do without having to spell it out. Awesome.'

Awesome. *So are you, my girl.* Who'd have believed the excellent chef he'd once known would turn out to be such a good paramedic? Especially when the sight of blood used to turn her white and giddy. She never ceased to surprise him.

He held the passenger door open for her. As she ducked around him he smelt peonies and smiled. That scent had been made for her. Evocative, sensual, very feminine. Nik.

He'd better get into the car and drive before he took her in his arms and held her for ever. Shutting her door, he strode around the car and slipped inside.

Nikki sighed. 'So much for a day off. It's like a busman's holiday.'

Fraser turned the engine over, at the same time jerking his thumb towards the back seat. 'I don't think those bags have anything to do with being an AP but all to do with looking gorgeous when you're not in your uniform.'

'Take me home, then. I've got a lot of unpacking and putting away to do.' She grinned, more relaxed with him than he'd seen her in the past couple of months.

'Yes, ma'am.' Fraser grinned back before slowly easing between two cars in preparation for heading on up the hill. Three steps forward. None back? Again. Progress was being made. His grin stretched wider.

CHAPTER TEN

FRASER watched Nikki from under half-lowered eyelids as she read a magazine. Except she hadn't turned a single page in the past twenty minutes. So far their shift had been very quiet for a Friday night. Too quiet. Without work to focus on, his brain was running riot with images of Nikki.

Nikki driving the ambulance.

Nikki holding that guy in his car on the Whangamoas.

Nikki burning the scrambled eggs, and another time walking in here with enough chocolate brownies to feed half the town.

Nikki in his arms, kissing him.

His chair crashed against the wall as he stood up. Damn it, he needed some air. He pushed out through the main door into the parking area and dragged in a lungful of warm evening air. Thank goodness for spring when there was no need for heavy jackets or jerseys.

He needed to get away from her. She'd gone back to being a work colleague and nothing else since their day in Nelson, which was starting to irritate him. It was as though she regretted the kisses they'd shared, and the love-making. As if she had more issues to clear up but wasn't outright asking him about them. If they were even about him. He suspected they were. So why couldn't she say what was on her mind? She'd harped on about not believing he had returned permanently, mentioned on more than one occasion that he should return to his medical studies. What did she want from him?

Hands on hips, he leaned back and stared up into the clear night sky filled with stars. Three steps back. Talk about being all over the place.

At least his mum and dad were back home after the endless rounds of discussions with doctors, specialists and rest-home managers. His mum had finally conceded it was time to let his dad go into care, but it was breaking her heart to do it, so he'd made a point of being at home every moment he wasn't here.

With one exception. The day he'd visited the Page clan. He'd planned on seeing Allan and Rose before tracking down Jay and Beau, but when he'd turned up at the homestead everyone had been there. Including Nikki. His heartfelt thanks for what they'd done in helping to find his dad had been well received. Like old times. Once again he was completely at home in the Page house. It felt good, great.

Even Nikki hadn't been as distant as she was at work. Probably secure with her brothers all over the place, minding her business for her.

The way she'd stayed with him when he'd learned his dad was missing had got to him, reminded him again how badly he'd treated her all that time ago. Nik had not backed off from a potential problem, supporting him instead of leaving him to his own resources. Gawd, he loved her. But until she learned to trust him again he wouldn't make any headway. Only time was going to show her he meant everything he had said.

In the office the radio squawked at the same moment his pager vibrated on his hip. At last. Locking the door, he hurried to the ambulance, unhooked the power supply and climbed inside.

Nikki slid into the driver's seat. 'What's the address?'

'Holdsworth Road. Know it?' Fraser read the screen.

'Yes.'

'Asthmatic with chest pains. Sixty-nine-year-old man.'

'Who?'

'David White. The head of science at the boys' college was a David White. The age seems about right.'

'Could be the same man, then.'

A neighbour let them into the house. 'I came over when I saw the lights still on. He's never up after ten and it's now gone midnight. He's struggling to breathe.'

Fraser placed the pack on the lounge floor and knelt down beside his old teacher, the man who'd inspired him to keep following his dream. 'Hello, sir. Got yourself in a spot of bother, have you?'

'Fraser…' David tried to inhale. 'Is that you?' he gasped.

'Yes, it is. Bet you never thought I'd be turning up to help you out. Have you taken any asthma meds in the past hour?' Fraser was taking obs as he talked.

David moved his head sideways. 'No,' he mouthed. Then his eyes widened. 'Nikki? With you.' David wheezed. 'Good. Back together.'

'Only working together,' Nikki was quick to reply as she prepared the nebuliser to administer salbutamol.

'I'm going to give you a shot of adrenaline, David.'

David nodded once. 'Getting worse,' he squeezed out.

Fraser rapidly rechecked his patient's obs. 'Slipping in and out of consciousness. I'll set up an IV port ready for more adrenaline if he goes under.'

Nikki nodded. 'Wait twenty minutes before a second dose if you can.'

'Will do.'

'As soon as you're done we'll get him on the stretcher and loaded up.'

Fraser drove away from ED after they'd handed their patient over to the night staff. 'I wonder why David let his attack get so bad?'

'Didn't want to be a nuisance?' Nikki mused. 'We get plenty of those.'

'I wouldn't have thought he'd be like that. He's severely compromised himself now.'

She'd seen how it had upset Fraser to see his old teacher in such a state. 'The nurses in ED will give him a lecture, believe me. I've heard them do that on more than one occasion.' Nikki stretched her legs as much as possible in the confines of the cab. Her stomach rumbled—loudly. She grinned. 'Can we go by a burger bar?'

'Anything to stop that racket.'

'Cancel the burger.' Nikki reached for the handset. 'Blenheim One, go ahead.'

The coms operator's voice crackled loudly in the truck. 'Priority-one call. Male, eighteen years, Eugene Clark, heavy blood loss from right arm. Be aware, possible stabbing, police have been notified.'

'Roger, Coms. And thanks.' Nikki grimaced. 'It's one-thirty in the morning. We've got to be dealing with drunks.'

'Possibly.'

She hadn't finished. 'I just love stabbings. Everyone will be off their heads with booze and drugs. They'll be angry and looking for another fight. The patient will be belligerent and swearing fit to bust. And us? We'll be trying to be nice and helpful.'

Fraser winced. 'Sounds like a heap of fun.'

She watched Fraser as he sped through the dark, empty streets, ever watchful of the road and looking out for walking partygoers thinking they had the street to themselves. Hopefully the flashing lights were enough to warn anyone out and about of their presence. At this time of night the siren was a last resort.

Nikki nibbled her top lip, feeling more uneasy than usual. 'Remember the first priority is our own safety. If the crowd looks dangerous, we wait for police back-up or leave.'

'Gotcha.' He indicated a left turn. 'I've been to these sorts of situations before, Nik. Often.' He reached across, gently squeezed her thigh. 'We'll be careful.'

'Sure.' Of course they would. But she had a bad feeling about this one.

'Here we go.'

Nikki peered through the dark. 'That's one hell of a crowd. All young men, by the look of it. I hope they're not going to give us any grief.'

A policeman opened her door. 'Hey, Nikki, how're you doing?'

Relief loosened the tension gripping her. Thank goodness for the boys in blue. They weren't quite so alone now. 'Just fine, Grant. What's the mood here?' Nikki slid to the ground.

'Tense, but they'll leave you alone, I think. We'll be watching your backs.' Grant nodded at a line of three of his colleagues. 'The victim's behind our men.'

Slinging her pack on her back, Nikki closed the back door firmly. 'Can someone keep an eye on our truck?'

Grant said, 'Absolutely.'

Keeping close to Fraser, she pushed through the jostling young men. After one crude remark Fraser took her elbow and whispered, 'Ignore them.'

'I am,' she replied, but the shiver rolling through her body undermined her conviction. The atmosphere heaved with loud rock music and something else. Something she couldn't put her finger on. It worried her. One wrong move from any of these guys and she was leaving. Ambulance crews were told time and again not to put themselves in any danger.

And tonight things felt dangerous.

Then they were looking down at their patient and she pushed her concerns aside.

Eugene lay sprawled on the pavement, his arm bound tightly with a towel in an attempt to slow the heavy bleeding. It wasn't doing the job. He was groaning and cursing everyone in sight, especially the police. Patches of vomit were mixed with the massive pool of blood next to the lad's body.

Nikki knelt beside him. 'Eugene, my name's Nikki and this is Fraser. We're paramedics from the ambulance service. I need to look at your arm.'

She reared back at the expletives that spewed from Eugene's mouth, her shoulder slamming into Fraser's knees and knocking him off balance. 'Sorry,' she muttered when he crouched down beside her.

Leaning forward, he said as calmly as he could manage, 'Listen, we're here to help you so stop carrying on like that and let us get on with it. The sooner we're done the sooner we can get you to hospital and out of pain.'

Following Fraser's example, Nikki drew a deep breath to calm her thumping heart and looked around the immediate area then back at their patient. 'By the amount of blood covering the pavement, Eugene's in serious risk of going into shock and organ failure,' she said quietly.

'Aren't you going to give me some drugs now?' Eugene's eyes widened. 'I'm hurting real bad.'

'I'm sure you are. We'll give you some gas in a minute, but we also need to stop the bleeding.' Fraser had a face mask ready.

Nikki reached into the bag for some scissors and asked quietly, 'Want to tell me what happened?'

'What's that got to do with you, cow? Just fix me up.'

Beside her Fraser drew an angry breath then stood to ask the cops if they knew what had happened. When he returned to crouching beside Nikki he told her, 'Knife wound. Grant put this towel in place before being edged away by some of Eugene's mates.' He reached for the lad's good arm, wrapped a cuff around it. 'Eugene, I'm going to take your blood pressure. Can you stay still for a moment?'

Nikki murmured, 'Unfortunately that towel isn't stopping the bleeding. I'm going to have to risk removing it to put a tourniquet on.' She began snipping at the soaked towel.

'Hey, lady, what are you doing? You can't take that off his arm. You'll kill him.' A young man, bouncing from one foot to the other, loomed up on her other side, anger glaring out at her from his mean-looking eyes. Then he stuck his fingers in his mouth and let loose with a piercing whistle.

She shivered, glanced behind, heard shouting break out on the opposite side of the crowd. The cops took off, heading for the fracas. Three menacingly silent youths slid in beside Nikki and Fraser.

Her tongue moistened her lips. 'We're helping your friend.' If Eugene wasn't their friend, she and Fraser were in trouble.

The biggest and meanest of the trio grabbed Nikki's shoulder, his fingers digging in so hard the knuckles were white. 'You think we're stupid? You're gonna make him bleed to death.'

'Hey.' Fraser spun on his feet. 'Let her go, mate. She's trying to save Eugene's life.' Anger glittered from his eyes.

Light glinted on the wide blade of a knife in her assailant's hand. 'Not if she takes that towel off she's not. I know you have to put pressure on a cut to stop the bleeding.' His fingers dug deeper and he carved a pattern in the air right before her face.

Nikki could feel her knees knocking. The air in her lungs caught. Her skin went icy. What could she say to deflate this madman's attitude? Her mind was blank.

Fraser stepped closer, glared into the man's face. 'Let her go or your pal isn't going to get any help.'

'That so?' The young man splayed his legs, waving the knife between them. He jerked a thumb at Nikki. 'She your woman?'

Fraser didn't hesitate. 'Yeah, man, she is.'

I am? Did he mean it? Or was he just saying it to defuse the situation? She tried moving her shoulder free.

The guy gripped harder, spun her round. 'Let's show him what it's like when his woman's hurt.' And the hand holding the knife rose, the blade flashing in the light.

Nikki watched, breathless, with her feet rooted to the ground, appalled as the blade descended, fast, aimed directly at her. Then she was shoved sideways, slamming onto the road. Her elbow cracked hard, pain ricocheting up and down her arm. Her hip thumped hard, more pain hitting her, winding her.

Then something, someone, toppled, fell over her feet. 'Fraser,' she screamed. And scrambled to get clear and reach for him.

The knife handle protruded from the side of Fraser's chest. Nausea roiled up her throat. She swallowed hard. *Don't be sick now.* Fraser needed her. What to do? Her brain was not functioning. Remove the knife? Wrong. Load him and drive like hell for the hospital? Made more sense than anything else. She needed help getting him to the ambulance.

'Fraser, talk to me,' she pleaded, and looked at his face.

Blood pumped from a head wound, tracking over his fore-head, down his cheek. When she touched him, his head lolled sideways. He was unconscious. Had his head hit the tarmac?

'Hey, Nikki, move over, girl. We're here now. We'll take care of Fraser.'

She blinked, took a quick sideways glance. 'Mike? Rebecca?'

'We heard on the radio there was a problem here so thought you could do with some support.' Mike already had Fraser's shirt cut away from the wound.

Nikki wobbled on her haunches as she gripped Fraser's hand. 'Hang in there, Fraser, love.' She knew she sounded desperate. She didn't care. 'You have to save him, Mike.'

'We will. I promise.' He gave her a quick hug. 'Now, move a bit so I can get to your man.'

The second person to have called Fraser her man. Maybe they were right, and she should just get over the past. Completely. She blinked and looked around. 'Where is everyone? What happened to the crowd?' Strength had returned to her voice now that Mike and Rebecca were here and she wasn't dealing with this alone.

'Disappeared in a flaming hurry, from what Grant told us. No one's sticking around to take the rap for this.' Rebecca knelt on the other side of Fraser, calmly working on him.

Tears pricked Nikki's eyelids and streaked down her cheeks. 'Thanks, guys. I lost it. I didn't know what to do.' Her thumb stroked Fraser's hand without stopping, willing him to be all right. How? He had a ruddy great knife sticking out from between his ribs. She knew all the implications of that. She shivered as her skin chilled.

'Who would remember anything in these circumstances?' Rebecca smiled.

Mike turned to Nikki. 'I know you don't want to leave Fraser's side but could you ask Grant and his colleagues to load the other patient and drive him to the ED?'

She didn't want to. 'Okay.' Letting go of Fraser's hand was difficult, peeling one finger back at a time. But Mike was right. Eugene was entitled to be helped, regardless of what his mate had done to the man she cared for most in this world. But before she stood up she placed the softest of kisses on Fraser's cold lips. 'Hang in there. You and I are not finished yet.'

CHAPTER ELEVEN

NIKKI curled up uncomfortably on a chair beside Fraser's bed. The beeping of the machines monitoring his breathing reassured her. Something had to tell her. Fraser wasn't. He lay so still. Too still. Nothing like his usual active self.

His hand lay in hers, not reacting to any of her light squeezing. Bruises covered his forehead and his left cheek was swollen. A shaved patch on his head showed a wound stitched together. According to the surgeon, Fraser had been very lucky. A concussion but no lasting damage to the brain.

Add to that a punctured lung and one nicked rib, and he was lucky?

Her bottom lip quivered. He *was* lucky. He could've been killed. 'He saved my life.'

On the opposite side of the bed Molly smiled wearily. 'Don't go blaming yourself. Fraser would never let anything happen to you if he could help it.'

'Aren't you angry at him for leaping between me and that knife? At me because he cared enough to do that?' Dang, *she* was angry. Fraser should not be lying here. She should. It was her that guy had wanted to hurt. Not Fraser.

'The only person I'm angry at is the man who did this. I know I sound old when I say it wouldn't have happened when we were your age.'

Nikki couldn't stop the chuckle that rolled off her tongue. 'Remind me not to say that when my kids are getting into trouble.' She squeezed Fraser's hand and looked at his mother. 'Thanks, Molly, you've cheered me up.'

Molly pushed off her chair. 'I'd better go and see Ken. He'll be fretting because I'm late.'

'What are you going to tell him about this?'

'I doubt I'll say a word. It will only distress him when there's nothing he can do about it.'

'But you must tell him. Ken has a right to know, surely? Wouldn't you want to know? I would, if it was me.' Like mother, like son? Had Molly always kept things from Ken, or was her reaction due to his illness?

Molly flushed. 'I'm protecting Ken, saving him added stress. Stress only makes him so much worse. And I don't want that.'

Placing Fraser's hand on the bedcover, Nikki went to his mother and embraced her. 'I should mind my own business. You're right. Ken's already got enough problems.' She leaned back and looked into Molly's sad eyes. 'So have you. Anything I can do to help, make sure you ring and tell me. Okay?' She shook this lovely woman gently. 'I mean that.'

Molly looked down at her son. 'You're already doing lots.' And then she was gone, leaving Nikki to puzzle the meaning of her words.

'Hey, sis, how's he doing?' Jay strode into the room and engulfed her in a bear hug. 'You okay?'

Sniff, sniff. 'Couldn't be better. And Fraser's going to be all right.' Dang, she hadn't cried all night and now with Jay holding her, concern in his voice for her and Fraser, it was as though someone had opened the floodgates.

'Now, what did I do to deserve this?' Jay pushed her down into the chair and reached for a box of tissues. 'Here, use these,' he said gruffly, 'then tell me all the details. I hear the cops arrested the guy who stabbed Fraser.'

Her eyes widened, spilling more tears down her face. 'They have? Good.' Nikki filled Jay in on everything. 'Fraser was protecting me, Jay.'

'I'd be stunned if he hadn't.'

Her gaze returned to Fraser. 'Yeah, you're right. He'd never let anyone hurt me.' Funny thing, that.

Fraser tried to stretch but stopped as pain stabbed his chest. Gingerly lifting his eyelids, he peered out at the white room, the metal bedrails. Hospital. That explained the pain. Sort of. Turning his head to one side, he bit down on an oath as a bomb went off inside his head. Lights flashed in front of his eyes.

What had happened to him? Was he all right? As in not seriously injured?

Closing his eyes, he concentrated on his body. Wriggled his toes. No problem there. Stretched his calves. Good. Lifted his left arm, and sucked air through his clenched teeth. That cranked up the dull throbbing in his chest, making him want to stop breathing for a while till everything settled down again. His right arm felt heavy, weighed down.

He popped his eyes open, turned his head slowly to avoid another explosion, and stopped. His whole body softened, warmed. Nik. Beautiful Nik. Sitting on a chair, leaning so her top half was sprawled on the bed, she slept. Her head lay against his arm, her breathing warm on his skin.

And then he remembered. The knife. Aimed at Nikki. Going for her. His frantic leap. Then the hot pain as the blade had slammed into him.

Thank goodness. Or it would be Nikki lying here. Or worse.

Carefully, so as not to wake her, he shifted his arm and placed his hand on her head. Threaded his fingers through her messy hair, feeling the silky tangles on his skin. He closed his eyes again. Drank in the sweetness of the moment. He and Nik. Together. However temporarily.

'Nikki, there's something I have to tell you.' Fraser sat up in bed, the robe he wore revealing more chest than was good for her heart rate.

'You sound serious.' Hadn't they had enough serious stuff to last a lifetime? Two days after the stabbing and the police had finally stopped calling in with questions, their colleagues had found their smiles, and her brothers had stopped suggesting she go back to cooking for a career.

'I need you to trust me, believe I'll never deliberately hurt you, so there is one more thing you should know about why I called off the wedding.'

Nikki leaned close, kissed those seductive lips that weren't smiling. Running her forefinger along his jaw, she asked, 'Do you think I care about that any more? I love you, and that's all that matters.'

His eyes widened in surprise. So did hers. She felt her eyebrows lifting. When had she come to that conclusion? Some time during the long night waiting for Fraser to come out of surgery, to regain consciousness. But talk about springing it on him, on her. Shouldn't she have taken her time to get used to the idea first?

'Say that again,' he whispered. 'The bit about loving me.'

She wasn't taking it back. 'I love you.'

He caught her hand, kissed each fingertip. Then he reached for her, slipping his arms around her in the gentlest of hugs.

Her badly bruised elbow ached as it rubbed against his thigh, but she daren't move it for fear of knocking the drain in Fraser's chest wound. Instead, she lifted her mouth to his, glad of the distraction for both of them. Then the kiss took over and she was lost in the heat of Fraser's mouth claiming hers. A breathless kiss due to Fraser's pierced lung. But a kiss nonetheless.

'You won't be wanting a cup of tea, then,' an aide called from the doorway.

They jerked apart, Fraser gasping at the sudden movement. 'Not at the moment,' he finally managed to mutter.

When the woman had taken her broad smile and the tea trolley away Fraser grinned. 'How could I drink tea after kissing you?' Then his mouth straightened. 'You distracted me. But I haven't forgotten what I was going to tell you.'

Nikki shifted uneasily at the serious look in his eyes. He loved her, right? She hadn't exposed her heart to have him tell her they weren't ever getting back together. 'Dang. Do you have to?'

'Yes, Nik, I do. Because, my lovely, despite what you say, you still don't believe my reasons for not telling you about the cancer were justified. And you're right. I probably would've told you right from the get-go if not for one thing. I truly wanted you with me, desperately needed your strength, right from the start. Every time I thought I could tell you, only one thing made me stay away. And staying away was as hard as dealing with the news, believe me.'

Her heart slowed, almost stopped. This was not working out how she'd hoped. This did not sound like a declaration of his love for her. She leaned back so she could see every emotion that crossed his face, wanting to see exactly how he felt as he talked. 'Go on.'

His chest lifted, and he opened his mouth. 'My oncologist was so truthful it was gutting. He warned that after the surgery there was a likelihood that I'd be impotent.'

Nikki gasped, pressed the fingers of one hand to her mouth. She stared at him, stunned. 'Oh, my God.' Reaching with her free hand, she cupped his cheek.

'That's why I stayed away.' He turned his mouth to kiss first her thumb, then each finger, then put her hand away from him. Stared deeply into her eyes. 'Now do you understand? Can you see why I couldn't tell you?'

She swallowed. Nodded. Tears welled. For him? For them? Finally, she whispered, 'I still wish you had told me, but I understand why you felt you couldn't. What an impossible situation.'

'It was.'

'We could've put the wedding on hold.'

'You really think so? The tension between us would've been horrendous.' He flinched. 'Hell, when the time came I probably wouldn't have been able to perform anyway, I'd have been beyond nervous. There'd have been far too much riding on the outcome.'

'You were doomed if you did, doomed if you didn't. But don't you see how disappearing with hardly a word was so painful for me? How it nearly destroyed both of us?' Fraser winced. 'You shut me out. You didn't give me a chance to choose, you just decided for me.'

'I know, and I'm sorry. I'm sorry for everything I put you through. I wasn't exactly coping very well at the time. I wanted to save you from having to make that decision, from living with your choice.' He looked up into her eyes. 'Please believe me when I say that I was trying to protect you.'

Nikki laced her fingers on her lap. She stared at her manicured nails, remembering another time she'd had them done. Light pink to match her wedding bouquet of peonies. She'd never worn anything remotely pink since.

She shivered. Impotent. Fraser? Impossible. It would've destroyed him. She understood the difficult situation he had been in, and why he had struggled to tell her the truth. How could a man tell anyone that, least of all the woman he was about to marry? Raising her head, she said in an unsteady voice, 'I'm glad you're okay.' Then she blushed crimson. 'I mean, in all respects, the cancer, everything,' she blustered.

'I'm glad, too. Very glad.' His gaze was fixed on her. Watching every nuance on her face? He added, 'More than glad. In all respects.'

'Spoken like a man.'

He smiled, a deep smile that warmed her through, that teased and promised so much. 'How else would you have me say it?'

She couldn't answer.

'Nik,' he said softly, 'I never stopped loving you, not for one moment. There were times, I swear, I wouldn't have got through it if I hadn't carried a picture of you in my head. All those wonderful memories we created gave me the strength to fight, made me realise how much I had to live for.'

'Really?' she croaked. Clearing her throat, she tried again. 'You mean that?'

'I understand your disbelief but, yes, sweetheart, I love you. Always have, always will.'

Her lips were trembling when she placed them on his mouth. Her hands shook as she held his shoulders, her body soft against his. 'You love me.'

She tasted so sweet. So Nik. So much his life. Stirring him, heating his blood in a slow, loving way, making him long to be joined with her.

'Huh-hum.'

The second interruption of the afternoon. 'Can't a man get any peace in here?'

His surgeon shook his head in amusement. 'Anyone

point out that you're in hospital? You know, where sick people go?'

'Every minute of the day.' Fraser grinned and let Nikki sit up. Her face was scarlet as she crossed to sit on the chair.

But as Fraser discussed his wound and treatment with the surgeon he was very aware that Nikki's gaze never left him, and that the sparkle produced when he'd told her he loved her was slowly evaporating.

Fraser woke late in the afternoon to the sound of someone moaning in the next bed. Sleeping in hospital wasn't the greatest. Usually the moment he nodded off someone came along and prodded him or took his temperature or lifted the sheet to see his wound, which had become infected.

'The guy could've at least cleaned the blade before sticking it into me.'

'Be thankful the first man he used it on didn't have hepatitis A or something equally nice,' Jay drawled from by the window.

'How long have you been here?' One member or another of Nikki's family was always dropping in. 'Where's Nikki?'

'Long enough to know you talk in your sleep but not long enough to hear anything juicy. And Nikki said she had to go see Mike about starting back at work.' Jay sat on the end of the bed. 'Any more questions?'

'The vet clinic not doing very well at the moment?' Fraser asked. Apart from Nikki, Jay was his most frequent visitor. He didn't believe Nikki had gone to see Mike. There'd been a strange look in her eyes when the surgeon had been with him. Wait till he saw her next. He'd dig for some answers.

'Flat out, actually. I don't know why people think their dogs and cats should partake in the pre-Christmas nibbles. We're seeing so many pets with tummy trouble, it's not funny.'

'Not a lot different to our job, then.'

'Anyone told you when you're getting out of here?' Jay asked.

'Hopefully tomorrow. But I'm on sick leave for at least another week. They won't even allow me to work in the office. Probably not stupid. Paperwork is definitely not my forte.'

'You'll have plenty to do at home. According to Mum, Molly's getting stuck into clearing out the house. You mightn't have a bed by tomorrow.'

Fraser swallowed the flare of annoyance. 'I wish she'd waited. That's not a job to do alone. But it's like she's decided to make a completely new start and doesn't want to waste any time moving into the townhouse she's bought near the retirement village.'

'If you think she's doing this on her own, you don't know the Page women. Mum and Nikki are with her. And Dad's been taking trailer loads of furniture to the second-hand gear shop and a whole heap of other stuff to the tip.'

'I'm glad Rose and Nikki are helping.' His hands curled into fists. 'It should've been me, though.'

Jay stood up. 'Time I went. But for the record you can't be there for everyone and if I had a choice I'm glad it was Nikki you were there for the other night.'

He shuddered. 'Me, too.'

He watched Jay saunter out of the room and gave a thankful sigh. He'd come a full circle, back on side with Nikki and her family. Definitely getting ahead now.

And Nikki loved him. How lucky could he get? As soon as he was up and about he had plans of his own to get under way.

* * *

Nikki sauntered into his room that evening, a covered plate containing chicken enchilada in one hand, two take-out coffees in the other. 'Thought you'd like some real food for a change.'

'What I'd really like is to go home and keep an eye on what Mum's throwing out.'

'Who's a grumpy boy, then?' Nikki popped the top of one coffee and blew on the liquid. 'What's bugging you?'

'List everything that's gone to the tip. I bet there are things that I'd like to keep.'

'I doubt it. Old and broken shovel handles, rusty saws, a chainsaw that had to be the first ever produced. A thousand bent nails. Blown light bulbs. Why did Ken keep all that anyway?'

'He's always been a hoarder.' Fraser took a bite of his supper. And some of the tension gripping him since Jay's visit receded. 'This is wonderful. I don't suppose you sneaked a beer in to go with it.'

The way her eyes rolled told him she hadn't. 'You're not like your dad, are you? You won't spend your life filling sheds with junk?'

No, I'm going to spend it filling my house with a wife and kids. 'Not likely.'

'Thank goodness.' She pulled the chair across to the window and sat down, nursing her coffee. A frown creased her forehead. The same frown that had been there when she'd left after their discussion about his possible impotency.

He'd thought they'd finally gone through everything they needed to so they could move on. 'What's up?'

Her head twisted at an angle as she looked at him through her long eyelashes. Her mouth was tight, not unfriendly, not overly loving either. He couldn't read her. Her hand was steady when she raised the paper cup to her lips.

'Nik?' His heart started thudding. Was she about to retract her love? He couldn't bear that. Anything but that.

Those blue eyes focused directly on him, boring into him. 'When you decide to go back to med school, I'll help you.'

When he opened his mouth to deny her words she held her hand up. 'Spare me your denial. I've seen in your eyes the hunger to be a part of the medical system whenever we've brought a patient into ED.' She sipped her coffee. 'You're meant to be a doctor. You want to be one. Going away to med school to finish your degree isn't going back on your word about staying here. The moment you qualify you'll be on the first plane home. Follow your dream, Fraser. Isn't that why you fought so hard for your life?' Tears glittered in her eyes.

They, more than her words, moved him. Did she think she was letting him go? Freeing him? He stared at her in wonder. She loved him and yet she was telling him to do what he hankered after. 'I promised you I'd stay. And Mum. She needs me.'

'Molly is moving into a low-maintenance property that she can manage easily. Anyway, there are enough men in my family to take care of any problems. And if you went to Wellington you'd only be twenty-five minutes away by air.' She drained her coffee and scrunched the cup tight. 'And if you need funds to get through, I've got money put aside. Grandma left me a healthy amount in her will.'

'I bet that's for your cake shop.' He wasn't taking that. 'You can't give away your dream for mine.'

'The cake shop idea is years away from happening, and by then you'll have paid me back.' Standing up, she tossed the cup into the bin and headed for the door. 'Think about it, Fraser. You know I'm right.'

CHAPTER TWELVE

'HEY, Mum, what's all this stuff?' Nikki asked as she surveyed the piles of cartons in the spare bedroom. It was
Christmas Eve and Fraser's parents were coming to stay
for the next two nights. With all her family around to keep
an eye on Ken it hadn't been difficult to persuade Molly
or his caregivers of the idea. 'It would take until Easter to
clear this room.'

Her mother appeared at her side and reached for the
door, pulling it shut. 'Just some things I've been collect-
ing lately at the second-hand shops. I'll show you after
Christmas once everyone's gone.'

'Second-hand what? Clothes? Cups and saucers?' This
was so unlike her mother, a woman who lived by the adage
that if you hadn't used or worn something in the past year
then you no longer needed it, and off to a charity shop it
went. 'And that many boxes? You're not starting your own
shop, are you?'

'When would I have time for that? With my grandchild
due to arrive any day, I'll hardly have time to get my gar-
dening done.'

There was another thing. 'What's going on, Mum? I've
never see the gardens looking so wonderful. The roses
are amazing. And I'm taking an armful of those pink and
white peonies home with me at the end of the weekend.'

'I'm sure there's plenty out there so I won't notice some missing.' Her mother headed down the hall towards the kitchen. 'Now, come and help me polish the glasses for tomorrow. And don't worry about Molly and Ken. I'm putting them in Jay's old room.'

Perplexed, Nikki studied her mother. Why was her mum talking so fast, jabbering on about anything as though trying to sidetrack her? Aha, her mum had ducked the question about what was going on. Why? 'Here, use this.' A polishing cloth was pressed into her hands.

In the kitchen, Nikki delved into the back of the large walk-in pantry for the boxes of wine glasses and champagne flutes. 'What's this?' She spied a box right at the back she'd never seen before and carefully tugged it out.

Her mother was immediately at her side, reaching for the box. 'Oh, just a couple of glasses I bought the other day.' She put the box back where Nikki had got it from. 'We're not using those tomorrow.'

Nikki turned to stare at this woman she'd known all her life. 'You still look like my mother.'

Red spilled through Rose's cheeks. 'I am your mother.'

'Really? I'm not so sure.' Nikki shook her head. This was getting way too weird. But right now there was a lot to do before tomorrow's festivities. Maybe by the time they had everything ready her real mother would be back and this stranger would've caught the bus out of town.

Then suddenly she was enveloped in her mother's arms, hugged fiercely. 'I'm very proud of you. You're special. My girl.'

Nikki hugged her back, blinking rapidly. Weirder and weirder.

'Merry Christmas.' Fraser walked up to Nikki and kissed her on both cheeks when he and his parents arrived at the

Page farm early Christmas morning. Then he kissed her on the mouth, softly. His stomach squeezed with nerves. What if this didn't work out? What if she threw him off the farm? He felt a hand on his back. Not Nikki's. Her father's. Suddenly, he knew deep down inside that everything would work out just fine.

'Merry ho-ho to you too,' Nikki murmured against his mouth before turning to Molly and Ken. 'Merry Christmas to you both.'

His mum enveloped her in a hug. 'This is special, being here with your family. Thank you for inviting Ken. I know he's become a handful.'

Nikki gave his mother one of her heart-stopping smiles. 'We don't ignore people once something happens to them.'

His mother blinked and smiled back. Fraser knew she'd just been given the best present of the day. Unconditional acceptance of her beloved husband.

He caught Nikki's hand, drew her back to him. 'You look absolutely stunning.' Dressed in a clinging red dress that barely reached mid-thigh and a wide silver belt that accentuated her tiny waist, balancing on red shoes with impossible heels, she looked perfect. Good enough to eat. The Santa hat perched cheekily on her flowing hair brought a mist to his eyes. He loved Nikki more than he'd thought possible.

The scent of peonies wafted through the air. Peonies, bright and colourful, fragile and silky, the perfect perfume for Nikki. He watched as his father hugged this woman who'd shown him so much care and compassion, even love, over the past few months. Both his parents adored her. Even his dad—who had fewer and fewer lucid moments as the weeks progressed, hurtling towards a total fog and a shadow of the hulking man he'd once been—fully understood how special Nikki was. Her whole family had taken his small one in, making them welcome and a part of them.

Like today. It was Christmas Day on a grand scale with the McCalls. People everywhere. Nikki's parents, her brothers and their wives or partners, the partners' parents, and Amber, who was on duty on Boxing Day so she couldn't go down south to share the day with her folks.

Later in the day, Allan and Rose would open their home to all the local strays and waifs—as Nikki called the neighbours who had nowhere to go or no one to share Christmas with—for a dinner that had to be seen to be believed, going by what Nikki had told him. Even Morag and Bryne had been invited to come along later in the morning.

Morag now worked on the farm and, along with Bryne, lived in one of the farm cottages. Another happy ending for someone Allan and Rose hadn't known until an accident had brought them all together.

'Good, I'm glad you've arrived.' Rose bounced down the steps. 'Now we really can get Christmas under way.'

'It's only eight o'clock.' Allan clasped Fraser's mum in a hug. 'I swear this is Rose's favourite day of the year. She's like a big kid, waiting for the presents to be opened.'

'Yes, well, we're all waiting for that today.' Fraser heard his mum say.

Fraser's breath caught in his throat. He'd hardly slept a wink last night waiting for the sun to come up. He'd have come around at five if he'd thought Nikki might be awake. Anything to get the gift giving out of the way. He couldn't believe how nervous he felt. Terrified even. What if—? *Quit the what-ifs. What would be would be.* He was done with doubts about the future. He knew what he wanted and he aimed to get it.

Thankfully, Jay thrust a glass of champagne into his shaking hand. 'Here you go, pal. You look like you could do with something strong under your belt.' His over-exaggerated wink made Fraser grin self-consciously.

'Bit early for that.' Even if he did feel like something to anesthetise the gnawing hope and worry churning his gut.

'Maybe we should have brunch first,' Allan teased, a cheeky grin so like Nikki's on his face.

'Definitely presents first.' Nikki clapped her hands and began shooing them all up the steps and along the wide veranda to where the huge Christmas tree stood in pride of place.

There were truckloads of presents. Fraser gaped. Never in his life had he seen anything like it. 'Blimey.' This was going to take hours.

Nikki giggled as she slipped her hand into his. 'Told you Mum goes overboard. Anyone who comes up our drive today will receive a little gift, even if they haven't been invited.'

A lump blocked Fraser's throat as his eyes searched the pine tree for the gift he'd placed there yesterday. There, near the top, sharing a tiny branch with an angel, hung the precious object. So small and yet monumental in its significance.

'Are you all right?' Nikki nudged him. 'You've gone all pale.'

If only you knew. 'I'm fine. Who'd have believed four months ago we'd be spending Christmas together?'

Her laughter tinkled on the air. 'Not that I regret any of it.'

Thank goodness. 'Coming home turned out to be the most right thing I could ever have done.'

'Hey, are you two joining us?' Allan called from his Santa seat. 'I'd like to start handing out the presents.'

'Go ahead, Dad. Sorry, Santa.' Nikki tugged Fraser to

a cupid chair and pushed him down, then sat on his knee. 'Ready when you are.'

Fraser gulped his champagne and the bubbles shot up his nose, causing him to sneeze. The moment was getting closer. There was no escaping now. Not that he wanted to. But he'd certainly jumped in the deep end. What had happened to doing things quietly and privately? Nikki had happened, that's what. This was about her, for her.

Presents were passed around to everyone and the delighted cries of thanks and excitement momentarily distracted Fraser. The girls especially seemed ecstatic, getting enough presents to keep a small nation going. Even he had never had so many. He unwrapped CDs and DVDs, an All Blacks jersey, a pair of cricket shoes, and from Nikki a voucher for a mystery weekend away for two.

'You're taking me, of course,' she chirped, and for once he saw no uncertainty in those azure eyes studying him from under long lashes.

'Do you know where we're going, or is it a surprise for you too?'

'I know exactly where we're headed. I didn't want to go anywhere not romantic enough.'

'We'd make it romantic no matter where we went.'

'Aw, you say the nicest things.' Her lips brushed his. Her scent filled his nose, tipped his world sideways. He was such a lucky man.

'Okay, you two,' Jay chipped in. 'That's the presents done.' Then he banged his head with the palm of his hand. 'Oops, wrong. Seems like there's one more at the top of the tree.' He looked around at everyone, his cheeky grin finally aimed at Fraser. 'Eh, mate. Your turn, I believe.'

Fraser froze. The moment he'd been anticipating with excitement and a dash of trepidation had arrived. Everyone was watching him, waiting with happy anticipation. Everyone except Nikki.

'What's going on? Fraser, what does Jay mean?' She squirmed around on his thighs, peered at him with a big question in her eyes.

For the life of him he couldn't move. Not because Nik was sitting on him but because his muscles had forgotten how to work. His legs were like custard. His arms gripped the sides of the chair, unable to manoeuvre him upwards.

'Nik, shift your butt and let the man up.' Jay ducked as a wad of scrunched wrapping paper flew at him.

But at least Nikki stood up, turning to stare down at Fraser again. 'Please tell me what's going on.'

The tiniest wobble in her voice propelled Fraser out of the chair and had him reaching for her hands. 'It's okay, sweetheart. It's all good. Trust me.'

She squinted at him, her mouth twitching as though she was trying hard not to smile at him. 'You've hung some of that terrible plastic mistletoe somewhere, haven't you?'

'It's right up here.' He tugged her with him as he approached the tree and reached up to remove the last present. Then he sucked a huge breath, winced as his injured lung protested, and knelt down in front of her. 'Nikki Page, please, will you marry me?'

Nikki gasped. The hand he still held began trembling. Her eyes widened in astonishment. She didn't say a word.

There was utter silence on the veranda. Not even the cattle in the nearest paddock had anything to say. The world was waiting on Nikki.

In his chest his heart was trying to pound its way out through his ribs. *Say something, please.* Yes. No. Anything but this awful silence. He could barely wait.

Nikki blinked. A tear escaped, ran down her cheek.

Her mouth widened slowly into the most beautiful smile he'd ever seen. 'Yes.'

Relief surged through him, lifting him back on his feet. 'Really?' His mouth was split wide in a grin. 'Really?'

'Yes, Fraser, I will marry you.'

The whole room erupted in clapping and cheering.

Nikki leaned in against him, wrapped her arms around him and kissed him long and tenderly.

He kissed her right back, long and tenderly.

Of course, it was Jay who interrupted them. 'Haven't you forgotten something, you two?'

Pulling his mouth from Nikki's, Fraser stared at him. 'What?'

'The small matter of the last present.'

Fraser rolled his eyes. What a dope he was. He took one of Nikki's hands and placed the tiny box in her palm. 'Nikki, sweetheart, you need an engagement ring now.' And he closed her fingers around it.

Her one tear turned into a torrent as she tore the ribbon off and then snapped the lid back. 'Oh, my goodness, it's beautiful. Stunning, fabulous. A bigger version of the first one.' She sniffed.

'You like it, then?' Fraser took the sapphire and diamond ring from its cushion and slipped it over her finger.

Nikki gazed at her hand, holding it out to the sunlight. 'I love it. But nowhere near as much as I love you, Fraser.'

Then they were surrounded by everyone trying to shake hands, hug them, see the ring. The melee finally stopped as Allan and Jay began handing around more glasses of champagne, this time top-shelf champagne.

Allan raised his glass. 'A toast to Nikki and Fraser.'

Nikki hesitated, understanding finally dawning. 'You all knew Fraser was going to propose today. Did he ask you all for my hand in marriage?'

As everyone answered in the affirmative, she turned back to Fraser with a cheeky smile. 'That was very brave of you.'

'You're telling me!'

'I suppose you've all decided when we're getting married too?' Then her gaze turned on her mother, and when Rose's face turned crimson Nikki gasped. 'You have. All those boxes in the spare room. They're to do with our wedding, aren't they? Nothing to do with second-hand shops at all.'

'Not a thing. It was the only explanation I could come up with when I found you about to delve into those cartons of table settings.' Rose gave her daughter an understanding look. 'It is your day, love. There're still lots of things to organise and decisions to make about colours, flowers, the dress.'

Nikki looked around for Molly. 'I think we can sort the dress out right now.'

Molly brushed tears from her face and came to give Nikki a kiss. 'At least we know it fits.'

Fraser looked at the two women he loved most. 'What's going on?'

'You're not the only sneaky one around here. When we were packing up your mum's things while you were lying on your back in hospital, we came across Molly's wedding dress.'

'And you just had to try it on?'

'Of course. It's beautiful.' Nikki frowned. 'When are we getting married?'

'How about New Year's Day? Start the year off as we mean to go on.'

This was where everything could go pear-shaped. Nikki liked to be in charge, and to have partially organised her wedding without her knowledge had been a risk, but there'd been no other way to have the wedding so soon. The licence had been arranged, the caterers booked, the marquee ordered. But Fraser knew they had to get married quickly for Nikki's sake. He couldn't stand for her to fret that he might opt out before the day. Even waiting a week might seem an age for her if she was worrying he might not show up. She loved him, trusted him, but if there was even a smidgeon of doubt about her own worth, that would fester away within her. He wasn't taking the chance.

'We've got a date, Fraser McCall.' Her kiss was sweet and sexy and loving and all the things that made up his woman. 'Second time lucky, eh?'

New Year's Day

The sun shone brightly from a perfect summer sky, glinting off the sides of the huge white marquee erected on the front lawn of Nikki's family home. All the lawns were immaculate, the grass no doubt scared to grow a millimetre since Fraser and Jay had mown and raked them two days ago. The rose beds were stunning with their bright red, yellow, pink and white blooms. In the paddocks to the west of the house the vines were covered in bright green foliage.

A trail of scattered rose petals led from the house to a huge oak tree under which the marriage celebrant stood patiently waiting in front of at least a hundred guests. Among those guests were all the full-time crews from the station and, biggest surprise of all, his friends he'd travelled with, who'd flown out from England two days ago.

Fraser's mum and dad grinned and waved to him as his gaze found them at the front. He hadn't seen them look as happy in years. Thankfully, today was one of his dad's better days and he knew exactly what was going on.

Everything was going perfectly. Even the baby had

obliged and arrived between Christmas and today, giving Yvonne time to recover for the wedding.

Fraser crossed to his favourite garden—the peony bed. The heady scent filled his nostrils, and he snapped off a pink bloom and poked it into his buttonhole. The breath caught in his throat. Never in a million years had he imagined this day quite like this. It was the perfect backdrop for his beautiful bride.

'Where *is* Nikki?' Jay had followed him and now stood beside him, tapping the toe of his shoe on the path. 'You'd think she would be on time today of all days.'

'I'm the one who's supposed to be nervous, not you.' Fraser grinned at this man who was standing up with him at the ceremony. 'She'll be here.'

And there she was, standing at the top of the three steps leading down to the lawn, her hand on her father's arm. Fraser forgot to breath. Beautiful didn't begin to describe Nikki. Dressed in ivory satin that highlighted her blue eyes, she looked perfect. 'Wow.'

'That's my sister?' Jay grinned. 'She does scrub up all right, doesn't she?'

'All right? She's stunning,' Fraser croaked.

'Amber looks awesome too.'

Amber? Oh, yes, tucked in behind Nikki, she looked pretty in her long pink-and-white dress, but his eyes returned to Nikki. He couldn't get enough of her. He heard the guests gasp as they turned to watch Nikki descend the steps and fully agreed with them.

'I've never seen Amber in a dress,' Jay muttered.

Fraser decided he'd be telling Amber to wear one all the time if the star-struck expression on Jay's face meant what he thought. Amber had spent months trying to be noticed by Nik's brother and all she'd had to do was wear a dress. He grinned to himself. What a great day.

Finally, Jay nudged him. 'Come on, man, time you got hitched.'

Then he was being tugged by his future brother-in-law to the front of the excited guests, where he turned to watch the progress of his bride. His heart leapt with joy within his chest and a lump the size of a brick blocked his throat. Everything that had happened over the past five and a half years had been worth it to experience this moment.

When Nikki and her father reached him, Fraser couldn't resist leaning in for one little kiss. 'You're absolutely beautiful, my love,' he whispered around the lump. 'You're everything to me.'

My future, my life, my everything. Thank goodness he'd come back to Blenheim. If there was one thing in his life he could thank his father for it was forcing his hand to come home. Home was where their families were.

'Let's get married.' She smiled that sweet smile that he'd dreamed about every night since he'd first set eyes on her trying to catch tadpoles in the pond behind the farmhouse.

Taking her hand, he smiled back. 'Let's.' And he gave her another wee kiss for luck before turning to the marriage celebrant. 'I think we're ready.'

A few years later

Fraser slowed for the turn into the drive leading up to the farmhouse. 'Are you ready for this?'

Nik shook her head at him. 'This is family, Fraser, nothing more, nothing less.'

He grinned. 'Exactly.' Pressing his foot down on the accelerator, he added, 'Hope someone's got the beer cold.'

'This is my family.'

True. 'It will be icy cold.' They rounded the bend. 'Oh. My. God.'

'Fraser, Little Miss Big Ears.'

'Sorry. But—' He waved a hand in the direction of the house. 'That's over the top.'

'That's my family.' Nikki chuckled. 'Though they seem to have gone overboard today.'

WELCOME HOME
DR AND MRS MCCALL
AND WEE CINDY

The banner stretched from one end of the house to the other. Underneath crowded all their family, holding glasses of champagne.

'Marry one Page and get a whole book.' Fraser brought the car to a halt and leaned over to pat Nik's expanding belly. 'You might want to stay in there, little man. It's a lot quieter.'

'Daddy, lots of people.' Cindy leaned forward in her child car seat.

'Tell me something I don't know, little one.' He opened the back door. 'Come on, sweetheart, time to catch up with all your family.' He kissed the top of his daughter's head. 'You don't know how lucky we are.'

* * * * *

ONE NIGHT
THAT CHANGED
EVERYTHING

BY
TINA BECKETT

For those who embrace life.

All the characters in this book have no existence outside the imagination of the author, and have no relation whatsoever to anyone bearing the same name or names. They are not even distantly inspired by any individual known or unknown to the author, and all the incidents are pure invention.

First published in Great Britain 2012
by Mills & Boon, an imprint of Harlequin (UK) Limited.
Harlequin (UK) Limited, Eton House, 18-24 Paradise Road,
Richmond, Surrey TW9 1SR

© Tina Beckett 2012

ISBN: 978 0 263 89213 0

Harlequin (UK) policy is to use papers that are natural, renewable and recyclable products and made from wood grown in sustainable forests. The logging and manufacturing process conform to the legal environmental regulations of the country of origin.

Printed and bound in Spain
by Blackprint CPI, Barcelona

Dear Reader

There are times in life when every person comes face to face with his or her own mortality. As I brainstormed Greg and Hannah's story I thought about people who overcome incredible challenges, and how they seem to relish life with an intensity others can only dream of. I wanted Hannah's character to have this same passion as someone who's faced down a life-threatening illness and made a conscious decision to live every moment to its fullest. Even if some of those moments have unexpected consequences...

Thank you for joining Greg and Hannah as they experience the joy and heartbreak of working in a difficult field. Their dedication to their patients and to each other helps them rise to meet each new challenge. Best of all, this special couple finds love along the way.

I hope you enjoy reading about their journey as much as I enjoyed writing about it!

Sincerely

Tina Beckett

CHAPTER ONE

"MRS. BROOKSTONE went under hospice care last night."

The words met Hannah Lassiter the second she pushed through the glass doors of the Alaska Valley Oncology Center. She glanced at her watch, her shoulders slumping. Only seven-thirty, but she had no doubt her boss was already here. Had already heard the news. "Oh, no. Where is he?"

She didn't really need to ask. Dr. Gregory Mason would be holed up in his office until his first appointment. Dedicated to providing the best care possible, news like this—even when it was expected—had the power to bring Dr. Mason's world crashing to a halt for an hour or two. At least until he rose from his chair, closed the door on this particular compartment in his head and got back to work. It was eerie, really, how he could seemingly wall off certain portions of his brain at will.

The receptionist answered her question with a jerk of her thumb.

Hannah sighed. "When's his first patient due in?"

"Martha Brookstone *was* his first patient. We've cancelled the appointment."

"Don't put anyone else in her slot, okay? I'll check on him."

Easier said than done. Her employer, a brilliant doctor,

insisted on doing much of the scheduling himself, which was a nightmare for his staff, who had to scramble to keep up with him.

Yet every single person in that office had benefitted from his indefatigable nature, including Hannah herself.

A year in remission and counting. She'd never even seen it coming. A routine checkup two years ago had uncovered enlarged lymph nodes.

Cancer.

She'd moved from her position at a tiny clinic in the Aleutian Islands to Anchorage for treatment. Dr. Mason had convinced her to stay on as one of his staff afterward.

Today, of all days, though, she was going to have a tough time keeping her mind on her job. She'd had her own doctor's appointment yesterday. Her chance at a new beginning.

Rounding the U-shaped receptionist desk to check the printed schedule, she frowned. The list stretched well into the evening. Seven o'clock. And the word *hospital* was penciled in after the last appointment.

How did he do it?

While some doctors crammed in as many patients as possible, Dr. Mason worked long, hard hours but his patients were spread out, most covering an entire half-hour block, some up to an hour—especially the newly diagnosed. She ran a finger down the list. Three new cases. Blowing out a breath that fluffed her bangs off her forehead, she again wondered why she'd agreed to work for a doctor who represented every fear she'd ever held.

Except for today. Even with the sad news about Martha still floating in the air, this was one day she'd force herself to flatten the past and let the hope of a shining future take hold and grow into something wonderful. Just as she hoped that little blast of sperm she'd received yesterday would grow and multiply.

Too bad that blast had been from the end of a syringe. But it was the only kind of action she was likely to get. Especially with the schedule she'd been keeping lately. It was almost as bad as her boss's.

And if the little swimmers hit their mark, she'd have to talk to Dr. Mason about cutting back and possibly finding a replacement as her time got near.

A lot depended on the damage the chemo had done to her eggs. Dr. Mason had put her on a lighter regimen in an effort to preserve her fertility, but even so, she'd banked some of her eggs beforehand, just in case. But she'd decided to start with the easiest option—artificial insemination—and work her way toward the hardest and most expensive procedures. If those all failed, adoption was always an option.

Going to the coffee carafe they kept in the far corner of the office, she poured two cups, one for herself and one for Dr. Mason, who'd probably already let his first cup go stone cold.

"Wish me luck," she said to Stella, who was already busy fielding calls for the nurse who'd arrive soon. The receptionist gave her a thumbs-up sign and went back to writing on the neon green notepad in front of her. The only way she could keep track of things, she'd said.

Stella buzzed her in, and Hannah used her shoulder to push through the metal door that led to a short corridor of exam rooms, at the end of which lay Dr. Mason's cramped office. She didn't know why she bothered going back to see him. He would emerge when he was ready and not a second before.

His door was closed, but since when had she let something like that stop her? Um…never.

Using her elbow to push down the stainless-steel lever, she waited for the click that would allow her to ease it open. Lucky for her, the thing wasn't locked. Kicking it repeatedly wouldn't be the most dignified way of letting him know she was there.

He sat behind an ornately carved mahogany desk, forehead resting on steepled fingers, eyes closed. He didn't bother looking up. "Don't you ever knock?"

His low voice was gruff, and she had to strain to hear it. The sound pulled at her heartstrings, but she couldn't let him know it. They'd played this little dance several times since he'd hired her. No, even before that. The day he'd declared her to be in remission she'd impulsively thrown her arms around his neck and hugged him tight, thanking him. He'd stiffened for a second or two before sliding warm hands across her back and returning the hug. Just as quickly he'd moved away, not quite meeting her eyes during the rest of the appointment.

None of the other staff dared come into his "lair"— as they called it—without an invitation. But Hannah had been raised in a house with five boys. Impulse control and subtlety were not on the menu. Neither were privacy and quiet. And the last thing Dr. Mason needed right now was to sit here alone and brood.

"My hands are full. Besides, would you have let me in?"

His head came up, twin indentations from his fingertips marring the broad surface of his forehead.

How long had he been sitting like that?

"What do you think?" Deep brown eyes met hers. Eyes that had been filled with compassion when he'd treated her Hodgkin's disease were now glittering with annoyance.

"I brought a peace offering." She set both the cups of coffee on his desk, spying a matching paper cup off to the side. It was still full, but when she touched the side of it…

Yep. Icy cold, just as she'd suspected.

Carrying it into the tiny restroom attached to his of-fice, she dumped the contents into the sink, rinsed out the dregs, then threw the cup into the wastebasket.

She joined him again, taking her own cup and sliding into one of the twin chairs on the other side of his desk.

Dr. Mason groaned. Out loud, which made her smile.

"I'll drink it, I promise."

"You're right. You will." She crossed her legs and took a sip of her own coffee. Waiting.

"Damn it, Hannah. You're not my mother."

No, she wasn't. But she was grateful for everything he'd done for her, and this was the only way she could think of to return the favor. It was all he'd allow. And, grudgingly or not, he usually let her have her way.

Right on cue, he picked up the cup and took a sip.

"Stella told me about Mrs. Brookstone. I'm sorry."

He nodded.

Hannah knew the recommendation not to continue che-motherapy had been an agonizing one for Dr. Mason. He never made those kinds of decisions lightly, which was why he was in here, probably going over each step of his patient's treatment with a fine-toothed comb, wondering if he could have done something differently.

"She's seventy-five, and the cancer had already spread to her lungs by the time her general practitioner diag-nosed her."

His eyes closed for a second before sending her a glare. "I've read the chart."

Many times, if she knew him.

"Yes, you read it. But did you accept it?"

A muscle worked in his jaw. "I'll never accept no hope as a diagnosis."

Her heart squeezed at the tightness behind the words.

She wasn't saying he should just write the most serious cases off. "That's what makes you the perfect man for this job."

"I sometimes wonder."

She set her coffee on the edge of the desk and leaned forward. "You need to cut back on your schedule. Take some time off just for yourself. You're already on the road to burnout as it is."

His brows went up. "I've been doing this job for ten years. I think I know my own limitations."

"When was the last time you took a vacation?" She held up a hand before he could answer. "A real one. One that doesn't involve a medical conference or giving some type of lecture."

"You mean like the one you're giving me right now?"

Her face heated. Okay, so he had her there. "Sorry."

He picked up a pen and twirled it, giving her a chance to study him. Dark hair, conservatively cropped, lay thick against his head. Not a hint of grey yet. His broad shoulders were strong and imposing, despite the slight stoop from spending hours bent over operating tables and examining patients. She knew those shoulders led to narrow hips, which were now safely hidden on the other side of the desk.

The fingers that gripped the pen were long and delicate, nimble enough to separate healthy tissue from diseased. She gulped, remembering the gentle way they'd touched the bare skin of her midriff as he'd drawn a permanent marker across the vulnerable surface in preparation for taking a biopsy of one of her thoracic nodes. The way her abdominal muscles had rippled at the contact. Even through the thin latex gloves, his hands had been warm and reassuring.

This isn't what you came back here to do, Hannah.

She stood, taking another sip of her coffee. "Lecture's almost over, then. Drink your coffee, Dr. Mason."

"Greg." His head tilted to the side. "How many times do I have to ask?"

A hundred? A million?

That crazy hug all those months ago had changed something between them. Had left her with a frightening awareness of his scent, of the solid feel of his body against hers. She was only too eager to keep those memories locked up tight.

Calling him by his first name might just undo all that hard work, despite the fact that everyone else in the office called him Greg. Most of them would also admit to having a bit of a crush on their handsome employer. Or at least a good dose of hero-worship.

Some of his patients claimed he was a miracle worker.

In reality, Dr. Mason was just a man. He even had a pretty big flaw: despite his best efforts, he couldn't remain completely objective about his patients. And it ate him up from the inside out.

Mrs. Brookstone was a prime example of that.

He grieved. Deeply. For each one he lost. Even though he didn't let others see his pain, she suspected he kept a private scorecard inside his head that recorded those he'd been able to snatch from death's door…and those he hadn't.

"Dr. Mason—"

His brows went up.

Okay, she was weak. Stupid. Would probably come to regret doing this very, very soon. But he was hurting right now.

"Greg," she corrected, her voice soft. "You can't save them all."

He dropped the pen onto the top of his desk, the sharp

ping as it struck the wooden surface as loud as a guillotine strike. *Off with her head!*

Why had she said something he was already well aware of?

"Thank you."

His answer didn't track with what she'd just said. Unless he was being sarcastic.

But there was nothing in his face to indicate he was. In fact, his eyes met hers for a second or two before moving lower. Her lips tingled, sending an answering heat washing across her face.

He was *not* looking where she thought he was.

To cover up her embarrassment, she said, "What are you thanking me for?"

He picked up his prescription pad in one hand and his coffee cup in the other then stood. "For bringing me coffee." His lips curved up at the corners, sending more heat sloshing around her tummy. "And for saying my name."

CHAPTER TWO

THANK you for saying my name.

Greg rolled his eyes and scrubbed a hand across his head as he wrote up notes from his last patient of the day. What kind of lame comment was that?

He refused to admit he'd waited with bated breath, wondering if his physician's assistant would rise to the subtle challenge.

She had, which had shocked him. At first.

But hearing his name uttered in those husky tones had washed away his surprise and done a number on his gut. He'd been hounding her to adopt the informality of the rest of the staff for months now, but she'd steadfastly refused.

Until today.

And now he wondered if the policy he'd instituted hadn't been the most idiotic idea known to man.

She just felt sorry for you, that's all.

He slammed the folder shut, hoping to God she'd already left for the day. Unlike the first-name-basis rule, one of his smarter decisions had been to request that the staff leave once they'd finished inputting the last patient of the day, with the exception of his nurse. He might work long hours, but that didn't mean he should expect them to as well. Most of them had families to go home to.

Except Hannah.

He could still remember her gripping his neck, the softly whispered "Thank you" against his skin when her last set of test results had come back. And, like a fool, he'd returned her embrace…had—

Damn it. Why couldn't he get her out of his head today?

Maybe because she'd rarely given in once she'd made her mind up about something. Like not leaving his office this morning, until she'd watched him take a few sips of his coffee. He'd learned the hard way not to go head to head with her.

Her determination to make the most out of life had struck him even when he'd been her oncologist. It was still there now that he was her boss.

She hadn't been able to make the transition from patient to employee as well as some of his other staff had.

And yet that *"Greg"* had seemed to slip between her lips effortlessly, as if she'd said it to herself hundreds of times before.

That thought made not only his collar tighten but other, more dangerous parts.

As her mouth had formed the word his thoughts had strayed, along with his eyes.

The pink color rushing to her face had told him she'd realized the exact second his gaze had touched her lips. Paused there.

He shook his head. What was wrong with him? He still had work to do and wanted to run by the hospital before it was too late to check on his patients.

Mrs. Brookstone's case had weighed on his heart like a rock all day. The last time he'd seen her, three of her grandchildren had crowded around her hospital bed, looking up at him with such hope. She'd had a pair of knitting needles balanced in her hands, in the process of making yet another hat for one of his patients.

But the news he'd brought had been anything but good.

Life was fragile. As he'd learned from experience. When Hannah had stood there in his office, all he'd wanted to do was pull her into his arms and relive the warmth of her breath washing across his cheek, the steady beat of her heart.

He'd resisted the impulse. Thank God.

Tucking a few files into his attaché case, he slung the strap over his shoulder and headed out, locking his office behind him. When he got to the closed door of the reception area, a strange blend of scents hit his nostrils. Garlic. Tomato sauce. It smelled like...lasagna.

What the...?

Someone must have brought pasta from home and heated it in the microwave at lunchtime.

His stomach gurgled in sad protest, and he realized he hadn't eaten anything other than the ham sandwich that had been mysteriously deposited on his desk at lunchtime.

Maybe he'd swing by the hospital cafeteria after making his rounds. He had nothing at home, other than the bacon and eggs he'd bought a couple of days ago. And neither of those sounded very appetizing right now. Especially with his nose still twitching in anticipation.

Pushing through the door, he blinked at the quartet of aluminum containers lining the reception desk. And the lights were still on.

"I was just about to come and get you." The voice came from his left. He didn't have to look to know who it belonged to. Hannah.

He turned. Sure enough, there she was, her printed work smock gone and in its place a soft green blouse, cinched at the waist with a belt. The deep V-neckline drew his eyes down. He forced his gaze to stay above her collarbone, which was not quite as prominent as it had been during her treatments a year ago. That was a good sign. She was putting on some of the weight she'd lost. There were now curves that…

Clearing his throat, he met her gaze, noting the pink tinge from earlier was back in her cheeks. The color contrasted with her hair, the deep mahogany locks still fairly short, even after a year's regrowth. He liked the choppy style she'd adopted. It matched her personality. "I thought you'd left a while ago." He motioned toward the desk. "What's all this?"

"I figured you wouldn't stop to eat before going to the hospital, so I ordered takeout. Manicotti."

Huh. So his nose hadn't been too far off the mark. "I don't pay you to babysit me."

Her teeth came down on her lip, making him regret the words almost as soon as they'd left his mouth.

"I was trying to help. You work too hard."

One shoulder went up in irritation. "I think we've already covered this territory. I'm not married. No kids. So I don't think it's anyone's business how many hours I put in."

"Your patients count on you." Her voice was soft. Hesitant. And he had no idea what she meant. His patients were what motivated him to work so hard. Along with his sister's faith in him.

"I'm trying to make sure they have reason to."

She took a step closer. "No, I don't mean they need you to work harder. They count on you staying healthy enough to make good decisions."

Good decisions. A thread of anger unfurled inside his chest. He didn't need this today. Especially after Mrs. Brookstone. "I didn't hear you complaining when I treated you."

"No. But I didn't know what your office hours looked like back then." Her gaze went to the desk, and she picked her handbag up from a nearby chair and hitched it on her shoulder. "I didn't stay to argue with you. I just wanted to make sure you had a decent meal for once. I'll see you tomorrow."

"Wait." He put a hand on her arm, the shirt just as soft and silky as it appeared. He let go once she looked up at him. She'd said she was trying to help, and all he'd done was gripe and complain. "At least stay and eat with me. It'll be good to have a conversation that doesn't revolve around malignancies and treatment options."

She shook her head. "I don't think… There's only one plate."

"Then we'll improvise." Why was he insisting? Because her thoughtfulness had touched him? Because the perks of not having anyone waiting for him at home came with a hefty—and lonely—price tag?

He had no idea, but he knew he wanted some company. He didn't want to sit here by himself and dwell on his patients. What he'd said was true. There were times he craved conversation that had nothing to do with his job or his struggles—something his sister had intuitively known. But she wasn't here to make him smile anymore.

"Okay. Wait here."

The ease at which she'd given in surprised him almost as much as it had earlier. He smiled. He noticed she hadn't once said his name again, though.

She would before the meal was through. He'd see to it.

Punching the buzzer that unlocked the back area, she dragged a chair over to the door and propped it open, then disappeared for a few minutes. When she came back, she was holding a pink emesis basin.

"You're kidding."

She shrugged. "It's clean. I've eaten chili out one of these more than once."

Greg's lip curled half in disgust, half in amusement. "Have you ever thought of bringing in a package of paper plates and stashing them somewhere?"

"Yep, but I never got around to it. You said to improvise." Her head tilted, a quick smile forming. "This is me, improvising."

Okay, she had him there.

"And silverware? Are we supposed to share?" The thought made something heat in his chest.

She pulled a clear plastic package out from behind the desk. "Nope, the girls always keep their leftover plastic ware in case of an emergency."

What kind of emergency, other than eating, required sets of plastic knives and forks? He didn't think he wanted to know. "I guess we're all set, then."

Greg helped her dish out the food, noting she took the emesis basin for herself and gave him the plate and silverware provided by the restaurant. Besides the manicotti, there were two kinds of sauce, white and red, as well as a Caesar salad and garlic rolls. She'd expected him to eat all this himself?

"I see I owe you some money."

She shook her head, spooning white sauce over her own portion. "I took money out of the petty-cash drawer."

His brows went up. "We keep that much in there?"

"Fifty bucks." She dropped the spoon back into the container. "But this pretty much cleaned it out."

He couldn't remember the last time he'd spent that much money on a meal for himself. The warmth in his chest grew, bringing with it the uncomfortable awareness that he was in a deserted medical building with a woman he couldn't begin to understand. One he found dangerously attractive.

She was also one of his employees. Asking her to stay and eat with him had been a big mistake. Huge!

But he couldn't very well ask her to leave now.

So he sat on one of the brown leatherette chairs in the waiting room next to her, balancing a flimsy plate across his knees.

Hannah, on the other hand, looked perfectly at home, cutting into her manicotti with a plastic fork and popping a piece into her mouth. "Mmm." Her lids came down for a brief second as she seemed to savor the food.

He swallowed, despite the fact that he had nothing in his mouth other than the lump that was currently stuck in his throat.

Incredibly long lashes swept back up, and green eyes regarded him. "Aren't you going to taste it?"

The only thing he wanted to taste were her lips.

Ah, hell.

He forked up a big bite and shoved it past his teeth, dumping the food onto his tongue before he could do or say anything stupid. He chewed. Swallowed. His stomach gave another fierce rumble.

Okay, so she'd been right. He was hungry. And evidently that fact was going to trump any other urges for the moment. He relaxed into his seat, figuring he could eat and then get the hell out of there before his belly figured out it was full and let his other instincts out of their cage. "It's good."

"I know. It's my go-to place for takeout. I order from there at least once a week."

He didn't like to think of Hannah at home alone, eating from disposable metal containers. But it wasn't much better than what he did day in and day out. He was content with it, so why would he assume someone else wouldn't be?

Greg just couldn't imagine her having weekends free,

figuring she'd be out making up for the year she'd lost. There was something inside her that burned brightly. That glow could have been snuffed out in an instant. Not something he wanted to think about right now.

He covered by saying, "I normally just grab something from the hospital cafeteria."

"I know."

She did?

Before he could ask, she added, "I used to see you walking down the corridor with a sandwich container in your hand."

"When…?"

"When I was getting my chemo infusions. I saw you sometimes." Her hand went to her collarbone area and fingered the pale scar where her port had once been. Greg was so used to seeing those that he hadn't even noticed it.

He also hadn't realized she'd been in that treatment room. Had seen him. How many other patients had he walked by without noticing? Another brick of guilt settled into place. "I'm sorry. I'm normally so busy, I don't stop in there all the time."

Putting her fork into her bowl, she reached out and touched his hand. "I wasn't trying to make you feel bad. I've just learned how important it is to eat a balanced meal."

She was right. Again. He often preached to his patients that they needed to strengthen their bodies as much as possible to help during the chemo treatments as well as to aid in the fight of their disease. That meant making healthy choices when it came to food. And yet, just like a pulmonologist who indulged in the occasional cigarette, Greg was unwilling to abide by his own advice.

"I don't have cancer, but I also don't cook."

She picked up her fork again, avoiding his eyes this

time. "That's why there are places like *Piazza Toscana*." The comment, unlike her lighthearted ones from a few moments ago, was tight, as if…

I don't have cancer.

How damned insensitive could he be? She'd spent a year undergoing chemotherapy. Hadn't known for sure if she'd live or die.

Maybe she was right. He worked so hard that he no longer paid attention to social conventions or cared how his words might affect someone else.

No, that wasn't right. He did care.

Setting his plate onto the chair next to him, he shifted sideways to face her. "Hey." He waited until she looked at him before continuing. "I'm sorry for saying that. There's no good reason, other than I'm tired and not thinking straight."

She blinked, and he wasn't sure whether the light was playing tricks on him or if there'd been a trace of moisture rimming her lower lids. But when he looked closer, it was gone.

"How long will you be at the hospital tonight?" she asked.

"About an hour."

Glancing at her watch, she set her own plate to the side and went over to the low sofa and picked up one of the leather pillows. Coming back, she lowered herself to the padded loop carpet at his feet.

His mouth went dry as she set the pillow down and patted the area next to her. "It's only seven. Why don't you stretch out for a while? Take a quick nap. I promise I won't let you sleep longer than an hour."

Was she crazy? After the thoughts that had just gone spinning through his head? There was no way he was going to lie down on the floor and—

Even as the words slid through his mind, a wave of exhaustion washed over him, staggering him with its force.

It was the food. The heavy meal was making him sleepy.

What would it hurt? If his eyes were shut, he could block out her face. No more trying to make small talk. No more worrying about how he was looking at her. About what her kneeling on the floor with that pillow had made him imagine.

Before he was fully aware of what he was doing, he'd done as she'd suggested and stretched out on his back, his head on the pillow she'd laid next to her hip. Every muscle in his body seemed to go boneless, and he glanced up to see her leaning over him with a smile. Her fingers brushed across his forehead, the touch light. Comforting.

He pulled in a deep breath. Let it out.

"Close your eyes, Greg. I promise I'll be right here."

Even as his lids seemed to obey her every command, a tired sense of triumph went through him.

He'd been right. She'd said his name. Again.

CHAPTER THREE

THE trill of Hannah's watch alarm registered in her ears, but it took her brain a little more time to place the sound.

Opening her eyes, she punched a button before noticing Greg's dark, mussed hair, his even darker eyes regarding her with a slight smile. He was upside down. No, wait. She was. Hadn't she been sitting up while he'd slept? Why were they now reversed?

Ack. Because she'd fallen asleep, too. Had evidently just keeled over sideways and was lying on the floor, looking pretty much like she'd looked sitting up. Bent at the hips, legs straight out.

Greg's lips curved higher. "Looks like I wasn't the only one who was tired."

Only he didn't seem tired. Not anymore. His eyes glittered with life, and the dark circles beneath them had eased. He also looked much more relaxed. Or was that still due to the topsy-turvy world she'd awoken into? Maybe his smile was really a frown.

"Did you sleep well?" She cleared her throat when her voice came out as a hoarse squawk.

"Like a rock. Good thing you set that alarm."

He could say that again. She'd only set it so she wouldn't be tempted to wake him with the proverbial kiss. Like a reverse Sleeping Beauty. That analogy fit her current mixed-up thought processes to a T. "Sorry. I had no idea I was that tired."

"I should be the one saying sorry. I don't expect you to keep the same hours I do."

Her eyes narrowed slightly, and somewhere in the back of her mind, she realized she should be moving. "Don't you think I'm capable of it?"

He gave a soft laugh. "Oh, I know you are. I just don't want you to run you off before I've…"

His words trailed away.

"Before you've what?"

"Before I've proven I can take better care of myself."

That made her smile. But when she did try to sit up, the awkward angle at which she'd been lying made her back muscles give a warning twinge. She eased back down, licking her lips as she waited for the spasm to pass.

He frowned. "What is it?"

"Nothing." Lord, what was she going to do? She couldn't very well wave him off and send him on his way while pretzeled on the floor. What if she couldn't get up after he left and he returned in the morning to find her still here? Still folded like a crazed contortionist? "I'll be fine in a minute. My…er, foot's asleep."

He angled away, his gaze sweeping down her pants' legs. He reached down and plucked off one of her white leather slip-ons and then the other. "Which one?"

"No, don't touch it!"

Okay, that screech hadn't been exactly the calm tone she'd been going for. But her feet were seriously ticklish—one wrong move and she'd wrench her back even further.

"Shh. I won't." He propped himself on one elbow as he continued to regard her. "Your foot might keep you from walking but it wouldn't keep you from sitting up. Why didn't you at least get a pillow for yourself?"

Because I didn't expect to crash to the floor like a felled tree. Was so busy watching each breath you took that...

No, that wasn't right. She'd been merely biding her time, letting him get some much-needed rest.

"I just closed my eyes for a second or two."

"Or more." He paused, still watching her face. "Do you want me to help you up?"

Her body tensed, her back already sending up a frantic mayday. "No." She even managed to smile, although she could only imagine what it looked like to him. She'd better come clean before he did something that made the situation worse. "My back is a little...sore. From lying in this position."

"I thought it was your foot?"

"I lied." The admission came with a real smile this time.

"Hannah, Hannah, what am I going to do with you?" The soft murmur trailed across her senses, making her back tighten further.

She pulled in a careful breath. "How about leaving me to die in peace?"

His face stilled. "Don't say that."

"Don't say...?" It hit her. Mrs. Brookstone's turn for the worse. How hard he'd worked to keep that from happening to any of his patients. "Sorry."

"It's okay." He stood up and carefully lifted the chair behind her out of the way. Then the two on either side of it.

"What are you doing?"

"I'm going to help you sit up."

"I don't think that's a good idea."

When he knelt on the floor behind her and put his hands on the muscles on her right side, a quick flicker of fear went through her. But he didn't try to jerk her upright. Instead his fingers played over the different areas of her back before muttering something under his breath. Then he said, "I can't feel anything through your shirt. I need bare skin."

Her heart went into overdrive, threatening to hammer its way out of her chest. "Wh-what?"

"Sorry. I meant your muscles." He paused. "Where does it hurt?"

"Below my right shoulderblade."

His fingers shifted, testing. "Can you roll onto your stomach?"

"I don't know." She tried, inching to the right, his palms taking some of the work off her back muscles. Then she was there, legs stretched straight behind her, feet bare, all the while a group of muscles sizzled with fire. Even drawing too deep a breath caused it to tighten further. A tiny whimper made its way out before she could stop it.

His fingers began exploring her back again until he reached the ball of agony around which her world currently swirled.

"Oh, God, don't. Please." She was horrified at the hoarse plea in her voice.

He swore softly.

"Stay here. I'm going to get a muscle relaxant and a heating pad. I'll be right back."

As he walked away, Hannah heard him talking softly to someone, giving them his cell number and asking whoever it was to call him if there was an emergency. The hospital? His answering service?

She hadn't wanted to interfere with his work. She'd just wanted to leave some food for him and be on her way.

He could have just left her, like she'd suggested...

But he wasn't that kind of man.

She heard him come back. "I don't want you to take the pill lying down like that, so we'll see if we can loosen you up a little first."

Despite the pain, she giggled. It sounded more like he was trying to get her drunk than help her get back on her feet.

"You find this funny?"

"No. It's just… Never mind."

A second later he draped something across the sore part of her back and the sound of a switch clicking hit her ears. Soft vibrations made their way through her back, not hard enough to hurt but enough that she knew it was there.

"It'll warm up in a minute or two."

"I'm sorry. I don't normally have back spasms." The last time had been after her biopsy, when lying in one position for a prolonged period of time had left her muscles stiff and sore. She'd moved too quickly and driven home in quiet agony, too embarrassed to tell anyone at the hospital what was going on. It had taken two days for the pain to ease—she hadn't even been able to lift her arm to brush her hair. And it had been in the same muscle group as now.

What if she were laid up for two days again? No. If she could just get up, she'd be fine.

Greg's voice came back to her. "It's okay. Just rest a few more minutes."

Unable to do anything else, she watched as he cleaned up the remainder of their shared meal, tossing containers into one of the trash cans and drawing the plastic bag up tight.

Sure enough, the vibrating pad began to warm, the heat working its way into the affected muscle. It didn't completely relax but the pain wasn't quite as severe as it had been moments earlier. Maybe she could… Shifting a bit, she gasped as the muscle contracted again.

"Lie still. You're not going anywhere for a couple of hours."

A couple of hours? A second ago he'd said to rest for a few minutes.

"Why don't you go to the hospital and then head home? I'll be fine in a little while. Promise."

"Not going to happen, Hannah. The hospital can do without me for one night. I've already told them to call me if there's an emergency."

Guilt rolled through her. He never skipped his rounds that she knew of. Always did them every night. Even weekends.

And here he was, stuck at the office, babysitting the person who'd told him to get some rest. Having to take care of her. Again. Just like during her treatments.

The thought brought tears to her eyes. She never wanted to go back to those days of fear and pain and that dark hole that had threatened to close over the top of her.

Stop it. You're not sick. It's just a muscle cramp.

The pain would soon be gone then she'd be strong and healthy once again. Free to live every day to the fullest. She visualized those words, made them her reality. Added an image of herself with a rounded tummy and pink, glowing cheeks. She was happy. Content.

Pregnant.

She blinked, remembering the procedure she'd undergone just that morning. She also realized her back was feeling better, at least while she was lying still. If she could just stay where she was a few minutes longer…

A half hour later, she found herself again nodding off, the pain finally sliding away. The vibrations stopped and she was aware of the heating pad being lifted off and gentle hands again moving over her back, this time right where it had hurt. She pulled in a deep breath and felt nothing but that contentment she'd reached for a few minutes earlier. "It's gone." She whispered the words, afraid the pain would find her again if she spoke any louder.

"I'm sorry. Do you want me to put it back?"

"Put it...?" She realized he was talking about the heating pad. "No, I meant my back feels better. Can you help me sit up?"

"Yes, but we're going to roll you onto your back first so you won't have to twist at an awkward angle. I don't want to give that muscle any reason to flare up again." He placed his hands on her right shoulder and hip. "Ready?"

His fingers were almost as warm as the heating pad and a tiny shudder went through her. "I'm ready."

"On three." He counted slowly and when he reached three, before she could even brace her hands on the floor and help, he'd gently rolled her over.

Moving a tiny bit, she tested her muscles. Nothing felt out of place or sore.

His brown eyes slid over her face. "Everything okay?"

"I think so."

"Let's just wait a minute or two." He nodded toward the reception desk. "I have some carisoprodol, just in case."

She shifted again, a little more this time, to see if anything acted up. Still nothing. "I think the worst is over. And I'd rather not drive with that kind of medication in my system."

"I'll take you home."

"Muscle relaxants knock me for a loop, and I'm never myself the next day." She didn't want to tell him that her year of treatment had conditioned her throat to constrict at the sight of anything that resembled a capsule. "I have to work tomorrow, remember?"

"Stay home."

She lifted her hand, feeling at a distinct disadvantage

lying flat on her back. "Help me up, and then we'll talk about it."

Greg stood and then curled his hand around hers. She sensed a slight hesitation on his part before his grip tightened and his arm bent at the elbow as he applied steady pressure. Their connected palms were doing crazy things to her stomach so, in an effort to hurry the process up, she braced her feet and launched herself into a vertical position.

Her momentum carried her straight into his chest where she landed with a thump.

Ack!

Greg wrapped an arm around her waist, holding her against his solid body as she tried to catch her breath.

At least her stupid move hadn't sent her back into another spasm.

Something she couldn't say about her heart, which was pumping at an alarming rate. A hundred and twenty beats per minute at least...and rising by the second.

She tried to act nonchalant, as if falling against her employer was something she did on a regular basis. And it was no big deal. She'd hugged him before after all. "Sorry. I guess I shouldn't have gotten up so fast."

"I'll say." The murmured words ruffled her hair and sent her heart on another race for the finish line. "How's your back?"

She wiggled the upper part of her body back and forth to feel it out, then realized she'd just done a quick shimmy against his thorax.

Her nipples contracted in reaction, and she blurted out the first thing she could think of: "Can't feel a thing."

The hand at her back tightened. "Can't you?"

Um, yeah. And it wasn't good. Because she was suddenly aware of every inch of male flesh pressed against her. Muscular chest, firm abs, taut thighs, and…

No, it couldn't be. She licked her lips, telling herself to pull back now before he realized that *she* realized that he was…

He was…

Yes. He *was*.

And if she shifted one millimeter, she'd be rubbing right against his *was*. Lord, did she want to press just a little bit.

And like that horrible thing that often happened when you told yourself not to do something—like not to eat that whole pint of ice cream in one sitting—your body did the exact opposite.

She pressed.

And the sound of his breath hissing in through his teeth met her ears.

Okay. Now he knew that she knew.

She slowly lifted her head and met eyes that were sizzling with something she hadn't seen in a very long time in a man. Especially not directed at her.

Desire.

Steaming. Naked. Toe-curling need.

"Greg?" She had no idea why she said his name, but his gaze darkened further.

One hand came up and slid into her hair, his thumb resting along her jaw. "How's your back?"

"Better." The words came out in a whisper, because suddenly she knew why he was asking. She emphasized her point. "*Much* better."

"Hannah." His thumb applied gentle pressure to tilt her head up, even as he angled his own down until only a breath of space remained between them. "You know this is a very bad idea."

"Worse than playing with matches?"

"Much worse."

It was. But the fascination of running that match across a strike plate and watching it flare to life proved too much to resist. Besides, she wasn't sure she even had what it took to light that particular fire. Closing her eyes, she bridged the gap between them, deciding to prove him right…and herself wrong.

He didn't want her. Couldn't.

The second her lips met his, though, and the hand at her nape hauled her even closer, she knew.

He could.

And he did.

CHAPTER FOUR

GREG wasn't sure who kissed whom first, but he knew with certainty there was nowhere he'd rather be right now. First she'd coaxed him to eat. Then to sleep. When he'd awoken, he'd found her right there beside him—even if she had been folded into something reminiscent of a cube. Her mouth had been slightly open, one hand curled softly against her chest. Her breasts had slowly risen and fallen as she'd breathed. The sight had sent his endocrine system on a rampage, pumping chemicals through his body. Then she'd looked up with those big green eyes, and he'd been lost. He'd stayed where he was, when he should have run.

No, that wasn't completely true. He'd been pretty sure he could walk away without a problem, until that singular moment when her hips had seemed to zero in on a certain part of his anatomy. The part that was now issuing all sorts of commands he wasn't sure he could resist.

He tilted his head, deepening the kiss, ready to pull back at the first sign of hesitation on her part.

Damn it, what was he thinking? Her back had just gone through hell and back, and here he was, mauling her to within an inch of her life.

But wasn't she mauling him right back, her fists buried in his starched shirt and hanging on for dear life?

Still, he had to be sure.

"Your back," he whispered against her lips.

"Forgotten."

"But—"

She pulled him close and cut off his words with another lingering kiss.

Okay, if that's the way she wanted to play this, who was he to complain? Besides, he was tired of warring against his emotions, trying to keep them in check so as not to alarm his patients, or hand out undue hope, if things took a turn for the worse.

Like with Martha Brookstone?

No, don't think of that right now.

He was with someone who'd fought the disease. Who'd won. He gloried in that. Celebrated Hannah's life. Her health. It was why he'd surrounded himself with people just like her, to remind himself that cancer could be beaten. Not all of the time. His own sister had...

His fingers tightened in Hannah's hair, desperate to feel the life force coursing through her body, her heart pumping strongly against his own.

Life! This was what it was about. The need for closeness, to reaffirm your own existence.

Surely just this once he could block out the real world. The blinds were closed. Door locked. Alarm set.

And, most of all, there was a beautiful, willing woman in his arms.

Her low sigh melted his resistance even further, and Greg gentled his kiss, taking the time to taste her, to measure the softness of her lips against his. His tongue slid in a slow arc across the surface of her teeth, then back again, his senses roaring to life when she opened her mouth in invitation. Stunned by the force of his reaction, he hung around outside for a second or two, until her tongue touched the underside of his, leading him inside.

Coaxing him, just like she'd done with his meal. Before he knew it, he was right there, the interplay of textures and heat making it impossible for him to retreat again.

His hand left her hair, sliding down her back until it lay just above the curve of her buttocks. A very dangerous place to be. Once he took that leap there'd be no going back.

On that note, he lingered in her mouth, needing to show her exactly what she was doing to him, and that if she intended to call a halt to things, it needed to be soon.

She didn't. She met each stroke by moving closer, protested each withdrawal with a soft bite to his lower lip. His hands slid down and over in unison, his fingers curving on the rounded flesh he found there. It filled his palms, set his whole body on fire.

He pulled her up and against him, hoping to relieve a little of the ache that was growing steadily worse. And hoping the shock would knock them both back into the realm of reality. Except Greg didn't want reality. He wanted the fantasy…to keep her here. With him. Wanted to wish their clothing gone and to drive every last inch of himself into her—to fill her to capacity and beyond.

Hannah released her hold on his shirt, and at first he thought she meant to pull away. Instead, the top button of his shirt popped free, as if…

His lips left hers in question, and he caught her smile. Then another button was plucked loose.

She was undoing his shirt. There went the third button. It was either allow her to keep going or let go of her and stop her.

Her hands settled on his bare chest, upping the ante. Especially when they wandered down, purposely sliding over his nipples in the process. His eyes squeezed shut as he tried to hold on to some small portion of his sanity.

When her fingers seemed to want to stay and visit for a while, teasing and testing, he had no choice. He let go of her, reaching up to capture her wrists and carry them behind her back.

"You're treading on dangerous ground."

Her brows went up. "I hadn't even gotten to the dangerous part yet."

Greg couldn't stop a quick laugh of surprise. This was a side of Hannah he hadn't known existed. But he liked it.

He took her mouth again. Harder this time. His free hand slid beneath her blouse and claimed the very thing he'd just denied her, the lacy bra providing almost no barrier. And he reveled in it—in the tightly drawn nipple that pressed against the fabric and scraped lusciously against his palm. When he rolled the bud between his thumb and forefinger, she moaned into his mouth.

Yes.

God, he wanted her. Now.

He let go of her and grasped the bottom of her blouse, holding her gaze as she slowly raised her arms above her head so he could take it off. Her shirt was as far as he got, though, because she reached back and unhooked the black bra herself, letting it fall from her body. Still no sign that her back was bothering her. But, hell, if the sight of her naked breasts didn't hurt him in a very different kind of way.

When he started to move forward again, she backed up a step and reached for the button of her slacks. "Here's where it starts getting dangerous."

Holy hell. Surely she didn't mean to...

In an instant she'd unzipped them and pushed them down her hips, kicking them away from her. Her black panties were barely there, just a scrap of lace with a crisscrossing of strings on the sides. He had no idea where they led or what the back looked like, and he wasn't sure he wanted to know.

"Hannah," he warned, when her fingertips slipped beneath the ties.

She gave a soft laugh. "Your turn, then."

His turn to what? Take off his clothes? Remove her last article of clothing himself?

He assumed she meant for him to start shucking his own clothes, so he finished unbuttoning his shirt and slung the garment to the side. His fingers weren't quite as steady as hers, but it had been a long time since he'd been with anyone. A very long time. His hours were too crazy, and he was too exhausted by the time he got home.

And yet right now he seemed to have the energy of an eighteen-year-old boy.

Hannah moved back in before he could go any further and slid her palms up his chest, and rested them on his shoulders, leaning in to kiss the base of his throat.

That wasn't where he wanted her. "Hey."

When she looked up, he took her mouth, wrapping his arms around the bare skin of her back, trying to absorb everything at once. The heat of her skin against his, the softness of her breasts.

Breasts he wanted to devour.

He gripped her hips, intending to ease her back so he could cup them, but the strings on her panties sidetracked him. He followed them around. The back had a satiny feel as opposed to the lace in front. Part of him was relieved, part of him disappointed. He'd half hoped to find nothing there.

But it didn't matter, because he could just do this…

He slid his fingers between the elastic band and her skin and repeated on her bare bottom what he'd done earlier when she'd still been wearing pants. He squeezed, trying to get his fill, then pulled back enough to push her underwear halfway down her legs, his mouth having to leave hers to do so. This time when his hands returned to their perch, he pulled her tight against him, her bare flesh pressing directly on the hard bulge at the front of his slacks. He ground against her, once…twice, swallowing hard when she gave a tiny whimper, her fingers digging into his shoulders.

Enough!

He scooped her up in his arms in a quick movement and carried her past the still-propped-open doorway in back. His office had a couch.

And a desk.

Yes.

That's where he wanted her. On his desk, legs splayed open, with him between them. His flesh tightened beyond belief.

That decadent image would carry him through many a lonely night.

And there'd be no danger of hurting her back.

He gave a rough laugh.

Sure. That was the reason.

He pushed on the handle, but it didn't budge. Damn. Locked.

"Where's the key?" she whispered.

"Left front pocket." Thank heavens he'd kept his trousers on.

"I think I can get it." Hannah scooched her arm between their bodies, her breasts jiggling in a way that made his mouth water. She found his pocket, dipped in and instead of finding his keys and retreating, her hand drifted to the right and curved over the tight ridge of flesh. The fingers massaged and squeezed and drove the breath from his lungs.

"Those aren't my keys, woman."

She gave a soft laugh. "I know." Her nails scraped down his length, the fabric keeping it from hurting while also making it the most erotic sensation he'd ever felt. He almost did the unthinkable standing right there in front of his door.

"Hannah...please."

She kissed the side of his neck and retrieved his keys. "I like it when you say please."

That "please" now encompassed asking God to help him make it inside his office.

"Unlock the door."

He turned his body sideways to allow her to reach the lock, which she undid in record time. Pushing his way past the door, he carried her over to his desk. He surveyed it, trying to figure out where to put her. "Push the pencil cup onto the floor."

Her brows went up, but she did as he asked, the offending object flying off the side of the desk, shedding pens and pencils as it went. He then set her on the edge and stepped back to watch her as he undid his own pants.

He was afraid she'd get up, but she didn't. She sat there, panties still halfway down her legs, her arms going back to prop herself on the wide wooden surface. The act pushed her breasts up and out, while pushing his self-control to the breaking point.

Making short work of the rest of his clothes, he moved over to her and rested his arms on either side of her hips. He gave her a long, slow smile. "My turn to get a little dangerous."

"Believe me, you already are."

Her tongue came out to moisten her lips. He leaned in and did the same, drawing his tongue slowly across her already wet mouth. He then kissed her chin, before nudging her head back so he had access to the underside of her throat. Working his way down to her shoulder, he dipped further until he reached her right breast.

The second his lips closed over her nipple, he knew it had been worth the wait. Her reaction was immediate. She arched toward him with a moan. But when she went to lift her arms, he put his hands over hers, trapping them on the desk.

She thought she could drive him crazy with no recourse? Well, he was about to get a little of his own back. He suckled and nibbled, holding her in place with his teeth while his tongue lapped over her. When he finally released her, the nipple was slick and tight.

Just like she would be when he finally entered her. And it had to be soon.

He finally stood upright. Hannah's teeth were digging into her lower lip, eyes sealed shut. Her hips made tiny movements on the surface of his desk.

He wanted to be right in the middle of that.

He slid her panties the rest of the way down her legs, and as soon as they were gone, her thighs spread apart. He swallowed as he moved between them, trying to think about anything other than what was about to happen, and failing miserably. Instead, he gave her a deep openmouthed kiss, settling against her and finding her just as slick and ready as he'd hoped.

To be sure, he slid his hand between them, thumb seeking the right spot and then stroking gently. She pressed closer, moaning against his mouth. Her flesh enveloped his tip, the heat and tightness driving him to the very edge of insanity. It was all he could do not to thrust into her and lose himself in a fiery rush. As if reading his thoughts, she reached around to grab his butt, pulling him even deeper.

She was so wet, so hot. Her hips were still making those

tiny thrusting motions against his arousal…against his thumb. Growing stronger. Quicker.

He sped up the motion of his thumb, knowing that the second she went over the edge, he was going with her. And he'd be able to push deeper. Harder.

No! Wait. Condom!

He started to withdraw, only to have her hands pull at him desperately, her calves wrapping around him, hips sliding forward until she had him fully within her. She lay back on the desk, her eyes pleading with him.

"Greg, now. Please."

The sight of her lying naked on top of his desk drove every rational thought he'd had a few seconds ago from his mind. Grasping her hips, he pushed into her, reveling in the tight heat that gripped him to perfection. She put her heels on the edge of the desk and rose to meet him stroke for stroke, beads of sweat breaking out on his forehead as he fought for control.

Control he couldn't seem to find.

No need because Hannah was at the end of hers as well, pushing herself onto him, her hips now leaving the desk every time he drove into her. Within a few seconds she arched up and gasped, her body tightening around him in a series of explosive waves. He gave up and held on for dear life, hands braced on the desk as he thrust into her again and again, her name falling from his lips as he found his own release deep inside her.

He went down onto his elbows as the world slowed, as time began to trickle back to normal. Hannah's breath floated past his cheek, her sweet, womanly scent washing over him as he struggled to piece together what had just happened.

No need to ask. He already knew.

Hannah had happened. And he realized he'd been trying to avoid this moment for months. Definitely since that fateful hug. Maybe even the entire time he'd known her.

And as reality crystallized, hardening into a rock that blocked his throat—filled his chest—another realization swept over him. This one much more deadly.

His wallet contained an object around which his thoughts and regrets now circled like vultures.

A single, unopened condom.

CHAPTER FIVE

HORRIFIED.

The word she'd been searching for all morning finally came to mind. The one adjective that described Greg's face when he'd caught his breath enough to stand upright and look down at her. Not regret. Not joy. Not satisfied exhaustion.

Horror.

It was an expression she'd never forget.

Her cheeks burned as she balled up the used exam-table paper and tossed it in the waste receptacle to prepare the room for the next patient. How was she going to get up the nerve to walk into his office and look at that desk? The second she did, would her mind picture him going down on his elbows in those final few seconds, would she remember her own soft cries of pleasure filling the room?

Oh, God.

The man had helped her up afterward, and they'd dressed without a word. Had collected their things, walked through the office and out the front door in silence. Until she'd inserted the key into her car door, only to have a hand cover hers, stopping her from fleeing into the night.

"Hannah, I'm sorry. We'll talk…later."

Sorry. The very word she'd dreaded hearing. It ranked right up there with *horrified* and *talk.*

She didn't want to talk. Or even face him.

He was in surgery this morning, leaving Hannah with a full slate of patients who needed her to be on her game. And no time to plan what she'd say when she eventually saw him again.

And she would.

Unless she quit. The idea had come to her the night before, tickling her with temptation before she dismissed it as ridiculous. She needed this job, especially now. What had happened last night was a fluke. Greg had been hurting, and she'd botched her attempt to comfort him by sending out the wrong signals.

No. That was a lie. They had been the right signals, and he'd picked up on them as easily as the PET scan had homed in on the cancer in her lymph nodes.

Stella poked her head into the room. "Are you ready for the next patient?"

"Yep." She forced a smile, knowing it probably looked as strained as she felt.

"You okay?" The receptionist's concern only made her feel worse, because she was far from all right.

Why couldn't her little encounter with Greg have happened two weeks from now? A month? Anything outside the five-day lifespan of sperm? And with the washed sperm used during inseminations, that window was even narrower.

If she got pregnant now, nothing other than a D.N.A. test could prove whether the baby was the donor's or Greg's.

"Hannah?" Stella's voice broke through her thoughts.

"Sorry. I'm fine. Just daydreaming."

Or nightmaring, whichever you chose to call it.

The receptionist stepped inside the room and closed the door. "About anyone I know?"

"No." The word came out on a strange wobbly note, and

she decided some kind of explanation was due. "I had an I.U.I. procedure yesterday, and I was thinking about the possibilities."

And that was the absolute truth.

"Oh, honey, congratulations!" Stella enveloped her in a bear hug, and if the fifty-year-old's ebullience was in direct proportion to the tightness of the squeeze, it was off the charts, since she'd just wrung the last molecule of air from Hannah's lungs.

Her brain a bit woozy from the lack of oxygen, she hurried to add, "I don't even know if it took yet or not, so please don't tell anyone."

Especially not their boss.

All she needed was for Greg to hear she was pregnant the second he walked into the office.

He'd immediately wonder if she was angling for something, since there's no way she could know twelve hours out whether or not he'd knocked her up.

Right.

Horrified would be the least of her worries, if that happened. And *looking for a new job* would be the order of the day.

"Don't worry. My lips are sealed."

Since those lips tended to flap around like pancakes tossed from a cast-iron skillet, this could mean trouble. Which meant she'd have to talk to Greg, like it or not.

Too bad she couldn't rewind to yesterday and go back to calling him Dr. Mason. Only if she did that now, he'd assume she was doing it because of their little interlude, and he'd be right. No, the less emphasis she placed on what had happened, the less likely it was to change their working relationship.

"Okay, Stella, where's our next patient?"

* * *

The next two hours passed in a frenzy of work and worry. She forced the latter to remain in the background, only letting it surface when she had five minutes to spare, which was thankfully not often.

Her last patient of the day sat on the exam table, a jewel-toned silk scarf artfully draped around her head. The woman's blue eyes sparkled with life. Claire Taylor had already defied the odds once and was well on her way to doing it a second time. The lumpectomy she'd had three years ago was now a mastectomy scar, but she was cheerful and positive. Since her first diagnosis, the twenty-six-year-old had gotten married and was already looking ahead to a bright future.

"I talked to a plastic surgeon last week about reconstruction."

Hannah glanced up from her examination. "I didn't realize you were even thinking about it." Claire had opted not to have the reconstruction right after the surgery. She'd been through a chemo regimen once before and didn't want to have to worry about anything but getting through that ordeal. She was halfway through her eight-treatment cycle—heading down the home stretch.

"I wasn't. But I haven't been as sick this time as I was the last time. Or maybe I just remember it being worse because I didn't know what to expect."

Hannah could relate to that. She'd saved her scarves—all fifty of them—as a reminder that she was a survivor, and that she intended to keep on living. Every once in a while she wore one around her neck and talked about it with her patients. As one survivor to another.

Maybe Claire was at that point as well—gearing up to tell the world she was ready to enjoy the rest of her life. "What did the surgeon say?"

"That he could take some skin from my stomach to

construct the breast. So I'd get a tummy tuck and a perky new boob at the same time."

"Wow, a twofer—you lucky girl."

Right as she said it, she winced, realizing she'd also gotten one of those: two batches of sperm for the price of one. But in this case she could have done without the figurative tummy tuck and been perfectly happy sticking to the lab-generated portion.

Claire laughed. "I know, right?"

"What does your husband think of all this?"

"Oh, you know how they are. He claims to love me just as I am, says I don't need it." The woman's lips twisted. "So who said I was doing it for him, anyway?"

It was Hannah's turn to laugh. "Did you tell him that?"

"No way. Let him think it. It'll add some spice to our love life."

Hannah could feel the heat crawling up her stomach on its way to her face. The sound of a knock and then the door opening didn't help, especially when Greg strolled in, his face a study in exhaustion. But when he saw Claire, his eyes softened, the edges of his mouth turning up in a smile. "I couldn't let one of my favorite patients get away without a single hello."

Claire laughed. "Okay, then. Hello."

Had he really come back to the office to say hi his patients? Or was he here to have the Dreaded Talk?

Why hadn't he just gone home? This could wait. She was tired too, and she wasn't up to a conversation about regrets.

He continued talking to his patient, not giving Hannah a second glance as he listened intently to Claire's plans for surgery. He held out a hand for the chart, which Hannah gave him. A moment passed as he perused the contents, flipping pages. "I'd like it if you waited until after you complete the regimen, just to be sure. You'll be stronger and there'll be less worry about infection."

"That's what the surgeon said, as well." Her hand crept up to the robe, and the hollow left by the mastectomy. "It's healing well, and he says I'm a good candidate."

"I agree. There's no reason to think you wouldn't be. Let's just get you through the next couple of months."

Maybe that's what she needed to focus on: getting through the next couple of months. Well…nine, in her case.

Standing in the hallway with Greg while Claire got dressed, she cast about for something to say that would send him on his way. But he didn't seem in a hurry to leave, leaning against the wall, watching her.

Why was he doing that? Why hadn't he just gone straight to his office and let her finish up with the patient?

"How did surgery go?"

"Pretty well."

"This was the Hodgkin's patient, right?" She tried to get him to keep talking, in part to prevent the silence from growing more awkward but also because this was a diagnosis close to her heart.

At his nod, she pressed forward. "Did you have to perform a splenectomy?"

"She was in the early stages, so yes." He paused and glanced down the hallway toward his office. "I don't like doing them, but…"

"I know." Her fingers itched to go to his arm and reassure him, but she didn't dare. "I'm doing fine without mine, though."

"Sometimes it's the only way to know for sure how much lymph-node involvement there is."

Hodgkin's cells tended to collect in the spleen early in the disease. Hers had been removed for the same reason.

Before she could reply, Claire came through the door,

her huge handbag slung over her shoulder. "Thanks, guys. I appreciate it."

"I'll try to peek in on you at the hospital during your next treatment. When do you go in?"

Hannah's brows went up. Since when did he do that? He'd never come into the chemo room when she'd been having her infusions. And it wasn't like his time wasn't sucked in every direction under the sun already. They saw Claire off and then she turned to face him. "Are you doing that for all your patients now?"

"Doing what?"

"Checking in on them during chemo treatments."

He pulled his shoulder off the wall and stood straighter. "When I'm at the hospital, I try to."

A small ache went through her heart. "You're going to kill yourself, you know." She wasn't sure whether or not she should follow that thought, but the words just kind of came out. "I know what it's like to wonder if you have a tomorrow. It's made me grab at life and enjoy every second I have."

His eyes met hers, and his jaw tightened. "Some of us don't have that option."

"That's ridiculous. You have as much choice as the next person."

A hard laugh echoed through the hallway. "I see. And your way of enjoying life is to do whatever strikes your fancy at that particular moment—especially after business hours—no matter what the consequences?"

The inference was plain.

She glanced down the hall, hoping no one was within earshot. "Maybe that's what's needed sometimes. Less thinking, more doing." Hannah didn't believe that for a second, but she wasn't about to admit how much his attitude hurt. There was almost an accusatory slant to his tone that made her wonder if he really felt that way about her.

He stared at her for several seconds then sighed. "I think we need to have that talk before this goes any further."

Afraid he was going to suggest going to his office—the last place she wanted to be right now—she almost sagged in relief when he motioned toward the door of the exam room Claire had just vacated. Maybe he felt the same reluctance to share his office space with her. Fine, as far as she was concerned.

She swept through the doorway ahead of him, grabbing up a few items and starting to stow them away. The snick of the lock stopped her cold. Swinging around to face him, her eyes went to the door, which was indeed locked. What was that all about?

"I didn't think you wanted anyone to overhear this particular discussion."

He was right. Stella already knew too much, and she didn't know the half of it. "Thanks."

His chest rose as he took a deep breath. "About yesterday…"

"It's fine. Just call it a combination of exhaustion and sleep deprivation. We were both half-asleep at the time."

One corner of his mouth quirked up. "Are you sure about that?"

"About being exhausted?"

"No, about being half-asleep." The low rumble of his voice curled her toes. "Because I seem to remember you being very much awake."

The image of just how awake she'd been swept over her.

Her face heated, and her teeth clamped down on her lower lip. Maybe she should be a little more careful about choosing her words in the future. She drew a careful breath. "Well, regardless, it won't happen again."

He took a step closer. "Sometimes once is all it takes."

Her mouth opened, her brain working furiously to figure out what he was referring to, because it almost seemed like he was about to say he… "Once is all it takes to what?"

Only a foot separated them now and, try as she may, she couldn't stop the sudden pounding of her pulse in her temples as she waited for his answer.

He reached out and slid his fingers under her chin, searching her eyes. "We didn't use any protection."

Protection. Protection. *Protection*. She finally got what he was saying, and suddenly realized why he'd been so very upset after they'd finished. They'd had sex without using a condom. He, evidently, *had* realized the implications almost immediately.

"I'm sure it's fine." Uh-huh. That's what she'd been telling herself all day, right?

"If it ends up not being…fine, you'll let me know, won't you?"

A wash of tears appeared from nowhere, and she fought not to blink, hoping they'd drain right back down her tear ducts. She wanted this pregnancy so badly, and hearing Greg talk about it in those terms made her insides spasm. What was she supposed to do, turn her hopes into a plea for the insemination to fail…to lose this chance at being a mother?

No. She drew herself up straight. "Not necessary."

"Oh, but it is, Hannah." The words were soft, but a thread of steel ran through them. His brown eyes bored into hers. "If you end up pregnant, I want to know."

She tugged away from him, her arms going around her waist as if holding whatever was inside her in place. "The situation might be a little more complicated than you think."

CHAPTER SIX

Complicated?

How could the situation possibly be any more complicated than it already was? Greg had already resigned himself to doing the right thing if Hannah became pregnant. He'd do right by the child, be a part of its life where he could—but even the thought of that made his chest tighten. One careless slip-up and he found himself at the end of a dark tunnel with the distant roar of a freight train sounding at the other end.

Hell.

He was tired, hungry and the last thing he wanted to do right now was stand in an exam room and talk about responsibility. But having this conversation in his office was out of the question. He hadn't been in there since last night, and one glimpse of those pencils scattered over the floor would do him in. He'd eventually have to go in and pick them up, a task he wasn't sure he was up to, even if he was all alone in the clinic. Knowing Hannah was somewhere nearby would make it that much worse.

He could always ask her to transfer—find her a position at another oncologist's office. But that would be copping out. And he had never turned his back on his responsibilities. Besides, she was damned good at her job. He didn't want to lose her, if he didn't have to.

"Do you have any plans for this evening?" he asked, when she continued to stand there without explaining what she meant by her words.

"I'm sorry?" The hint of panic in her eyes made his gut churn. Surely she didn't think he was coming on to her. Again. This would be a good time to knock that notion right out of the ballpark and let it stay there. There would be no repeats. "I mean, it's almost seven, and I haven't eaten. I'm guessing you haven't either."

"No."

No, she hadn't eaten? Or, no, she didn't want to get anything with him?

"Are you up for grabbing a bite? We can talk on the way."

She hesitated before giving a simple nod.

Halfway to the Seafood Bistro, about five miles from his office, he still hadn't opened his mouth and tackled the subject at hand. And neither had she. Instead, she stared pensively out the window, her right elbow propped on the window ledge of the vehicle, chin cupped in her palm. She'd avoided looking at him since he'd cornered her at the clinic, except when he'd taken hold of her and forced her eyes to his in the hallway. Was it better to talk now, or after his dinner had time to sink to the bottom of his stomach like a rock?

Tightening his fingers around the wheel, he glanced over at her. "Okay, we both agree this situation is compli-cated. So what are we going to do about it?"

She shrugged, still not looking his way. "I suggest we adopt a watch-and-wait attitude."

Watch and wait? He was an oncologist so, yes, there were times when it was wise to sit back and see what hap-pened. But other times you had to plan ahead, take aggres-sive measures before things got out of hand.

Like what? Exactly what kind of measures could he take, besides setting up some kind of trust fund? And there was no way he'd ask her to get an abortion. His chest tightened even as the thought went through his mind.

Would she, if the opportunity presented itself?

Complicated was right.

So, maybe he could start with a trust fund, although he chafed at the idea of something so impersonal. Sticking a sizeable sum in an account once a month seemed cold and distant, hardly the kind of "taking responsibility" he'd talked about earlier.

His sister would have frowned at him for even considering it, would have said he was taking the easy way out. Just like when his father had wanted him to skip college in order to take over the family business. Greg had been on the verge of giving up his dreams, until Bethany had dropped the application for medical school on his bed and told him to do what was right, not what was easy.

Time to do the right thing.

"How long do you intend to wait before verifying things?"

She finally turned and looked at him. "You didn't get me pregnant, Greg, I'm almost sure of it, okay?"

"Almost sure doesn't cut it, in this situation."

"It's possible my body is still so messed up from the chemo that I won't be able to conceive. Ever. So I hardly think one quickie is going to do the trick."

Quickie. Okay, that stung. Even if she'd been as quick as he had.

And, damn it, he'd tried to do the right thing then, too, had tried to stop and get a condom. He hadn't just thrown caution to the wind. Was she really so sure that she couldn't get pregnant?

"Have you talked to a doctor about your fertility?"

Her elbow came off the window, her hands clasping together in her lap. "Yes."

"And what did he say?"

There was a long pause before she answered. "*She* said there are no guarantees."

The soft wistfulness in her voice made him sad, even while he physically relaxed into his seat. Maybe the situation wasn't the tragedy he was making it out to be. Although something inside him mourned for Hannah. They'd both known at the beginning of her treatment that the drugs could render her infertile. But when your life is at stake, you do what you have to do to give yourself the best possible outcome.

He took the turn-off to the restaurant and tried to think. They could always watch and wait, like Hannah suggested. But he really needed her to know he was there for her if she needed him. Just like his sister had been there for him.

The parking lot was just starting to fill up. Greg found an empty spot and switched off the engine, trying to decide what to do. Just then a rumble came from Hannah's seat. He blinked. "Was that your stomach?"

She gave a quick laugh. "Sorry. I think it knows we're here."

With that, the decision was made. Any further conversation could wait until she'd at least gotten something into her system. "I keep telling you, you don't have to work the same hours I do."

She stepped out of the car and waited for him to join her. "You were in surgery, and we had patients scheduled."

And Greg was normally responsible for scheduling them, which made him feel like a first-class heel. He knew he'd have to spend the day in surgery from time to time, and yet he still scheduled himself till he was up to his eyeballs in patients. In the past, he hadn't had a PA and could do his own thing—they'd simply juggled patients on days he had an emergency come up. But as his practice grew, he found himself pulled in too many directions. Hannah being available had been a godsend. One he'd taken advantage of. Maybe too much.

"Sorry, I should have kept track better. I'll try to cut back on the workload."

She touched his arm. "I like working. I want to keep doing it right up until I…" Her voice trailed away, eyes widening.

Was she planning on quitting? "Until you what?"

She hesitated. "I have something to tell you, but it can wait until after we eat."

And let him worry about it the entire meal? No. Not happening.

"Are you leaving the practice?" If she was, he wanted to know it now. Up front. Except even the thought made something in his chest dive toward his gut. Dammit. It would be easier for everyone if she did leave.

"No, not unless you want me to, or…" She blinked a couple of times. "Please, let's talk about this once we've both had something to eat. Maybe I can figure out how to say it by then."

Great. Now he was imagining all kinds of scenarios. Was she involved with someone?

Hell, he hadn't even thought about that. It would make what he'd done ten times worse. Was that the complication she'd been talking about? Had he just ruined something between her and a significant other?

Her quick glance toward the restaurant said she was serious about eating first and talking later. He remembered her stomach growling and cursed himself again. He was handling this whole situation like an idiot. No wonder he steered clear of relationships. Not only did he not have the time but he was doing a terrible job of moving this conversation in the right direction. "Okay, after we eat. But we are going to talk."

Once they were seated at the table, the server took their order and brought a cutting board loaded with a fresh loaf of pumpernickel bread. Greg nodded toward it. "Help yourself."

Hannah sliced a generous hunk and slathered it with butter. She bit into the bread with a groan, a tiny crumb landing on the outside corner of her lip. A quick flick of her tongue swept it away again.

He swallowed hard, even though his mouth was currently empty, because all he could think about was the hot kissing they'd done in the reception area of the clinic, the way she'd coaxed him into her mouth, had kept him there with the same kind of noises she was currently making. And how all he wanted to do was drag her off to some dark corner and do it all over again. This time going a hell of a lot slower.

A perfect way to repeat the same mistakes.

"Try some," she said, holding out the knife. "It's soft and very delicious."

Just like Hannah was.

He took the knife and was somehow able to hack off a chunk of bread. Shoving it into his mouth before anything he said tipped her off as to his thoughts, he chewed then swallowed.

He could have been eating shoe leather for all he knew—he couldn't taste a thing.

"Don't you like butter?"

Okay, so maybe that was why he'd had to choke it down.

She cut another piece and buttered it, then handed it to him. "It's honey butter. Try it."

Greg already knew what it tasted like, he'd been to this

particular restaurant many times before, but he couldn't resist taking it from her and biting into it as she watched him. This time, he forced himself to taste the food, to let the flavors swirl on his tongue.

"Isn't it wonderful?"

His eyes held hers. "Yes. Very."

Neither of them moved or talked for the next few seconds as they stared at each other. Then the waiter came over, and the soft clinking of a plate being set down in front of him dragged his attention away from her.

Except he didn't want this food. He wanted her to keep buttering his bread and watching him as he ate it. Wanted her to keep watching as he leaned across the table and put his lips to hers.

Greg closed his eyes and tried to force the image away. They had a serious situation on their hands. Kissing was the last thing they needed to do. So they'd eat. Have their little conversation, then he would drop her off and drive away. Intact. With a contingency plan in place in case the unthinkable actually happened.

The only thing was, he hadn't the foggiest idea what that plan was. Maybe it would come to him as he ate.

He'd ordered the fresh grilled salmon, while Hannah had claimed she was throwing caution to the wind and having the seafood Alfredo. Despite the weight she'd put on since her chemo, she was still more slender than she'd been a year ago—her hip bones had pressed into his abdomen as they'd ground together...

And that—he rotated his neck to relieve the growing tightness in his spine—was not something he should be remembering. Not now. Not tomorrow. Not ever.

"Are you involved with someone?"

He wasn't quite sure where the words had come from, but the effect was immediate. She froze, her fork and its burden of creamy noodles stopping halfway to her mouth. "I'm sorry?"

"If I've made things awkward between you and a boyfriend, I want to apologize."

"A boyfriend?" She set her fork down and leaned forward, eyes flashing. "You think I would have…done what we did if I'd been seeing someone?"

The words, although soft, rang between them like a gong, and he immediately wished he could take back his question.

"I didn't think you were, but what happened wasn't planned. It was so sudden… I just wanted to make sure that's not what you meant by complicated."

She nodded, her lips still tight. "It's not. And since you seem so determined to do this now, I'll just come right out with it." Her fingers curled around the edge of the table. "I had an I.U.I. done yesterday morning."

"An…" His brain scrambled to find the words that went with the acronym. Found it. "Intrauterine insemination?"

"Shh." She glanced around. "Yes."

She was *trying* to get pregnant? "Are you taking fertility drugs?"

She nodded again, her fingers now toying with the tablecloth.

Which could explain why she'd seemed so eager for him last night. The hormones tended to up the libido. That might be the reason for *her* reaction, but what about his? He seemed to be a walking commercial for Viagra whenever she was around.

Something else occurred to him. She'd said her system could be so messed up that she might not be able to conceive. If she'd had an I.U.I. that morning, surely she hadn't been trying to up her odds of getting pregnant by sleeping with him.

Hannah wouldn't do that. Would she?

"How badly do you want a pregnancy?"

"What do you mean?"

"That wasn't what last night was about, was it?"

If he'd thought his question about a significant other had raised her hackles, this one had done that times ten, if the angry color marching along her cheekbones was anything to go by. "I think I'd like to leave now."

When she reached for her purse, he put his hand over hers. "Don't. I don't know why I asked that. I just had no idea you wanted to... The timing seems so..."

"Convenient?"

"Yes." A sense of shame washed over him the second he admitted it. "But I should have known better."

"I can see how it might look but, I promise you, I didn't want what happened any more than you did."

Complicated. She'd hit that word on the head.

He nodded toward her food. "Go ahead and eat, Hannah, before it gets cold."

"I'd rather just get this over with, okay? I didn't use you to boost my chances. But even if I am pregnant, there's no way to know if it's yours or the donor's. Let's just leave it alone."

He took his hand off hers. "There's always D.N.A. testing."

"I won't go that route. Not before the baby—if there even is a baby—is born. I won't take that risk, especially since the fertility specialist couldn't promise the I.U.I. would even work. If it does, I don't want to lose it. I might never get another opportunity to have a baby. Let's just assume that the donor's...er contribution is the only player in the game. It had at least a twelve-hour head start."

She was handing him an easy way out, one he should grab with both hands. But his sister's face appeared before him, that little furrow cutting between her brows. This time he didn't need the warning, however. Something in him wanted to know if the child was his. He wouldn't be able to look at Hannah's growing body without wondering. And he'd have a hard time looking at himself in the mirror if he closed his eyes and pretended none of this had ever happened.

"What about after it's born? You can have the testing done then. It's as easy as swabbing the inside of the child's cheek."

"Why bother, Greg? No matter whose D.N.A. the baby carries, I'll be the one raising it, nurturing it. That's what I wanted when I started down this road. It's still what I want. This was my decision. Not yours."

A flush of anger crept through him, growing stronger as he realized what she was saying. So much for taking responsibility for his actions. Hannah was going to try to shut him out completely.

"That's where you're wrong," he said, fixing his attention on those gorgeous green eyes of hers. "It may have started out as your decision, but that changed the moment we had unprotected sex." She flinched at those words, but he kept going. "I was as much a part of that particular decision as you were. If this child is the result of our coming together—no matter the hows or whys—then it won't be just *your* baby. It'll be mine, as well."

CHAPTER SEVEN

SNOW.

Hannah scrunched her nose when she pulled aside the drapes. It was just a light dusting of the stuff, and she'd seen worse in October. Much worse. But dark skies promised more of the same. She'd hoped winter might hold off a little longer.

She glanced over at the rustic wooden settle she'd made a couple of years ago, just before her illness. Hopefully her red ice grippers were still inside the storage area beneath it and would hold up for one more winter. She'd have to dig them out and make sure. Although how much hiking she'd get in this year was yet to be seen. But if she wound up pregnant, they could come in handy as she grew larger and weather conditions began to deteriorate. Walking across an icy parking lot to the grocery store was treacherous enough even when her center of gravity wasn't pushed forward by a foot.

Her work schedule was still busy, although, true to his word, Greg had cut back on the number of patients they saw after six o'clock. At least on days he was scheduled to be at the hospital. All other days, he continued working like a crazy person.

She sighed. It had been a week since they'd had their last

big discussion, when he'd insisted he wanted a role in the baby's life, if there was a baby and if it ended up being his.

How? She barely saw him during office hours these days, and she worked with the man. How did he expect to make time for a baby? Was that really the role model she wanted for a child? That of a workaholic whose job came before everything else?

To be fair, he was helping a lot of people, and he was right when he'd said she hadn't complained when she'd been on the receiving end of that help. But Greg had never had to face the harsh reality that life didn't go on forever. It was up to each person to make the most of their time on earth.

He was certainly doing that by giving back to those around him, but what about his own life? When did he start living? Really living?

Maybe he hadn't really meant his offer—maybe it was just the obligatory "take responsibility for your actions" spiel that faded away once the guilt loosened its hold.

Hannah swallowed. She'd seen the look in his eye, had heard the quiet anger in his voice after she'd insisted the baby was hers alone.

What a mess.

And it was Saturday. Not even a day when she could throw herself into work and not have time to think. Her pregnancy test that morning had yielded nothing, which didn't necessarily mean the I.U.I. had failed. Her doctor said it was better to test at the two-week mark, but she hadn't been able to wait.

What if she wasn't pregnant?

While it should be a relief to know she couldn't possibly be carrying Greg's child—and that she'd be able to have another procedure done after her next cycle—she couldn't convince her heart it was for the best.

Sigh.

She turned away from the window and headed for the kitchen, where she had a batch of sunshine muffins baking. A perfect foil for the gloomy day. The wonderful scent of citrus washed over her as she dug her oven mitt from one of the drawers. Peeking inside the oven, she noted the muffins were just starting to set, their swollen tops curving over the edge of the pan, like twelve pregnant little bellies.

Great, was this what she was in for? Picturing her future body at every turn?

Just as she pulled the muffin tray out of the oven, the phone chirped. She dropped the pan onto the stovetop and hurried into the living room, tugging the mitt from her hand as she went.

"Hello?"

"Hannah Lassiter, please."

The brisk voice stopped her cold because she immediately recognized it. Greg. Why on earth was he calling her at home on a Saturday morning? "Th-this is Hannah."

"I know it is. Habit. Sorry."

What was a habit? Asking for the person, even when you knew who it was? Her heart took a dive when she realized why he was calling. "Where are you?"

"At the office. I've had an emergency come up and need to pull some records off the computer. I already tried calling Stella, but nobody's home."

"Is the computer on?"

"No. I can't find the damn power button on the system."

"It's on the front of the tower, under the reception desk."

"I've already tried pushing that and nothing happened."

She licked her lips. Oh, no. That thing could be ornery at times. "Try it again."

There was a pause, and then a low curse. "Still nothing."

"I'll be there in a few minutes." Was she crazy? True,

she'd just been complaining about having nothing to do, but this wasn't quite what she'd had in mind.

There was a lengthy pause over the phone. "Greg? Are you still there?"

"I'm here. If I could just reach Stella... You don't happen to have the number to her cell, do you? It's not on the pad with the other numbers."

"No, sorry. It might be in the personnel records, but those would be on the computer, as well. The system's temperamental. Stella showed me a few tricks, so hang tight."

"I don't want you to have to come in."

Hannah could pretty much swear he didn't want her anywhere around, since he'd steered clear of her as much as possible over the last week. "If it's an emergency, I don't mind. Who is it?"

"Claire Taylor. Her husband thinks she's having a reaction to the chemo and wants me to take a look."

Oh, no. The breast-cancer patient she'd seen a week ago. "Are they headed in now?"

"Yes."

"I'm on my way." Before he could hand her any more arguments, she pressed End, cutting off anything he'd been about to say.

She ran to the bedroom and threw on the nearest set of scrubs she found. How was it that more than half her wardrobe was made up of the comfortable clothes? She even slept in a clean set most of the time.

Giving her hair a quick brush, she shoved a plastic headband up over her forehead so she wouldn't have to blow-dry her bangs into any semblance of order. She decided to forgo makeup as well, in the interests of time—resisting the little voice inside her that urged her to make an effort. Neither Greg nor the patient cared how she looked. She'd stay long enough to get that computer system up and running, then she'd take off again. Fifteen minutes in and out, tops.

The image of her and Greg and their quick "in and out" session ran through her head and she groaned aloud. *Stop it.*

As she ran back through the kitchen, she grabbed a canvas grocery bag and slid the entire tray of muffins inside. She could eat in the car as she was starving. And since Greg's call had come in just after eight o'clock, she doubted he'd fixed himself much of a breakfast either. He'd probably been at the office for at least a half hour, fiddling with that computer, before being forced to call for help. Besides, there was no way she could eat a dozen muffins by herself. She'd leave some there for him to take home.

The trip to the clinic took less than ten minutes. Thankfully the light snow hadn't turned into ice, so the roads were clear and dry so far. She hadn't gotten a chance to listen to the forecast, so she could only hope the weather held until she got out of there.

She found the front door to the clinic unlocked, so she pushed through it, muffins in one hand, purse in the other. Greg popped up from behind the desk, where he'd evidently still been trying to figure out the computer. His eyes skimmed over her and he blinked a couple of times.

Did she look that bad? Because he sure didn't. His hair was sticking up a bit, probably from dragging his fingers through it in frustration as she'd seen him do many times before. He was more casual today in a dark T-shirt that hugged his chest and arms.

Setting her things on the counter so she didn't end up staring, she slid the muffin pan from the bag. "Here, eat."

He stood the rest of the way, and she noted that his lower half was as casual as the upper. Worn jeans gripped his lean hips and thighs, the color fading where the fabric followed a certain decadent curve. One that had her biting her lip in an effort to rip her gaze away from it.

A throat cleared, the sound shocking her back into action. "What are they?"

They? Oh, the food.

"Sunshine muffins. They have pineapple and orange zest. They're happy tasting."

His lips curved as he took the napkin-wrapped muffin she held out. "I don't think I've ever heard anyone refer to food as 'happy.'"

"Wait until you taste one." She took a muffin for herself, realizing she hadn't eaten in the car as she'd intended.

Greg's white teeth cut the miniature cake in half, his brows going up. He swallowed and then studied the muffin. "Okay, so maybe there's something to that description."

"Told you." She took a bite of her own piece, loving the way the pineapple chunks provided a little extra spurt of moisture. Anyone who'd ever eaten these knew they were about as close to heaven as you could get.

She swallowed. Well, she used to believe that. Up until a week ago.

"Well, I'll see about that computer." Taking her muffin with her, she edged past Greg, who'd finished his first one and was reaching for a second.

"Thanks for these. I forgot to eat."

Just as she'd suspected. Kneeling in front of the computer, she took another bite as she felt around the back of the CPU box and jiggled one of the many cords snaking behind the equipment to make sure it was tight in its slot.

She pressed the power button and heard the promising whine of success.

"It's coming up." Greg's voice came from beside her and, as she knew they would, her eyes paused as they traveled up his leg—even though it was obvious he was talking about the computer monitor coming up and not something else.

Gawd. What was wrong with her? Wasn't she in enough trouble as it was?

She forced herself to look at his face. "Come here, and I'll show you what to do the next time it happens."

The second he crouched beside her, she realized asking him to do so had been a huge mistake. Ducked down behind the desk together, their knees touched, making the space seem smaller and much more intimate.

She held up the attached cord, horrified to note it shook in time with her hand. "This one comes loose periodically. Stella says that if you bump it the wrong way, it shuts everything off. The thing drives her crazy."

"I'll have to have it fixed," he murmured. "Where does the cord lead?"

His fingers touched hers for a second before sliding along the piece of wiring, her heart crashing around in her chest as the scent of soap and cool aftershave hit her senses. She could lean three inches to the left and her cheek would slide along his jaw. She forced her body to go rigid instead and held her ground.

"Ah, there you are." He withdrew his hand and turned to look at her, their faces now inches apart. "So all I need to do is make sure there's a good connection?"

"C-connection?" Her brain struggled with the word, since the only connection she could think of involved having her lips mashed up against his. "Oh, the power cable."

"What did you think I was talking about?" His voice was impossibly low, his breath gliding across her cheek.

He didn't want to know.

"The computer, of course."

"Ah, and here I thought you were talking about matches."

As in the "playing with matches" comment she'd made a week ago?

His lips curved with a secret knowledge. He knew exactly what she'd been thinking.

"Hannah." The chiding tone should have made her smile back, but it didn't.

Instead, the tip of her tongue came out to moisten her mouth just as Greg's fingers walked up her nape then curved around it, the warmth of his hand sending a shiver over her.

Lord, was he going to kiss her? Again?

The sudden tinkle of the bell over the front door made Hannah rear back so quickly she landed on her backside with a grunt. She then jumped up from behind the desk, her hand automatically going to her hair as if she'd just been caught doing something naughty. Which she hadn't. At least, not yet.

It was the patient and her husband. She could only hope that Greg had crawled away on his hands and knees and made his escape, because if he stood up right now…

As if on cue, her boss unfolded his long length and casually climbed to his feet, brushing dust from the front of jeans, while she cringed inwardly.

He came around the counter, and offered his hand to each of them. "One of our computer connections seemed to have come loose, and I couldn't switch it on. Hannah was showing me which cable it was."

Not a tremor or a warble affected his voice, and even Hannah believed him. What he'd said was true, after all. So why did her face burn like the inside of a kiln? Because her boss could quite possibly be the father of her child? And she'd been about to let him try for a double. Ack!

In the background, she heard Greg asking about Claire's symptoms in low, soothing tones. By now they were all seated in the waiting room's leatherette chairs, with Greg leaning forward as if trying to catch every word his patient said.

Hannah could remember him doing exactly the same thing when he'd visited her in the hospital that first time. He hadn't written anything down, instead he'd let her pour out all her hopes and fears and had answered each of her questions. A little black book had sat in his lap, but he'd never opened it until the very end, when he'd scheduled her appointment.

That appointment book was nowhere in sight right now, but she had no doubt Greg would remember everything spoken in that room.

She wasn't sure what to do. Did he want her to leave now that the computer problem had been fixed? She could at least look up Claire's chart, as that's what he'd wanted the computer for in the first place. She sat behind the desk and flipped through screens until she came to the patient's information. Hitting Print, she went over and retrieved the small stack of papers that contained digitized test results and observations. Then she padded over to Greg, who held out a hand for the packet without taking his eyes off his patient.

"I want to take a look and see what's going on, okay?" He glanced at the woman's husband. "Why don't you come back with us?"

A wave of relief washed over her. She could escape while everyone was in the back.

Right before Greg walked through the door, he glanced back. "Would you mind waiting around for a while? I could really use another of those muffins."

A muffin? He really expected her to believe that?

"Um…no, not at all. I'll be happy to stay."

As soon as he left, Hannah sank into a chair, leaning

her head against the cream-colored wall behind her with a roll of her eyes. She'd be happy to stay? Why hadn't she just said, "And where would you like me this time, sir? In your office? Or shall we climb back under the front desk?"

Greg wasn't sure why he'd asked Hannah to stay, other than to find out if she'd heard anything about her hormone levels. Had her HCG spiked? Or remained level?

His patient lay on the exam table, her husband murmuring softly to her. She looked so remarkably like his sister that he often found himself staring as if she could suddenly morph into Bethany at any moment and start laughing about old times. Even the eternal spark of optimism was something his sister had had. He was convinced that if Bethany had lived, she would have turned out very much like Claire—a kind, giving, cheerful person. She would have had a happy life…had a husband who adored her, just as Claire's husband obviously doted on his wife.

Watching the pair, he saw nothing of the grasping greediness he'd felt when he had gone after his PA last week.

There was so much he should regret about that night, but he couldn't seem to wring that particular emotion from his brain, or any other part of his body. Instead, he had been ready to move in for another sample just before his patient had walked through the door.

Luckily she had, because seeing her had snapped him back to the present and reminded him exactly why he was there. Especially when he saw how pale she was, how tired looking. He hadn't been able to save his sister, but he was damned well going to do everything in his power to help Claire. Was he using his patient as a substitute? Doing for one what he hadn't been able to do for the other? Maybe, but in the end it didn't matter as long as it worked.

He forced his attention back to Claire. He could have asked Hannah to come in with him, but he needed a little breathing space. Besides, taking blood pressure and temperature gave him something concrete to do with his hands, and with his thoughts.

He glanced at the readout on the tympanic thermometer and frowned. One hundred point one degrees. A low-grade fever. The beginning of an infection? Not good when dealing with a chemo patient's weakened immune system. A thread of worry twisted inside him. "Have you been exposed to anyone who's ill?"

"I don't think so. I had chills last night, and stomach cramps. I had a little fever, but nothing too terrible."

He felt her abdomen for signs of tenderness. "Does anything hurt right now?"

"No. I actually feel better, but Doug insisted on calling."

Good man. He nodded at him in reassurance.

"And he was right. You still have a slight fever. I'm going to prescribe some antibiotics, just in case, but if your temperature climbs above one hundred and two degrees, I want you call me and then head straight to Anchorage Regional and let them give you some intravenous meds."

Her husband placed his hand on her shoulder. "Do you want her to do her chemo treatment this week?"

"When's it scheduled?"

"Friday morning."

Almost a week away. She needed to stay on the regimen if at all possible. "If her fever's gone completely, then go ahead, as long as her blood count looks good." He glanced back at his patient. "Can I check the incision?"

He knew this was hard for her, but he had to be sure nothing was acting up.

Claire swallowed, but opened the gown so that he could check the mastectomy site for signs of redness or infection. Her husband held her hand and leaned down to whisper in her ear again while Greg studied the area. It looked clean and well healed. Her pulled her robe closed and gently squeezed her shoulder. "I don't see anything here to worry about."

Grabbing a pad from a nearby drawer, he scribbled a prescription for antibiotics.

Claire spoke up. "Sorry to drag you away from whatever you were doing."

It took him a second to realize she was talking in generalities and not about catching him and Hannah under the figurative boardwalk. Being able drop everything at a moment's notice to help patients like Claire was the exact reason he'd chosen not to have a wife and family. His sister had stayed on his case until he'd agreed to at least try med school for a year. She'd been right. He was meant to be a doctor.

His throat tightened. She hadn't lived to see the completion of that dream. But he could honor her memory by being the best damned doctor he could be. Especially since the doctor who'd ultimately treated her during her illness had been everything he'd learned to despise in a physician. He'd cared more about his golf swing than his patients.

Maybe that wasn't an entirely fair assessment, but that particular specialist's reputation—as he'd discovered later—left a little to be desired.

"Don't apologize. I wasn't doing anything special today. And I always want you to call if something's worrying you. It's usually easier to head problems off than to try to fix them once the wheels have been spinning for a while."

He helped her sit up and handed her the prescription.

"Thank you. Your patients are lucky," she said.

He smiled. Luck had nothing to do with it. If she wanted to thank anyone, she should thank his sister. Without her, he wouldn't be where he was today. He'd be on a commercial fishing boat, freezing his ass off and hating life. Instead, he was doing a job he loved—one that gave him immense satisfaction.

For that reason and a myriad of others, Greg had fashioned his practice differently than most oncologists. He hired people whose lives had been touched by cancer. Survivors. He found it was the best way to keep his head clear of distractions and fixed on the task at hand. And helped him remember his sister.

And it had worked. At least until Hannah had come along. Her murmurs of concern had worn him down little by little, until he'd thrown himself on the rocks, just as sailors of old had when confronted with the sirens' song.

He went into the hallway to wait for his patient to get dressed, knowing that as inwardly battered and bruised as he might be right now, he was eventually going to have to walk into that waiting room and face down temptation all over again.

CHAPTER EIGHT

"Congratulations, Hannah, you're pregnant."

The fertility doctor's voice confirmed what her own home pregnancy test had indicated. She was carrying someone's baby.

But whose?

Be happy, Hannah. This is what you wanted.

It was. But not like this. Where she'd anticipated the ability to raise her child as she saw fit, sharing her new-found zest for life, dread had oozed in, infecting her happiness. The fact that she couldn't wholeheartedly celebrate this moment made her angry. Angry at Greg, but even more angry at herself.

Why was he so persistent?

I want to know if this baby is mine, one way or the other. I don't care how long it takes to find out.

His parting words last Saturday echoed through her head. He'd asked her to wait at the clinic until he'd finished examining Claire, but when he'd finally emerged, keys in hand, he hadn't mentioned the muffins, confirming her suspicions that it had merely been a way to get her to stay. Instead, he'd made that statement before holding the door open and watching her walk toward her car. Once she had been safely inside, engine on, heat cranked up, he'd turned away to lock the clinic door.

And that had been it.

They'd passed each other in the hallway this week, but neither had said much to the other. The clinic was busy, although, true to Greg's word, the overall hours remained shorter. Hannah had her suspicions about that, too, as he stayed behind every night. Notes added to certain patients' files upped those suspicions. He was seeing more patients after hours.

That brought her back to her original question. Why was he so insistent on knowing whose child this was, when he wouldn't have time to spend with it? There was no way she wanted to introduce a two-year-old to a man and tell him or her, "This is your father," only to have Greg continue on with his life as he'd always done. That was not the message she wanted to send to her child: you're not important enough for Daddy to spend time with.

God. What a disaster.

"Hannah, did you hear me?" The fertility doctor touched her shoulder, making her jump.

She glanced up, seeing the concern on the woman's face. "Sorry. That's wonderful news."

"Then why don't you sound ecstatic?"

"It's complicated." As soon as the words came out of her mouth, she snorted in disgust. That seemed to be her new favorite phrase. "Let me ask you something. Is it possible to do D.N.A. testing before the baby's birth?"

Dr. Chaquir leaned against the cabinet behind her. "Is there something I should know? A genetic problem in your family?"

Another thing Hannah had never thought of when she'd had sex with her boss. Was he carrying some kind of defect? Was that why he was so fired up about knowing one way or the other? Surely he'd have said something before now.

No. Why would he? If the child wasn't his, he had no reason to tell her anything.

Her hand went to her stomach as if she could protect the tiny fetus from some kind of horrible problem. Maybe she did need to find out.

She sighed. "I…um, did something stupid."

The doctor frowned. "How stupid?"

"Stupid enough to not know if this baby is the result of donor sperm or someone else's."

"I don't see how. Unless you were with someone immediately afterward, I'm pretty sure the donor sperm reached the egg first."

"But the life cycle of washed sperm is shorter than… um, the other kind, right?"

Dr. Chaquir nodded. "Six to twenty-four hours on average, compared with up to five days for fresh ejaculate. I'm taking it you were intimate not long after the I.U.I. was performed?"

Hannah's face heated. "Within that time frame you mentioned."

There was a pause. "I see."

Those two words told her all she needed to know. The doctor was not going to heave a dramatic sigh and say, "You lucky thing, it's definitely not your boss's baby."

"So, as far as prenatal D.N.A. testing goes, how risky is it?"

"You're going to want to talk with your OB/GYN about that." She paused. "Are you sure you want to go through with this pregnancy, Hannah? It's still pretty early."

Did she?

Yes. This was her baby. The one she'd dreamed of as she'd sat in the recliner in the chemo room, having toxic substances pumped into her veins. The "happy place" she'd traveled to during some of the unpleasant side effects. This was something she'd wanted more than anything, and she might never get another chance.

"Yes, I want to go through with it." She forced a smile and stood. "Thank you, Doctor. If you could give me a referral for an obstetrician, I'd appreciate it."

On the drive back home, a sudden rush of joy—in the form of tears—dumped whatever dread she'd felt right out of her body. She pulled off the side of the road as moisture cascaded down her cheeks. The bad emotions might come back soon enough, but right now she could celebrate. She *would* celebrate.

She was pregnant. *Pregnant!*

No matter what came next, she would soon hold a new being in her arms and glory in the miracle of modern medicine that made it possible. Maybe some deity had seen how badly she wanted this and had sent Greg to her at just the right time. What did it matter?

She scrubbed at her cheeks. Okay, so it did matter. A lot. But she could deal with that later, once the reality sank deep and she had to face Greg with the news. But for now it was Friday afternoon and she didn't have to face anyone for the next two days. Not until Monday morning. By then she'd have come up with the perfect words to toss at Greg.

"Any news?"

Greg had come up behind her silently, and she gave a muffled scream before whirling around to face him. "When did you get here?"

"About an hour ago."

Her two-day search for a quick and easy answer had been fruitless. She'd come up with zilch. Maybe even less than zilch. Because she'd dreamed of herself—very pregnant—in a flowing wedding gown on Saturday night and when she reached the altar, the faceless groom had yanked a sign from beneath his tuxedo coat that read, "Is that my baby?"

She'd awoken in a cold sweat, unsure if the accusing figure represented the sperm donor or Greg.

She turned her attention back to the man in front of her, whose face was very real and who was asking much the same thing as the groom from her dream. Only she didn't have a better answer now than she'd had then.

"Yes. I found out on Friday."

"You're pregnant." He'd evidently seen the truth on her face.

"Yes."

He leaned a shoulder against the wall as if needing the extra bit of support. "So what do we do now?"

Hannah glanced to her left, hoping Stella wasn't going to suddenly pop out of one of the exam rooms. "I have an appointment to see an obstetrician in a couple of weeks."

"Will you ask for testing?"

"I'm going to ask *about* testing." In her mind, asking for information was very different from asking to have it done. "I'm really not holding you responsible, Greg. It was a fluke, something neither of us expected to happen. Please, can't you just leave it at that?"

His jaw tightened. "You might not hold me responsible, but I do. I knew what the consequences could be, knew I had a condom in the wallet not five feet away from me. I went ahead without it."

As opposed to her, who hadn't thought about anything but having him inside her as soon as possible. A condom had never even crossed her mind, maybe because in her head she had already been pregnant, which was ridiculous. If this was anyone's fault, it was probably hers. "I was there, too. I didn't exactly give you the opportunity to stop."

Something dark flickered through his eyes before it winked back out. "I could have handled the whole situation differently—never let it go as far as it did."

How? By shoving her away when she'd reached for him? That would have been the ultimate humiliation. Even worse than having to stand here now and hear him imply that had been one of the options.

"Knowing the truth isn't going to change anything. Not really. You live to work. I live…to live. Like it or not, cancer changed me. I don't expect you to be able to understand that, but I want to share what I've been given with others. That includes my child. I want it to know my hopes and dreams. To teach it the same values I have. I want the baby to know how precious each and every second of life is."

He folded his arms across his chest and waited as a nurse made her way past them. "You don't think I want those same things?"

"Quite frankly, no." She glanced pointedly in the direction the nurse had gone seconds earlier. "And I'd really like to keep the pregnancy to myself for the moment—I haven't even told my parents yet—so can we please not have this discussion in the middle of the hallway?"

Greg stared at her for a long minute. "Fine. So you tell me when and where, and I'll be there."

So much for hoping he'd walk away and leave things on some vague, undefined terms. She needed time to think about how much involvement she was willing to let Greg have. Ultimately it was her decision, but she also needed it to be the right one. She didn't want to have to explain to her child someday why she'd kept his biological father—if that turned out to be Greg—from being a part of his life. That didn't seem right either.

Maybe he was right about the D.N.A. testing. If he knew

for sure the baby wasn't his, he'd stop pressuring her. And, in all honesty, he'd probably be hugely relieved to boot.

"How about you go with me to the obstetrician and hear what she has to say about the testing? I don't promise I'll have it done, if it's risky to the baby, but I don't want you to think I'm being disingenuous about anything either."

"Sounds reasonable. Let me know when the appointment is and I'll shuffle my schedule around."

She blinked in surprise. He would? Greg had never once canceled a surgery or patient's appointment since she'd worked at the clinic. Even when he was in the operating room or had an emergency with another patient, someone on the team kept the other scheduled appointments. Maybe he wasn't quite as intractable as—

Before she could finish the thought, Stella stuck her head through the door in the reception area. "The office furniture guys just called. They should be here with your new desk in around a half an hour. Will you be here to sign for it?"

Dark color washed up Greg's neck and infused his face. "Yes. I'll be here."

Stella nodded. "Oh, and one more thing, they want to know what you want done with the old one…said you mentioned something about needing it out of here as soon as possible." She paused. "Didn't you just have your office redecorated this past summer?"

"I can't remember." He pushed away from the wall and began stalking toward his office. "Let me know when they arrive."

"Will do." Stella withdrew, leaving Hannah to stare at Greg's retreating back, humiliation and hurt jockeying for first place in her head.

That desk. The one where they'd made love.

Was it really so easy to erase what had happened between them? It evidently was for Greg. One flick of his wrist and he made the desk—and everything it represented—vanish forever.

CHAPTER NINE

"CHANCES of miscarriage are one in a hundred."

The obstetrician continued explaining how chorionic villus testing worked and what to expect during the procedure, but Greg's mind fastened on the risk factors. The phrase ran through his head time and time again.

Hannah, dressed in a standard hospital gown, sat on the exam table and listened intently to the doctor. Her face was a blank slate, giving Greg no indication of what she was thinking. Her appointment had been the first one of the day, and if Dr. Preston was surprised to see him accompanying her new patient, she didn't show it.

Greg had stepped outside the room during the internal exam but had been called back in during the explanations. Everything with the pregnancy seemed to be normal. Hannah was six weeks along, but that time was calculated from her last period, not the date of conception, which had been two weeks after that date. But, still, how had four weeks passed from the fateful encounter in his office? Time had kind of become a vague BC/AD delineation of time in which BC stood for "before condom" and AD meant "after dumbass."

Hannah had been given a tentative July due date, which seemed both way too soon and an eternity away. His life would be turned upside down until he knew for sure whether or not he was the father.

But at a one-in-a-hundred chance of losing the baby? Was his peace of mind really worth that much?

He moved closer to the exam table and touched Hannah's arm, interrupting the doctor's litany. "Don't do it."

Hannah blinked up at him. "I'm sorry?"

Her question made him realize just how far they'd traveled away from the subject of D.N.A. testing. Greg had no idea what the current topic was, but he had to make his wishes clear. "I don't want you to do the paternity testing."

The doctor glanced from one to the other. "Do you want me to give you a moment?"

"Do you mind?" Hannah's voice was soft, her eyes still on his.

"Not at all. I'll get started with my next patient." The doctor squeezed Hannah's shoulder, gave Greg an enigmatic look and slid through the door.

"I thought you wanted the testing done," Hannah said as soon as they were alone.

"It's too risky."

"But when I mentioned that earlier, you just brushed it aside."

Greg dragged a hand through his hair. She was right, he had. He didn't know what had changed between then and now, but something had. Maybe having tangible evidence the pregnancy was real. "I think hearing the actual numbers made me rethink things. If they weren't so high…"

Where exactly was that line? If the doctor had said the chances of losing the pregnancy were one in a thousand, would he want her to have it done? One in a million?

He wasn't sure. But a hundred to one. That wasn't a risk he was willing to put Hannah through. Not for the selfish reasons he had.

"Maybe later on," she said. "An amniocentesis could carry fewer risks."

"You're not old enough to warrant testing for genetic defects." He frowned. "Unless there's something in your family."

"No. And the donor didn't list any kind of problems." She hesitated. "Is there anything in your family?"

Was there? Greg had no idea. He'd long since given up on the idea of having kids, so he'd never bothered checking his family tree for inheritable conditions. Although he seemed to remember reading that myeloid leukemia—his sister's illness—could be caused by a defective chromosome in about thirty percent of cases. Hell, something he'd never even bothered to think about. Selfish bastard. All he'd worried about were the ramifications to his own life if he were the baby's father. What about the ramifications to the child's life?

"My sister had myeloid leukemia. If I'm the father..." His voice trailed away. Hell, what if he'd passed on some kind of time bomb?

"Is myeloid inherited?"

"I think it can be." He thought about it for a second. "I'll see a geneticist and ask about testing."

Hannah's face drained of color. "Oh, God. Even if there is a test, it could take weeks or longer to get the results."

He took her hand and squeezed. "I'm so sorry. If I could take it all back, I would." He'd had strange, uneasy dreams about that night ever since. He'd wake up drenched in sweat, wanting her with a fervor that shook him. Worse was when he reached for her upon waking, only to find the other side of his bed empty. Cold.

And now this.

"It's not your fault." She gave him a shaky smile. "I've often wished that night had happened a whole lot earlier, or later. But I was taking hormones and they…well, they probably affected my thinking."

In other words, if she'd been in her right mind, she'd have never had sex with him. Fantastic. And that made him feel a whole lot better, because he had no excuse, other than having had the hots for his beautiful PA almost from the moment he'd laid eyes on her. Even as a patient, there'd been something special about her, something that drew him.

Hiring her had been a mistake. He'd felt it at the time but had figured the attraction would fade. He'd felt a twinge of lust for a woman from time to time. It never lasted. And that attraction had certainly had never made him lose his head before.

"Are you sure it wasn't just my charismatic personality that did the trick?" He'd been abrupt with her when she'd brought him coffee that fateful day. He wasn't sure making a joke was the right thing to do under these circumstances, but it was all he had.

"That was probably it." She lifted her brows and regarded him for a moment or two. "What ever happened to the desk?"

Heat sifted up Greg's neck. So she had suspected the real reason he'd swapped it. Not that it had helped. The white pickled wood—so different from the rich mahogany of the previous desk—still seemed to be burned with the image of Hannah splayed across it.

And come to think of it, she rarely ventured into his office nowadays, whereas before, hardly a day had gone by that she hadn't brought him coffee or stopped to chat about a patient. He used to be irritated by her apparent lack of boundaries, like the impulsive hug she'd given him when they'd still been patient and doctor—something his sister might have done.

His reaction to Hannah's embrace, however, had been anything but brotherly. But as much as she confused him and caused him to forget himself, he found he missed those daily visits. And as for that old desk...

"It's in storage." He hadn't quite been able to get rid of it entirely. The men had offered to haul it to a consignment shop, but he'd balked at the last second and instead rented a unit in one of the pricier, climate-controlled facilities. He figured he'd take care of it by the time the next rental payment was due.

"Oh." Hannah's face turned a delicate shade of pink. "Well, I guess I'd better get dressed. I'm sure you need to head back to the office."

"I don't have an appointment for another couple of hours." He hadn't been sure how long these initial obstetrician visits took, and he hadn't wanted to leave in the middle of it. Not that he'd even needed to be here in the first place.

Yeah, he had. He'd needed to hear the risk factors in person, and to see Hannah's reaction to them. He'd come away certain of one thing. She wanted this baby. Who was he to jeopardize that possibility?

And if he'd passed on some defective chromosome? Could he handle seeing his child go through the same thing his sister had endured somewhere down the road? He didn't think so, but that wasn't his choice to make. It was Hannah's. And he wouldn't have given up knowing his sister for anything. Her steadfast solidarity—after he told his father of his decision to go to med school—had been his rock during a time of seething turmoil and anger.

Hannah's voice cut through his thoughts. "Unless you want me to get dressed in front of you, you might want to wait outside."

Ah, okay, so that's what she'd been getting at by telling

him to go back to the office. He needed to pull himself together. Something about this woman made him say and do things that were completely out of character. "Sorry. I'll…go. Out there." He jerked a thumb in the direction of the door.

"I drove, so why don't I just meet you back at the office?"

A wave of tension he hadn't even been aware of rolled off his shoulders. "Do you want me to send the doctor back in?"

"That's right. I forgot about her." She paused, her eyes going to his. "You've never talked about your sister before. Did she…?"

"She didn't make it." The sorrow from years past gathered in his throat, and he had to swallow hard.

Hannah took his hand again. "I'm so sorry. How long ago?"

"About ten years."

"So you weren't a doctor at the time?"

He sighed, not liking the way her hand wrapped around his or how natural it felt. "I was in med school when she was diagnosed. It happened faster than anyone expected." It was ironic that the very profession she'd encouraged him to pursue hadn't been able to help her in the end.

"And yet you specialized in oncology. Isn't that hard?" The compassion in her eyes was hard to face. And yet it wasn't pity, simply a deep understanding. Of course. How stupid of him. Hannah had traveled the same road as his sister, only her illness had veered down a different fork and had had a much better outcome.

"It's why I specialized. My sister was my biggest cheerleader when I decided to become a doctor. It seemed like the best way to thank her." Why he'd blurted that out, he had no idea. He'd never told anyone his reasons for going into this particular field, not even his parents—although they probably knew.

"Of course." The words were soft, carrying a hint of surprise, as if she'd just figured something out. "I need to get dressed."

She let go of his hand, leaving an emptiness in its wake that he didn't like. This was ridiculous. Even if she ended up carrying a human being that contained his D.N.A., that didn't change their relationship. He was her employer, nothing more. And he'd yet to decide what he would be to her child—if it was even his. And that was pretty unlikely. At least he hoped it was. Because if that was the case, his life could go on unchanged, continue exactly as it had for the last ten years.

As he went through the door, he knew he was telling himself the worst kind of lie. His life—no matter what the outcome of any paternity test—would never be the same again.

"Itsy bitsy spider climbed up the water spout…"

The sing-song tune—coming from the next aisle over—was followed by the quick giggle of a child. Hannah couldn't stop her lips from curving at the cheerful sound, despite her confused jumble of thoughts about Greg, his sister's cancer and her own pregnancy.

As Greg had shared about his reasons for becoming an oncologist, memories of her own terrifying struggle had roared back to life, swamping her with memories of pain and fear. Those fears had stayed with her for the past week, refusing to seep away like they normally did. Maybe because she was now responsible for someone other than herself.

She'd come into the cavernous baby supercenter on a whim, hoping to replace the bad emotions with happy ones. But standing in the middle of the store, she'd been overwhelmed by the quantity of paraphernalia surrounding her. A chaotic jumble. Just like the feelings she'd been trying to escape.

That tiny giggle did what her own frantic attempts to tame her fears couldn't: turned everything right side up so it could settle back into place. That happy laughter was why she'd wanted to get pregnant…why she was willing to go through all the doubt and uncertainty of being a single mom. She wandered over to where the sounds of singing continued and found a young mother, her dark hair shining as she leaned over a fancy baby stroller.

Hannah could almost imagine the woman's fingers walking up her child's belly as the song continued and another happy shriek filled the air, followed by the mom's light chuckle.

Hannah's smile widened. That would be her someday. At least, she hoped it would. But at the moment the thoughts of illness and fear still seemed terrifyingly real. Her hand went to her stomach, which at the seven-week point hadn't begun to expand yet. But she knew the baby was there. She might even get to hear its heartbeat at her next scheduled appointment.

In the week since her initial check-up, Greg hadn't said anything else about his sister's illness or whether or not he'd spoken with anyone about testing, and Hannah was afraid to ask. She finally understood why he'd thrown himself headlong into his work. Doing what he hadn't been able to do for his sister. No wonder he wasn't involved with anyone. He was like a monk…someone who'd thrown aside his own creature comforts in order to seek a higher purpose in life.

And what of this child, if it was his? How could she expect Greg to change who he was? What he wanted out of life? She couldn't. Another reason she'd come into the store today.

She wanted to be able to spend a few moments not thinking about the horrible possibilities and just enjoy being pregnant—but the thoughts had followed her inside. A year ago she'd wondered if it would even be possible for her to have a baby. And yet here she was. Expecting one. The thought should make her happier than she'd ever been.

She took a deep breath and let it out slowly. Some of the tension left her. And as she watched the mother and baby interact, a sense of rightness washed over her. Nothing else mattered at the moment. She'd live for the here and now. Worrying about the future was futile, as she'd learned through her own fight. She couldn't change the outcome, could only do her best to optimize her chances for survival.

That's what she'd do for this baby, as well. She couldn't change what might or might not happen in the weeks or years to come, but she was making an effort to eat right and to do what she could to stay healthy in the present. She'd worry about the other stuff as it came up.

The mom, a few yards away, suddenly looked over her shoulder as if sensing someone was watching her. "Sorry," she said, her smile big. "I didn't realize anyone could hear me."

When she straightened, Hannah realized the woman not only had a baby in the stroller but that she appeared to be pregnant again, as well. "I was enjoying your baby's laughter. I just found out I'm expecting."

"So am I. Congratulations." The woman nodded at her own stomach. "My husband couldn't be here for his daughter's birth, but we're hoping he'll be home for this one."

Hannah's mind was working on the first part of that statement, when the young mother explained. "He was deployed to Iraq. I found out I was pregnant with her—"

she reached into the carriage to stroke the child's head "—right after he left."

"I'm glad he'll be here for the new baby."

The woman laughed again. "Me, too. I didn't get to yell any profanities at him during labor."

Hannah smiled. "Who was with you?"

"My mom. Cussing your mother out isn't quite the same." She shook her head. "And, no, I didn't."

"I didn't think you did." Hannah didn't want to think about the fact that her own baby's father probably wouldn't be there for the delivery either. Definitely wouldn't be if it was the donor's child, but even if it was Greg's, she couldn't see him wanting to be there for such an intimate event. The more businesslike they kept things the better for both of them. Something in her chest started aching all over again at the thought.

She'd chosen this route, and she would not allow herself to regret it now. And, honestly, she didn't. Not knowing the father's identity made life a little bizarre at times but she wouldn't go back and undo the pregnancy, even if it was a result of that night.

"I hope your pregnancy goes well," the woman said.

"Thank you. I hope yours does, too."

The baby in the carriage started to fuss, tiny mewling cries replacing the happy laughter from a few moments earlier. "Sorry," she said. "I have to get moving or she's going to let loose. I just came in to pick up some diapers, but couldn't resist looking around for a while. Unfortunately, big sister is getting hungry."

"I understand completely. I'll let you get back to it."

As the woman moved away from her, the sound of soft singing again floated through the air as the young mother tried to hush the child's cries. A wave of longing went through Hannah. That's what she wanted for her newborn.

Not the baby daddy drama she was currently embroiled in but the simple happy singing of a mother to her child. She touched her stomach as if she could somehow transmit some of the woman's joy to her own child.

She started walking again, whispering, "Hey, baby. Be happy, okay?"

But Hannah neither heard not felt anything within her, except a deep sense of loneliness that grew steadily stronger with each step she took.

CHAPTER TEN

STELLA glanced in Hannah's direction as she spoke to whoever was on the phone and pointed toward the receiver and then toward Hannah. "I'll send her right over."

She hung up. "Greg wants you over at the hospital for some reason. Do you mind?"

"Did he say why?"

Her boss never sent for her, always wanting at least one of them at the clinic to attend to patients. But, then again, since he did a lot of the scheduling, he'd know by looking at his little black book that there was a lull for the next two hours. Her nose crinkled. It was also lunchtime and she'd been hoping to sit and eat in peace, gearing up for the afternoon patients.

"Sorry, he didn't give a reason."

"Okay." She sighed and went to get her purse. Was there an emergency with one of their patients? With Claire Taylor, the woman who'd come in a couple of weeks ago?

Hannah arrived at Alaska Regional in fifteen minutes and made her way to the oncology building at the far end of the hospital campus. Greg was waiting for her just inside the entrance, along with a man in a lab coat—so it wasn't about a patient, unless the man was there on a consult. If that was the case, why did they need her?

"I'd like you to meet Bill Watterson," Greg said. "He's a medical geneticist."

Hannah blinked, her mind whirring in confusion. Why would he be introducing her to a…?

Things clicked into place. She shook hands with the newcomer and murmured a greeting she hoped didn't relay her growing anger. He'd never mentioned meeting with a geneticist today. She gave a tight smile and turned to Greg. "Could I speak to you for a minute?"

Bill Watterson, evidently picking up on the tension between them, excused himself, saying he was going to get a coffee and would be back in a few minutes.

As soon as he was out of earshot, Hannah propped her hands on her hips. "You told him?"

Greg frowned for a second, then his face cleared. "I didn't tell him about the pregnancy, no. I wanted his take on my situation, whether or not my sister's myeloid leukemia could be the familial version. If so, I was looking for some reassurance. I thought you might want to hear what he had to say, as well."

"Oh." All the anger seeped away. "Sorry, I just—" She'd thought he'd gone behind her back, but somehow admitting that now didn't seem like a wise thing to do.

"I'm trying to respect your privacy here, Hannah, but I'd be irresponsible if I let you think your child was free from risk when that might not be the case. I did a little research and familial myeloid leukemia is autosomal dominant."

"Meaning it only takes one parent to pass down the gene?"

"Yes."

A blip of fear appeared on her radar screen. "Did your sister have the familial version?"

"I don't know, that's why I talked to Bill. My grandfather also died of leukemia at a relatively young age, but it was never identified as to type."

"And your parents?"

"Neither have had it, but they're in their late fifties. There's still time for it to appear." Greg touched her hand. "Will you meet with Bill? Talk to him with me?"

What choice did she have? She couldn't just turn her back on something this important, not without educating herself on the possibilities. "Yes."

"I thought we'd talk in one of the exam rooms here at the hospital. I didn't think you'd want Stella and the rest of the staff overhearing."

She appreciated him thinking about that, even if he'd just scared ten years off her life. "Thank you."

Bill stood off to the side, sipping a cup of coffee, and she followed Greg as he went over to him. "I think we're ready."

They went to one of the far exam rooms. There were already three chairs set up, so Greg had been prepared, just in case. They each took a seat.

Greg started the conversation. "I've already told you about my sister's and grandfather's leukemia."

"You wanted to know more about the familial version, right?"

"Yes."

Bill glanced at Hannah, who by now was sitting with her icy hands clasped in her lap, another invisible hand clenched tight around her heart. He gave her a reassuring smile.

He knew. Without anyone having to say a word.

"Familial acute myeloid leukemia is fairly rare. I'm assuming you've already looked up some information."

"I did, but wanted to hear directly from someone with some expertise in the field, otherwise I'm just guessing."

"Well, if you carry the mutation, it'll be in the CEBPA gene. Was your sister tested for type?"

"I don't know. I was in med school at the time, and things were…tense between me and my parents. They played down the seriousness of her illness—at my sister's request—until it was late in the game."

Greg had talked about his sister being his biggest cheerleader when he'd made his decision to go to med school. Had things been tense with his folks because of that decision?

"I see," said Bill. "We might be able to look up her records and see if her doctors identified anything. Any other cases in your family?"

"Just my maternal grandfather. I don't know of anyone further back, although it's possible."

Bill nodded. "The familial cases I've followed have all had an affected parent, as well. If yours are both healthy, I'd say it's unlikely you carry the defect."

"But you couldn't say for sure."

"No, not without sending a sample of your marrow in for testing."

Hannah spoke up. "That's ridiculous, Greg. Why would you do that? If your parents are healthy, then you probably don't have it. Even if you did, the possibility of passing it on is only…" She glanced at Bill, hoping he'd fill in the blank for her.

"It would be roughly fifty percent."

Hannah's heart stalled. "A fifty percent chance that any child he fathered would contract leukemia?"

"No. Just that they'd carry the gene. I would never recommend prenatal testing unless a definite familial link had been determined. In other words, I'd recommend testing for the affected family first." Bill turned to Greg who'd gone pale.

"If you can get me your sister's records, I'll take a look. I really don't think it's going to go any further than that. If it does, we can have you tested. Familial myeloid follows a pretty set pattern, though. From what you've told me, I'm not seeing any cause for concern here."

Greg stood. "Thanks. I'll make sure you get Bethany's records."

Bethany...such a pretty name. A wave of sorrow washed over her. She hadn't even known Greg's sister's name. But hearing him say it suddenly made her real. Made Hannah even sadder for Greg's loss. The urge to reach across and squeeze his hand came over her.

She stood as well, in an effort to banish the need. "Yes, thank you for talking to us. I appreciate it."

Bill looked from one to the other and smiled. "You're welcome. And good luck. Call me if you have any further questions. Either of you."

With that, he handed Hannah a business card and excused himself, closing the door with a soft click.

"There, do you feel better now?" she asked.

"Not really, no. I still don't know who the hell the father is. Or if I've unintentionally passed something on to it."

This time she didn't resist the urge. She wrapped her hand around his and squeezed. "Look. I wanted a baby and went to a fertility clinic in order to have one. Yes, not knowing whose child it is has put a spanner in the works, but I still want the baby, regardless. If you're feeling guilty, don't. This child is going to be loved more than you could possibly imagine, no matter who the biological father is. Please believe that."

Greg's fingers tightened around hers. "I know it is. You're going to be a wonderful mother. I just wish I could undo what happened between us. That you could have the child you planned to have."

"I already do. Please believe me."

He released her to brush back a short wisp of hair that had fallen over her forehead, smoothing it back with gentle fingers. "Thank you."

"For what?"

"For being you." He leaned over and kissed her cheek. "I'll let you get back to the office."

The meeting had only lasted a half hour so after phoning the clinic to make sure their two o'clock patient hadn't arrived early, Hannah decided to drive the long way back. She needed some time to think before facing anyone at the office. Tiny snowdrops floated across the windshield and blurred the road in front of her. Perfect for her current state of mind, which was just as hazy and indistinct as the view ahead.

Greg's voice had sounded strange when he'd thanked her for being "her." No more insisting that he was going to do right by the baby. If anything, he seemed to be checking things off some invisible list and with each mark he made he backed a little further away from the situation.

It's what she wanted, right? She'd wanted things between them to go back to being simple and uncomplicated. Hadn't wanted any involvement in her life—in her child's life.

But something inside her heart cramped at the thought.

Why? Greg didn't have time for anything else in his life besides work. He'd proven that time and time again. He wasn't likely to change. Not for her. Not for an accidental pregnancy.

It would still just be her and the baby.

She switched on the windshield wipers, and noted a car about a hundred yards in front of her. As she adjusted her speed to maintain a safe distance, something dark and large loomed out of nowhere, moving directly in front of the other car. The vehicle swerved, missing whatever it was—probably a bull moose after a female—but in trying to stay on the road, the driver over-corrected, sliding sideways into a dangerous skid.

Hannah tapped her brakes, praying for the other driver, even as she saw the vehicle leave the road, its passenger door slamming into a nearby tree before coming to a sickening stop. The moose paused, looked in the direction of the accident and then trotted toward a neighboring field as if it hadn't a care in the world.

Oh, God.

After clicking on her hazard lights, she dug for her cell phone, dialing 911 and reporting the accident. She then edged her car forward, getting as close to the other vehicle as she could. Keeping her eye on the moose, which was still visible, she opened her door and half stumbled down the slight embankment as she made her way to the other car. If the moose really was chasing a female, he could turn aggressive in the blink of an eye. As if taunting her, the creature stopped halfway across the field and turned to glare at the two metal interlopers.

Please stay there. She did not want to have to face down a thousand-pound animal while trying to help the occupants of the other vehicle.

She peered inside the driver's side window and saw a woman leaning against her seat belt, the air bag having done nothing to cushion the sideways force of the crash. A trickle of blood made its way down one side of her mouth and dripped from her chin. Hannah tried to open the door, but it was locked.

A cry from somewhere in the back caught her attention, and her eyes widened as she saw an infant carrier strapped into the backseat. It was facing the rear of the car so she couldn't tell what age the child was, but the baby had to be young. The cries grew louder, cutting through the soft plinking of falling snow, which was coming down faster now.

She heard a car stop and glanced up, hoping it was an emergency vehicle, but there'd been no sirens. Nope, it was just another car like hers. Just then a female voice shouted something out the window that sounded like, "Hey, watch out! He's coming back."

She straightened to look, and the blood thrumming through her head rushed straight to her feet. Because the car wasn't the only thing she saw.

The bull moose hadn't drifted away, like she'd hoped it would, but was now headed their way. Although he wasn't moving particularly fast, Hannah knew that could change at any second. He was still on the other side of the road but it wouldn't take much to rile him up. Not at this time of year.

It was then she saw the other moose—a female. The bull had evidently scented her, as evidenced by the animal's head swaying from side to side, white puffs of mist rising from his nostrils as he exhaled. Maybe this was what he'd been after when the woman's car had cut between him and his goal.

Several things went through her mind at once. The car's windows and doors were locked tight, so she couldn't get in, neither could she get the occupants out. The baby inside the car was crying louder now, his wails turning to piercing shrieks, which could serve to further agitate the moose.

And the most terrifying thing of all was the realization that she was standing directly between the huge bull moose and his prospective mate.

Just as that last thought registered, the moose lowered his head and charged.

CHAPTER ELEVEN

GREG'S head swiveled to the right as a familiar name hit his ears.

Hannah Lassiter. The words *moose, roof* and *unknown injuries* also came through. His blood turned to ice in his veins just as the cell phone at his hip began to vibrate.

He glanced at the readout, noting it was the office. He punched the talk button, but before the person on the other end of the line could get in a simple hello, he barked into the receiver, "Where's Hannah?"

Stella's answer came through the line. "I was calling to let you know she phoned here a few seconds ago. She's at the scene of an accident."

"Is she hurt?"

"I don't think so. But a moose has evidently gone on a rampage, and she's trapped. State troopers are on their way and Dispatch is sending an EMT unit, as well."

"Where?"

"Mountain View Road."

"Mountain View? Are you sure?"

"That's what she said."

"Okay, Stella, thanks. I'm heading up there. Page me if there's an emergency."

He clicked off and raced to the hospital parking lot, where he gunned the engine of his BMW and tore out. He had no idea how far out she was, but he could already hear the wail of a siren, probably heading to the scene. He'd just follow behind them.

Hell, had the meeting with Bill Watterson upset her so much that she'd needed to get away from everything? There was no other reason for her driving up Mountain View Road when Debarr was a straight shot to the clinic. Unless she'd needed to think about things.

He pressed the gas pedal in an effort to catch up to the emergency services vehicle. Not many cars were on the road at the moment, so he wasn't worried about creating a problem. All he wanted to do was reach Hannah and make sure she and the baby were okay…that they'd simply come across an accident and had called for help.

Five minutes later, he saw he was wrong. Hannah was perched on top of the roof of a small SUV while a bull moose—as big or bigger than the vehicle itself—stood a few feet away. The black car had a big dent in the driver's side door, whether from the accident or from being charged by the moose, he had no idea.

Even as he thought it, the animal snorted then lowered its head and pushed against the vehicle with its enormous spread of antlers. The wheels on that side of the car left the ground, sending Hannah scrambling for a handhold on the roof racks. The vehicle came crashing back down as the pressure was suddenly released.

Damn.

The EMT guys got out of their vehicle but remained behind the open doors, not daring to make a move toward the enraged animal.

His heart in his throat, he knew if the moose somehow flipped that vehicle, Hannah could be crushed in the process. Or if she wasn't, moose had been known to stomp people into the ground, killing them. Even as he thought it, the moose repeated the act and the vehicle tipped higher than it had the last time.

Without thinking about the consequences, Greg opened the door to his car and got out, rounding the hood as he yelled. "Hey! Over here! Come this way!"

The moose's head came up and the car dropped back into place so fast that Hannah was thrown sideways, her legs coming over the edge right in the space between the moose's antlers. If the animal's glance swung back that way...

Even as he thought it, Hannah kicked, scrambling back onto the roof and hunkering down low. She was from Idaho, from what he understood, but he had no idea how much experience she had with large game.

Moose could be unpredictable, appearing calm one second and then striking out with shocking speed the next. He'd heard of instances where tourists had tried to approach a resting moose, not realizing the calm demeanor could change in the space of a heartbeat. Tragedy had happened on more than one occasion.

Greg took another step, anger rising up fast and quick in his gut. Where the hell were the state troopers? He yelled again, waving his arms to keep the animal focused on him. Maybe it would abandon Hannah and come after him instead. The moose swung around in a ninety-degree arc, one of its massive antlers scraping along the length of the SUV as it did. Hannah looked at him, her frown apparent even from this distance. She shook her head, silently trying to warn him off.

The EMT guys had ventured a little farther from their truck, probably wondering what the crazy cancer doctor thought he was doing.

Just then Greg heard the sound of twin sirens and before he had time to think, two state troopers squealed off the road and in front of his car.

The noise and growing number of bodies was evidently too much for the moose to handle, and he gave one last snort, before whirling and trotting away from the vehicles. Greg waited a second or two to make sure he wasn't coming back, then hurried around the police cars, shouting that he was a doctor when they acted like they might stop him. He met the EMT guys at the stricken SUV and reached up toward Hannah. She let him wrap his hands around her waist and pluck her from the roof.

"You okay?"

She leaned against him for a moment, her body trembling in reaction. "Fine, but we need to get inside the car. There's an injured woman."

One of the EMTs tried the doorhandle then called for everyone to stand back. Greg, his arm around her waist, edged Hannah back and to the side so that she was facing away from the vehicle. The paramedic broke the window with a metal instrument and then reached in to click the automatic door locks. The child in the back, who'd finally stopped crying, started up again at the sound of the glass shattering.

Hannah pulled away and went to the back door, opening it. She quickly checked the child for injuries while he was still strapped into the seat. Her heart wrenched when the child's arms went up in an age-old request to be picked up, "Just a second, sweetheart. I'll get you."

"We've got a broken left clavicle and possible rib fractures up here. Get the back brace." The EMT met her eyes from across the seats. She recognized him from the hospital, and he evidently recognized her as well, because he didn't even question her qualifications. "What have you got back there?"

"I'm not seeing any obvious injuries, the car seat did its job. I think he's just scared."

"Great. We'll transport him anyway, just to be safe."

Hannah unclicked the car seat and gingerly lifted the child from it, ducking down to bring him out of the damaged vehicle. She propped him against her shoulder, rubbing his back through his thick layers of clothing and murmuring softly to him.

The whole world seemed to fade away as she held him, a sense of magic and mystery flowing from his small frame to hers. His crying stopped almost immediately. She turned to Greg with a smile she couldn't contain.

He came forward a step. "He's okay, then?"

"I think he's perfect."

Some dark, powerful force flashed through his gaze as he eyed the pair of them, one side of his mouth finally curving up in a half smile. He started to reach toward her, then his smile faded and he averted his eyes. Without a word he moved away to check on the woman's condition, although the EMTs looked to have everything well in hand.

The two troopers came over and asked for a quick rundown of events, which Hannah relayed to the best of her ability, although she was still shaking both inside and out. One of the officers jotted everything down on a clipboard and then turned it, asking her to sign the statement. She couldn't. Not while holding the baby. "Hold on for a second."

She hurried over to Greg and held the infant toward him. "Can you take him for a minute? I need to sign something for the police."

He looked like he might refuse, but finally took the child from her, holding him awkwardly under the arms. The poor thing's legs dangled straight down, a bemused expression coming over his tiny face.

"No, like this," she instructed, helping him slide an arm under the baby's legs while guiding his other hand to the baby's chest to stabilize him in a kind of modified swing position. Greg seemed stiff and uncomfortable, but something in her chest melted at how he looked holding the baby. He looked...

Like a father.

Biting her lip, she swung away before he saw anything in her eyes. Going back over to the officers, she signed the paperwork. "Let me know if you need anything else."

"We will. Thank you, ma'am. We'll call for a tow truck for the vehicle. Do you have a ride home?"

"Yes, I have my car." She motioned to the emergency lane of the highway, where her car was still sitting, emergency flashers engaged.

As the officers each got into their respective vehicles, filling out papers and talking on their radios, she wrapped her arms around her waist, realizing how very cold she was all of a sudden. She'd leaped out of her car without her coat when she'd seen the accident, her thin turtleneck and camisole the only coverings she'd had on. Everything was damp, including her hair.

The snow had stopped falling at least, but the temperature felt like it was still dropping, or was that because she'd been trapped on top of a freezing car for the past half hour?

Something warm and familiar settled across her shoulders, his scent filling her senses. Greg. But where was...?

"The baby?" she asked.

"The EMTs are loading him and his mom into the truck. They're both going to be fine."

Another hard shiver went through her as more of the cold air made it through her sweater to her skin. A soft curse ruffled her hair. "You're half-frozen. Where's your jacket, Hannah?"

She had to think for a second. "The accident happened so fast, and I wanted to make sure everyone was okay. There was no time to grab it from my car. Then the moose came back…there was no time to do anything but get on top of the SUV."

"Come on, let's get you someplace warm."

Pulling her away from the gathering crowd of onlookers, he helped her into his vehicle and reached over to switch it on. The still-warm engine sent heated air swirling around the interior and Greg got in the other side, holding her icy hands in his own. Between the car's heater vents and the body next to her, warmth slowly penetrated her frozen core.

"Better?" he asked.

"Mmm…" she murmured, leaning closer with another shiver. "Your hands are so warm."

He shifted to put an arm around her and pulled her toward him. Hannah had no idea how his body could generate so much heat, especially as he was coatless and hatless as well. All she knew was that if she could wriggle her way beneath his skin right now, she would.

They sat there for what seemed like forever then he broke the silence. "Give me your car keys."

She sighed, not moving, as the heat continued to work its magic. "They're in the car, along with my purse." She needed to go, but couldn't work up the energy to prise herself from Greg's body or from the interior of the car.

"Wait here. I'll be right back."

She cringed when he pulled away, depriving her of his warmth. The sensation was even worse when he opened the car door and slid out. Then he shut it again and Hannah leaned back in her seat, letting her eyes close. The combination of the meeting with the geneticist and the adrenaline from the moose attack did what several sleepless nights had been unable to accomplish: send a wave of exhaustion over her. She yawned and let her body go utterly limp.

Just a second or two, that's all she needed. Then she'd be able to drum up enough energy to drive back to the clinic and see to the rest of their patients. She tried to remember whose names she'd seen on the schedule that morning, but there was nothing inside her head but a big black hole. It was as if she'd been drained of everything. Her hands went to her stomach, rubbing it softly as she gave way to the tiredness seeping through her.

Vaguely, she was aware that Greg had returned and that his car was now in motion, but no power under heaven could have wrenched her eyelids apart. Instead, she sat there, her head lolling back and forth on the seat as the vehicle made gentle turns for the next several minutes before stopping.

The clinic. They must have arrived. Time to wake up.

But her muscles felt as floppy as a piece of lettuce that had been frozen and then defrosted. The car pulled forward again for a few seconds, then the purr of the engine cut off. A door opened and closed, but this time no icy gusts of wind blew across her cheeks, just slightly heated air.

Her eyelids finally obeyed her commands to open, her brain struggling to make sense of what she was seeing. They were inside some kind of white enclosure. The clinic didn't have a parking garage.

Didn't matter. Maybe Greg would just let her sit here and sleep a while longer. Then her door opened.

No such luck, evidently.

However, instead of nudging her to get her to move, her seat belt unclicked—when had she buckled it?—and something soft and fluffy enveloped her before she was lifted from the car.

Lifted?

Oh, but the girls at the office were going to have a field day if Greg carried her into the clinic. She tried to protest, shifting in his arms, only to have a soft voice shush her, tell her it was okay to sleep for a while.

It was?

Well, she wasn't going to argue with him. Besides, her lids were already sliding shut again.

A minute later something soft met her back, her shoes came off, and the fluffy object from the car was tucked around her. She could have sworn warm lips pressed against her forehead for a long second but that must be part of the wonderful dream she was having. Whatever it was, she was willing to sink deep into it for a few minutes.

Then she'd rouse herself back to the real world and all of its worries.

Right now there was just her and Greg and this decadent sensation of…of… She struggled to put her finger on it, before settling on the only word that came to mind: *peace*.

Greg's patients were at the clinic, and he was at home. Something unheard of.

But from the moment he'd felt the sheer iciness of Hannah's hands, he'd known what he was going to do. He asked one of the police officers to see to it that her car made it to his house. The officer had glanced toward Greg's car, where Hannah was half-asleep, and nodded. Then Greg retrieved her handbag and called Stella, giving her an abbreviated version of the story.

"Poor thing," the other woman said. "We can cover for you this afternoon. There are only three patients left. Take her home and let her get some sleep."

Greg was pretty sure Stella was referring to Hannah's home and not his own, but somehow that was where they wound up.

He didn't dare stretch out beside her on his bed, and there were no guest bedrooms in his house. His hours precluded having any overnight visitors—female or otherwise. His parents had never asked to stay with him, opting for a nearby hotel room on the one occasion they'd come from Ketchikan to visit.

One visit in ten years.

Damn. He hadn't been a very good son since his sister had died. It was easy to blame it on the distance between Anchorage and Ketchikan, but how hard was it to pick up a telephone and give them a call? Then again, his father had held a grudge for a very long time after Greg had turned down his offer—maybe he still did. It was something they'd never talked through and resolved. And his mother had been unwilling to take sides. Bethany had been the only one who could see through to Greg's heart. And now she was gone.

Shaking away those troubling thoughts, he moved back to the situation at hand. What was he going to do about Hannah? He'd allowed her to eat into his office hours in a way he'd never let anyone else do, not even his parents.

It was because of her pregnancy. It had to be.

You don't even know if the child is yours, Greg.

When does it stop? When you have a patient go into crisis and die because you aren't there for them—just like Bethany's doctor had done?

No. He'd vowed to be different. To be someone his patients could call day or night. Just like he'd urged Claire Taylor to do.

He remembered Hannah's comment about seeing him rush past the chemo room from time to time. Yes, he'd begun peeking in there in recent weeks and greeting his patients when he saw them, but what about before? What about when it had been Hannah sitting in one of those chairs?

He'd been oblivious, just like he'd accused his sister's doctor of being.

Hell. His thoughts jumped from one thing to the other, but that assurance that he was doing the right thing was no longer in the spot it used to be.

The situation with Hannah had messed with his head, and he wasn't sure he was ever going to be able to go back to who he was before. Neither was he sure he wanted to.

So what did he want?

He glanced toward the dark hallway leading to his bedroom.

He wanted something he couldn't possibly have. But that didn't stop him from wanting it just the same.

CHAPTER TWELVE

THE smell of bacon roused her from a blissful dream. One where Greg held their child in his arms and slid beside her on the bed, leaning over to kiss her forehead.

She smiled up at him as she drew her fingers across his cheek and murmured that she loved him even more than…

Bacon?

Her eyes flew open. Yes, she'd just told a man she loved him more than a strip of nitrite-loaded meat. Okay, so it had been in her dream, not in real life.

And she didn't love him…not more than bacon, not less than bacon. Not at all.

She blinked as the room came into focus. Wait. This wasn't her bedroom. The beige microfiber blanket wasn't hers either. She remembered the moose ramming the car, the injured woman inside, the cold and this very blanket being carefully folded around her as she'd been lifted from the car.

Lifted from the car…

Oh, no! She hadn't gone back to work. And what about their patients?

Had Greg returned to the clinic and finished the workday without her?

Great. He now thought she was less than useless. It had to be all the messed-up hormones that went along with a pregnancy. She was just going to have to push through them. She couldn't just curl up on a cot at the office whenever the urge hit her.

Turning her head, she looked at the pillow on the other side of the bed. It was still flat across the top. No indentation from a head, and the bedspread hadn't been pulled back. Greg hadn't slept here at all.

Maybe it was still today. No, wait, yesterday. She glanced at the clock. Seven...squinting, she noted there was no red glowing dot beside the p.m. symbol, which meant it was morning.

So she'd slept here all night.

And the scent of bacon meant Greg was still at home. He was normally in the office by now, catching up on paperwork.

Except it was Saturday. At least she thought it was. She did the math in her head. Yes, Saturday. She assumed Greg didn't normally work weekends, although she wouldn't put anything past the man. He'd certainly gone in that Saturday when Claire had called.

A soft knock sounded at the door, and she realized he'd closed it at some point. "Come in."

The door opened and her boss appeared in the entrance, his hair damp, a plaid flannel shirt rolled up his forearms. She hadn't taken him for a flannel kind of guy, but she kind of liked the rugged air it gave him.

"How are you feeling?"

She cleared her throat before answering. "Guilty."

His brows went up. "Why?"

"Um, I was supposed to be working yesterday, and instead I conked out in your car on the way back. Sorry about that. Did you have to see to the rest of the patients on your own?"

There was a short pause before he responded. "Stella took care of it."

"Took care of…" Another wave of guilt washed over her. "You didn't go back either?"

He took a step inside the room. "There was nothing urgent. I'll go in for a few hours later today."

So he did work on weekends. She vaguely remembered him coming into her hospital room the day after her surgery. That had been a Saturday, as well. At least, she thought it was. Her memories of those days were a little suspect as she'd been an emotional wreck.

He had to work, and here she was lounging in his house. No wonder he was trying to wake her up. "Sorry. I'll get dress—" Okay, so she'd never gotten *un*dressed. And exactly how was she supposed to get home? "Where's my car?"

"It's in the driveway."

That was strange. She remembered him asking about her keys but just, like her surgery, those memories were cloaked in a foggy haze that she couldn't quite penetrate. "How did it get here?"

"One of the police officers said he'd see to it. He put the keys through the mailbox slot on the front door."

She sat up. "Have you heard anything about the woman and her baby?"

He smiled and leaned against the doorpost. "You mean the ones currently in my bed or the ones from yesterday?"

Yesterday. So she had slept all afternoon and all night. In Greg's bed, of all things. "Yesterday."

"I checked this morning. Mom has a slight concussion, broken collarbone and some bruised ribs. The baby is with his father, who flew back from a business trip to be with them."

Hannah's heart tightened. What if something similar

happened to her? There would be no husband to come running. Where would her baby go?

Her parents would fly in and take care of the child.

Why did that thought bring her no comfort? "So she's going to be okay."

"Yes. They'll probably keep her for observation one more day then they'll release her."

"I'm glad she's okay."

Greg moved the rest of the way into the room and sat on the edge of the bed, smoothing a few strands of hair back from her temples. "As for you, let's try not to bait any more moose traps in the near future, okay?"

"Believe me, if I'd known that big guy was going to come at me, I'd have had second thoughts about getting out of my car."

"Sure you would."

Okay, so he had her there. She hadn't known how badly hurt the other car's occupants had been. There's no way she'd have waited around for the moose to decide the vehicle wasn't worth its trouble. But she also wouldn't have purposely gone running across its path either. "I wasn't trying to get myself killed."

"That's good." There was a pause. "I wouldn't want to have to replace you."

His eyes held hers, and she tried to decipher the changing emotions she saw in them, but failed. All she knew was that he wasn't angry, and that fact made her relax. "Admit it. You kind of like having me around." When his eyes darkened to black, she realized how that had sounded and quickly added, "At the clinic, I mean."

He didn't respond for a second or two then his hand withdrew. "Of course."

A sudden awkward silence fell between them, which

she tried to break with the first thing she could think of. "Is that bacon I smell?"

"It is. I've also whipped up an omelet. Interested in sharing?"

The words brought back memories of another time they'd shared food. At the clinic. She'd fallen asleep there as well, and disastrous things had happened afterward. Better not to keep sitting here, especially not after the dream she'd had before he'd knocked on the door. "Definitely, if there's enough."

He stood and held out a hand. "There's plenty."

She let him help her out of bed, the tangle of blankets causing her to career forward when she tried to get her feet underneath herself. He caught her, a hand at her back holding her against him for a second or two before releasing her again and taking a step back.

"I, ah, need to use your restroom first, if that's okay," she said.

"It's right through there." He nodded at a door on the other side of the bedroom. "I'll get the plates ready, so come out when you're ready. Do you take butter or jam on your toast?"

"Both?" Bad for her, she knew, but something about the taste of warm melty butter mixed with fruit was one she hadn't been able to give up.

"Both it is. I'll see you in a few minutes."

Hannah went into the restroom and put her hands on the sink as she stared into the mirror. She must have slept like a rock, because her hair wasn't sticking up at all angles like it normally did. She'd be glad when it grew out enough to rake back into a ponytail or put up in a clip. For now, she settled with dragging her fingers through it and coaxing it to settle into place. She found a tube of toothpaste in a cup and squirted a dab on her finger, scrubbing her teeth as best she could. She wasn't about to ask if he had a spare toothbrush in a package somewhere. Not because she wouldn't love to clean her teeth but because she didn't want to think of him keeping spare toothbrushes on hand for occasional overnight guests—of the female variety.

She had to admit she didn't hear a whole lot of rumors about her boss being paired up with women at the hospital, and she knew he wasn't involved with anyone at the clinic as everyone there was either married or spoken for. But that didn't mean he didn't meet people somewhere else.

When would he even have the time, though, with a schedule like his?

Sighing, she finished washing up the best she could before following her nose. She found Greg sliding the second half of a fluffy-looking omelet onto a plate. "I thought you said you didn't cook."

He glanced up, his eyes going over her from head to toe. "You're seeing my entire repertoire. I don't normally eat anything but breakfast at home."

"What do you eat when you're off duty?"

"I manage."

That sounded suspiciously like wolfing down takeout food night after night.

He set a plastic disposable plate in front of her across the small bar. Strange. Did he not have a set of real dishes? The sink was empty as well—and there was no sign of a dishwasher—so they weren't all dirty.

Now that she had a moment to look around, she saw that the great room was as sparsely furnished as the bedroom had been. A couch and an easy chair sat across from a large-screen television, which was hung on a wall, but there were no coffee tables or end tables. There was a beige washcloth resting on the hardwood floor beside the recliner, which she could imagine him resting drinks on.

A state-of-the-art treadmill was pushed against the far wall, a handtowel slung over its digital panel. The machine's incline was set to a painful-looking angle, but that was it—no other furniture except the two barstools they were currently using.

And other than the floor, there were no flat surfaces to set pictures or knick-knacks on. "Did you just move in or something?"

He sat across from her at the bar. "No, I've lived here for about five years, why?"

"It's just…empty."

Five years. And he had nothing to show for it.

Greg's glance trailed around the room before he shrugged. "I'm not here that much."

If she'd had any doubts about him pushing himself to the point of neglect, he'd set them to rest. Her own house was filled with things that made her happy—baskets of soft quilts and afghans beside a comfortable couch. Just right for settling in with a book or a chick flick. Some of her grandmother's things were sprinkled here and there, and an old Victorian rocking chair sat in a place of honor in her living room.

Her front room drew her in the moment she hit that front door and helped her relax. The first thing she did was kick off her shoes in the entryway—symbolic of leaving her workday behind her—and pad across the deep-pile carpet on the floor.

She didn't have time for a pet other than three fish in a large terracotta pot on the back patio. The constant sound of trickling water from the submersible pump was soothing, as were the goldfish—rescued from the kill tank at a local pet store—who came up to greet her, their mouths opening and closing to an internal beat. She liked to imagine them dancing and singing, moving to the tune of the falling water. She'd gotten her little guys soon after her treatments had finished and they'd grown and flourished. Just like her.

Greg's sterile environment, on the other hand, made her feel lonely, somehow, even though it wasn't her house.

"Hannah? Are you okay?"

Greg's voice interrupted her thoughts, and she realized she'd been staring off into space—or, worse, staring at him. "I'm fine. Just feeling slightly out of it still."

"You had quite a day yesterday." He forked a bite of omelet into his mouth, and she glanced down at her own plate. Eggs filled with what looked like a creamy mixture of broccoli and cheese, expertly folded and cut in half. Toast with…yep, butter *and* grape jelly, and four neat slices of bacon.

"Wow, I never eat this much in the morning."

"It's probably time you started to."

She blinked for a second then realized he was talking about her pregnancy. "I guess you're right. It's not all about me anymore."

Greg's fork faltered on its way back to his mouth, and he set it on his plate. "I guess it's not," he murmured.

Something about the way he said it made another wave of loneliness hit her. Not for herself this time but for him. "Sometimes it's good to be reminded of that."

If he understood what she was getting at, he ignored it, steering the conversation in another direction instead. "I forgot to ask. Do you want to put a call in to your doctor and have her check you over after what happened yesterday?"

"It's Saturday."

"So?"

"I feel fine. Besides, I'm sure she has a life outside work." As soon as she'd said it, she realized he really *didn't* see what the big deal was. Did he assume that all doctors kept the kinds of hours that he did? Surely he knew better.

"It's her job."

"Are you serious?" She took a bite of her omelet to stifle the flow of words that wanted to pour out of her mouth.

"She's an obstetrician. I'm sure she's used to working crazy hours. Babies can't be programmed to arrive during a nine-to-five workday." The words came out with a bitter edge she didn't understand.

She swallowed her food. "Exactly. Which is why I don't want to call her for any little thing."

"You were attacked by a moose—banged around by him. Isn't it better to be safe than sorry?"

"I'm fine. Not even bruised. I think my recovery consisted of sleeping." She set her jaw. "I'm not calling her."

"Fine." A flash of anger went through his eyes, but he didn't say anything more.

There was no sound for the next few minutes, other than eating. Hannah kept her head down, wishing her hair was long enough to shade her face and afford her a bit more privacy.

"I'm sorry. You're right." Greg's soft voice came across the bar, and she looked up in surprise as he continued. "I forget that other doctors don't get the kind of satisfaction from their jobs that I do."

"Just because they don't work themselves into the ground it doesn't mean they don't find satisfaction in what they do. I enjoy having weekends off. It helps me recharge my batteries."

"I'm not judging you or anyone else. It's simply how I've chosen to live my life."

How he'd chosen to live his life. So he'd made a conscious decision at some point in time to work this hard? If so, she thought she knew when that had been.

"Because of your sister?"

His fork stopped halfway to his mouth. "What do you mean?"

"You said you became an oncologist because of her." She forced the words past the lump in her throat. "Is that why you work so hard?"

"Yes." The word came out as simply and smoothly as silk. Things clicked into place a little bit further.

"You once said it was because you wanted to help others like her, but is it more than that? Do feel guilty for being alive? Are you paying some type of penance?"

He seemed to consider that for a minute. "No, but we were pretty close. Her death came as a shock—it was more sudden than anyone expected, a couple of days after one of her chemo treatments. Her doctor was nowhere to be found when she got to the hospital. I never want that to happen with my patients."

"You can't be available every second of every day."

"No, but I also don't have to live at the golf course or the ski slopes, depending on the season."

"Are you saying that's what your sister's doctor did?"

"He has quite a reputation in Ketchikan, from what I've learned."

"That's terrible. I'm so sorry."

His left shoulder lifted and fell. "It was a long time ago. I'm over it."

Was he? His behavior said he wasn't.

"It never seems that long ago." She spoke from the experience of her own health crisis. Maybe someday in the distant future she'd look back at her cancer as some tiny speck in her rearview mirror instead of the huge black mass that stood just off to the side, waiting to slide into her path and derail her dreams. Just like that moose from yesterday had sent the other car careening off the road. It could happen suddenly. Without warning.

Even as she thought it, the fear inched closer, rising in front of her.

You're fine, Hannah. Healthy. Strong.

She pulled in a deep cleansing breath, let it back out. Sucked down another.

A hand covered hers. "Hey, I'm sorry. I keep forgetting you've been down that path, too."

"It's stupid. I just can't seem to get past it, to…" Horror of horror, tears washed up her throat and gathered in her eyes. She blinked furiously, trying to suppress them in any way she could.

Greg got up from his seat and came around to the other side of the bar, wrapping his arms around her shoulders and pressing her face into the solid warmth of his chest. "I know the feeling. I promise you, I do. If I could do something to make sure the cancer doesn't ever come back, I would. I swear it."

"I know." She sniffed. "It's not you. It's me. And I know you'd do the same for your sister, if you could. You're trying to make it up to her with each patient you save."

He cupped her face, tilting it so she was forced to look at him. His thumbs stroked across her cheekbones sending a slow shiver through her that had nothing to do with the cold. Nothing to do with fear. "You're probably one of the few people who could ever understand that. One of the few who could fathom why I never wanted children…a wife."

A stabbing pain went through her chest, and she tried to pull away, only to have him hold her in place. She'd known this all along, was a fool to believe him when he'd said he wanted to be involved with this child, if it was his.

He didn't want a baby. Any baby.

"Let me go, Greg, please." Otherwise the tears she'd

successfully fought back could start gushing through the crack in her soul.

"I can't." His eyes bored into hers. "I didn't want kids, but the thought that this—" one hand left her face to splay low across her tummy "—might be mine has messed with my head in ways you can't even imagine."

Maybe that kiss on her forehead yesterday hadn't been her imagination after all. Maybe he was just as confused as she seemed to be. She'd gone from wanting to stay as far away from him as she could to wanting to be closer to him than any human being possibly could. If nothing else, she could admit it.

"Mine, too." She forced a smile. "It was a whole lot easier when I thought those cells came from the end of a catheter."

"Easier." He smiled back at her. "But not quite as much fun."

Any remaining tears receded at his gentle, teasing tone. "You know what they say about natural being better than modified. We could always put a stamp on you and call you organic."

He laughed, then his head dipped, his cheek sliding against hers. The still rough whiskers from last night scraped across her skin, and his scent filled her nostrils. Then his lips were at her ear, causing gooseflesh to rise on her arms as he whispered into it, "I think what's going on between us is pretty organic."

His words sent a jet of raw need spurting through her system, sweeping along her senses until every cell in her body was waiting in hungry anticipation.

Those cells didn't have long to wait because he soon retraced the same path his cheek had taken, only this time with his mouth. When he reached her lips he hovered there for a second or two as if debating options.

Only there was no option, even he had to see that. "Kiss me, Greg."

Very slowly, his hand moved to her nape, fingers sliding into the short strands of her hair. "I don't want to do this."

Oh, yes, he did. She could feel it in the tension radiating from him, in the way his hand applied just enough pressure to keep her from moving away from him. And Hannah gloried in it. Rejoiced that a man—*this* man—could be so attracted to her that he was willing to ignore his rational side just to have her. And he wanted her in spite of the effects of the chemotherapy that were still very evident in her body and mind—her short hair, her scars, her moments of unbridled terror.

He didn't seem to care about any of that.

And hanging in the balance was everything he claimed to want in life—everything he said he *didn't* want.

That didn't stop his head from beginning that fatal descent, didn't stop his lips from meeting hers in a delirious, electrifying kiss from which there was no hope of escape.

And the last thing Hannah wanted was to escape.

All she wanted, was him.

CHAPTER THIRTEEN

Five seconds after Hannah wrapped her arms around his neck, strong hands swept her off the barstool and carried her somewhere. She didn't open her eyes to look. Didn't care where they were going.

All she knew was that there was nothing like the sensation of this man's lips on hers, the crazy things his touch did to her on the inside—and on the outside, where her nipples were already pressing against her shirt, her body moistening in anticipation of what was going to happen.

What she *hoped* was going to happen.

Greg moved her in a way that no other man ever had. From the moment he'd come onto the scene, her life had gone topsy-turvy. In some ways those changes had been terrible beyond belief, and in other ways they had been more wonderful than words could express.

This was one such moment.

He kicked at a door, muttering a curse under his breath when it evidently bounced back and caught him in the shoulder. She smiled against his lips. "Oh, an ouchie. Do you want me to kiss it?"

"No." The growled word was followed by a quick hard press of his mouth to hers. "I have better places for you to kiss."

A wave of need rose up inside her, and just like the time

in his office she wanted him to consume her in a fiery rush, wanted him so badly that she shook with it. It made her crazy, confused her in ways that she'd never been before.

She loved it. And hated it.

And where she should grab on to the latter thought and start waving it like a white flag in front of her raging libido, her mind embraced the former, to the point where she didn't know if the idea of love referred to the man himself or what he did to her.

Please don't let it be the man.

The plea had barely been processed when her back met the same soft surface it had yesterday afternoon, only this time Greg followed her down. And his reassuring kiss was not on her forehead but had moved to her throat where the touch was anything but comforting. Instead it made her squirm against him, arching her neck to give him better access.

"I thought you had places you wanted *me* to kiss."

"I lied." One of his jeans-clad legs nudged between her thighs, the weight of it resting on her most sensitive spot. She resisted the urge to shift her hips to increase the pressure.

His mouth slid down to her collarbone, licking across something before kissing it gently.

The scar from her port.

The almost reverent act made her breath catch and tears once again appeared on the horizon, but he'd already moved lower, to where the V of her shirt dipped, showing the slightest curve of her breast.

His lifted his head, all teasing gone. "Do you want me to use protection?"

Her mind whirred. She was already pregnant, had already had him without anything between them. It seemed silly to backtrack at this late point. "No."

Greg moved back up and took her mouth again, showing her with his tongue and teeth that he approved of her decision. Her own heart threatened to hammer its way from her chest as he mimicked the long strokes from a few weeks ago. She reached up to hold him against her, needing him to continue doing exactly what he was doing.

He didn't disappoint, sliding his left hand to her breast, finding her nipple even through the padding of her bra. Sensation arced from her breast to her center, where his leg was still exerting delicious pressure.

Moaning against his mouth, she couldn't stop herself from lifting her hips this time, and a wave of need hit her system when she did, moving through her like wildfire. She pressed closer still.

Greg reacted by shifting his weight and removing temptation.

"No! What are you doing?"

He kissed her mouth before answering. "Slowing things down a little bit. Last time was—" he paused "—great, but I want this to last."

Last? Who cared about lasting? She wanted him, and she wanted him now.

But Greg evidently had no intention of letting her call the shots because despite her low sound of displeasure he smoothed her hair off her forehead then kissed her eyes, her cheeks, the tip of her chin.

When he acted like he was going to avoid her mouth, she put her hands to the back of his head and pulled him to her. He obliged, his lips sliding across hers repeatedly, the subtle friction nearly driving her insane before he finally kissed her the way she wanted to be kissed.

She melted with a sigh.

"Better?" he whispered.

"Much."

Her neck, which had been straining up in an effort to reach him, relaxed into the pillows with a sigh as he deepened the kiss, following her down. Her hands, no longer needing their feverish grip on his head, wandered over his back, feeling the bunching of muscles as he moved in time with the give and take of their joined mouths.

The same way those muscles would react when they were joined in other areas. Would he have to get rid of the bed afterward, like he'd done with his desk?

She almost laughed. These little rendezvous could end up costing him a fortune if this became a regular event.

No. Don't think about that right now. Just enjoy the time you have together. That's what you vowed to do, right? Take life as it came and not worry about what might happen in the future.

Yes. That was better.

So much better that…

Her hands went from holding on to shoving at his chest.

His "What are you—?" was drowned by her laughter as she turned the tables, flipping him onto his back in a smooth move that would have made any ju jitsu instructor proud.

"I assume you had a reason for doing that?" His brows went up.

"Mmm-hmm." She wiggled her hips against his rigid length. "I'm taking charge."

He groaned. "I thought we'd already settled this. We're going slow."

"I'm not interested in slow." To prove her point, she sat up, her legs straddling his hips—where she could still feel a definite spark of interest—and stripped off her shirt. Her bra followed a second later. She trailed the garment across his lips, up one of his arms. He wrapped his hand around it and flung it to the side.

"Hannah…"

"Spoilsport." She leaned forward, her breasts flattening against his chest, and used her hand to cover his mouth. "I've already decided how this is going to go, so no use trying to stop me."

He nipped at her hand until she removed it. "Believe me, I have no intention of stopping you."

"Well, good." She sat up again. "Then you won't mind if I do this."

She slid higher, until she was on his belly, her hand reaching behind her to find the zipper of his jeans and that delicious hard ridge that lay just beneath it. Placing her palm over the swell of his flesh, she stroked him for a second or two, until he sat up in a rush, dumping her back onto his lap.

"My turn," he said, his breathing not quite steady.

His hands slid over the skin of her back, hot and urgent as they headed down, edging beneath the waistband of her slacks and cupping her bare butt.

She smiled. "Oh, I like that."

"Yes? Then how about this?" He jerked her forward until she was pressed tight against him, his strong grip rocking her along his length. The breath she'd been holding rushed from her lungs in an audible gasp as a sudden jolt of sensation gripped her center. From zero to a hundred in under a second and a half.

Her eyes closed at the heady knowledge that he was using her body to massage his own, to heighten his pleasure, even as hers skyrocketed, as well. Her thighs, forced wide by his hips, made her fully aware that only a few centimeters of clothing separated them, and even that couldn't stop the torturous friction that had her rushing closer to oblivion with each passing second.

She gripped his shoulders for all she was worth as he increased the speed and pressure, his own body static, while hers rose and fell. Her teeth dug into her lower lip, knowing if she was going to ask him to slow down, it needed to be now. But she'd started this…claimed she didn't want to go slow…so he was giving her exactly what she'd demanded. What she wanted. What she…

The black depths of his pupils appeared before her as she struggled in vain to stay afloat, but this wave was too tall, too wild, too…

She buried her face against his neck with a hoarse cry as everything inside of her seemed to implode all at once, her mind blanking out as her body shattered into a thousand pieces and then fell back together again in a rush.

Hannah was vaguely aware that while Greg's hands still held her tightly against him, he was no longer dragging her along at a punishing pace. But his body was still hard. Still tense.

She leaned back to look at him, trying to breathe as she gathered her thoughts. "Wh-what, exactly, was that supposed to be?"

His crooked grin was unrepentant. "That was fast. Just like you wanted."

Fast.

It had been that. And more. Her legs were still trembling from the force of her explosion.

"What about you?"

"Me?" His hands came up, one splaying across the middle of her back and the other cupping her head. "I already told you. I'm all about slow."

As if to demonstrate exactly what he meant, he laid her gently backward an inch at a time, until she was again lying on the bed, her head at the opposite end this time. Once she was there, he reached down and unbuttoned her jeans, the act taking her all the way back to the first step on the stairway she'd just climbed. She looked at the distance from here to where she'd just been and sighed.

Mmm.

Slow sounded like a very, very good idea.

"Annie, look what someone made for you." Greg brought out a neon purple hat one of his other patients—who'd seen Annie in his office a week ago—had knitted for her out of some kind of soft furry yarn.

The child's eyes widened as she reached for it, her fingers sinking deep as she hugged it to her. Her happiness contrasted with the bittersweet emotions circling within his own chest.

"It's so soft," she said. "Just like my kitty's fur. Are you sure it's for me?"

He smiled, the wonder on her face tugging at something inside him. "Is your favorite color purple?" He nodded at the lavender tank top covering her thin frame.

"Yes. But how did the person know what color I liked?"

He glanced up at Hannah, who stood in the doorway, a file pressed to her belly as she watched the scene unfold.

"A little birdie told her."

Annie laughed and, in a quick move, tugged the hat down over her bare head, showing it was a perfect fit. "I can wear this under the hood on my winter coat."

"You can wear it whenever you want to. And you'll stay warmer than I will, as I don't have a special hat."

Hannah's teeth came down on her lip, and her hand went behind her back. He only realized she was trying to find the doorknob when the door opened and she slid through it and around the corner. Was she crying?

Pregnancy hormones.

Even as the thought pressed in on him, he rejected it. Hadn't his own eyes moistened when Martha Brookstone's daughter had come by the office a week ago with an update on her mother? The hospice had been wonderful to them, she'd said. "Mom is weaker, but still insists on knitting hats for your patients." When she'd seen Annie in the waiting room she'd told her mother about her, and Martha had used some of her precious remaining energy to knit one last hat. She'd passed away yesterday morning, but her daughter had brought the hat in anyway, insisting her mother would have wanted Annie to have it.

His throat tightened with sadness and frustration. He hated cancer. Fought it with every ounce of strength he had, and yet it was never enough. He couldn't save every patient, no matter how hard he threw himself into his job.

He'd barely made it back to his office for his Saturday appointments after spending the morning in bed with Hannah. While the sex had been amazing, the closeness hadn't lasted longer than it had taken her to retrieve her clothes. She'd gotten up and showered, then slid out the door and out of his life.

Well, not out of his life because she was still here at the office a week later. But they'd both kept their distance, neither speaking about what had happened between them. In fact, Hannah was the consummate professional. Cool as a cucumber.

He should be glad. But he wasn't. He'd rather she came at him in a fury, asking what the hell he thought he was playing at.

Only he had no idea. All he knew was that whatever it was, it felt like fire...and silk. At the same time. Seducing him even while it burned him to the core. Hannah had hit the nail on the head: it was like playing with matches... thousands of them.

He brought his attention back to Annie and her mother. "That hat looks perfect on you."

Annie's mom smiled. "Tell the angel who knitted this we said thank you."

Greg wasn't about to tell her that Annie's "angel" had earned her wings and flown away, never to return.

He set up the next appointment and made sure the treatments were still on track. The child hugged him around the waist before she and her mother left, the fuzzy strands of the hat waving as she bounced her way down the hall. A very different little girl from the pale, despondent soul who'd sat silently in her chair.

Maybe he should see if he could find someone to knit hats for him on commission. If they could raise one person's spirits, it was worth it—because he was certain, no matter what the scientific world might say, the mind did play a role in a patient's recovery. Sometimes the illness was too great, but finding ways to rev up the immune system was a good thing. And if a simple hat could do that, then he was all for it.

Hannah came wandering down the hallway, another chart in her hands. "How'd it go?" she asked.

"You saw. She loved it." He paused. "You know, I've been thinking, maybe we could find someone who could knit those on a regular basis."

"That's a great idea. I used to knit, maybe I could—"

"No."

She frowned. "What?"

"I'm not putting anything more on you right now." He should have kept quiet about the idea, but he'd never expected her to immediately raise her hand and offer.

"You're not putting anything on me, Greg. I'm volunteering. Once I get home at night, I don't have all that much to do. Knitting would be a welcome distraction. I just need to practice to get back in the swing of things."

"You should be resting, not taking on more work. Especially now." His glance went to her stomach, trying to banish the thought that he knew exactly how it looked without a stitch of clothing. "When's your next doctor's appointment?"

"In a couple of weeks. She wants to do an ultrasound and check the position of the baby because I was on fertility drugs."

He glanced down the hallway to make sure no one was around, remembering Hannah saying she didn't want anyone to know yet. "What do the drugs have to do with position?"

There was a pause, and her cheeks lit up like red balloons. "Well…she wants to make sure there's only one."

"One?" A light bulb flashed inside his skull, blinding him for a second. Of course. Fertility drugs could cause more than one egg to be released. Oh, hell. "She thinks you're carrying more than one?"

She stepped closer and put a hand on his arm, making him realize his voice had risen to match his skyrocketing blood pressure. "Relax, she doesn't think anything at this point. She goes through the same procedure on all her fertility patients."

Relax? That was kind of hard when his brain was filtering through all kinds of scenarios. None of them good. What if Hannah did end up carrying more than one? What did that mean for him?

A nightmare, that's what. One that was increasing exponentially.

Even as he thought it, the opposite picture rose in his mind of Hannah propped up in bed with a baby in each arm, smiling up at him. There was a diamond on her left hand and the babies were a melding of their mother's facial features and his. Once inside his head, the image took hold, looking nothing like the nightmare he'd imagined.

Instead, the idyllic scene looked like a dream come true.

CHAPTER FOURTEEN

THE hat was lopsided, the lump along one side taking on the appearance of an ear flap, rather than a smooth round head covering. Maybe she could make one for her own baby this way.

Except there was no guarantee she could replicate the mistake—or have it come out the same for each ear. She needed a pattern to do that.

Hannah sighed and ripped the stitches out until she reached the part where things had first gone wonky, counting the rows carefully. The circular needles made for a seamless construction, which meant she wouldn't have to sew it together at the end, but keeping track of where she'd decreased her stitches was also more complicated. And she was only using regular knitting yarn right now. If she wanted to make those furry hats that were all the rage, it was going to be even harder because that kind of yarn had a lot of fringy fibers. Maybe Greg was right, she shouldn't be taking this on. Except hearing the constant click of the needles soothed her in a way that her own thoughts couldn't nowadays.

What Greg didn't know wouldn't hurt him. And once she brought in her first finished hat, he'd be so impressed with her talents that he wouldn't say another word.

Right. So why hadn't she just barreled her way through

that disagreement and stood her ground? Because it had been easier not to. And she didn't like fighting with him.

Yes, she liked doing other things with him instead. Just the memory of that day they'd spent together made her stomach tighten. He had gone slow that second time. And by the end she'd been quaking with need and asking him to hurry all over again. He had, and the result had been an experience that still had the power to wake her up at night and turn her into a blathering idiot when she saw him at the office day after day.

What did that make her?

Infatuated.

He was the doctor who had treated her during her cancer scare. When she'd hugged him all those months ago, her heart had zigged when it should have zagged, sending her to a place she didn't want to be. Wasn't that what this was all about? She saw it happen time and time again with patients. They got a crush on the person they credited with saving their lives.

And if anyone deserved all that adulation, it was Greg.

Only it wasn't right for her to add one more set of doe eyes onto an already overburdened doctor.

Except, as far as she knew, he'd never shown a hint of attraction for any other of his patients, not even Claire Taylor—for whom she knew Greg had a soft spot.

Instead, he'd been a perfect gentleman during her treatments.

All it had taken was one weak moment on both their parts to start an avalanche neither of them seemed capable of stopping.

But she had to. He'd made it plain he didn't want a wife and a family no matter what he'd said during their last encounter. Besides, what had he said exactly? That he hadn't wanted a child…until the thought of this one being his had messed with his head?

So he hadn't wanted a family, until one had been forced on him.

Maybe his whole overdeveloped sense of responsibility had switched itself on and tricked him into thinking he wanted the baby. As a way to make him step up to the plate.

That was the last thing Hannah wanted. Especially as her own feelings about her boss were jumbled and confused.

If she wasn't careful, her heart could be snared in a trap of its own making. And then where would she be? In love with a man who could never truly love her back—whose desire to honor his sister's memory eclipsed anything but the need to work for a cause.

Laying the knitting needles in her lap, she set her wooden rocking chair into motion, closing her eyes and gripping the armrests. But Greg's face was right there, smiling down at her as he told her he had better places for her to kiss. The tenseness of his jaw as he'd finally reached the limits of his control and let go.

Her lips curved at the memories and then her eyes popped open.

Oh, no!

What if it wasn't infatuation at all? What if she really did have feelings for him? Big, honkin', end-of-the-line feelings that wouldn't simply go away once the baby was born?

Her hands went to her stomach, pleading with all she had in her that her heart not go in that direction.

But it was hopeless. Her mind and her heart never saw eye to eye when it came to stuff like this. Her heart had wanted this baby while her mind had argued that she needed to wait a few years to be sure that her cancer really was gone for good.

Her heart had won in that instance.

Lord. She couldn't afford to let it win now. Not with everything that was at stake. The last thing her child needed once it was born was the tumultuous push and pull of an unstable relationship—one where she and Greg devoured each other one minute and avoided each other the next.

Neither did she want to end up as the "booty call" for a man who didn't have the emotional energy to nurture a relationship until it could withstand the wear and tear of normal life.

She deserved more than that. So did her child.

So what did she do? Find another job? Put her foot down and tell Greg that she was done with anything outside a professional working relationship.

The silence in her head was deafening.

Gee, thanks for the advice.

Picking up her knitting needles, she put one point through the first of the row of stitches and threw the yarn over them. For now, all she could do was knit and hope that—like the screwball stitches she'd just ripped out—she could go back undo the mistakes she'd made with Greg and start all over.

Only she had a feeling that returning to an earlier time was going to be a whole lot easier to accomplish with yarn that it would be with Greg.

A hat.

Greg had to look twice before he realized what the item in the brown paper gift bag was. There was a little card on the handle that listed the name of a patient—Dorothy Acres. There was no indication who had sent it, although he had a sneaking suspicion.

So three days after he'd asked her not to take up knitting, she was already churning out hats. Who knew how many hours she'd burned through, doing this?

He hadn't seen much of her as he'd spent the past couple of days in surgery at the hospital. He'd just gotten back from one, in fact, and had decided to write up his notes while they were still fresh in his mind. He'd closed his office door to have some privacy.

It wasn't like he was intentionally avoiding her.

But there was a kernel of discontent lodged inside his gut that just wouldn't go away, no matter how many antacids he'd consumed over the past couple of days. He'd stripped his bed and washed the sheets on the hot-water setting of his machine, trying to pretend he was washing away his own misplaced sentiments right along with the reminder of their time together. Like when he'd replaced his old desk?

It hadn't worked then, and it didn't work now. Finding the hat only augmented his irritability. And the thought of her sitting at home all by herself with a pair of knitting needles wasn't helping any. Because his nights had been spent alone, as well.

That had never bothered him. Until now.

He'd had women before—not every weekend, or even every month, but often enough to know that something was off with his reactions to this situation. It had to be the pregnancy. Or maybe it was just Hannah herself.

Bethany would have liked her. Would have liked Hannah's spark of life, the way she always tried to do the right thing, rather than just making it easy on herself.

He shoved his chair away from the desk and stood, picking up his phone.

He paged Stella and waited for her to pick up. "Is Hannah still here somewhere?"

"Um, I think she's with a patient," his receptionist said, as if that fact should be obvious to even a simpleton like him.

Okay, so the sarcasm was probably a product of his own guilt and nothing to do with Stella dissing him. "When you see her, could you ask her to come to my office?"

As soon as he put the phone down he cursed himself as an idiot. Hannah had not set foot in his office since their fiery encounter there six weeks ago.

Six weeks. Had it been that long?

He counted back. It had.

Hannah had gone from bringing him coffee every day to avoiding him as much as he appeared to be avoiding her.

Although, someone had put that bag in his office. He somehow doubted it was Hannah.

The last thing he needed today, though, was for her to stand in front of his new desk while he sat behind it and pictured her sprawled across it all over again. He quickly picked up the gift bag and his patient's file and went over to the sitting area on the other side of the room. There, that was better. They could still see the desk but they wouldn't have to look across it in order to have a quick conversation.

And he intended this to be a quick, non-emotional session that put both their minds at ease.

A knock sounded at the door. He frowned. It had been a rare day when his PA didn't just open the door and come in. Just like on that fateful day when he'd gotten the news about Mrs. Brookstone.

"Come in." He laid the file on the coffee table, letting it remain open, as if he'd just been casually reviewing it.

Hannah poked her head inside, but didn't enter. "You wanted to see me?"

His irritation grew. If he could handle this like an adult,

then so could she, dammit. "Would you mind coming in for a minute?"

You could have heard a pin drop in the silence that stretched between them. Finally, Hannah pushed through the door, making no effort to close it behind her. It was a telling move.

Was it him she didn't trust? Or herself?

That was a very dangerous question, and one he preferred not to answer right now.

He motioned to one of the wingback chairs that sat across from the leather sofa. Once she'd perched on the edge of it, her eyes went to the gift bag. So she already had an idea why he'd called her in. He nodded toward it. "Is this from you?"

"Does it matter?"

"I think you just answered my question. Didn't I say I didn't want you knitting hats?"

Her eyes narrowed slightly, she leaned back in her chair. "Were you ordering me not to make them or just suggesting that I shouldn't?"

A good question. He'd asked her not to, but was he so stupid as to think he could tell her how to spend her free hours and expect her to roll over and obey? Someone like Hannah? Not bloody likely.

Then what had he been doing?

He thought he'd been showing concern for her health. The baby's health. "It was a suggestion."

She nodded. "Okay. I found it…comforting."

She'd found what comforting? The suggestion or the knitting itself?

"I'm sorry, I don't follow."

"It gives me something constructive to do without brooding over the future."

The bald words reminded him of the ones she'd uttered

at his house. Was she really that worried about a possible relapse? Or was she worried that she might be stuck with him as the father of her child and wondering how much interference she'd get from him?

He leaned forward, planting his elbows on his knees, his chin on his fisted hands. "What part of the future?"

She shrugged, cheeks turning pink. "About the babie— baby. Whether or not everything will go okay with the pregnancy."

Had she been about to say "babies," plural? Was she actually expecting the doctor to find more than one during her next appointment? His mouth went dry.

"Did your doctor give you some cause for concern?"

"No, but you never know what could happen."

True. But other than finding multiple fetuses, Hannah was young and healthy. Her cancer was unlikely to return. She'd been able to get pregnant with the eggs she carried in her body, rather than the ones she'd frozen. It seemed like the odds were lining up in her favor. Then why wasn't she meeting his eyes? Was she still worried about Bethany's myeloid leukemia being passed down? If so, he could at least set her mind at ease regarding that.

"I talked to Bill Watterson a couple of days ago. He confirmed my family isn't one of those that carry the defective gene. So there's no chance of me passing it down."

"That's good. I wasn't worried, though."

But something was bothering her. He could see it in her face.

"Are you afraid I might interfere with the way you'll raise this child?"

She gave a soft laugh that sounded anything but happy. "Nope."

"What if it's mine?"

"What if it is?"

The words came out sounding like a challenge rather than an honest question—a kind of "so what are you going to do about it?" message.

He decided to tread softly. "What would you like me to do?"

"Nothing."

If he was closer, he'd reach out and take her hand. Touch her knee. Do something other than lean across a damn coffee table and try to get her to look at him—to really meet his eyes. "Do you want a marriage proposal?"

Her "No!" came at the exact same time his mind shouted, *What the hell are you doing?*

The horror in her voice, though, was a thousand times louder than his own. Because while he'd had this same inner tussle several times over the past couple of weeks, his heart had given a weird kind of sigh at his words. Like it might actually like the idea.

Well, *she* didn't. That much was obvious.

Hannah's words came tumbling out a second later, and she leaped to her feet. "Yes, I brought in the hat. And I want to make more of them, if that's okay with you. If it's not, I'll give them to the girls in the chemo room and let them hand them out as they see fit."

He got up as well and rounded the table until he stood in front of her. "Hey, I'm not going to stop you. If it makes you happy, by all means you should continue."

"Thank you."

He couldn't keep his eyes from trailing over her, acknowledging to himself that he was glad to finally see her up close, rather than just passing her in the hall for a few brief seconds. Despite the awkwardness currently between them, he missed having her barge in with a cup of coffee in the mornings. Missed the questions about whether or not he'd eaten lunch…or dinner. Missed her concern when a patient took a turn for the worse. But most of all he missed the easy camaraderie they used to have. It seemed like ages since they'd sat down and smiled and laughed like a couple of...

Friends.

Was that what he'd thought of her as?

Yes. Someone who knew who he was and who was perfectly okay with his shortcomings, with the energy he put into his job.

He wanted to tell her, but his throat felt paralyzed, unable to utter anything but meaningless questions.

"How many patients do we have left today?" Like that one. Meaningless. Not at all what he wanted to say.

She glanced at her watch. "I think two, why?"

Why? Because he wanted to see her. Spend time with her. And not just inside the bedroom—although he knew that was part of it. A big part. But he also wanted to hear about how her pregnancy was going and to know how she felt about it. Wanted her to want him to be a part of it.

But most of all he wanted to know where he fit into the scheme of things.

Suddenly he knew just the way to ask.

"After you have the baby, are you planning to come back to the clinic?"

CHAPTER FIFTEEN

"I DON'T know."

Hannah wasn't sure exactly how it had happened, but after the last patient left she found herself in Greg's car, the heater running as they discussed her work status at a nearby park. It was too chilly to get out and walk, and neither one of them had suggested going to get something to eat.

The thought of leaving the clinic caused something cold and hard to lodge in her throat, but she had no idea how she'd feel about working for Greg if the baby turned out to be his.

"What if I told you I don't want you to leave?"

A spark of joy leaped within her, only to fizzle out again. Was this the same type of offer as the "proposal" he'd mentioned earlier? Born of a sense of responsibility? He didn't want her as his wife so how did she know he still wanted her at the clinic?

"Is this because you somehow feel responsible for knocking me up? Because if it is—"

"Please don't use that term."

She blinked. Somehow she'd assumed that was all this was to him. A mistake. One that never should have happened. Hadn't he said as much?

No, actually, he hadn't. But surely he'd thought it. *She* had. "Sorry."

"And no, this isn't about feeling responsible, although I do, to some extent. But you're good for the clinic. Good for our patients."

Right. The cynical part of her mind gave her heart a knowing wink. Hadn't it told her that all along?

Before she could open her mouth to respond, he shook his head. "No, that's a lie. You are good for the clinic, but you're also good for me. You drag me back to earth when I've gotten my head too far up my…" He cleared his throat. "Too far in the clouds."

She couldn't stop her laugh. "I think I liked your first attempt better."

He smiled back at her. "See? You're also good for my ego."

"You mean by chopping it back down to a manageable size?" She relaxed in her seat, swiveling her knees toward him so she could look at him.

"Exactly." His face turned serious as he studied her. "I've missed this."

"So have I."

They looked at each other for a few more seconds, before Hannah glanced away. "If this baby does turn out to be yours, don't you think things could become strained?"

"Only if we let them."

Her brows went up. "Seriously? Look at us now, at the clinic. You can barely stand to talk to me."

"It's hard, I admit. But we could work through it."

Pain lodged in her chest and branched out, like crystals forming in a jar of sugar water. He'd just admitted to avoiding her. Was that why his hours at the hospital had suddenly increased? She'd gone from being a collaborator on cases to handling some of them on her own, just going to him for a quick consult when she was unsure of something. Was that how she wanted to continue? It gave her a lot more freedom to make decisions, but she liked the give and take as they'd brainstormed through problems. Instead, she felt like she'd been set adrift.

It was a lonely feeling. Maybe that's why she suddenly looked to knitting as a type of therapy. She'd even finished a brown argyle beanie hat, the pattern for which she'd found in a magazine. They didn't have any male patients at the moment, yet her fingers had found their way to that page time and time again, carefully selecting the shades and the layout—matching the color of Greg's hair. The finished product had come out just as she'd imagined.

You'll stay warmer than I will, as I don't have a special hat. The words he'd said to Annie when he'd given her Martha's gift ran through her mind. Something about them had grabbed hold of her throat and squeezed tight, which was ridiculous. He'd just been making idle conversation.

So why had the words stuck with her? It's not like she'd ever have the courage to give it to him.

"Are you sure you wouldn't rather just get a new PA?" The question sounded as shaky as her legs had become.

His brows came together. "Would I be sitting here in the damn car, asking you to stay, if I did?"

Why the sudden flare of anger? Maybe the thought of her leaving really did bother him.

"What would you do while I was on maternity leave?"

He took a minute to think about that. "I could cut back on my patient load until you got back."

"What? You always say that, but know you'd never be able to."

"I already have, remember? It's why you're able to leave here by six o'clock every night, rather than eight."

She pounced on those words. "Ha! I know for a fact

you sneak patients in after everyone's gone home." Several mornings she'd come in to find the paper on the exam tables rumpled from someone's body and had had to strip them before beginning a new day. She was pretty sure Greg wasn't snoozing on them at night. Not when he had that long couch in his office. And that comfy bed in his home.

Something she'd better avoid thinking about.

"You do? How?"

She tapped her forehead. "I'm psychic."

"Well, I wouldn't have a choice when you're gone. I'd have to cut back. I can't be at the hospital and the clinic at the same time."

He was right, he couldn't be two places at once. Which was why the thought of being married to someone like him was beyond absurd.

"That's true. You can't be." She heard the wistfulness in her voice and cringed inwardly. But maybe Greg hadn't noticed. He probably had too much on his mind to notice the subtle shift in pitch...the note of sorrow she'd unintentionally injected.

His throat moved, then his hand came out to squeeze hers. "I'm trying to do better, Hannah."

That was the problem. No matter how much he might want to change, he wouldn't. Not really. Not until he could temper whatever drove him to work so hard and so long. Only Greg knew if the compulsion was out of control or if he really could back away from it. Hannah loved the patients she treated, but she also knew there was a limit to how much she could do before her body and mind rebelled.

Greg's never seemed to, although she had no idea how he could stay focused for as long as he did.

But, like he'd said, he didn't have anyone else to worry about. And that's the way he liked it.

"It's not a matter of doing better. It's a matter of taking

care of yourself, so that you can take care of others. You don't eat right. You probably don't sleep well. When I was at your house, your refrigerator was practically empty."

Instead of taking offense, he laughed. "Thanks."

Huh?

"For what?"

"For fussing at me. You haven't done that in a while." He linked his fingers through hers. "Like I said, I've missed it."

Things between them *had* been strained lately. And she hadn't been in his office in a while. Was it possible he'd liked what they'd had before?

She squeezed his hand back. "So have I."

"So you'll at least think about staying once the baby is born?"

"Yes. I'll think about it."

"I appreciate it." He let out a huge breath. "I can't promise I'll be able to change overnight, but I'll at least try."

Maybe she'd been wrong. Maybe he really *would* try to make time for things outside work. A ball of hope formed in her chest.

"Promise?"

"I do."

The doctor stared at the ultrasound monitor, a frown of concentration on her face.

Hannah's anxiety level had been going up in steady increments for the past ten minutes. This was taking a lot longer than she'd expected. At eight weeks Dr. Preston should be able to find the baby and see its tiny heart pumping, even if she couldn't find it on the Doppler yet. "Is everything okay?"

"Just give me another minute here."

The same answer the doctor had given her the last time she'd asked. What if the baby was dead?

Her own heart stalled at the thought.

Greg had offered to come with her, but their patient load was heavy today and she hadn't felt right about dragging him away. Especially as he had been better about eating. They'd even started meeting in his office for coffee again in the mornings, like they used to.

And most days Greg had already poured and doctored hers up with creamer and sugar before she even got to the office, which was different from the way it had been before. Stella would just nod toward the door and send her on her way.

And now she was alone in a room, possibly about to hear the worst news of her life.

"Hannah, there're two of them."

"Two what?" Heads? Torsos? Babies...?

"You're going to have twins. Sorry for taking so long. I wanted to be sure before I said anything." She turned the monitor toward Hannah.

"Twins?" She'd known this was a possibility. Barb had even warned her ahead of time, but to actually hear the word was...

Terrifying.

Two babies. How could that be?

"You're positive."

"I am." She pointed out the babies, one of which appeared to be superimposed over the other. "The angle made it hard to see. I wanted to make sure they weren't fused."

"Oh, God. They're not, are they?" Conjoined twins would send her soul plummeting back to earth.

"No. There are two separate individuals in there. Oh, and they're fraternal, as there are two placentas."

"It's just so... I'll have to..."

To what? Tell Greg? Oh, no. Her fear grew even more. What was she going to tell him? He'd freaked out over one baby, what would he do with the news that he might have fathered two?

Maybe he hadn't.

"Any chance of knowing if these are the result of the insemination?"

Dr. Preston squeezed her shoulder. "No, sorry. There's no way to tell for sure until we do a D.N.A. test, and you said you wanted to wait on that, right?"

"Yes." She had. And Greg's quiet words came back to her, affirming it was the right decision. He hadn't wanted her to risk losing the baby just to put his mind at ease.

But now that there were two? Would he still feel the same way?

She gulped as another thought hit her. "You're positive there aren't any more in there, right?"

The doctor laughed. "Yes. I'm sure. I almost missed the second one as it was."

Maybe it would have been better if the second baby had remained hidden a little while longer. She and Greg were just getting back on solid footing. But withholding this kind of information wouldn't do anyone any good. And if he'd been able to come to her appointment, like he'd wanted to, he would already know.

Yes, she had to tell him.

But when?

Um, yeah. Like he wouldn't ask how the appointment had gone the second she got back to the office. Nothing to do but suck it up and tell the truth.

She got back during the lunch lull, which was both fortunate and unfortunate as it didn't give her much of a chance to prepare. Nonetheless, there was no time like the present. Armed with two fresh cups of coffee, she made her way to Greg's office, mumbling the words she wanted to say under her breath. She slid one mug in the crook of her elbow and knocked, heard his "Come in" and took a deep, deep breath before taking that final step.

If she'd been hoping he was immersed in paperwork and would give her a few more minutes, she was mistaken. He was sitting behind his desk, elbows propped on the flat, empty surface, staring off into space.

Brooding over his lot in life?

Lord, she hoped not, because it was about to get a whole lot worse.

She held out a cup. "I made a fresh pot."

Nodding an acknowledgment, he accepted it and took a fairly big sip. Bracing himself. Great. Brooding *and* bracing.

He set the cup on the desk. "How is he?"

"He?"

"The baby, sorry. Just using the generic term...unless you already know what it is?"

"I don't know the sex yet, no." She licked suddenly dry lips. "But I did learn something pretty significant."

A frown appeared. "Did a problem show up on the sonogram?"

The worried note in his voice made her rush ahead. "Oh, no. There's nothing wrong with...them."

He blinked. Stared. His Adam's apple took at least one dive, possibly two, before he said in a low controlled voice, "Them?"

"Yes."

"Them, as in more than one fetus?"

"Yes."

He leaned back in his chair, the springs protesting the sudden change. Then, as if he needed to distance himself even farther from the news, he swiveled half a turn to the left until he faced the wall. Planting his elbows on his knees, he closed his eyes and pressed his fingertips into his temples. His face was paler than she'd ever seen it. Hannah wondered for a moment if he was going to be physically sick.

"Greg? Are you okay?"

One hand left his temple to wave a warning, which she took to mean he needed another minute or two.

Oh, Lordy. She was beginning to feel a little nauseated herself, nerves causing her stomach to froth and twist.

He'd known this might be a possibility, so why was he acting as if it was a death sentence?

Then, in case he might be wondering, or might be trying to get up the nerve to ask, she forced herself to say, "I'm not going to ask about a reduction."

"Of course not."

He still hadn't moved. Hannah couldn't tell whether the words were meant as an affirmation or an indictment. Or maybe he was simply resigning himself to his fate.

She tried to explain. "I can't, Greg. Twins are easily managed, and if something should happen to one of them, I…I…" Even the thought brought a quick slice of pain.

He turned back toward her. "I wasn't asking you to."

She hesitated, trying to feel him out. "I know this must come as a shock."

"You have no idea."

He picked up a pencil and toyed with it as she searched for something else to say. Something that might make him feel at least a little better.

"They might not be yours, you know."

He set the pencil down with a click. "I'm going to assume they are, until I know otherwise."

He was? Why? He was obviously not overjoyed with the news. It would be so much easier to grab the lifeline she'd handed him and pull himself to shore—far from the likes of her and the babies. So why wasn't he?

Because that wasn't the way Greg did things. Not in his line of work. He evaluated the situation, identified the worst-case scenario and then fought to improve the odds. But this time there was no way to change course. What was done was done. They couldn't go back and undo it.

She almost laughed. Although Greg had certainly given it a shot by banishing the old desk and getting a light pine mission-style thing that clashed with all the other ornate mahogany pieces. If his decorator could see it, she'd cringe. She had to admit, though, it was a relief not to have to face him over that other desk or something that was almost like it.

"Maybe that's not a wise thing to do. If they end up not being yours, won't you be…?"

Sad?

No, of course he wouldn't be. He'd be hugely relieved, just like she would.

Wouldn't she? The empty place in her chest said otherwise.

"Will I be upset? Maybe. But things would be a whole lot less complicated."

That was one point they could definitely agree on. "Yes, they would."

He dragged a hand through his hair. "Any other exciting news you'd like to spring on me?"

"I did ask Dr. Preston if she was sure there weren't any more hiding in there."

He coughed, then cleared his throat. The first hint of a smile finally made its way across his face. "And?"

"There aren't. She almost missed the second one as it was. He or she was hiding behind the first baby."

"Probably afraid of my reaction." His gaze finally

landed on her face. "And I'm sorry for that." He hesitated. "Are you happy?"

She searched inside herself and found the answer. "Yes."

"Congratulations, Hannah." He leaned across his desk and held out his hand, waiting until she took it. "When are they due again?"

"July twelfth."

He squeezed her fingers then released them. "They don't usually let twins go to term, do they?"

"No. Dr. Preston said to plan for thirty-seven weeks."

"So now you have two baby names to come up with instead of just one."

"Ye-es." She drew the word out, wondering if she should do this now or let him recover a little while longer. But he seemed softer and more relaxed, even if he wasn't shouting for joy. She'd been holding on to the question for the last week, trying to get the nerve up—and that had been when she'd thought there was only one baby.

What if he laughed in her face or, worse, shouted for her to get out of his office? Well, nothing could be worse than the way he'd shut down on her a few minutes ago. At least, she hoped not.

Taking a deep breath, she forged ahead. "Can I get your opinion on something?"

He picked up his coffee and took another sip. A shorter one this time. "Sure."

Setting her own cup in her lap, she wrapped both hands around it, noting that the now-tepid brew was still warmer than her icy fingers.

"If one of the babies is a girl, what do you think about naming her Bethany, after your sister?"

CHAPTER SIXTEEN

His sister?

Greg wasn't sure he'd heard the words correctly—in fact, he wasn't sure he'd heard *anything* correctly for the past fifteen minutes—so he sat there trying to replay that last sentence. But all that kept running through his head was the word *twins*.

"Could you repeat that?"

"It's fine if you don't want to. I mean, I know it's really soon, so feel free to take some time to think it over before you—"

"You don't even know if the babies are mine. Why would you want to do that?"

"Because your sister was obviously a beautiful person. She's the reason you fight so hard for your patients. What a wonderful legacy. And if you decide never to have children of your own…" She shrugged, not quite meeting his eyes. "It's something I've been thinking about for the past week or so."

Hannah was right. He did fight for his patients, but only because Bethany had taught him how to—had always been the one person he could count on to understand. Just as Hannah seemed to, first at his house and now right here in this very office.

Hell. Something was wrong. Hannah's face blurred and

then came back into sharp focus. The problem wasn't with
her features, though, it was with his eyes. There was a
layer of moisture over them that was growing deeper by
the second.

Another happy little girl might carry Bethany's name.
The problem with his eyes had now spread to his lungs,
which burned with every breath he took.

Getting up from his seat, he went to the window and
stared out over the parking lot, scrubbing his hand over
his face. Last week's dusting of snow had melted but the
sky was overcast.

A gentle hand landed on his shoulder. "I'm sorry I upset
you. I won't do it, if you don't want me to, if it would hurt
too much."

Half turning, he wrapped his arms around her and laid
his cheek on top of her head, her soft scent filling his chest.
Despite his attempts to dash them away, the damned mist
covered his eyes again, this time spilling onto Hannah's
hair.

He took a deep shuddery breath, fighting to get himself under control. "It doesn't upset me. I don't think anyone has ever done a nicer thing for me or for Bethany.
Thank you."

Her arms circled his waist, and she rested her head on
his chest. "You're welcome."

For the first time, the idea of kids and a family didn't
send his heart racing into a state of panic or make him shy
away in horror. Instead, as he stood in his office, holding
Hannah in his arms, a sense of rightness flowed through
him.

He loved her.

How? When?

He had no idea. The realization hadn't hit him like a
bolt from the sky. Neither did it bring an unwelcome jolt

of surprise. It was something that had begun growing the moment she'd thrown her arms around him and thanked him at the end of her treatments, her soft scent sweeping through him then just as it did now, her trembling body awaking something in his heart. Or maybe it had started even before that.

Yes, he was terrified. He hadn't planned on falling in love any more than he'd planned on fathering twins. But the feeling was there, and he could at least admit it to himself for this one moment in time, even if he never did anything about it.

"I have something else to ask." Hannah's voice was muffled by his shirt.

What else could she throw at him besides twins and wanting to name one of them after Bethany?

"What is it?"

"If the babies end up being yours…" She paused for a long second before continuing. "And if my cancer comes back at some point, I want to make preparations in advance. Do you have any preferences about who should raise them?"

If her cancer came back…

A black spot opened up in his chest at the thought.

Nothing would happen to Hannah. He'd make sure of it.

Like he had his sister?

"You're going to be fine. The cancer's not going to recur." Hodgkin's was different from his sister's disease. It had a high cure rate.

"You can't know that for sure. No one does. I just don't want to leave things up in the air. If they're yours, you should have a say about where they go."

Just like he knew he loved her, Greg's heart whispered the answer that had been there all along.

"I'll raise them."

"What?" Her head came off his chest, and she looked up at him.

"I said I'll raise them."

He wouldn't have to, though. Hannah was going to be around for a long time to come. She'd raise her children and wave them off to college. But she wasn't asking for reassurances. She was making arrangements, it was as simple as that. And this was the right thing to do.

He gave an inward smile. *See, Bethany? I can* do *it.*

"Are you sure?" Hannah asked. "You're so busy, and that is a huge commitment."

He searched around inside himself. He could ask his parents for help—his mother would be thrilled, and maybe it would help to heal the rift between him and his father. He could even move his practice to Ketchikan to be closer to them if necessary. But the thought of Hannah no longer being on this earth…

Then don't think about it. Just answer her question.

"I'm sure." He paused. "What if they're the donor's children? Are your parents well enough to handle raising two children?"

"Yes. They're both still fairly active. But they're in Idaho, so the children would have to go there."

Idaho.

The lower forty-eight always seemed like another world to someone who'd been born and raised in Alaska. And Idaho was three thousand miles away. So he'd probably never see the twins again.

"Let's not talk about this right now, okay?" He allowed his right hand to stroke along her spine. "I'm still getting used to the fact that there are two of them."

Hannah smiled. "Yeah, me too. All I can think about is what I'm going to look like when I'm eight months pregnant."

"You're going to look beautiful, just like you do now."

Her smile faded. "Thank you. That's a really sweet thing to say."

Before he could stop himself, he dropped a quick kiss on her lips. "It might be sweet, but it's also true." He sighed. "And as much as I don't want to, I'd better get out there before Stella sends someone in after me. Or, worse, comes looking for me herself. We might have some explaining to do in that case."

"Speaking of explaining…" Hannah dropped her arms from his waist and took a step back. "I'm eventually going to have to tell everyone I'm pregnant. How do you want me to play it?"

He fingered the silver earring that dangled from a dainty lobe. "Play it by ear. Just like we've been doing with everything else."

Play it by ear.

That's what Hannah had done with his spontaneous kiss yesterday, and with his shocking offer to raise the twins should they prove to be his. And when he'd called her beautiful, her heart had almost stopped.

But she'd smiled as if it had meant nothing special, all the while wondering if his feelings for her might be growing. Just like hers were.

A very scary proposition when you considered it. Dropping the new gift bag on his desk, she ran her fingers along the wooden surface. Several patient files were now scattered across the top of it, unlike yesterday when it had been empty.

She hadn't wanted to fall for him. If she could go back and undo the sequence of events that had led her here, she would. She'd have continued calling him Dr. Mason and maintained that professional distance she seemed to

need. At least with him. She'd never had any trouble calling other colleagues by their first names. But she'd resisted with Greg.

Now she knew why.

The door opened, and she jumped when the man himself appeared. "I thought you were at the hospital."

"I was. I finished up early."

"You did?" With the way Greg lived his life, she'd never
have considered letting him raise these children.

Until he'd cried.

Oh, he didn't know she'd felt the moisture in her hair,
and she hadn't dared say anything. But at that moment
she'd known he could love them, if it came down to it.
Known he'd sacrifice everything for them, the same way
he'd made sacrifices in his sister's memory.

She pulled her mind away from those thoughts as he
came into the room and closed the door behind him.

"I only had two patients." He smiled. "And, yes, I
checked the chemo room. No one there from our practice."

Our. That was the first time he'd ever used that term.

Hannah motioned toward the desk. "I've gotten another
hat done." And his still sat in a little bag on her dining
room table. She would eventually have to give it to him.
What was the worst he could do? Laugh and think her
silly?

"That's two hats this week. You're going to run through
all our patients within a month or two."

His words were light, but Hannah didn't smile. "We'll
always have new ones."

"Yes, unfortunately." He took another step toward her,
sliding his fingers beneath her chin. "Are you okay?"

She scrabbled around for something to say. "Just feeling a bit melancholy today, for some reason."

"You need to get away for a little while." He glanced at his watch. "Do you have plans this weekend?"

Yes. Knitting. Staring at her fish. Pining after her boss. Full schedule. "Nope. Just relaxing."

The fingers beneath her chin trailed along her jawline, sending a shiver over her. "My folks have a little vacation cabin about an hour north of here. I was thinking about going up there." He paused. "Are you interested in joining me?"

He never left town, as far as she knew. What was behind his sudden need to clear out? "Since when do you leave for the weekend?"

"It's been ages since I've been up there. Maybe your moose encounter made me miss the woods. I don't know. I just know I'd like to head up there…and I'd like some company. We could talk about the babies and your plans for the future."

"M-my plans?"

He dropped his hand. "If you don't want to, it's fine."

"No, no, it's not that. You just surprised me." Her insides warred for a second or two, the "should" battling it out with the "want to," although there was never any doubt as to which side would win, really. "Thank you. I'd like to go."

"Great. Do you want to leave tonight or Saturday morning?"

"I need to pack, so could we make it tomorrow?"

"Sure."

Hannah thought she heard a note of disappointment in his voice, but surely not. He'd probably regret asking her as soon as she left the office. Maybe he'd even call to say he'd changed his mind.

"What time to you want to leave?"

"Is nine o'clock too early?"

"No, that's fine." Her head was whirling. She'd gone

from wondering how she could have avoided this particular train wreck to agreeing to spend the weekend with him. It was probably reckless and wildly idiotic, but she wanted to go. Wanted to head somewhere private where they could talk through things for once, instead of wondering where all this was leading. "Does the cabin have heat?"

If not, she'd have to bring some additional layers.

"It does. It also has linens and towels and everything we'll need to cook meals. Except the food."

Cooking. She hadn't thought about that. "Do you want me to pick up some groceries?"

"I'll do that. Or we can eat out for lunch and dinner."

But not for breakfast. She remembered the omelet he'd made them. Remembered the events afterward. Suddenly she thought of something that should have been apparent from the outset. He planned on them sleeping together, obviously. Why else would he have asked her? The thought should have made her uneasy, since she'd already given herself the "booty call" lecture, but it didn't. Instead a stream of anticipation began swirling through her stomach.

"Oh, and, Hannah…" His fingers slid through her hair, ruffling the short strands as he gave her a slow smile. "In case you're worried about my intentions, the cabin has two bedrooms."

CHAPTER SEVENTEEN

"IT's beautiful!"

Greg smiled as Hannah gave a small twirl, taking in the rustic entryway of the log cabin. He dropped their bags on the plank floor, his worries over asking her to join him dissipating. If she'd turned him down, would he even be here?

Doubtful. His decision to come had been an impulsive one at best, and although he was antsy about being so far from Anchorage, he'd traveled to medical conferences in the past and nothing terrible had happened. The world had continued its slow, methodical turn. His absence hadn't spawned any natural disasters.

Besides, he'd wanted some time alone with her to try to figure this thing out and decide what he should do about it. What was it about her that drew him time and time again?

Who was Hannah, really?

He knew exactly who she was. A survivor who, like his sister, challenged him to be the best he could be. Hannah was also kind and caring and made his blood turn to fire the second she walked—or barged—into a room. A woman who might be carrying his children. She was already a professional partner, but could she be more than that? He'd gotten things a little backward, but maybe that's what it had taken to get through to him.

"I'm glad you like it." He went to a nearby wall and

switched on the gas fireplace, even as he tried to see the place through her eyes. The foyer opened into a great room with sturdy leather furnishings and a rough pine table. He could remember his whole family coming up here during summer vacations—at least until he and his father had had that final big blowup. His mom had been surprised when he'd called, asking if they still had the place, but she'd been happy. The key was still in the same spot, she'd said. In that silly fake rock his father kept next to the front porch.

Hannah kept her coat on and made a beeline for the fireplace, holding her hands out. "Does this heat the whole house?"

"No, there's central heat as well, but this is a little more immediate."

"Brrr…I think winter is already moving in."

Frost had painted the landscape white that morning when he'd gone to pick her up, and the temperature hadn't warmed up much during the trip. No precipitation predicted, but the sky was grey and overcast. "You could be right."

Shrugging out of his heavy parka, he hung it on a hook in a nearby closet then picked up their bags again. "Which bedroom do you want?"

"Whichever one you don't want." She sank to her knees on the rug in front of the fireplace, sighing. 'I think I'm going to sit here for a minute or two and get warmed up. Where does it get its gas?"

"From a big tank out back. It should be fine for the time we're here. Do you want me to crank it up higher?"

"No, it feels wonderful. I could sit here all day."

So could he. Right next to her.

And as far as putting her bag in whichever room he *didn't* want, that was going to be a little tricky, because he'd immediately want to be in the one she was in. But that wasn't smart. He'd brought her here to be with her, to spend time with her. It was better to give her some space, not to mention the fact that he could do with some of that himself. Okay…easy solution. He'd give her his parents' room. That should put paid to any thoughts of sneaking into her bed in the middle of the night.

"I'll put these away and then see about lunch."

"Mmm. I'll help you in a few minutes. Once I thaw a bit more." She curled up on the rug in front of the fireplace, much as Bethany's cat would have done years ago.

Despite Hannah's words, she looked anything but frozen. He was sure if he touched her, she'd be warm and soft. Which was why he was heading straight to the bedrooms before he dropped onto the rug behind her and tucked her close.

Going first to the room he'd shared with Bethany when they'd been kids, he set his suitcase on the floor, staring at the place where the two single beds had been replaced with a queen-size one. He could still visualize the bedding and how she'd talked their parents into rigging a curtain to go between the beds so she could pretend to have her own room. The ceiling rod was gone, the area painted to look brand-new. In fact, the whole room had been redecorated, for which he was grateful. The outside wall was made of thick rustic logs, but the three inside walls had changed from pale yellow to nondescript beige. All traces of Bethany had been scrubbed clean. It was as if she'd never been here at all.

Only she had been. And, in a way, her presence was still here. It was one of the reasons he hadn't been to the place in years. But instead of the crippling sadness her memory had once dredged up, he found the pain had eased, even if it wasn't completely gone. He could now smile at the mischievous antics she'd once engaged in. Remember how happy this place had made her.

Something inside him relaxed. It was going to be okay.

Maybe that's why he'd needed to come. To get a sense of what his sister would have wanted him to do.

Hannah didn't want to marry him. Even if she hadn't said the words, her face had been a picture of shock and dismay when he'd mentioned it. Enough that he wouldn't pursue that avenue again. But it didn't have to be marriage, necessarily. Maybe she could grow to care for him—could trust him not only to raise her children in the event of her death but enough to let him be a part of her life, as well.

Was that what he wanted?

Yes. But he wasn't sure he could do it. Or whether or not he should. This weekend was meant to be a test run. And a lot rode on how he felt by the end of it.

"Is this where I'll stay?" Hannah's voice yanked him from his thoughts. He knew she meant "stay" as in temporarily, but the word made something shift inside him. The urge to ask her to share the room with him came and went without incident. He shifted gears.

"Weren't you going to warm up for a while?"

"Already done." She put her hand on his. "See? Warm as toast."

Yes, it was. And he was growing a bit heated himself. He cleared his throat. "I'm going to put you in the room across the hall. There's only one bathroom, so we'll have to share. My parents always meant to add a second one, but they never got around to it." And once Bethany had died, there'd been no need, as they'd no longer come here as a family.

"Okay."

That reminded him. He'd have to switch on the hot-water heater and let it run for a couple of hours before they could shower. "Let me show you your room."

He made the trek across the narrow hallway, suddenly glad to be moving. Opening the door, he let her walk in ahead of him. The room was chilly, but he could already feel heat gusting from one of the overhead vents.

A soft exclamation of surprise came from behind her. "You should take this room."

He knew why she'd said it. This bedroom was obviously the master suite, since the huge four-poster bed dominated the space—his mother's one big splurge. A system of mahogany slats cleverly attached to the four carved finials, creating a canopy that could be disassembled depending on the mood.

His mother had always liked them up, had even bought a lacy fabric covering that was probably still tucked in one of the closets somewhere, but Greg liked the bare wood. "No, I'm fine in the other one. It's where I used to sleep as a child."

"But this bed is bigger. And you're—"

"Don't say it."

She grinned. "I wasn't going to say you're fat. You're not. But you are a big guy."

Her cheeks colored almost as soon as the words left her mouth. His cue to back out of there, and fast.

"Do you want to unpack?"

"I think I'm going to leave my things in the suitcase. We'll only be here for one night."

"Right." Suddenly it wasn't enough. He wanted a week. A month.

A lifetime?

Stick with the plan, Greg. Take it one day at a time.

"I'll bring the rest of the stuff in from the car."

"Want some help?" She stood in the doorway as if unsure what to do next.

"I've got it. I thought we might eat lunch here at the cabin and then do dinner at a seafood joint in town."

"Sounds good." She patted her tummy. "I ate breakfast, but I'm already starving. Must be the air up here."

He could blame the air for his ravenous appetite, but this was a completely different kind of hunger—one that physical food wouldn't put a dent in.

"I've brought steak and potatoes. How does that sound?"

"Like a little piece of heaven. I'm so glad I haven't had any morning sickness yet. I'm eating all I can, just in case it eventually hits." She put one hand on the edge of the door. "Oh, are there sheets already on the bed?"

"No, Mom used to keep them in the dresser drawers in each bedroom—they're probably still there, in a zippered bag. We can throw a set in the washer, and then I'll help you make the bed."

Her brows went up. "I have made a bed before, you know."

He did know. And that was something else he didn't want to think about. The way she looked as she bent over the exam tables, pulling paper from the roll and tucking it beneath the strap at the bottom. How her perfect behind had called out to him, inviting him to mess up the bed she'd so meticulously made. But then he might have had to buy a new exam table, for the very same reasons he'd gotten a new desk. That might be a little harder to explain to Stella.

His perceptive receptionist had eyed him with one brow raised nearly to her hairline as they'd carried his old desk away. The thing was still tucked in a storage area, awaiting his decision on what to do with it. He couldn't bear to throw it out. Maybe he should move it to his house. There wasn't much furniture in the place.

And see Hannah's slim body stretched across it every time he passed by? Yeah, if he thought he was tired now, he'd be doubly exhausted if he did that.

Since when had he gotten so sentimental?

Maybe since seeing on a daily basis how fragile the thread of life was. He'd learned to notice little things about his patients that he might have overlooked before, like the soft glances between Claire and her husband. Or hands that gripped tightly as he talked about their particular illness. Or...

"Greg? Are you okay?"

"Yep, fine." He rolled his shoulders to relax some of the tension. "Like I said, linens are in the drawer. Choose whichever set you like and bring them to the kitchen. The washer and dryer are in a closet next to the pantry."

"Okay." Her gaze trailed over his face as if trying to figure out what he'd been thinking about, but she didn't ask. "Do you want me to get out a set for you, as well?"

"Sure. I'll be back in a few minutes."

Greg hightailed it out of there before she figured out that she was part of his salva—confusion. Hell, had he almost used the word *salvation?* He didn't need anyone to save him. Unless it was from his own recent thoughts and actions.

He'd done some things that were pretty out of character for him.

Rescuing the grocery bags from the trunk of his car, he brought them in the house and quickly sorted through them. He glanced at his watch. Almost lunchtime. Good. At least the food preparations would keep him from doing any more thinking.

Because right now thinking was the one thing that could take an otherwise cautious and controlled doctor and turn him into a type of Mr. Hyde.

One who only wanted one thing out of this trip.

Hannah.

CHAPTER EIGHTEEN

SHE was crazy cold, but it was so worth it.

When Greg had said he had a surprise for her, she'd glanced at her watch and blinked. Almost midnight. But now, seated on the whitewashed porch swing overlooking the front yard, she curled up in a ball and hugged her knees. And stared.

Lights.

The gorgeous green hues of the aurora borealis hung high in the sky, a soft misting of color that was perfectly visible from her seat. The swing creaked as Greg sat beside her, tossing a throw from the couch over both their shoulders and wrapping it around them. "To keep us warm," he'd murmured, when she'd looked at him.

She was. His body heat, trapped within the folds of the woolen fabric, quickly made the nippy temperature more bearable, even for her feet, which normally turned into heavy blocks of ice whenever she sat outside for extended periods.

"How did you know it would happen tonight?" she asked. You couldn't always predict when the lights would appear, and sometimes they only lasted for minutes before fading away again.

"I didn't. I glanced outside and there it was." He shifted on the seat, the move bringing him close enough that his shoulder slipped behind hers. She responded by leaning against him, automatically seeking the extra heat he was giving off. "This used to be Bethany's favorite part of coming to the cabin."

"Tell me about her." It wasn't often he volunteered information about his sister, and she was curious.

He shrugged. "She was feisty. Made me stand up to my dad when he wanted me to take over his fishing business."

"And you wanted to be a doctor."

"Yes." He gave a soft chuckle. "And Bethy nagged me until I told him the truth, that I didn't want to be a commercial fisherman. She knew I'd be miserable if I tried to force myself to be something I wasn't."

"That must have been tough." She couldn't imagine her parents pressuring her into taking over their cattle ranch. There'd never even been a hint that she should give up her own dreams and take on theirs.

"It was. Things have been shaky between my dad and I ever since." His arm went around Hannah's shoulders, drawing her closer. "But it was the right thing to do."

"I'm glad she insisted."

He paused, before saying, "Me, too."

She sighed, turning her attention back to the sky. "I think this is the clearest I've ever seen the lights. I've heard northern Idaho has displays from time to time, but I'm from the southern part of the state so I'd never experienced them before moving to the Aleutians. And then, after my diagnosis, there weren't a lot of opportunities."

The time she'd spent on the island of Dutch Harbor had been a magical, eye-opening period. The inhabitants knew how to make the most of what they had. She still missed the island, and her friends there.

Hmm... But not that much, she thought as she rested her head on Greg's shoulder. This was definitely something she could get used to. Sitting on a porch with him, watching the mysterious glow dance across the night sky, the silence broken only by the occasional shuffle of wildlife in the distance or the soft hoot of an owl in a nearby tree.

"I don't think I could ever get tired of seeing this."

Greg's warm breath slid across her cheek. "You don't get tired of it. But you do take it for granted. Forget it exists."

"Kind of like good health."

"Yes, unfortunately. In our practice we're suddenly more aware of things like the northern lights, aren't we?"

"Having cancer changes you. Sometimes for the better. Like appreciating the beauty of the lights, for example. You learn to treasure every second."

"Is that why you decided to have children?"

Hannah had sensed him wanting to talk about this earlier, but he'd never quite made it around to the subject. Maybe it was for the best. Because out here she felt a kind freedom she'd been longing for. "Yes. Putting it off until I met the right person just didn't seem like the best decision for me anymore."

"So you decided to go it alone."

"I was alone during my illness and treatment so this doesn't seem like such a huge step."

Warm lips touched her temple. "I'm sorry you felt alone. Your parents?"

"My mom came up for a couple of weeks, but when she realized she couldn't really help I talked her into going home. My dad gets nervous when he can't do something to make things better." She paused. "He's in the early stages of Parkinson's. It's another reason I didn't want to wait. I wanted my dad to be able to hold his grandchild while he's still well enough to."

"I didn't know."

She shrugged. "It's just something that's never come up between us."

"Anything else?"

"What do you mean?" She glanced up to see his eyes fixed on the lights.

"What about the twins? What are your plans once they're born?"

Leaning back, she took a moment to really look at his face. The slow muscle working in his jaw. "I don't have a lot of plans. I'm just taking life a second at a time. Trying to savor every step along the way. I'm afraid if I start really laying things out, I'll live for the future, instead of treasuring today." She struggled to find the words, but couldn't. "I don't know how to explain it, exactly."

"I think I understand. Maybe I should learn to be a little more spontaneous. My days do kind of run together."

Something funny settled in her tummy. "And right now? Right here? Is this running together?"

"No. I'm painfully aware of each tiny second ticking down."

"You are? Why?" She held her breath.

"Because…I don't want it to end." The words were so soft she had to strain to hear them.

When she realized exactly what he'd said, the air whooshed from her lungs in a big gulp, the puff of mist she caused obscuring her vision for a moment. She realized she didn't want it to end either.

In love.

The very thing she'd been avoiding—trying not to think about—seemed to be written in the sky in bold green ink. Oh, Lord. Could he have feelings for her, too? Was that what he meant by not wanting it to end?

Or was he simply talking about the lights in the sky?

She was afraid to ask—afraid she'd be very wrong.

He'd mentioned marriage at one time, and she'd dismissed it out of hand, not wanting a workaholic partner helping her raise two children. Not wanting the disappointment when he missed important milestones in their lives. Worse, she didn't want those same children growing up believing Greg's way of living was the right way.

But he was here with her right now, not at work—something she could have sworn was impossible a mere month ago. He'd even admitted that he hadn't been to this house in ages.

So why now?

"About the kids," he said. "I know we really haven't gotten a chance to talk about the particulars, and it's still early, but I'd like to help with them in some way."

In some way. "In what way, exactly?"

"Maybe I could… Well, if they're boys, I could take them to a hockey game or something. Teach them how to ride bikes."

"Maybe girls would like to ride bikes and watch hockey, as well."

"I know. I didn't mean it like that, I just meant…"

Her heart sloshed around in her chest, a gooey mass of emotion. "I know what you mean, and it's sweet. Yes, of course you can take them to a game, just don't—" she searched around for a tactful way to say it "—make promises you can't or won't keep."

"I know I work too much." He sighed. "I've been thinking about cutting back, I just haven't been able to find the right moment."

She licked her lips, knowing it was selfish of her to even ask. "Maybe this is that moment."

He looked at her then reached up to brush her hair off her forehead. "Maybe it is. Maybe I just needed to find a good enough reason." His throat moved as he swallowed. "Hannah, I—"

Something tinkled from inside the house, threatening to break the spell, but Greg waved it away. "It's the house phone. Let it ring. If it's important, my service knows to call my cell."

"Are you sure?"

"I am. For the first time in my life." His head came down, and his lips covered hers in a gentle kiss that was worlds away from that first desperate kiss at the clinic. This was a kind of slow exploration of dormant emotions, as if he was trying to figure out exactly what was happening between them.

She already knew, and it scared her spitless.

What Hannah needed was to figure out what to do with her newfound knowledge. Did she take a chance on Greg, knowing he could break her heart into a million pieces? Or did she back away and never give him the chance to hurt her or the precious lives she carried inside her?

But he'd ignored the phone. Had hinted that she might be the reason he was thinking about cutting back on work. And his kiss certainly didn't feel distracted, as if he was keeping one ear tuned for the ringing to begin again.

No, he was kissing her as if he wanted more.

As if he never wanted this moment to end. Those words, the ones he'd used earlier, sealed her decision, and she began kissing him back. Eagerly, allowing her own pent-up emotions to surge to the surface.

Her hands reached for him, bringing him even closer.

Greg groaned against her mouth. "I just wanted to talk. I swear. But I can't think straight when you're around."

She smiled. "Join the club. Sometimes there's a time to talk and sometimes there's a time to…do other things."

"Is this one of those times?"

"Oh, I think so. Don't you?" Her heart swelled with love. Talking could definitely wait. They had all day tomorrow to figure the other stuff out.

Greg dragged her to her feet, still kissing her. In a second he'd scooped her up in his arms. "We'll have to go to my room. My parents' room…"

She laughed. "It's okay. I'm sure they'd appreciate it if they knew."

"I think they already might. When I called to ask about the keys, my mom's voice turned kind of hopeful."

"What did you tell her?" She wasn't talking about the twins exactly, she doubted Greg would have mentioned the pregnancy to his mom.

"That I wanted to bring a friend up here to talk."

"Does she know what happens when you try to do that?" She nipped his chin. "All kinds of naughty things."

He gave a mock shudder. "Let's not use the words *mom* and *naughty* in the same conversation."

"Fine by me."

He carried her into the house, and Hannah gave the lights in the distance one last look, noticing the brilliant colors were just beginning to fade, as if they knew there was no longer anyone to witness their display.

Greg kicked the front door shut behind him, and the warmth of the interior of the house washed over her. Halfway down the hall, the phone rang again, but this time the sound was different. This one carried ominous undertones.

A trickle of fear went through her when Greg stopped dead. "What is it? Is that your cell?"

"I programmed a different ring tone for the hospital's number."

She stiffened. "Put me down. You have to answer it."

He did as she asked, striding to the credenza in the foyer and glancing at the screen as he picked up the cell. "Hello?"

His expression quickly darkened, until it matched the fear that had filtered through her a moment earlier. Something was terribly wrong.

Within a few seconds she had her answer. "I'll be there as soon as I can, but I'm an hour and a half out. Call Dr. Calhoun to handle it until I arrive." He clicked a button on the phone and then dragged a hand through his hair, a soft curse erupting from his lips.

The same ones that had kissed her a minute ago. "What is it?"

"We have to leave. It's Claire Taylor." He wheeled around grabbing his keys. "Perforated appendix. It's spewed bacteria into her abdominal cavity."

"Oh, God." For someone with an immune system already weakened from chemotherapy, a burst appendix could be catastrophic. "Let's go."

She paused just long enough to scoop up her purse and her coat. Greg waited, but didn't say a word.

Neither did he talk the whole agonizing way home. Hannah tried to boost his optimism with little anecdotes about other chemo patients who'd suffered massive infections and lived. Claire could be one of those.

She had to be. Because if she wasn't...

Hannah didn't want to go there. Instead, she thought about Claire's bubbly personality, which had persisted even while sick. Her excitement about starting the breast reconstruction process.

She'd be okay. Maybe it wasn't as bad as Greg thought. Maybe the appendix hadn't actually burst. But she knew that chemotherapy could mask the symptoms of appendicitis. The body's immune system wasn't strong enough to mount a good attack on the infection, which was where the pain from appendicitis often arose. So Claire might not have even known something was seriously wrong until it was…

No. It wasn't too late. It couldn't be.

The outcome would have been the same no matter where she and Greg were.

Something crossed her mind. If they hadn't been together at the cabin, one of them would have still been in Anchorage to get that call. One of them would have been within a stone's throw of the hospital.

Only they'd both been out of the area. And because of it, a woman's life could be in danger. The house phone had rung. They'd ignored it, figuring it wasn't anything work related. But would the ten-minute lapse from one phone to the other really make that much of a difference? Who knew?

The hospital had other doctors. Brilliant ones, like Dr. Calhoun. Professionals who were every bit as capable as Greg. He couldn't carry the weight of every single patient on his broad shoulders.

But wasn't she carrying some of it? She was riddled with guilt over not being in Anchorage, and she wasn't even Claire's primary doctor. The buck didn't stop with her. It stopped with Greg.

And from the tight, closed expression on his face, the whitened knuckles as he gripped the steering-wheel, he knew that all too well. If something happened to Claire, he'd never forgive himself for coming away to the cabin.

And because of her part in it, neither would she.

CHAPTER NINETEEN

SHE made him miserable.

Just like his sister said he'd be if he tried to become someone he wasn't. Like a commercial fisherman. Or a family man.

Claire was in Intensive Care, fighting for her life, and although Greg had come out a couple of times and squeezed Hannah's hand, she could see it in his face. The abject misery. The hopelessness.

If it wasn't for her, they both knew he'd have been in Anchorage to receive that call. He'd have never gone to that cabin by himself. He'd done it for her. Trying to be someone he wasn't.

In fact, he'd talked about needing a good enough reason to cut back on his patients, patients that were as important to him—no, *more* important—as eating or breathing. At the time she'd been thrilled, hoping she might be that reason.

And now he was paying the price. Would continue to pay the price each time he looked at her or the twins. How long before he couldn't stand it anymore?

Hannah had known who he was from the very beginning and yet time and time again she'd asked him for more. And when he tried to give it, she'd begin her trek up the mountain of hope, only to slip back down the icy slope as soon as she neared the summit.

She didn't want him to have to choose between being with her and doing his job. Didn't want him to give up something he'd devoted his entire life to. And he would. Whether it was out of responsibility or because he loved her, the outcome would be the same.

He'd be miserable. For the rest of his life.

She leaned against the wall, closing her eyes for a few minutes as she tried to come up with some kind of solution, but her mind kept leading her back to the same place over and over. Even here at the hospital Greg had been torn between his patient and Hannah, as evidenced by him having to leave his post to bring her news.

There was no flicker of relief when his eyes met hers, only a deep-seated guilt that might never go away.

Unless she did.

The whispered words slid through her mind so quickly she almost missed them—had to call them back.

Unless she did.

The terrible ripping sensation inside her had nothing to do with the babies and everything to do with the pain that sometimes came from doing the right thing.

And it was. If she went away, Greg could go back to the life he was meant to have. He'd never have to face choosing between her and his job. He'd never sit at home when he wanted to be at the clinic. Never feel that spark of love slowly turn to hate as the years rolled by.

And the babies?

No. She never wanted them to wonder if they were the cause of their father's unhappiness.

Hot tears spilled from her eyes, coursing down her cheeks. She scrubbed them away but more followed, until there was an endless river. Oh, God. She didn't want him to see her like this. Didn't want to give him one more thing to feel guilty about.

Before she could talk herself out of it, she moved away from her perch near the double doors of the emergency room and stepped onto the pad that caused them to swish open. Then, putting one foot in front of the other, she walked away into the night.

Where was she?

Two weeks and no word from Hannah. He'd gone back to the emergency room for the fifth time, only to find her gone. The fight for Claire's life had consumed most of his time and had kept him from really searching the hospital. He'd assumed she'd gone home, knowing she couldn't do anything more for him or their patient, but never in his wildest nightmares had he imagined her walking away from him. From the clinic.

He fingered the note he'd found on his desk the day after the emergency.

Sorry. I can't do this anymore. I'll let you know when they're born. Hannah

He closed his eyes as the pain squeezed around his heart again. She couldn't do what? Spend one more day with someone who was married to his job? Couldn't watch any more patients suffer? Couldn't bear the constant reminders of what she'd once lived through?

After two weeks he was no closer to deciphering the meaning behind those words than when he'd arrived at his office that Sunday night and found the neatly folded piece of paper. He'd stared at it uncomprehendingly for several puzzled moments before he'd realized it meant goodbye. And not just for a week or two.

Forever.

He'd contacted Dr. Preston but she hadn't heard from

Hannah, and even if she had, she couldn't tell him where she was.

Stella had pulled Hannah's personnel file for him. It was still splayed open on his desk. The phone number for the house in Anchorage was there, as was the address. He'd swung by to find her things were still there, as was her car, but there'd been no sign of Hannah's vibrant presence. Instead, the place was dark and empty, as if she'd disappeared off the face of the earth.

She hadn't. He even had a pretty good idea of where she might have gone.

Idaho.

There was an emergency phone number and address listed but until he could figure out the meaning of her note, he wasn't going anywhere.

Maybe she'd be back.

His fingers trailed across the indentation of her handwriting, the paper cold and lifeless under his skin. She wouldn't be back. Not unless he went and got her.

But if she didn't want to be here?

Damn.

A knock sounded at the door. For a second his hopes leaped, only to crash again when Stella's voice came from the other side. "Greg?"

"Come in." He flipped the note over, not wanting her to see what a colossal fool he was for wanting a woman he couldn't have.

She stalked through the door, holding a sheet of paper and waving it at him. "Can I ask what you're doing?"

"What do you mean?" He tilted his head, trying to see exactly what she was so riled up about. The schedule?

"I thought you told her you were going to slow down."

He realized what she was talking about and bristled.

"Hannah's not here anymore, so it's business as usual. You don't have to stay past six o'clock. I've already told you."

"She quit, didn't she?"

"You know as much as I do."

Her eyes went to the desk and landed on the sheet of paper his hand still rested on. She gave a knowing grunt. "I don't know what you did, but Hannah loved it here."

His jaw tightened. "Not enough to stick around, evidently."

"Does her leaving have anything to do with Claire Taylor?"

Claire. The woman who reminded him so much of Bethany. And she was better, the surgery and antibiotics had worked their magic.

Surely Hannah didn't blame him for leaving the cabin early to treat the woman? He could have sworn Hannah cared for Claire, as well. But what else could the "I can't do this anymore" mean, other than she was tired of his work pulling him one way and then the other?

But it pulled her, as well. She'd left her house to come and help him with the computer on her day off, had knitted hats in her spare time for patients—in fact, there was an unopened one on the coffee table right now—so wasn't it a little hypocritical of her to be miffed about their time together being cut short?

Greg looked up at Stella. "I don't know. Maybe."

"Did you ever think maybe she cares about you?"

If so, why did she leave, just as he was acknowledging his own feelings for her?

He shrugged. "It doesn't really matter at this point, does it?"

She sucked down a deep audible breath, her exasperation obvious. "You two are like stubborn little kids." She nodded at the desk. "You show me yours and I'll show you mine."

"Excuse me?" He stared at her, wondering if he'd worked her too hard.

"Your note. You show me yours—" she reached in the pocket of her scrubs and pulled out a slip of paper "—and I'll show you mine."

"Where did you get that?" He'd torn the office apart, looking for any other notes she might have left. He could have sworn there'd been none.

"Remember the computer that goes on the fritz periodically? It wouldn't start up on Monday morning so I reached down to wiggle the cord, and there it was. She knew I'd find it." Stella unfolded the note while she continued to talk. "You never got that computer fixed. Just like you never fixed whatever was wrong with you."

"What was wrong with…" He frowned. "What are you talking about?"

She glanced down at the paper and began to read. "'Stella, I'm so sorry to leave you in the lurch, but I can't stay. I'd just end up making him unhappy if I do. Please make sure he eats. But above all, don't let him kill himself.'" She looked up again and met his eyes. "'My love to you and the rest of the staff. Hannah.'"

He swallowed hard. *I'd just end up making him unhappy.* Was that what she really thought? Hell, he couldn't remember a time he'd ever been *more* unhappy than these past two weeks.

"Do you know where she went?"

Stella shrugged. "I imagine she's gone home to Idaho."

Exactly what he'd thought. "Her car is still in her driveway."

"So you did go over there. I wondered." She glanced again at his desk. "What did yours say?"

A hell of a lot less than hers did. He flipped the note over and turned it so Stella could read it.

She nodded as if she understood exactly what the words meant. "And that bag?"

He glanced at the coffee table where the gift bag sat. "Hannah's been knitting hats for the patients." He hadn't been able to bear to look inside it.

"Who's it for?"

"I don't know. There's no tag."

That was strange. Hannah had tagged each of the gifts, just like Martha Brookstone had done.

Stella went over to the table and undid the tie that held the decorative rope handles together. She pulled a brown hat from the interior of the bag. Greg couldn't even look at the thing. Hannah had turned her back on him and walked away without a single word of explanation—other than a damn note that said nothing at all. Suddenly furious, he crumpled the paper in his fist and chucked it into the basket that sat beside his hideous desk.

He vaguely heard Stella gasp and turn toward him.

Alarmed, he stood. "What is it?"

She brought the hat over to the desk. There hadn't been a tag on the package but there was one dangling from the item itself. This hat wasn't all fluffy like the others, with floaty little strings that danced when you walked. This was a sensible woolen affair made of dark brown yarn with some kind of beige diamond pattern running through it.

Stella handed it to him. "Read it."

He didn't want to touch it but as she'd thrust it into his hands, he didn't have much choice. Turning the little tag with a flick of his finger, the same handwriting that had been on the note came into view. *Everyone should have a special hat. I was worried you might be cold.*

When he looked back up, he noted that his normally stoic receptionist's eyes were suspiciously moist.

"I don't understand."

"Of course you don't." Stella sniffed. "She made it for you, you knucklehead."

He turned the hat over and over in his hands, still not comprehending. She'd made several hats for different people. Then he remembered telling Annie, his young patient, that he didn't have a special hat to keep him warm—Hannah had been in the room at the time.

She'd made him one. The special hat he'd said he didn't have.

Suddenly it didn't matter that he didn't understand why she'd done it. And it wasn't going to do him a lick of good to keep sitting here brooding about why she'd left. The fact that she'd mentioned letting him know when the babies were born was telling. She didn't mean to cut him out of her life entirely. She certainly could have made that note a lot harsher and a lot more final: *don't bother contacting me again.* Instead, she'd left him a hat—a little piece of herself—worried he might get cold at some point.

"Stella, what does our schedule look like this week?"

She raised her brows. "Exactly like it did before Hannah came into our lives, remember?"

And that was the problem. As much as he might try to go back to the way things had been before, it wasn't going to work. Because Hannah *had* come into their lives and nothing would ever be the same again.

"Can you book me a flight?"

Stella smiled. "Now you're talking. For what date?"

"We need to reschedule or refer all our patients. After that, I want the first available flight." He picked up the hat and tucked it under his arm. "Oh, and somewhere in my paperwork is the number for the storage unit where my old desk is. See if you can get them to bring it back here, will you? And donate this one to charity."

Hannah slid her left foot into the stirrup and swung herself into the saddle. Poncho nickered and tossed his head, ready to get home to his warm stall and the flake of hay that was waiting in his feed crib.

Leaning down, she rubbed the quarterhorse's neck. "Thanks for the ride, boy. Sorry there aren't any more cows to wrangle."

Her dad's time of working the cows had ended last year when his Parkinson's had begun to affect his time in the saddle. The cattle had been sold off, but her mom kept two of the horses, including Hannah's mount. Now pushing seventeen, the gelding had come a long way from the green-broke four-year-old he'd been when they'd bought him. Hannah had trained him herself as a teenager.

She missed riding. Missed the freedom that came with galloping across the fields after a stray calf or riding the fence line in search of breaks or gaps.

She missed a lot of things.

But most of all she missed Greg.

She put a hand on the slight bump on her abdomen and wondered again if she'd done the right thing in leaving. But how could she have stayed when each day she'd have wondered if he regretted being with her? Regret being tied down to a relationship and kids?

Something in her had hoped he'd come after her and prove her wrong, especially once he realized she'd knitted that hat especially for him. But he hadn't. She'd have to make a decision about her house in Alaska pretty soon. And there was a job in the Boise area that looked promising, at a pediatrician's office.

No more oncology. No more reminders of her past.

She stopped short as a realization struck her. Sometimes you *needed* to face the past in order to tackle the future.

Gathering the reins, she gave Poncho's sides a slight squeeze with her legs and he immediately responded. His walk was a bit more energetic on the way in than it had been on trip here. No need to guide him at this point, he knew the way home by heart.

Her own words came back to her. *Sometimes you need to face the past in order to tackle the future.*

Wasn't that what Greg had done? He hadn't turned his back on the pain of his sister's death. Instead, he'd faced it on a daily basis with every patient he treated. Patients like her, like Martha Brookstone. Patients like Claire Taylor.

How was Claire?

Hannah had flown out of Alaska almost immediately so she had no idea if the woman had recovered or not. She'd left Greg to deal with the situation on his own.

A wave of nausea went through her. She'd taken the coward's way out. Yes, she'd had Greg's best interests at heart but, thinking back on it, how much easier had it been to simply drop a note on his desk and clear out without ever having to face him?

Too damn easy. Her mom used to say that was a sure sign you were doing the wrong thing.

A sound in the distance brought both her and Poncho's heads up. Her mount gave a whinny of recognition as another horse made its way toward them. It had to be Glenda, her mom's horse. She squinted. The figure on the mare's back was too wide to be her mother. Surely her dad wasn't out here riding. Even the easy, collected canter Glenda was doing would be difficult for him to maintain for more than a couple of strides. And this rider was perfectly at home at the gait, his form flawless.

Poncho tried to break into a trot but Hannah held him

back, a feeling of unease rolling over her. What if something had happened to her father?

When the rider was about fifty yards out, Hannah leaned forward, trying to figure out who was in the saddle.

Oh, God. That's why the person looked so familiar.

It was Greg.

On a horse!

She pulled Poncho to a halt, half wondering if she'd gone crazy. Greg didn't know how to ride. He didn't have time to do anything other than work. She didn't want Poncho moving suddenly and spooking Glenda. Except Greg knew his way around a horse. She'd swear it from his posture, the way he held the reins gathered in his left hand while his right rested quietly on his thigh.

He pulled up beside her. "Hi."

"You ride." The inane comment drew a laugh from him.

"I haven't in a long time, and I'm pretty sure I'm going to pay dearly for it tomorrow but, yes. I do. It feels good."

"How's Claire?" Poncho stepped sideways, anxious to be on his way.

"She's almost fully recovered."

Relief washed over her. "That's wonderful."

"That's not why I'm here, though."

She licked her lips. "I kind of figured."

Greg turned his horse so they were head to head. "I came to ask what you meant by your note."

"I, uh…" She shrugged. "I could tell you weren't happy. I decided to make it easy on you."

"Easy on…" Greg swung off Glenda and held his hands out for Poncho's reins. "I'd rather not have this conversation on horseback."

Hannah didn't have much choice but to follow his lead so she dismounted and let him tie the horses to a nearby bush.

She stood still, not convinced this wasn't all part of some strange hallucination. But when he came back and she realized he was wearing her father's broken-down cowboy boots, she knew he was very real. In Idaho. Riding her mother's horse.

"You decided to make it easy on me?"

"Yes."

He took two steps forward and wrapped his arms around her, holding her tight against him. His scent washed over her, clean, earthy and smelling like horse, and she couldn't keep herself from leaning into him.

When he spoke, his voice was low. "If this was easy, I don't ever want to face hard." He paused. "I love you, Hannah. What on earth gave you the idea I was unhappy?"

Her heart flipped over in her chest. He loved her? Surely she hadn't heard that correctly. "I—I didn't want you to have to choose between me and your job."

He kissed the top of her head. "That choice was already made."

"But you looked miserable at the hospital."

Greg's hand slid through her hair. "I'm upset any time there's a problem with one of my patients. You saw what happened with Mrs. Brookstone."

"Yes." Although it made her sad that it had taken the woman's illness to bring them together, she thought Martha would be pleased if she could see them now. "But you didn't want a wife or children. You said as much."

He chuckled. "I did. Stupid people say stupid things sometimes." Holding her away from him, he looked into her face. "My life was so wrapped up with my work that I didn't think I had anything to offer anyone else. But I've realized that without you I don't have much to offer to *anyone*…not even my patients. My heart wouldn't be in it anymore."

"But your sister—"

"Would approve. All she ever wanted was for me to follow my heart. And my heart is here. With you."

Hannah sighed, believing at last. "I love you, too. Are you sure you can do this?"

He cupped her face. "For the past two weeks I've found out what I *can't* do. And that's live without you. I think Stella agrees with me."

"She found my note?"

"Yes. And she opened your present—which I hadn't been able to do." He pulled the hat from his back pocket. "Thank you for worrying. It gave me the nerve to finally come after you."

"I'm so very glad you did."

He leaned in for a long kiss. The parts of her that had gone into hibernation slowly came back to life. When he pulled away, he leaned his forehead against hers, one hand curving over her abdomen. "Will you come back to Alaska with me?"

"Yes, but first I have a better idea." She took him by the hand and led him toward the horses. "My folks have a little cottage that sits about a hundred yards from the main house. It's where the ranch foreman used to stay. I don't think they'll miss us if we spend an hour or so over there. We can sneak in through one of the back windows."

He laughed. "I don't think we'll need to use the window."

"Really? And why's that?"

He lifted his hand, something shiny dangling from his index finger. "Your mom gave me a key to the front door."

EPILOGUE

HANNAH stood over the crib and watched the twins sleep.

Simon and Bethany huddled at opposite ends of the space, still looking incredibly tiny, although at a little over five pounds each they were good-sized. "It's almost time, munchkins."

She held a sealed envelope in a shaking hand, wondering what news it contained.

Greg loved these little ones as much as she did, doted on them every second that he was home, which was a lot more often than she expected. He didn't seem to be able to stay away for longer than six hours at a time.

In fact, they'd bought a house closer to the clinic so Greg could come home for lunch or whenever there was a lull between patients. And it was also close enough to the hospital that she didn't worry about keeping him away from anything urgent.

"And he's not miserable after all," she whispered to the babies.

Neither was she. In fact, Hannah was insanely happy. She'd go back to work in another month, and the timing was perfect. Fishing season would be over, and Greg's parents had offered to come up and help out. Between the heart-to-heart talk Greg and his father had finally had and the birth of the twins, the hard feelings between the two men had been eased. They were both stubborn and prideful, but Bethany's memory would serve as a permanent link between them. Greg's mother was a sweet woman and Hannah knew the twins would be in good hands with both of them.

The front door clicked shut. "Hannah? I'm home."

Greg's voice reverberated around the house, and she winced when one set of eyes opened and then the other.

Awake. Again.

She smiled. It was all good. Sneaking from the nursery and hoping to get a few minutes alone with her husband, she padded out to the front room.

Greg caught her around the waist and pulled her against his body before kissing her breathless. After six months of marriage he still held her like he couldn't get enough.

And that was fine by her because she couldn't get enough of him either.

Once she caught his eye, she held up the envelope. "The results are in."

His smile faded as he looked at her hand. "Did you open it?"

"No. I wanted to wait for you to get home. I think we should do it together."

He brushed a long strand of hair behind her shoulder. Over the course of her pregnancy her hair had grown six inches and was shiny and healthy again. Just like she felt.

A thin cry from one of the twins went up.

"Oh, no. They were stirring when you got home but I was hoping they'd go right back to sleep."

"It's Bethany, I'll get her."

Hannah was amazed that he could tell their cries apart so easily, but he could. Thirty seconds later he strolled out of the room, a baby snuggled in his arms. Wide blue eyes stared up at her daddy and little fists waved from beneath

er blanket. Hannah smiled then went over to the couch
nd waited for him to join her. He did, kissing his daugh-
er's forehead as he sat.

He stared at Bethany for a long time then looked up
t her. "It doesn't matter, you know. It won't change any-
hing."

"Don't you want to know one way or the other?"

"Not really. Unless you do."

Hannah frowned, not sure where this sudden reluctance
ad come from. Was he afraid the twins weren't his? Was
e afraid he wouldn't feel the same way about them?

"I'm their father. It doesn't matter whose D.N.A. they
carry." He took the envelope from her hand and set it un-
pened on the coffee table. "We'll keep it in a file somewhere, in case they need or want to know someday. But
'm okay with never opening it."

"Are you sure?"

Securing Bethany in one arm, he reached for her with
he other, sliding his hand beneath her hair and pulling
er close. "As sure as I am that I love you," he whispered.

A wave of happiness burst over her as his lips touched
ers, and Hannah knew without a doubt this was where
he belonged. In the arms of the man whose love stretched
s far and wide as the northern lights across a dark
Alaskan sky.

* * * * *

& *A sneaky peek at next month..*

Medical Romance™

CAPTIVATING MEDICAL DRAMA—WITH HEART

My wish list for next month's titles...

In stores from 4th January 2013:

- ❑ The Surgeon's Doorstep Baby – Marion Lennox
- & Dare She Dream of Forever? – Lucy Clark
- ❑ Craving Her Soldier's Touch – Wendy S. Marcus
- & Secrets of a Shy Socialite – Wendy S. Marcus
- ❑ Breaking the Playboy's Rules – Emily Forbes
- & Hot-Shot Doc Comes to Town – Susan Carlisle

Available at WHSmith, Tesco, Asda, Eason, Amazon and Apple

Just can't wait?